wALS 2/16

D0512904

Once Upon a Book Blog

'Fast-paced and utterly romantic' *Book Angel Booktopia*

C333884234

By Jen McLaughlin

The Sons of Steel Row Series
Dare To Run
Dare To Stay

JEN McLAUGHLIN
DARE TO RUN

headline
ETERNAL

Published by arrangement with NAL Signet,
a member of Penguin Group (USA) LLC.
A Penguin Random House Company.

First published in Great Britain in 2016
by HEADLINE ETERNAL
An imprint of HEADLINE PUBLISHING GROUP

1

Cataloguing in Publication Data is available from the British Library

ISBN 978 1 4722 3482 7

Offset in 11.7/13.45 pt Times LT Std by Jouve (UK)

Printed and bound in Great Britain by CPI Group (UK) Ltd, Croydon, CR0 4YY

Headline's policy is to use papers that are natural, renewable and recyclable
products and made from wood grown in well-managed forests and other
controlled sources. The logging and manufacturing processes are expected
to conform to the environmental regulations of the country of origin.

HEADLINE PUBLISHING GROUP
An Hachette UK Company
Carmelite House
50 Victoria Embankment
London EC4Y 0DZ

www.headlineeternal.com
www.headline.co.uk
www.hachette.co.uk

This one goes out to my agent, Louise.
You said we could get me here, and we did.
Thank you for all that you do.

CHAPTER 1

LUCAS

The smells of rotting fish, salt water, and dying dreams on the docks of Boston Harbor were all too familiar to me, but even so . . . they made me reflect on my choices every single fucking time. I'd lived in the heart of Boston my whole life, but I'd never taken the time to enjoy the city the way the tourists did. For them, it was all about a celebration of freedom and liberty. It was all memories and American pride and all the shit that goes with it.

For me, the city meant jail time for assault, bloody bar fights, meaningless one-night stands, blackouts from binge drinking, money lost to gambling, lives lost to violence, and shady shipments on the docks at midnight. Which was why I stood here in the dark, with no moon shining brightly, watching a bunch of sweaty men struggle to unload crates from an incongruous shipping container that looked as if it carried car parts but held so much more. The lack of natural light made the job nearly impossible, but we weren't about to turn on the spotlights so they could see better.

As I watched, I crossed my arms and tapped my foot impatiently. We were well within the allotted time I'd scheduled of twenty minutes, but it felt as if I'd been standing on these smelly-ass docks for hours, watching men grunt and curse at one another for not moving fast enough. They'd probably move a little faster if they stopped throwing nervous glances my way, silently communicating with one another about the "new" guy, fresh outta lockup.

I didn't have the patience for this type of shit, which was why I didn't normally oversee this portion of the business. Supervising the weapons shipments was my little brother's territory, but word had come in that the ATF had been tipped off on the impending shipment of guns. So I'd told Scotty to keep his ass home and I'd take care of things.

To throw the feds off, I'd moved our delivery up, and now I was standing on the docks watching for any suspicious activity . . . in more ways than one. Scotty, on the other hand, had opted to spend his night off trying to get in the pants of some girl he "loved," attending some lame-ass event to prove he was a "decent" guy.

He wasn't.

None of us were.

Illegal guns were just part of what we dealt with, for fuck's sake. That didn't exactly scream decency to me. Knowing Scotty, he'd been up front about his employment, tossing the bad-boy element in the girl's face. It had obviously worked. Me? I tended to avoid anything that required more than a slap on the ass and a thank-you as she walked out the door, never to be seen or heard from again. I'd been locked away from society for too long to try for anything else.

Add that to the fact that some little shit had tried to kill me—and almost *succeeded*—the week before I got out and I was left with the utter inability to trust anyone. Anywhere. I couldn't afford to anymore. I hadn't figured out whether the attack in prison was personal or business yet, but I knew one thing. Some prick wanted me six feet under.

Working for our gang, the Sons of Steel Row, under the reins of Tate Daniels, entrepreneur and illegal arms dealer extraordinaire, had taught me a thing or two about when something belonged on the library's fiction shelves, and when to categorize it as real.

And the threat on my life had *nonfiction* written all over its cover.

One of the roustabouts tossed me a narrow-eyed look, trying to get a read on me, no doubt, and I stared right back at the little shit. I might be keeping my guard up, but that didn't mean I was sitting here wallowing away in fear of my impending death.

People lived. Then they died.

That was life.

And as the overseer of this godforsaken shipment, it was my duty to keep things running smoothly. We had imports and exports to manage, inventory to distribute, and cash to launder. Shit needed to get done, and it needed to get done right *now*.

A crate hit the ground, causing a huge *boom* loud enough to awaken a deaf man. I growled and stepped forward, my fists tight at my sides. Striding forward, I moved right up to the two men who'd made the racket. One was a new recruit who'd joined when I'd been locked up, and the other was a potential member. "Can you maybe manage to unload our merchandise without, oh, I don't know, waking the entire police precinct? I rescheduled this for a *reason*."

The potential, who'd dropped it, flushed and lowered his head. "Sorry, Mr. Donahue."

"Hey, it's not my fault he's an idiot," the worker bee said.

I didn't know him, but I knew for a fact he'd been born

and raised in the same shit hole we'd all come from in Boston—a neighborhood near Southie that had been coined Steel Row. Probably in his twenties, he was the same redhead who'd been eyeballing me earlier. His glare filled with an unspoken challenge, he wore a baggy shirt, a pair of ripped jeans, and a bad attitude. He had muscles that rivaled a linebacker's, but that didn't matter. I welcomed the confrontation.

The challenge.

That's what I used to like about this job. It kept me on my toes. But everything was too damn easy now. It bored the hell out of me. I cocked my head and crossed my arms. "Is that so?"

"Maybe you guys should get rid of the weak links every once in a while and this kinda shit wouldn't happen. What was Scotty thinking, sending you here to run things you know nothing about? Exactly how long were you in for, anyway?"

I closed the gap between us and stared the man down. He wanted to challenge the bear? Then he'd get the bear. "Loyalty is rewarded, you little shit. I did my time, and I kept my mouth shut. If the ATF came swooping in here right now, could you do the same?"

The man didn't speak.

"Answer me." Without another word, I unholstered my Sig P229 and pressed it dead center to his forehead. My voice was calm and deep and I made sure to speak slowly. "Because the way I see it, there's only one other option in this world." Staring him down like the rat he was, I tightened my grip on the trigger enough to make him sweat. "So. You tell me. What's it gonna be?"

The man swallowed hard but didn't back down. I almost admired that, but he was too much of a dipshit to appreciate the value of his courage. Instead of answering my question properly so his brains didn't end up on the dirty docks, he asked, "You gonna pull the trigger?"

My finger twitched even more. For a second, I wanted to do it just to shut the idiot up. A little peace and quiet would do a hell of a lot for the headache building behind my eyes. But even though I was in charge here tonight, this was my brother's crew. It wasn't my job to decide if I needed to rid us of yet another fuckwit. That choice would be up to Scotty.

But still . . .

The point had to be made that nobody should mess with me and that I wouldn't tolerate insubordination from an underling. All around us, the men watched, waiting to see what I would do after that blatant display of disrespect. I'd been challenged, and it was time to show the rest of them why they shouldn't do the same.

Forcing an easy grin, I shrugged and slid the gun back into my holster. "No, I'm not going to shoot you. That would bring the boys in blue on our heads, and I don't want to be behind bars again. Not yet, anyway."

"Yeah." The man looked at his buddies, grinned, then tugged on his shirt like he was some thug that had flirted with the devil and lived to tell of it, before turning back to me. "That's what I thought, man."

"*Sir,*" I said from between clenched teeth, still grinning.

"What?" The man laughed. "What did you call me?"

"I said"—I rolled my sleeves up, slow but sure—"you should be calling me *sir*. I am in charge of this run, and as such, I own your pathetic little soul tonight."

The man paled, watching my movements with wide eyes. When I took a menacing step toward him, he stumbled back one step before he forced his feet to stand still. "Y-You're not my boss. I work for your brother."

"My brother runs this little crew, yes. While I—?" I grabbed the front of the little fucker's shirt and hauled him close, nose to nose with the twat. "I'm higher up the food chain, because I've worked my way there by following the rules. That puts me in charge of everyone on this dock. Did no one teach you about hierarchy? About showing respect to those who can get your death written off as an acceptable loss?"

The man gripped my forearms, shaking his head. "I get it, man. I get it."

"I told you to call me *sir.*" I shook the man. "What's your name, dipshit?"

The man let out a scared little whimper. So much for that budding respect for the man's balls. They'd shriveled up into the size of raisins at the slightest sign of danger. "D-Doug. Doug Pearson. Look, I'm—"

"Shut the hell up." I shoved Doug backward, sick of hearing his voice already. "When you speak, it hurts my head."

Doug stepped back. "I'm—"

"Jesus Christ, you don't get it, do you? Let me show you how to listen to your superior's orders in this crew." Hauling back my fist, I punched him in the nose, grinning as the sound of his septum cracking into pieces filled the silent night. Still, that wasn't enough. Man, I'd missed the feeling of things cracking under my fists.

It had been too long since I'd had a good fight.

When Doug hit the ground, his hand pressed to his bloody nose, I grabbed his shirt, forced him to his feet, and punched him in the gut. As Doug doubled over, wheezing for breath, I leaned on the injured man's back as if he was a piece of furniture. To me, he was. He was here to do a job, and that was it. When he stopped being useful, I'd toss him in the garbage with the rest of the shit that was no longer of any use to me. "You stand the hell up when I'm teaching you a lesson, and you shut up, too. And next time, you damn well better call me *sir.*"

Doug wavered but managed to stand straight. "Y-yes, sir."

"Good boy." I grinned wider, knowing I looked maniacal

and not giving a damn about it. I patted Doug's cheek hard. "And you might want to think twice before opening your mouth to someone who doesn't give a shit if you saw Mother Mary herself over his shoulder. Understood?"

Doug nodded, his lower face smeared with blood. "Yes, sir."

"Good." I pointed at the crates. "Now, wipe the blood off your face and get the rest of these unloaded. And make sure you clean up after yourself. We don't need a blood trail." I threw a scathing glance at the rest of the crew, who'd done nothing but watch. "That goes for all of you."

They all jumped into motion like obedient worker ants, including Doug. No one spoke, but they exchanged silent glances as they moved the crates out of the container and into the truck that would carry the goods to the old warehouse outside Steel Row where we stored our inventory. I'd busted their buddy's nose, but in this world? That earned you respect.

They wouldn't mess with me again.

Chris, my best friend and another lieutenant, came over to me, crossing his arms as he got closer. He watched me with an appreciative light in his brown eyes. Chris was the one exception to my no-trust rule. He'd gotten me into this world, against all odds, and had been there for me when I'd needed him most. "You handled that well."

It was sick that beating some dude up was a way to earn praise in my career field, but it was what it was. This life was the only life I ever would know. And that was fine by me. "He deserved it for being a dick."

"That's because none of these guys take you seriously." Chris lowered his head, his brown hair hiding his eyes from me, and studied his nails. His green T-shirt pulled at his muscular arms, and his ink spread all the way down to his wrist. He'd been in the gang since he'd been a teen, like me. He'd joined because his pa had been a member, so this life had been carved out for him from the moment he came into this world.

Those weren't my reasons for joining.

Hell, I wouldn't know my father if I passed him on the street. When my mother was alive, God rest her soul, I'd doubted if she'd even known who he was, either.

"Yeah, well, that's their mistake." I straightened my sleeves. "Not mine."

He looked over at the crew, who definitely had a new sense of urgency in their movements. "Maybe because you've been in lockup the past two years. They didn't know who you were, besides the fact that you got put away for assault, and now you're here, bossing them around on the docks."

Chris and I had always been tight. When I'd been doing time, he'd come to visit me twice a month. Kept me posted on the happenings in the real world. He'd visited more than my actual brother had, but that was no surprise. I'd always looked out for Scotty, but Scotty wasn't exactly the sentimental type of guy who put a priority on family visits. And that was fine, too. "I hadn't been planning on being here at all. This isn't my department. I came because of the damn ATF. And Scotty has some chick on the line."

"Since when do you care what Scotty wants when it comes to this shit?"

I shrugged. "Since I spent some time behind bars . . . Scotty and I aren't as close as we once were. But that doesn't mean I'm going to let him play chicken with the feds. He's too damn cocky for his own good."

"So he's off fucking some girl while you stick your neck out for him? Like usual?" Chris rolled his eyes.

I moved my shoulders, wanting nothing more than to get the hell out of here. They were almost finished, so I'd be free any minute now. *Free.* Funny choice of words. I'd never be free. Not really. The closest I got to *free* was when I walked down the Freedom Trail. "Yeah. Basically."

"You've got to stop treating him like a kid. He's twenty-four now." Chris looked at me, studying me too close. Chris was the only one who caught glimpses of the real me. "He's not the little boy you need to protect anymore. He can take care of himself. A little too well, maybe."

"What's that supposed to mean?" I asked.

"Nothing, man. Nothing at all." He shuffled his feet and stared at the guys as they did a final check of the shipping container. "I heard you almost got taken down inside. What happened?"

I shrugged. "Someone jumped me from behind on the way out of lunch. I fought him off long enough to keep my life, but I didn't get a clear look at his face before the guards dragged him away. A buddy on the inside said he looked like a new guy but couldn't point him out. It all happened too fast."

"You almost died."

Laughing, I scratched my head. "Yeah, well, I didn't, did I? Good thing I'm out, safe and sound, now," I drawled.

Chris rocked back on his heels. "You suspect something, don't you?"

"Don't you?" I looked at Chris. "You can't bullshit a bullshitter. I see it in your eyes. You know something's up."

"Maybe I do. Maybe I don't. But a smart man never talks." Chris dropped his hands at his sides and whistled through his teeth. As he walked away, he said over his shoulder, "Not in this world."

"Not even for his blood brother?"

Chris paused, his broad shoulders tight. "Not even then."

"Glad to see you haven't forgotten me, *brother*," I said, pressing my fingers over the old scar in my palm. One of the two Chris and I had made all those years ago on the railroad tracks behind my home. Ma had been pissed at me for deliberately cutting myself. If it'd gotten infected, it would have meant medical bills we couldn't afford. I'd gone to bed without dinner that night. "Have a good night."

Chris spun on his heel and came back, his cheeks red and rage in his eyes. "You know nothing. *Nothing.* You weren't here, asshole. You were gone, and the whole thing went to shit. You left me to fend for myself in the damn Sons of Steel Row all by myself."

I cocked a brow. "Excuse me for getting arrested."

"Ha-ha, so funny, fuckwad." Chris clenched his fists. "You want me to tell you what I think? You want it that bad?"

I forced myself to shrug. "If you feel so inclined, sure."

"I think someone is putting all his players into motion, and it all started the second we got word that you got parole." Chris looked me up and down, his nostrils flaring. "And I suggest, *brother,* that you watch your back."

I held my hands out at my sides, forcing a carefree grin . . . even though I felt like anything but. "I always do. It would take a ghost to sneak up on me."

Chris shook his head. "Don't be so damn cocky. It just might be your downfall."

"Or it just might be my protection."

"Whatever, man," Chris said, locking eyes with me. "Whatever."

As he walked away, I dropped the grin and fisted my hands. "Thanks."

Chris didn't say anything. Just walked up to the newly loaded truck, the men in either the cab or their own vehicles. He tapped the back of the truck to signify that all was well, and the truck took off. Chris followed behind it in his car, the others falling in line behind him. He'd make sure everything got to the warehouse, unpacked, and inventoried. I stared at the convoy as it disappeared from sight, then turned around and left, making sure to keep my steps light and unhurried. As I walked away, I buried my hands in my jeans pockets and whistled "The Star-Spangled Banner."

No matter what I did, I couldn't show my certainty that Chris was right. I'd been thinking the same thing, so hearing it straight from the mouth of the only man I trusted in this world? Yeah, that pretty much answered my unasked questions. It seemed clear as day that this was an inside job, and that meant . . .

Someone in Steel Row wanted me dead.

CHAPTER 2

HEIDI

This whole city was going to hell, and it was determined to take me with it. I'd grown up here and all, so this really wasn't new information, but standing behind the bar, watching a bunch of gangbangers argue over who got to hit up the convenience store down the road first, only drove that point home.

Sometimes I could ignore the degradation and overall shittiness and just feed off the energy of Steel Row. Accept the slums of Boston for what they were. This was my life, and I was okay with that, but on nights like this one? It sucked.

Shaking my hips to the beat of the music pounding through the sound system, I attempted to ignore the pestering voice in the back of my head that screamed for me to strive for better.

There was no better. This was it. All she wrote. Cue the pig at the end of the Looney Tunes strip to pop up and say, "That's all, folks."

I'd always hated that little pig.

But really, I couldn't complain. I had a better deal than others. I'd run far away from home and had been living on the streets of Steel Row before I'd been taken in by an old man who became more of a parent to me than my parents ever had been. And when Frankie died, he'd left me the Patriot, his bar, *my* bar. I loved this shitty little bar more than I'd ever loved any person.

With one exception.

The man who'd given it to me.

A drunk asshole leaned across the bar, grinning at me. He came in every Friday night, and he never ceased to hit on me, despite the fact that I shot him down every time. "Hey, gorgeous."

"Hey, Jimmy," I said, grabbing an empty mug and filling it up with Bud Lite. "How's it going?"

"Good. It would be better if you'd go home with me, though," he said, eyeing my tits. Big shocker there. "*Much* better. What do you say? Is tonight the night?"

I rolled my eyes while I turned away from him. It wasn't that he wasn't hot. He was. But he was a dealer, and I'd be damned if I was going to date a guy who would end up dead in an alley somewhere right after my stupid self fell in love with him. I'd seen way too many women in Steel Row go down that road. There was no way I'd join their ranks. Before I turned around, I forced a smile. "Yeah, sorry. I'm not in the mood tonight. I have a headache."

"Aw, baby, but I can make you feel like new," he said, reaching out and gently tugging on a piece of my hair. I slid his beer to him, and he fumbled to catch it. "Oh, I like it when you play rough."

Holding my hand out, I leveled a look on him. "Sure you do. That'll be five bucks, hot stuff."

"One of these days, you're going to regret turning me away," he teased, handing me a ten.

"That day hasn't come yet," I said, reaching out for the ten. "And I don't think it ever will, but, hey, whatever keeps your juices flowing, man."

He caught my fingers, his grip tight. "I know exactly what will do that."

"Yeah, I'm sure." I yanked free and scowled at him. "Too bad it's never going to happen."

"I love the way you tease," he said, picking up his beer and heading toward his obnoxious buddies. "Keep the change, baby. It'll help with your headache."

I watched him go, flexing my hand. "Asshole."

"I heard that," my bouncer, Marco, said. His brown hair stuck up all over the place, but there was no doubt in my mind he styled it that way on purpose. "Was he bothering you again, Heidi?"

"Just being his normal cocky self," I said, shoving the ten into the register drawer. "Nothing I couldn't handle. How's the floor tonight?"

"Rowdy."

"I noticed that, too." I eyed the crowd, my eyes lingering on the group of gangbangers, who were watching me with alarming uniformity. "Trouble's in the air."

Marco cracked his knuckles, his green eyes locked on the same group of men I'd been looking at. "Don't go home alone. I'll walk you."

"Thanks, Marco." I put away clean wineglasses, peeking over my shoulder at him. "I appreciate it."

"Anytime, Heidi. Anytime."

Marco was one of my rare finds. When I met him, he was living on the streets, like I had at his age. He'd been asleep behind my bar, tucked in under a threadbare wool blanket. It had been freezing that night, well below ten degrees, and he'd been shivering uncontrollably. When I walked over to him, he woke instantly, and he'd had this haunting resignation in his eyes. I think I must have looked the same when

Frankie had found me. He'd taken me in. Given me a home. A purpose. A job.

It only felt right that I do the same for Marco.

Now that he was almost nineteen, he paid me rent for an apartment above the bar, while he waited to head off to college. He'd been accepted to Boston College, and had been offered a dorm early as part of his grant. He would leave in a few days, and he was going to do great things with his life. He'd been given the chance I'd never had, to go to college and *make* something of himself, and was getting out of this hellhole. I'd never been happier for anyone. He was such a good kid.

All he'd needed was a chance.

I might be only five years older than him, but I felt like a mother hen around him. I watched him walk away, smiling, before glancing at the guy who'd just sat down at the end of my bar. As soon as I recognized him, my heart picked up speed. There was something about him, something I couldn't put my finger on, that made me hyperaware of his very being whenever he was in the same room as me. I didn't know his name, but I knew he had danger written all over him. In permanent marker.

He watched me with narrowed eyes that did bad things to my equilibrium. I knew from memory that they were green. Like, really green. They looked clean and fresh and happy, but he was none of those things. He always came in wearing jeans and a muscle-hugging long-sleeved shirt, which he always rolled up to just below his elbows to show off his strong arms covered in a thin dusting of fine hair. I'd stared at those freaking arms way too many times. I'd never been one for arms, for the love of God, but on him? They just worked. Everything did. In truth, he looked raw, gritty, and dangerous. And he had the faintest hint of a Boston accent.

As if he hadn't already been unfairly sexy.

He'd been in every night for the past week, but before then, I'd never seen him. When he came in, he barely spoke two words to me and mostly communicated with grunts and money. He wasn't rude or anything. Just the strong, silent type.

The only personal thing I knew about him was that he ran the mechanic shop across the street. I wanted to know more, and there was only one way that was going to happen. Straightening, I made my way over to him. "Whatcha drinking tonight, Lucky?"

He shrugged out of his dark brown leather jacket—another item he was never without—and dragged his hands through his dark brown hair. Although it wasn't *completely* brown. It had a tinge of red . . . not that I'd noticed, of course. Once he settled his jacket on the stool, he eyed me with those bright Irish eyes of his. "My name's not Lucky."

"Are you sure?" I cocked my head. "It fits. I mean, you practically scream Irish. Reddish hair, light eyes. Devastating charm."

He cocked a brow. "Devastating charm, huh?"

"Sure." I leaned on the bar. His eyes dipped south but shot back up almost instantly. "You come in here, scowl at everyone, and barely say a word. If that's not devastating charm, I don't know what is."

"Then you need to get out more, Heidi." He tapped his fingers on the bar and locked gazes with me. "That's your name, right?"

My stomach clenched tight at the sound of my name on his lips. With his accent, it sounded almost musical. "Yeah. How did you know?"

"I pay attention . . ." He trailed off and gave me a charming—yes, *charming*—smile. "In between bouts of being lethally charming, that is."

My heartbeat picked up speed, but I ignored it. I would

not swoon over the guy just because he smiled my way. I would *not*. "Sure. Or you're a stalker. One or the other."

"Darlin'?" He leaned in. He smelled good. Like Dolce & Gabbana cologne, leather, cars, and a healthy dose of pure man. And when he said *darling*, with the hard *r* dropping off like that, it melted my insides into a puddle of hot want and desire. I bet he knew it, too. "I've been coming here all week. You of all people should know I don't need to stalk women to get them to come home with me."

I reared back and widened my eyes, doing my best to look offended. It wasn't easy, because I was pretty much impossible to offend. "Excuse me?" I feigned. "Who said anything about me going home with you?"

For a second, he looked embarrassed. A brief, tiny second. Then the smirk slipped back into place and he tapped his fingers on the bar again. The leashed power behind such a simple gesture sent a shiver down my spine. "Oh, that's just adorable. You didn't have to say a thing. I've felt you watching me every night."

He was right. I had been. I had a feeling I'd be watching him more closely from now on. My cheeks heated, so I pushed away from the bar. "You never answered me, Lucky. What are you drinking?"

"Whiskey." He pulled his phone out of his pocket, his eyes narrowing on the screen. "Fuck. Make that a double."

"Sure thing." I turned my back to him and prepared his drink, making sure my hands stayed steady the whole time. I'd never let him see how much he affected me. "Bad news, or news that was so good you need to celebrate?"

"Does it matter?" He reached into his pocket and slipped a twenty across the bar. "I'm paying either way."

I handed him his drink and took the cash. "Nope. Doesn't matter at all."

"Thatta girl." He took a sip of his whiskey and looked

over his shoulder. His strong fingers held the glass, but it was clear his attention was elsewhere. "Who are they?"

"Who are who?" I asked, ringing him up and taking his change out of the drawer. "You'll have to be a little more specific."

"The guys who have been watching you and whispering since I walked in," he said, his hard words echoing his rocky accent.

I gave him a slow smile. "Again, you'll have to be more specific. I've been stared at once or twice in my life."

His eyes slid down my body. My black tank top and shorts, paired with black knee-high boots, suddenly felt as if they'd evaporated into thin air. But instead of giving me some contrived come-on that was supposed to sound original, like all the other guys in this joint, he looked me in the eye and said, "The ones at the table in the left corner. They're not Steel Row guys."

I stiffened. Did he not like what he saw? It shouldn't matter, but it did. "I don't know. They've been acting shady all night."

"More than shady." He raised the glass to his lips. "They're up to something, and it involves you."

"Well, unfortunately for them, I'm not interested."

"I don't think they give a damn if you're interested or not," he said, his voice hard. "Do you live upstairs?"

"No. Marco does." I blew my hair out of my face impatiently. "I live about three blocks down."

He frowned. "Do you have someone to go home with at night, or do you walk alone?"

"That's none of your business," I shot back. "I don't even know you. You don't get to go all GI Joe on me."

His lips twitched, but he didn't smile. "That might be so, but I've never been one to care about that. And you didn't answer my question."

The music seemed to get quieter and the barroom chatter faded as I held his gaze. My fingers tightened on his change.

"You didn't ask me very nicely."

"I won't." He raised a brow, giving me a look that made his eyes darken. But beneath that scrutiny, there was something else. Concern? No. That couldn't be right. "Are you walking alone, or no?"

"No." There was something about him that demanded brutal honesty. "But I can take care of myself."

He gave me another once-over. My skin heated. Why did he persist in treating me differently than the rest of my customers did? "I'm sure you can."

"Whatever." I held his slightly wrinkled money out, but he just stared at it. "Take your change."

"It's yours, darlin'."

God, that accent, those eyes . . . he was trying to kill me. It was a ridiculously high tip, but whatever. If he wanted to throw money at me, I wouldn't turn him down. I tucked it into the tip jar under the bar and then patted his arm. It was as hard as I'd always imagined. "Thanks, Lucky."

"I told you . . ." He caught my hand with a firm grip. The sensation of his skin on mine was electrifying. There was no other word for it. I might have been imagining it, but I'd swear he looked surprised, like he felt it, too. "That's not my name."

He didn't have soft hands. They were rough and callused, a man's hands, and the feel of them was hot. Of course, everything about him was. But I was not a woman who liked to be restrained, and his grip was stronger than I usually allowed. I didn't try to tug free, not because I didn't care, but because I didn't want to seem intimidated. And I wasn't. "What's your name, *Lucky*?"

"Lucas," he growled, a muscle in his jaw ticking. "My name is Lucas."

"Well, hi, Lucas." Leaning in, I stopped when our noses were practically touching. Something sparked in his eyes, something dangerously sexy, but he didn't react to my proximity in any other way. "Didn't your mama teach you that it isn't nice to grab girls without their permission?" He might be bigger than me, but I wouldn't back down. Call it a Napoleon complex if you must, but he would succumb or I'd die trying.

"My ma doesn't tell me anything lately. She's dead," he said, cocking a brow. From anyone else, it would have sounded sad. From him, it sounded matter-of-fact. His mom was gone, and he'd accepted that. For some reason, that made his words even sadder. "Has been for ten years."

I blinked. "I'm sorry."

"You didn't kill her." His fingers tightened on me and then his eyes met mine, and I don't know what he saw, but somehow . . . I knew he saw *some*thing, because his look softened. "But thank you, Heidi."

I swallowed a moan. That accent wasn't fair, man. "You're welcome."

We stared at each other, neither of us speaking.

Dishes clanged in the kitchen behind me, and the cook laughed as he teased one of my waitresses. The door behind me swung open, and the blond waitress I'd hired the other day pushed past me with a plate of wings in her hand. Still, I didn't move.

I caught sight of Marco watching and he shifted his weight toward us. I gave the slightest shake of my head, to keep him at his post. I could handle this on my own. I looked back at Lucas, to see the barest hint of amusement on his face. I cleared my throat. "Are you going to let go of me anytime soon, or nah?"

He laughed. My stomach tightened in response to his raspy chuckle. "I don't know." He loosened his grip to trail his fingers over my wrist. My pulse leapt at the deceptively soft touch. Despite the fact that he held my arm captive, nothing about what he did was threatening in any way. "I'm still deciding. Give me a second, darlin'."

"Well, I've got people to wait on."

He grinned. "You aren't worried about them. You want me to let go because you're helpless in the face of my devilish charm and soft Boston accent."

Damn it, he was right. But I wasn't about to confirm it. "I don't give in easily. I think you have me confused with someone else."

"Maybe. Then again, maybe not. Either way, I love a good challenge. And that's exactly what you are, Ms. Greene." He skimmed his thumb over my pulse again, grinning when it leapt traitorously. "That's why, when you ask me to touch you again, I'll make you admit you want me before I give you what you want."

With that, he let go.

I backed up, resisting the urge to rub my wrist where he'd held me. It hadn't hurt. His touch had been firm, yet gentle. But the urge to rub away the electrifying pings he'd left behind was still there. He didn't look affected at all. Maybe I was the only one who'd noticed our chemistry. I had to regain control over this situation. Forcing a laugh, I tossed my hair over my shoulders. "I won't be asking you to touch me again, Lucky."

"Lucas," he said. "I told you my name, which is more than I give anyone else free of charge, so you can damn well use it."

Resting my hands on my bar, I forced myself to be calm despite my fight-or-flight instinct clicking to life. Something told me this man was used to issuing an ultimatum and having people obey him. I wasn't going to be one of those people. Not in my own bar, anyway. "When you're on my turf, I'll call you what I want, when I want, and there is nothing you can do to stop me."

"We'll see about that," he said, his eyes full of promise and something else I didn't want to examine too closely. His gaze made my heart quicken and my breath come faster. He gave me a sexy smile, his eyes heated and green, and *ugh*. "I love a challenge almost as much as I love hearing those three little words." His voice was raspy.

"What words would those be?"

Lifting his hand, he counted each word off on his fingers. "You. Were. Right."

I snorted and lifted my own hand, mimicking his countdown. "Never. Gonna. Happen."

He laughed. Actually laughed. And it was as irresistible as he was. "I think we'll have to agree to disagree. Until you say the words to me, anyway."

"I wouldn't hold your breath," I said, winking at him. "You'll die waiting."

"Oh, I doubt that. I've been able to go without oxygen for long periods of time. My brother used to tell me I was part fish."

That was . . . *adorable*. Suddenly he became a lot more approachable . . . After all, how could someone who was part fish be . . . *bad*? And he had a brother. Another customer sat down at the other end of the bar. "I've gotta go take care of the other paying customers now. It was nice talking to you . . . Lucky."

He let out a growl, and I walked away, swinging my hips, hoping it looked like I didn't have a care in the world. The other customer was an old guy who came in at ten on the dot every night for a Sam Adams and was none too happy about having to wait. I could feel Lucas's gaze burning into my back as I moved.

And twenty minutes later, when he left, he left alone. Not that I'd been watching or anything. Because I hadn't been. I'd specifically forced myself not to watch him walk to the door. I almost succeeded, too, but then . . . I *looked*.

And what I saw almost stopped me in my tracks. I thought he'd been watching me closely before. That was *nothing* compared to how he looked at me now. As he stalked across the dark, wood-paneled bar, he watched me as if he was a predatory hunter . . .

And I was his prey.

CHAPTER 3

LUCAS

The next night, I sat in an overpriced diner in a touristy part of town, hidden behind a trendy dance club that I normally would avoid at all costs. I'd spent all afternoon in solitude, counting my cash and packing up a bag in case I had to run. A guy like me always had an escape plan at the ready—especially when someone tried to knock him off while he was still locked up. I covered a yawn with my hand, shifting restlessly on the worn pleather booth we'd settled into.

Across the table from me sat Chris, who was holding his steaming mug of coffee with both hands and blowing on it gently. Red-and-white-tiled walls surrounded us, and waitresses in fake fifties clothing skated around the crowded restaurant.

He wouldn't meet my eyes and kept glancing out the window as if he expected company, despite telling me it would be just us tonight. He took a sip from the mug before putting it down. He tapped his fingers once, then twice, on the table before he picked up the coffee again.

Everything about him was off, and it made me uneasy.

I patted my waist, feeling the hard edges of my holster. It was a violation of my probation to carry a gun, but if something was going down, then I damn well needed to be ready. I thanked God that throughout this fucked-up betrayal I had coming my way, I'd have Chris. He was the one person in this world whom I actually trusted without a second thought. As much as I could, anyway.

"Enough. If you look out the window one more time, I might shatter it." Shifting in my seat, I met his stare. "Why did you ask me to come here tonight?"

Chris shrugged. "Do I need a reason?"

"When you're acting more skittish than a virgin turning her first trick?" I picked up my own coffee with my left hand. "Yeah, man. You kinda do."

Across the restaurant from us, a family of four sat enjoying ice cream sundaes. They were laughing and smiling and looked so damn happy that it almost hurt to look at them. The stereotypical happy family of four, complete with a son and a daughter. The American dream. I'd never have that.

I'd probably never have kids at all.

All I had to hand down to my hypothetical kids was a world built on blood and other people's tears. Who wanted to give that to their children? Not me. And I didn't want anyone relying on me or crying when I was found dead in an alley.

Because that was the endgame for men like me: violent deaths, with a side order of heartbreak. Just another scumbag crossed off the Boston PD's most-wanted list. That's all I'd be. But did some minuscule part of me secretly wish I could have it all? The wife? The kids? The dog? The Cape Cod house with the white picket fence? Hell, yeah.

I also used to wish I could fly like Superman.

That didn't happen, either.

Chris sighed and set his coffee down again, but he didn't let go, and he leaned in. I did, too. After pressing his lips into a tight line, he said, "Do you remember that show we talked about yesterday? The crime drama?"

I cocked a brow. We certainly hadn't been watching television on the docks, so this had to be some code for our conversation about someone making a move against me. "The one we watched at the bar on the wharfs?"

"Yeah." Chris cleared his throat. "That one."

A little girl's laughter rang out through the diner, coaxing smiles from the other patrons, but the tension at our table was too thick for it to penetrate.

"I remember, yes. What about it?"

"You hear what happened in the first episode of the new season?"

I shook my head. "Nah, man, but you know I don't mind spoilers."

"Well . . ." Chris looked over his shoulder before turning back to me. "Well, the *mayor* was really impressed by how *Leo* handled his shit last season and wants to promote him to commissioner for the whole fucking city. Rumor is, he's even eyeing up Leo to be his successor, when he's done."

I blinked. It didn't take more than a moment to realize who Leo was. That was huge, and I hadn't expected to get anything even remotely that prestigious. Hell, I wasn't even sure if I *wanted* it. "Why?"

"Because Leo gets the job done with no muss, no fuss, and he's trustworthy. Last season, he proved he could keep a secret. The mayor likes a guy who's focused on business and not running his mouth in an effort to snag wet and willing."

"Holy shit," I muttered.

Chris shrugged. "But Leo's younger brother thought he

was the next in line for the job. And he ain't happy about being passed over. He's not willing to stand down for his older brother, and he's been looking for ways to cause trouble for Leo. Been *jumping* at opportunities."

I stiffened. That was a huge accusation to make, on the back end of some pretty seriously surprising news. Scotty had always been a little shit, and I'd loved him despite that, but *murder*? I didn't believe that of him. Not without concrete proof. "How did you find this out?"

"People are talking about it. I was . . . online, and somebody asked me, brother versus brother, who I wanted to win the city." Chris latched gazes with me. His brown eyes were grave. "This shit's real, man, and there's no doubt there's going to be an attack on Leo in the upcoming episodes."

Leo. Aka me. "God damn."

"Yeah. I know."

I leaned back in the booth, my heart thudding against my ribs, and tapped my fingers on the table. If Chris was telling the truth, then my brother had it in for me. And if Scotty was gunning for me, I didn't have a lot of options that didn't leave a bad taste in my mouth. "You realize what you're saying, right?"

"I wouldn't be saying it if I didn't." Chris latched gazes with me. "I have it on good authority that Leo is about to find himself under fire, in an episode airing *very soon*."

"Fuck," I said, glancing out the window, not sure what to say to that. I should come up with something cocky to show I didn't give a damn, but for once, nothing came to mind. "Do you know when that will be?"

"I'd say a week from now, at most." He picked his coffee up again and took a long swig. "But there's more."

"I can't wait to hear it. You're just a ray of motherfucking sunshine today, aren't you?" I said dryly. "Does he drown Leo's puppy and make him watch?"

"He doesn't have a puppy," Chris said matter-of-factly.

I rubbed my temples. "Yeah. I know. It was a joke."

"Funny. Anyway, there are whispers that the younger brother is playing at being traitor, feeding the feds bad intel on Leo," Chris said, ignoring my gibe. "So there's a chance he might get Leo locked up instead of outright killing him."

That made me sit up straighter. "Bullshit. How would he even—?" I froze. "Oh shit. The shipment. It was a setup."

"Yeah." Chris winced. "Last night's episode. Someone was running surveillance on the area, and he knew it, and Leo almost walked into a trap."

Motherfucker. I forced a smirk, even though I wanted to kill someone right then. "Wow, sounds like he's awfully threatened by Leo's presence. If I was Leo, I'd be honored that someone went to so much trouble to get him outta the picture."

"This isn't some stupid joke," Chris snapped. "Stop acting like it is."

I held my hands up. "Easy, man. It's just a show, all pretend."

"Yeah. Sure it is." Chris took out a twenty and tossed it on the table. "That's all life ever is to you. Some big fucking game."

I picked up the twenty, shoved it back at Chris, and threw my own twenty on the table. Even though I wasn't sure if I believed him or not, he'd risked his life to tell me his information, so the least I could do was pay for his coffee. I'd also repay him by watching his back, no matter the cost. But that was a given. "You know why I treat life that way?"

Chris eyed the cash, shrugged, and stuffed his money back in his pocket. "Why's that?"

"Because I don't like to lose." Opening the door, I shoved my hands into the pockets of my brown leather jacket. "I hardly make it a habit."

Chris fell into step at my side. "Yeah, I know. You punched me when we were eight because I sunk your battleship."

"And I'd do it again," I said, grinning. "No regrets."

"I know you would."

We pushed out into the night, the temperature slicing through our bones. It might be early spring, but it felt more like winter to me. I huddled into myself. It was cold as a witch's tit at sundown, and it was only going to get colder. The sun had just set, and there was a steady wind that would be sure to freeze anyone stupid enough to venture outside.

Chris sobered and glanced at me. "Seriously, though. What are you going to do about Scotty?"

"No more cryptic codes?" I asked.

"We're the only idiots taking a stroll tonight. It's fine. I was just being cautious." Chris huffed out a breath. "You never know who's listening."

"Agreed." I lifted my shoulders and exhaled. It made smoke in the cold night. "And I don't know. The way I see it, I have three options. Fight, go to jail again, or run. Leave this shit hole, and everyone in it, behind."

Chris laughed. "If you do that, take me with you. I've always wanted to live somewhere warm. I hate winter."

"You and me both," I said.

He stopped at his red Porsche. "You drive here?"

"I walked."

Chris unlocked the doors. "Want a ride?"

"Nah, I wanna walk. It's why I left my Mustang at home in the first place. Sometimes I like to pretend I'm one of them for a little bit." I gestured toward the Freedom Trail. "And the cold clears my mind."

"All right." Chris opened his door. "But, Lucas?"

I hunched over against the cold, keeping up my carefree exterior. "Yeah, man?"

"Watch your back."

"Always."

I watched Chris back out of his spot and drive off. As soon as he was out of sight, I dropped the act. My carefully crafted unconcerned expression faded away, replaced by rage. So much fucking rage. My little brother was an idiot. He thought he could just kill me off and then take over Steel Row? He was insane. The Sons wouldn't stand for it. Neither would Tate. No one would respect a man who killed someone in his bloodline to get the position.

Then again, in this life? Maybe they would.

Bastards.

Shaking my head, I cursed under my breath and turned onto the Freedom Trail. I tended to avoid this area, but tonight it felt fitting. Besides, it had emptied out a lot once the sun had gone down. All the tourists were either in a bar getting wasted or tucked in their hotel rooms with their kids, safe and sound till morning.

I stepped around all the metal plaques that lined the way, not wanting to dirty them with my feet. Tourists loved to walk these miles to celebrate the birth of our country, land of the brave and home of the free. Paul Revere and all that shit. I walked them to escape the chains I was bound by, to be free.

It was such ironic bullshit.

They also liked to take pictures of their feet on the plaques for some weird reason. I didn't get that, but then again, I didn't get what most people did. Selfies. Love. Twitter. It was all inane to me. I dealt with jail, extortion, death plots, and betrayal—between my hard decisions and even harder consequences. I'd never be the type to take pictures of my feet on the ground and post them all over the Internet.

And I didn't know what to do with this latest possible betrayal, either.

What would I do if it turned out to be credible intel?

Kill my own brother to save my life? The little brother I'd practically raised, the one who'd followed me everywhere when he was growing up, including right into this life? Sure, I could kill. I'd done it before, and I could do it again. But did I want to be that guy who kills his own flesh and blood without blinking an eye? Fucking Cain and Abel. I couldn't be considered "good" by any stretch of the word, and I never would be, but even I had to draw the line at fratricide.

But if I didn't kill him, that left two other options. Go to jail or run. Neither of those options suited me. Despite my packed bag waiting for me back home, I wasn't a runner, and I'd be damned if I willingly went back to prison.

Scotty had me backed into a corner, and there was no way out. No matter which I chose, Scotty won. Fuck that. And fuck him. I'd do it my way.

Whatever that was.

I stopped in front of St. Stephen's, my heart picking up speed. I hadn't been to Mass since before I'd been arrested. Something told me that no matter how forgiving God might or might not be, he had no room in his life for men like me. I didn't regret my life or what I'd done with it, but I wasn't blind to my faults.

And neither was he.

Tentatively, I reached for the handle, tugging. Locked. Of course. The gates of heaven were closed to me, as I'd expected. Hell, I half expected to burst into flames, just for daring to stand on holy ground. I shook my head. "This is stupid. I shouldn't have come here."

I was two steps away when someone spoke from behind me. "Sometimes it's the times when we think we shouldn't have come to pray that we need to pray the most."

Whirling, I reached for my gun. When I saw who stood behind me, I relaxed slightly. "Sorry, Father."

The old priest looked at me and I shifted uncomfortably under his knowing gaze. I started to back away.

"You don't have to go," the man said. He had white hair, blue eyes, and wrinkles all over his face. "We closed a while ago, but God never turns away visitors, and neither do I."

"You don't know me," I said, meeting his eyes. "If you did, you wouldn't say that."

"I doubt that," he said. "What are you seeking, my son?"

I suddenly thought of my mother, the gentle lilt of her voice, the cool touch of her hand on my forehead. How she'd told us that despite our poverty and our shitty rat-infested home in Steel Row, we had the chance to be anything we could be. Yet I'd fucked that up. I cleared my throat. "Nothing. I just . . . I just wanted to get warm."

"There is no judgment here." He opened the door to the church. "We're here for you."

His words were like a slap in my face. Aside from Chris, no one supported me. No one helped me. What I needed, I took. If I wanted something, I made it happen. *Me*. Just me. And that wasn't about to change.

Letting people in was one challenge I wasn't about to take on.

"Thanks, Father." I tugged on my collar. "But I don't need anyone."

"Spoken like a man who doesn't trust," the priest said.

I shrugged. I wasn't about to get in a philosophical argument about my psyche with a priest. "Good night, Father."

I walked away, my steps slow and steady. I embraced the cold night again once I was alone. That's how it needed to be. When you let people in, it gave them a chance to betray you. And in the end, they always did. People were greedy assholes like that.

Scotty, whom I'd spent my life protecting since my

mother hadn't been well enough to do so, was trying to get me out of the way by either killing me or sending me back to jail. No way. I'd avoid that iron hellhole or I'd die trying.

And that was that.

The whole way home, I tried to think of the best course of action. Kill or be killed. Stay or run. Fight or flight. That envelope of cash hidden in my place burned into the back of my mind, refusing to back off. By the time I got to my apartment, I still didn't have any answers. I stopped in front of the ratty old red-wood door of the Patriot. The fogged-up window obscured the inside of the bar, but I knew it was still open. I bet that sexy blond bartender who had challenged me last night was inside.

She was always there.

Ms. Heidi Greene.

There was something about her that called to me. In a way, she reminded me of Ma. Stubborn, strong, beautiful, and unafraid. She was like a fresh breath of spring air rising above the stench of my life. And when I touched her, I felt alive.

I'd forgotten how that felt.

She was a challenge, and things had been entirely too easy since I'd left jail behind. It was almost closing time. The bar would probably be emptying out, so she wouldn't be able to use other customers as an excuse to ignore me. She'd intrigued me last night, with her attitude and those sparkling eyes of hers.

Dipshit Doug had practically wet himself on the docks last night, but Heidi, now, she had balls.

I liked that she wasn't afraid to take me on.

I could go inside. Sit down on one of her wooden chairs at the bar and flirt with her. Try to take her home and fuck her. Forget about my brother and my job. The rest of the world. But I didn't. I went home alone instead.

Unlocking the door, I entered my apartment above the mechanic shop. I ran the place, but buried beneath layers of paperwork, it belonged to the Sons of Steel Row—namely, to Tate Daniels. It was a front for money laundering. Just like everything else in my life, nothing was as it seemed.

Never would be.

After shrugging off my jacket, I rolled my sleeves up and poured myself a whiskey. Picking up my packed bag, I tossed it by the door. After a moment's hesitation, I knelt down and unzipped the black duffel. Two blue shirts, a couple pairs of pants, my Sig, and a white envelope stared back at me. I grabbed the envelope of cash—everything I had to my name—palming it. With a sigh, I zipped the bag up and stood. Crossing my apartment, I slid the cash back into the kitchen drawer it had been in before, and bumped it closed with my hip.

I wouldn't be running tonight. Not till I got to the bottom of this. Not till I found out if my little brother *really* wanted to kill me.

Tossing back the shot of whiskey, I immediately poured another. Kicking my bag aside, I stood at the window, glowering out into the darkness. From up here, I could see the alley behind Heidi's bar. As if on cue, the door opened, and she stepped out with a bag of trash. My heart accelerated, and I watched her as I sipped my drink. She tossed the bag into the Dumpster and swiped her blond hair out of her eyes.

So beautiful.

In the moonlight, her hair looked almost white. I couldn't see them, but I knew her eyes would be shining, too. She was that kind of woman. Shiny and pretty.

All the things I couldn't have.

Just as I was about to turn and walk away, I saw shadows move toward her. No, not shadows. *Men*. Three of them. She saw them, too, and backed up one step before lifting her chin and glaring at them.

Brave. Foolish, but brave.

She should have run back inside and barricaded herself in. Her breasts rose and fell with each accelerated breath, and she held her short frame stiff.

I watched, my grip on my glass tightening. "Go inside. Don't fight."

The men moved closer, and she clenched her fists at her sides. She was obviously going to stand her ground. *Stupid, stupid, stupid*. What were the men up to? I stiffened when I recognized them. They were the ones who had been watching her last night.

The guys who I'd later figured out were Bitter Hill guys.

One of the guys went for Heidi, and she swung at him. I tensed, because the guy from Bitter Hill easily dodged the blow and delivered one of his own. For what it was worth, she barely looked fazed. If anything, she looked annoyed as she said something to them—more than likely an insult. I couldn't help it. Her actions filled me with pride.

She was a fighter. So was I.

It made me like her even more.

The Bitter Hill prick roughly shoved her face-first against the wall, the fury on his face way too easy to read. I'd seen that look before, way too many times, to not know what it meant. I set my drink down and took a step toward the door, but forced myself to stand still, gaze locked on the confrontation in the alley. It was harder than it should've been. No matter how much I might want to help Heidi . . .

I couldn't just charge down there and demand they release her.

The Bitter Hill Crew bought guns from us. Guns I knew they were packing as they closed in on Heidi. I tried to relax.

This could just be a routine shake-up. They generally dealt drugs. Maybe she used and owed them money. If that was the case, I wouldn't—couldn't—interfere. We did business with this gang, and the consequences of messing with their cash flow would be ugly. But still . . .

For the first time in my life, I wanted to help someone without any thought to the cost.

I wanted to help *her*.

CHAPTER 4

HEIDI

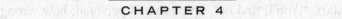

I ignored my racing heart and paralyzing fear. Even though I would do my best to fight the men off, I knew I could do only so much. At some point, they would overpower me. And I would be helpless to escape it. Would be helpless, period, because no help would be coming for me.

I was on my own.

Earlier, I'd sent Marco up to his apartment. I wanted to deep-clean the floors after closing so I'd told him I'd crash on the couch in my office when I was finished. Even from down here, in the alley, I could hear his music blaring. I could shout. Scream for help. But he wouldn't hear me. No one would. People shouted for help in this part of town every night. Gangs tagged future hits with red and black graffiti and no one cared. Guns were fired on a nightly basis, and no cops came riding to the rescue. Residents turned up their TVs to drown the cries out and went about their lives as if it were just a movie playing outside their window instead of real life.

"Okay, okay," I said, trying to keep my voice calm even though my cheek was being torn by the bricks of the building I owned. "I get it. You don't like when I say your dick's as small as your brain."

He smacked my head into the wall again, and I legit saw stars. "You'll find out, up close and personal, how wrong you are."

Fear crept down my spine, making my whole body go numb. So that's what this was about. They intended to rape me. Well, then, I intended to fight like hell. I didn't get where I was today by being scared to fight back. "Whatever you say."

"That's more like it." The guy who slammed me into the wall let go of me, chuckling. "You're learning."

His laugh sent shivers down my spine, because I *knew* this was all a game to him. And I was his next plaything. Now that I was free, I faced them, pressing my back against the wall, and blinked away the fuzzy vision the last head slam had given me.

But then I forced myself to stand still.

If they were here to find trouble, then I'd give it to them. If I cowered now, I'd always seem like an easy mark. This wasn't my first run-in with assholes like these guys. I knew how to handle this, and showing fear wasn't the way. All that did was make their dicks get hard.

I forced my eyes off Star Tattoo and located the other attackers. When I'd pegged down all three men—they had me fully surrounded, of course—I saw it. The graffiti by the Dumpster. They'd tagged my bar earlier tonight, and I hadn't seen it. I'd walked into their trap blind. I dug my nails into my palms and ignored my racing heart.

Time to pretend I was the one in control . . . when I *so* wasn't. "Guys . . . you clearly made a mistake coming here tonight. We can pretend this never happened. Go home."

"Go home?" The man to my left laughed, and the other two joined in. Greasy blond hair fell over his eyes and the Boston accent that sounded so hot from Lucas was menacing coming from him. "You hear that?"

The other two men made affirmative replies.

They closed in on me.

The one on my right, with a star tattoo on his neck, blocked the bar's back door.

"What's this really about? You want a cut of my earnings?" I fisted my hands at my sides, trying to watch all three of them at once. They weren't from the Sons, so I wasn't sure who they were. But I knew one thing: They were *trouble*. "You're welcome to try, but the last guy who came looking for my money left with a limp and a sore dick."

Dark Eyes grinned and pulled out a gun. "I'm not worried about my dick."

I cast a scornful look down and swiped blood off my jaw. "Obviously."

"And we didn't come here for money."

"Then leave before I call the cops." I cast a quick glance around for an escape route but came up empty. They still had me surrounded, and it was only a matter of time till I was face-first into the wall again. "Now."

"We're not done yet," Blondie said. "In case you failed to notice earlier, we came here for you. And we're not leaving till we get what we came for."

My heart pounded, loud and booming in my ears, but I refused to show them how terrified I was. "I'm not interested. Go home."

"We don't care if you're interested." Blondie closed the distance between us, fisted my hair, and yanked me off balance. I swung for him again, but he slapped me hard before I could connect. *Again.* "Oh, she's got claws. I love it when they fight back."

"Go to hell," I snarled. He'd busted my lip even more. "And take them with you."

And then I spit a mouthful of blood in his face.

He swiped his forearm across his jaw, spun me, and slammed my body face-first into the brick wall even harder than the last time, his fist still tight on my hair. "Bitch, you're gonna pay for that. You stand behind that bar all night, teasing all of us with that tight little body of yours, but you never let us touch. Well, tonight? You will."

Stars swam in front of my eyes and pain exploded across my skull, but I bit back the cry that almost escaped. "Over my dead body."

Star Tattoo came up to my left as Blondie held my hands behind my back and shoved me even harder into the wall. Dark Eyes came up on the right, unclasping his belt. "That can be arranged." Any second, they would all jump on me like vultures. I swallowed down the vomit that threatened to spill forward. No matter what, I would go down fighting.

Pleas nearly bubbled from my mouth, but I bit them back. I wouldn't beg for mercy when they clearly had none. I'd fight, and I'd die before begging. I turned my head and forced myself to laugh. It sounded manic. Strained. "What's the matter? Can't get a girl to go home with you without raping her? How sad for you. How *pathetic*."

"We'll show you who's the pathetic one." Star Tattoo closed his hand on my breast and squeezed cruelly. I slammed my head back, trying to break free by head-butting the jerk, but Blondie held me too damn tight. "Nice."

Nice. *That's* what this snake said while feeling me up.

My stomach rolled even more, seconds from expelling its contents. I swallowed it back because I refused to show them how much they'd gotten to me.

Gritting my teeth, I threw my head back again, this time successfully connecting with Blondie's nose. He cried out and let go of me, and I quickly spun away from him, swinging as I did so. I connected with Dark Eyes, but before I could do any real damage, Star Tattoo captured me again.

I kicked back but missed.

"Damn it." He adjusted his grip and my arms were pinned to my sides. "You little bitch."

"Let me go," I snarled, "or you're dead."

He laughed and bit down hard on my shoulder. It hurt like hell, but I didn't make a sound. Then he shoved me to the ground and was on me, the weight of his body so heavy that I couldn't *breathe*. As if that wasn't bad enough, he pressed a hand against my throat, cutting off any hope of oxygen. I struggled beneath him, arching my back and kicking my legs, but he didn't budge. Just grinned down at me.

Black crept into the corners of my vision, painfully taking over, and I fought more frantically. Unfortunately, he didn't budge, and as I ran out of air, my movements slowed. I hit him again, but my arm felt as if it weighed a thousand pounds, and instead of hitting him, my hand just kind of fell on him and stayed. I stopped struggling. It became clear that he was going to suffocate me before he ever got around to raping me.

That might actually be a merciful thing.

Just as the black was about to take over my world, Dark Eyes flew backward, landing almost directly next to me on the dirty ground with a sick, bone-crunching sound. The hands that had been cutting off my air supply eased a bit, and I gasped in a deep breath. It hurt more than the actual strangling had, and I coughed so hard my lungs almost came out of my chest.

I turned my head to the side and took in a deep breath, but I choked on it.

Dark Eyes wasn't moving.

Blood gushed out of his nose, and his eyes stared sightlessly into the night sky. You could still see the color in his eyes, but the rest of him was empty. He looked . . . *dead*. I couldn't see who, or what, had done this, but I could only assume it was Marco. And if it was Marco, then he'd go to jail. After he'd worked so hard to start a life. A real life. One he could actually be proud of.

Pins and needles filled my veins instead of blood, and I gasped in a deep breath, coughing and choking on the thing that was supposed to save me. Air.

Star Tattoo still pinned me down, but his head was turned toward the man attacking his buddies. Rearing up, I bit down hard on whatever I could reach. He yelled in pain as Blondie came crashing to the ground in a heap. Star Tattoo's attention was squarely on me, but before he could retaliate, he was gone. Just *gone*.

A man shoved him into the building, much like they'd done to me earlier, and slammed his head into the wall. It definitely wasn't Marco; that much I knew. This guy was too big. Too tall. Too muscular. And almost . . . *familiar*.

Star Tattoo whimpered. "Look, man, you don't have to do this. She's just a whore that we were—"

The man growled. "I know exactly what you were doing, asshole."

I sat up and hugged myself. My shirt had been ripped in the fight. I needed to get to my feet, needed to be in a better position to fight if I had to, but I . . . I needed a minute.

Soft Boston accent. Domineering tone. I knew that voice. Lucas. He had saved me. But why? Where had he come from? My mind struggled to make any sense amid all the uncontrollable panic that now bubbled to the surface. They were arguing between grunts and punches.

"You may have been locked up for a while, but that ain't no excuse for forgetting how this works. You got no right barging in here, Mr. Donahue. With all due respect, this ain't your, or Tate's, business." Star Tattoo looked over his shoulder at Lucas. "Nothing to do with you or the Sons of Steel Row at all, matter of fact."

Wait. Lucas *Donahue*? Now I knew why he looked familiar. He worked for the most violent arms dealer in the area. He was in a *gang*. He was in the Sons of Steel Row.

While I stayed far away from that life, I knew a few people who didn't. Those still alive kept me up-to-date. When I met him in my bar, I'd known he was trouble, but I hadn't known he was *that* much trouble. His crew was known for their violence and brutality. They owned Steel Row and pretty much everything in it.

Why, then, did he save *me*?

"It's my business because she's mine." Lucas fisted his hand in Star Tattoo's hair and slammed his head into the wall. "She's my girlfriend, you fucking idiot, and she has my protection."

Wait. I was his *what*?

The man nodded as best as he could. "S-sorry, Mr. Donahue. We didn't know she was property of Steel Row."

"Now you fucking know. You come near her again, and I'll kill you and everyone else in Bitter Hill, and then I'll kill some more." He yanked on the man's hair. "Got it, prick?"

He nodded again. "Yes."

"Clean up the bodies before she gets in trouble for something she didn't do. I'll expect them to be gone within the hour." Lucas slammed the guy's face into the wall one more time and shoved him in the opposite direction from me. "Now, get out before I change my mind and kill you, too."

The man fell but stumbled to his feet and took off as if hell itself chased after him. It probably did. Lucas watched him go, his hands still fisted. His back was to me, and his frame was illuminated by the streetlights. He stood there for a second, his entire body stiff. Then he kicked Dark Eyes's dead body and snarled, "Son of a bitch."

I watched him, cautiously remaining quiet. Yeah, he'd been a hero tonight, but he didn't exactly look *happy* about that. When he turned to me, he held out his hand as he kneeled beside me. He reached out to touch me and I flinched. Not because of him, but because I was having a delayed reaction to what had just happened. It had all happened so *fast*. Lucas's eye was already blackening, and he had blood running down from a gash in his forehead. He was sweaty and bloody and he'd saved my life.

By killing two men.

His mouth tightened into a flat line and he cupped my cheek, despite my knee-jerk reaction. "Are you okay? Did they . . . did he . . . ?" He scanned my torn clothes with angry, concerned eyes. "Shit."

"I'm fine." I held my ripped shirt together with a tight grip. The sensation of his hand on my cheek was comforting. Never thought I'd put him and that thought in the same sentence together. "You were just in time." I choked back tears of relief.

Big girls weren't supposed to cry.

"No." He swept his thumb over my cheekbone. "Not fast enough."

I rested my hand over his, holding it in place. Gratitude for what he'd done for me filled me, and I knew there was no going back to pretending he didn't affect me. "Thank you. Seriously."

Something flashed in his bright green eyes. "There's nothing to thank me for. I'm not your hero. I'm not anyone's hero."

He stood up and towered over me. I tilted my head back, and he watched me with a dark look in his green eyes—one that etched itself into my soul. With one look at his dangerous jawline, I knew that I'd never forget who he was, or his real name, ever again. I let him help me stand, my knees shaking so uncontrollably I thought I might fall over, which pissed me off. I hated weakness. It didn't look good on me. Glancing down at the bodies on the ground, I swallowed hard. "Are they both dead?"

He didn't let go of me but started leading me toward his shop. "They won't bother you again."

"They're dead." I followed him, more out of instinct than anything else. He tugged me along, so I followed him. "You killed them."

"They were going to hurt you." He stopped walking, our hands still entwined. "Of course I did."

I blinked at him. He thought that made perfect sense. They'd done me wrong, so they deserved to die. It was so black-and-white for him. "Why?"

"I told you why." He scratched the back of his head and glanced over his shoulder impatiently. "They were hurting you."

"But why do you care? Something tells me you don't normally jump into fights that aren't yours," I said.

"How would you know?"

"I heard him say your name. I know you're in the Sons of Steel Row," I said, not needing to explain further. "Why did you help me?"

"I don't know," he admitted. Averting his gaze, he dropped his arm back at his side. "Does it matter? Would you have rather I ignored it and let them attack you?"

"Of course not," I whispered.

"Then let's go." He tipped his head. "Up there. My place."

I blinked at the mechanic shop. "You live where you work?"

"Above it." His thumb brushed over my knuckles. "You need to come up with me. He'll be back with others, and I want you outta sight."

"I'll be—"

"*Now*, Heidi."

He pulled me behind him, ignoring me completely. I could argue, but I didn't really see the point. If he wanted to play knight in shining armor, then I could let him. For tonight, anyway. I was fine, now that I'd gotten over my initial shock, but he seemed to be worried, which was . . . sweet. Really freaking sweet.

And unexpected for a ruthless killer.

I snorted internally. The dude had just killed two guys in front of me, and I was thinking how sweet he was? What kind of crazy juice had I gotten into?

He unlocked his door and held it open for me. I peeked inside at the unlit staircase, swallowing past the fear that remained lodged in my throat. After what had happened earlier, I needed light to chase away the shadows. Lots of it.

As if he could hear my thoughts, he switched on the hallway light. "Go on in."

I fisted my hands and climbed the stairs. "You don't have to do this. I'm fine, I swear. I've handled worse than that on my own before."

"That's not right. From what I saw, *that* was pretty fucked-up. Someone like you—you should never have to deal with that, let alone anything worse. Ever." He followed me up the stairs. "And you really shouldn't try to take on three guys at once."

"Thanks for the tip," I said, stopping at the second door, which stood at the top of the stairs. It was dark blue, like the walls. "Next time I'll politely request they come at me one at a time, as good guys should."

He stopped directly behind me, his hard chest brushing my back. Despite everything I'd been through, I was all too aware of his very being. "There won't be a next time."

Annoyance crept up my spine. "What should I have

done? Cowered in the corner? Begged for my freedom? My virtue? My life?"

"I don't know." He flexed his jaw. "All I know is one girl against three men is not a fight you can possibly win."

"But I can try," I argued. "What would you have done if it was you?"

He opened the door, turned the light on, and gestured me inside. "The same damn thing I did when it wasn't."

"Exactly," I said, rubbing my arms and glancing around. He had a couch, a coffee table, a TV, and a table. That's it. But it was clean. *Really* clean. I'd expected it to be messy. Not a single thing looked out of place. "So why expect anything different from me?"

He didn't answer. Instead, he walked into the kitchen and washed his hands. I followed him, watching the water turn pink from all the blood he washed off. When he was finished, he dried off and then turned to me. The force of his stare made my heart quicken. A silent communication happened between us. Despite his notorious name and his past, he couldn't stand seeing me get hurt, and no matter what he said, that meant something. He might not think of himself as a hero, but he'd been heroic tonight.

He stepped closer and skimmed his hands down my arms. I shivered but held my ground. "What are you doing?"

"Checking for injuries," he murmured. His low voice did weird things to my body. "You could be in shock and might not feel the pain."

I forced back a groan. He might be trying to help, but he was killing me with those light touches of his. He was also making me feel like I mattered to him, but men like him didn't care about other people. "I'm okay."

And I was now. Especially here, with him.

"I'll decide that for myself." He clutched my hands. "Squeeze my fingers." I squeezed. "Good." Kneeling at my feet, he gently ran his hands over my legs, steering clear of my inner thighs. I had shorts on, so his fingers never touched my skin up there, but I could feel his heat straight through the denim. "Everything looks good."

"That's because it is." I cleared my throat. "Your turn."

He glanced up at me, brows raised. "For what?"

"Care." I pointed at the couch. "Sit."

His lips twitched. "Yes, ma'am." He stood and walked over to the sofa, glancing over his shoulder at me as he went. "I'm fine, though."

"You're less fine than I am. Do you have a first-aid kit?"

He turned and headed for the other room. "Yeah. In the bathroom."

"No, you sit. I'll get it."

He sat and watched as I crossed the room. I turned the light on in the bathroom, doing a quick once-over. It was as clean as the rest of the apartment. Blue walls again, freshly painted. I could still smell the slight scent of paint in the room. Guess I knew what his favorite color was.

"It's under the sink," he called out.

I opened the cabinet. A bunch of hydrogen peroxide and some scary-looking needles were under the sink, right next to the first-aid kit. I didn't want to know what the needles were for. Swallowing, I grabbed the kit, closed the cabinet, and stood up. When I glanced up into the mirror, the image reflected back at me made the contents of my stomach churn. A woman who looked more like a girl, in a blood-stained torn tee. It was the tee that did it, and I didn't want it on for another second. Didn't want anyone's blood on my hands, even if that somebody had been trying to kill me. Setting the kit down, I violently removed my shirt, walked to the kitchen, and shoved it into the garbage.

He still sat on the couch, but he watched me with heated eyes, his fingers gripping his knees. "Heidi, you need to put a shirt on," he gritted out.

His eyes were dark, and he perched on the edge of the couch as if he was ready to pounce without a moment's notice. The way he was looking at me, like I was actually *his*, should have pissed me off, especially on the heels of what had happened just minutes before. On a normal day, I hated dominant men who thought they could control women once those women were "theirs."

But right now, it didn't piss me off.

It *absolutely* didn't.

CHAPTER 5

LUCAS

I tightened my hands on my knees, fighting the impulse to cross the room and take the rest of her clothes off. I knew why she'd taken her shirt off. Through the open bathroom door, I'd seen the horror on her face when she saw the blood on the fabric. But, damn it, she was wearing only a sheer black bra and a pair of tiny shorts that looked as if they'd been painted on.

It was enough to tempt a saint, and I was no fucking saint.

My mind might know why she was half-naked, but my body hadn't gotten the memo. It hadn't even been in the same damn office as my brain at the time of delivery.

I knew she had to be shaken up from what those pricks in the alley had wanted to do, but I still couldn't take my eyes off her. Her hair cascaded down her back, inexplicably curling at the ends. Those blue eyes I'd been fantasizing about didn't have the same sparkle in them that they'd had earlier, and that pissed me off.

Those little assholes had stolen her sparkle.

She watched me, her dimples currently hidden. Her large breasts were clearly visible through the fabric of her bra, and she didn't even bother to try to hide her rosy nipples from me. Her *hard* rosy nipples, which were practically begging for my mouth.

Jesus, Joseph, and Mary, she was trying to kill me.

Her waist tapered in, and her generous hips flared out. Hips that were meant for a man's hands to hold while he was making her scream out his name.

No, not *a* man.

This man: me. Only me.

The shorts clung to the curves of her ass and her upper thighs, leaving the rest of her legs bare all the way down to her blue Converse sneakers. And she was in my apartment. Staring at me.

"Heidi . . ."

She fidgeted with her hands in front of herself. "Okay, in retrospect, maybe I shouldn't have done that. But I couldn't wear that shirt for another second. You know?"

Something twisted hard in my chest at her choked words. If I didn't know better, I'd swear it was my heart. But I knew I didn't have one anymore. I had a hunch that her admission hadn't come easily to her. It wouldn't have come easily to me, either.

She and I were a lot alike.

Standing up, I crossed the room and cupped her cheeks, brushing a thumb over her split lip. The gesture was tender and way too gentle for me, but I couldn't help it. Not when she looked so scared and uncertain. "It's okay, darlin'. I'll get you a shirt."

"Thank you," she said, still not looking away from me.

Reluctantly, I let her go and walked into my bedroom. Grabbing my favorite shirt, I handed it to her, balled up in my fist. "Here."

She took it, a small smile lighting up her pale face. "Blue. Of course."

"Yeah." I cocked a brow. "And?"

"You like blue," she said.

I did, but I couldn't remember telling her that. "Put it on."

"Oh. Right." She slipped it over her head. After she had her arms through the holes, she hugged it close and whispered, "Thank you, Lucas."

It was the first time she'd willingly used my name. I liked the way it sounded on her lips. All soft and sweet and seductive. But the way she looked at me, with her sparkling blue eyes, made my stomach clench tight and roll into one big knot. "Don't look at me like that."

She blinked her blue eyes at me. "Like what?"

"Like I'm your hero or something." I tugged on my hair and glanced away. "It's not like I saved you out of the goodness of my heart. I don't have one anymore. I'm not that guy. I'm the type of guy that attacks people in alleys—not the other way around."

She shook her head, those blue eyes never leaving me. "Your halo may be tarnished, yet you still saved me. That means more than if you were the hero type."

Again, something twisted in my chest. She was trying to turn me into a pansy, and I wasn't going to let her. "No. It doesn't."

"Sit down." She gestured to the couch impatiently. "I need to clean that wound."

Without arguing, I sat down. She sat on the table in front of me, situating her legs on either side of mine. It took a hell of a lot of control not to grip her thighs and spread them even wider for me. "You're mine now."

She pulled out the pad soaked in rubbing alcohol, ripping the packet open. "Excuse me?"

"What I mean to say is that since I claimed you as mine,

you have to pretend to be with me. Bitter Hill is gonna check into my claim, guaranteed." I closed my eyes, letting her fuss over me. It burned like a bitch, but I didn't make a peep. I didn't need her to take care of me, but I had a feeling *she* needed to take care of me. To calm her nerves. So I let her. "You need to be mine now."

"So romantic," she muttered under her breath.

"I'm not asking you to actually hook up with me," I said, my voice hard. "I'm not a relationship type of guy. I don't do love, or the whole boyfriend shit."

She laughed. "Yeah. I kinda got that impression already."

"I like variety in my life," I said, opening my eyes. She watched me with a softness I hadn't managed to chase away yet. But eventually I would. I always did, in the end. "You're doing it again."

She threw her hands up. "You can't tell me how I'm allowed to *look* at you, for the love of God."

"Actually, I—"

"I'm not one of your crew who you can just boss around, Lucky." She pulled out the Neosporin, squirted it on her finger, and rubbed it into the gash on my head. I barely kept from wincing. "What's it like?"

"What's what like?" I muttered.

"Having everyone in Steel Row terrified of you and the Sons?"

I could give her a cocky answer. Say it was the way the whole world should be. But I didn't want to give her the generic answer I gave everyone else. "It's the way my life's been since I was fourteen. It's all I've known since, and all I'll ever know."

Without welcome, the bag I'd packed came to mind. It reminded me I didn't have to stay. But the thing was—now I *did*. I'd gone down there and claimed her as mine. She needed my protection, or they'd rip her to shreds.

I couldn't run now.

"But you don't like it?" she asked, pulling out a Band-Aid now.

I wasn't answering that question. We weren't schoolgirls bonding over a makeover, for fuck's sake. Why did she give a damn if I was *happy* or not? How was I supposed to even know what that felt like? "I don't need a Band-Aid. What am I, six?"

"It'll get infected."

"I'll be fine." I stood and walked over to the window, minus the Band-Aid. Movement in the alley behind her bar caught my eye. "Cleanup is here."

She came up beside me, her breaths becoming shallow when she saw the men below. "What will they do with the . . . ?"

"Corpses," I offered, mildly amused at her discomfort with the idea of them being dead. To me, it was just another day on the job. "I don't know and I don't care."

She rubbed her forehead, not looking away. "They're really dead."

"Yeah. They're really dead." I stiffened beside her. Something rolled off her, and for the first time after a fight I'd won . . . I almost felt ashamed. When I killed, it was usually for the job. Not for a fucking girl. What the hell had I been thinking? "Do you think I could have made them a cup of tea and asked them to kindly please stop hurting you?"

She wrapped her arms around herself and shook her head slowly. "No."

"Exactly."

They went to the back door of the bar and tried the door. She tensed. "What are they doing?"

"They're looking for you. Looking for a plot hole in our story."

She rubbed the goose bumps off her arms. "And if they find one?"

"Then you won't be safe." I tipped her chin up, forcing her to face me. Her skin was soft. So soft it felt almost wrong to touch it with my rough hands. As if I dirtied her by doing so. "You have to stay with me. We have to make it look real."

She tapped her foot, looking anywhere but at me. I knew why. We were close, I was touching her, and I'd bet my last dying breath that she felt the same electricity I did. That same undeniable urge to get closer. Much fucking closer.

"Do you have a spare bedroom?" she asked.

"No." I tipped my head to the left. "I'll sleep on the couch; you can have my bed."

"I couldn't ask that of you. I'll take the couch."

I forced a smirk. "Aw, come on, sweetheart. What kind of gentleman would I be if I allowed that to happen?"

"I thought you weren't a gentleman," she shot back.

"I'm not." Letting go of her, I took one step back. I tried to put enough distance between us to help keep my undying urge to touch her in control. It didn't work. I still wanted her. "But for you, I decided to be one tonight. Sleep well. I'll be an asshole again in the morning."

She shook her head, a small smile tilting her pink lips up in the corner. "That's not something you can turn off. You're either an asshole or you're not."

"Oh, I am." I strode to the couch and sat down, setting my feet on the table and crossing my ankles. "Don't ever think otherwise. You saw what I do to people who fuck with something that's mine."

Her nostrils flared, and she marched up to me with narrowed eyes. "I'm not yours, *Lucky*. Stop thinking I am."

"It's cute that you think that. Really, it is." I stared up at her, forcing the same *I don't give a shit* smile to my face I'd perfected when I was ten. "Because you're wrong."

She laughed and shook her head. "You have this whole thing down to a science, don't you?"

"This whole what?"

"The tough-guy act," she said, leaning down and looking me square in the eyes. "You say something nice, realize you did it, and then say something ludicrously ignorant to even it out. To make people not like you."

I snorted. She was uncomfortably close to the truth and I couldn't let her know it. At least one piece of her logic was wrong. How could I possibly be some kind of nice guy masquerading as an asshole? It was the other way around; tonight, I was an asshole masquerading as a nice guy, and that was much more dangerous. "Run off to bed, sweetheart, before I decide to show you just how much of an asshole I can be."

"You don't scare me." She placed her hands on her hips and stared me down. "And furthermore, I don't require your protection. I can take care of myself, just like I always have. I'll sleep here tonight, but tomorrow this thing we have going on between us?" She pointed to me, to her, and back again. "It's *over.*"

"If you hadn't just been brutally attacked in an alley, I'd show you exactly what we have between us." I stood slowly, my gaze locked on her the whole time. She flushed and didn't back off. "You started something last night when you came up to me in your bar and called me Lucky. You knew exactly what you were doing, and you know exactly what you're doing now. You're fucking with me."

She lifted her chin. "Yeah. So why are you smiling, then?"

"Because I have a secret." I skimmed my fingers down her arm, watching the goose bumps rise as I went. She stood her ground, not retreating from my touch. "I know exactly what I'm doing, too."

"And what, precisely, is that?"

Leaning in, I brushed my lips across her cheekbone. Just a featherlight touch, enough to show her I wasn't messing around. Enough to make her slightly afraid of me, because she needed to be afraid of me. If she wasn't, I'd have no defenses against her.

"Oh, funny you should ask," I said, grinning against her temple. I cupped the back of her head, threading my fingers through her silky curls. "Even funnier? I have no intention of answering. You'll just have to wait to find out, like a good girl. But I'll give you one hint."

Her breathing increased. "What's that?"

"We're not over and you're not refusing my protection. I didn't stick my neck out for you to see you get jumped in an alley tomorrow night, without me there to save your pretty little ass. I own you now, darlin', and you'd best accept it."

She stepped to the side as far as she could with me holding on to her hair, glaring up at me. "God, you're so—"

"Devastatingly charming?" I let go of her completely, rubbing my jaw and grinning at her show of anger. "You've told me that once or twice."

"Annoying. Insufferable. *Cock*—"

Her cheeks turned red as soon as she started to shout that last one.

I spluttered before bursting into laughter. "I have one of those, yes. But don't think you'll be seeing it anytime soon. Now, go to bed before I change my mind."

She scowled at me and spun on her heel. As soon as she cleared the bedroom door, she slammed it behind her. I dropped the smirk and sat down, letting out a shuddering sigh. This was a fucking mess. Not only had I broken my code of keeping my nose out of other people's business, but I'd done it with another gang.

One that was a reliable repeat customer.

I'd killed two of their men and almost killed the third.

I should have just finished the third asshole off, too, so there would be no one to talk. If this wasn't a shit storm, I didn't know what was. I'd just declared war on Bitter Hill, a gang that was our ally, and over what? A girl? A challenge?

The door opened and she came out. She'd taken my shirt off and stood clothed in that damn see-through bra again. "I no longer want to sleep in this. It feels dirtier than the blood-soaked shirt did, because it's *yours*. Unlike *me*."

With that, she stalked across the room and chucked my shirt at me, hitting me dead center in the chest. "Heidi, put the damn shirt back—"

"No." She tossed her hair over her shoulders, her blue eyes flashing beams of fire at me. "And when I'm asleep in your bed, think of this. I sleep nude . . . but you'll never get close enough to see that for yourself. Because this is *over*."

With a dramatic hair flip that only a woman like Heidi could pull off, she turned on her heel and went into my room, shutting the door behind her. As I held my shirt— which now smelled like peaches—she slid the lock into place.

Okay, yeah, I'd started a war over a woman.

But what a woman she was . . .

And she was all mine.

CHAPTER 6

HEIDI

The next night, I cleaned the same spot on the bar for what had to be the millionth time, my motions jerky and rough. Jimmy sat on the corner stool, watching me like usual, but that wasn't what had me on edge. I could handle him with my eyes closed and my hands tied behind my back. All night long, from a table toward the back, a few guys had been staring me down all night. Watching. Waiting. Planning. I could tell from their clothing that they were from the same gang as the assholes who'd attacked me—Bitter Hill.

And the man Lucas had let get away?

Yeah, he was here, too. Watching me.

I had a feeling they were lingering to see if Lucas showed up, whether he'd really staked his "claim" on me or not. If he didn't, I'd be fair game. Lucas had told me as much last night, but I'd refused to accept it. Refused to pretend to be his "property" to scare off a gang that had suddenly decided I was *interesting*. I didn't know what I'd done to earn this level of attention, but I didn't want it. Even so, I had a feeling the scrutiny wasn't going anywhere.

The second Lucas had claimed me, the wheels were set in motion.

And the fact that he'd killed two of their guys to protect me? Well, that didn't help, either. I'd seen enough to know that a challenge had been thrown down, and now I was going to be smack-dab in the middle of it, whether I liked it or not. It was becoming clear that I was stuck with Lucas, *and* his protection. And I didn't get a say in that, either.

The biggest guy at the table kept staring at me, so I raised a glass to him and downed the water I'd gotten myself moments before. As soon as I set the empty glass down, he smirked and rested a hand at his hip. On his gun, no doubt.

Then he stood and moved toward me, one cocky step at a time.

My heart sped up and my muscles stiffened, but I forced myself to remain calm outwardly. When he stopped before me, he leaned on the bar casually, his back to the wall and his front to the door. Watching out for Lucas, more than likely. I knew how men like him worked. Always on guard. Always ready for the next fight.

"Where's your man?"

I stared back into his eyes, not backing down. He was tall and muscular, but I didn't care. It was all about appearance with guys like this, and to show him weakness or fear would be the biggest mistake I could make. "I don't know. Working, maybe? I'm sure he'll come in soon. He always does. It's why we started dating in the first place. The guy just kept showing up, like a bad penny. Eventually, I gave in. Romantic, isn't it?"

Shaking his head, he chuckled. "For your sake? You better hope so. I need to talk to him. He crossed the line last night, and this needs to be settled. I understand he felt the need to protect his girl, but thing is? No one knew you

were his to protect. And if you're not, and he lied to us . . ."
He let his words trail off, staring at me menacingly.

He didn't need to finish his sentence. I knew exactly
what he inferred, and exactly how much danger I would be
in if the lie was exposed. Damn it, Lucas had been right. I
still needed his protection. Tossing the rag down, I crossed
my arms. "That's all fine and dandy. What can I get you to
drink . . . while you're waiting for him to show? I see you
didn't have anything on the table back there, and this isn't
a charity establishment, so . . ."

"Is that so?" He glanced down and tapped the paper on
the bar that had tonight's specials printed out on it. "Well,
then . . . I'll have four of these two-dollar Sam Adams,
please."

I gave him a small smile, being careful not to reopen my
wounds. It didn't hurt much anymore, but I figured better
safe than sorry. "Of course."

As I walked away, I felt his eyes on me. Everywhere.
The attack still fresh in my mind, I had to fight back a
telling shudder. I knew exactly how men like him got what
they wanted . . . all too clearly. And I didn't want him anywhere near me or my bar. But business was business, and
the Patriot needed all the money it could get. As it was, I
barely managed to make ends meet. The past few months
had been particularity tough, but I'd be damned if I'd let
it go down without a fight. I owed that much to Frankie.
According to him, the Patriot had been around since the
birth of our country. The way he told it, the Founding
Fathers themselves had sat in this bar, plotting and planning for this very country. Whether it was true or not? I
didn't care.

This was my baby, and I wasn't about to send paying
customers away when I had bills to pay, booze to buy, and
employees relying on me. I'd watch them, sure, while waiting for Lucas to show up and scare them away. But still . . .

Relying on a guy to swoop in and rescue the day didn't sit well with me.

I took care of myself and my own *on* my own. I didn't need some guy helping me. Protecting me. Not until now, anyway. What the hell had I gotten myself into? I slid the beers onto the bar and met the man's eyes. Or tried to, anyway. He was too busy staring at my boobs to notice. I found myself wishing that I hadn't sent my waitress and cook home when the kitchen closed at nine. But since we weren't serving food, no service was needed, so I couldn't just pay them for sitting around and doing nothing. I was on my own. Holding my hand out, I cleared my throat. "That'll be eight dollars."

"Yeah." Slowly, his gaze lifted. "I figured that out by myself."

I arched a brow. "I wasn't sure if you could. I mean, math can be confusing for guys like you. So can the word *no*."

"I never had a problem with math, but you're right. I don't like the word *no* or what it stands for. Never have." He handed me a five and four ones. "Keep the change."

A whole dollar. "Gee, thanks."

He nodded to me once, grabbed the mugs, and walked off. Swaggered off was more like it. As soon as he was back at his table, I released the breath I'd been holding and went to the register to put the eight dollars in, tucking the lousy tip away safely.

Marco came up behind me. "They gonna be trouble?"

"Nah." I blew out a breath. There was no way in hell I wanted Marco anywhere near this mess. Not when he was about to leave all this crap behind him, once and for all. "Nothing to worry about. I thought I told you to go upstairs. I'm fine on my own."

"Are you sure about that?" He leaned on the bar, his eyes on the Bitter Hill Crew. They stared right back, challenging him without words. Marco straightened. "They look like trouble to me."

I stared down at the register, taking a second to compose myself. I hadn't told him about the attack last night, and I had no intention of ever doing so. I told him I slipped on the wet floor, and busted my face on the bar on my way down. If he knew the truth, he'd confront those guys. And if he did that, someone would get hurt. Him, more than likely. He was a good kid and an effective bouncer, but he wasn't a match for guys like them, who killed without blinking.

Guys like *Lucas*.

And even though Marco had lived on the streets, he wasn't made for that life. He wasn't going to be stuck here, dealing with gangs and murder and rape. He was going to get out of here in five days and make something of himself. Do something *real* with his life. Sure, he'd done his share of petty thievery to get by while he'd been living on the streets, but he had dreams and goals. And I was determined to make sure he got them. Determined to see him thrive in a world full of shit and evil.

He *had* to.

"Of course they're trouble. Men like them always are." I shrugged and turned my back to them. I was sick of watching them stare at me as if I was their next meal. "But they'll keep to themselves, I'm sure. And if they don't, I'll handle them."

He looked less than convinced. "I don't know. They're watching you closely."

"Nothing new there," I said dismissively, waving a hand. "Enough about them. Did you start packing yet?"

He ducked his head and peeked at me from beneath his lowered lashes. "Yeah, but let's be realistic here, Heidi. I'm not going to fit in there. All the other students will be . . . you know, normal. Rich. Spoiled."

"But not better than you."

He rolled his eyes. "I bet they'd disagree."

"I don't give a rat's ass what they'd say. Not after that

essay you wrote, which your guidance counselor said was *the best* one she's *ever* read. I guarantee they didn't get any others that looked even half as amazing as yours." I rested a hand on his arm. "And you can't think like that—thinking they're better than you. They're not. You have just as much right to be at that college as anyone else does, and you'll see that when you get there."

He smiled, but I could tell it was forced. "You might be right. But until then, I'm going to head up to pack since you don't need me. I'll be down later around closing just to make sure you're okay."

"Okay." The door opened behind me, and I knew, without looking, exactly who had walked in. I could *feel* him, even without confirming that it was indeed Lucas. "Be safe."

"You, too. Speaking of which," he mumbled, eyeing the door, "that redheaded guy is back."

My heart kicked up a notch. "Yeah . . . about him?" I smoothed my hands down my jean shorts. It might be cold outside, but it was hot as hell in here, so I dressed accordingly. The whole bar consisted of one smallish room, so body heat added up quickly on a busy night. "He's my boyfriend, in a way, for a little while. Sort of."

Marco's eyes narrowed. "What do you mean, *sort of*?"

"It's a long story, and nothing you need to know, since you'll be outta here soon." I smiled, but I had a feeling it looked as strained as his smile had. "I just didn't want you worrying if you saw him touching me, or talking to me too long. That's all."

"All right . . ." He stepped back, his attention still on Lucas. "He's not your type, though."

Laughing, I pushed off the bar. "Do I have a type at all? I don't exactly date a lot."

"True. But when you do?" He walked away and said the last bit over his shoulder. "It's not guys like him. Be careful."

"Always am," I called out. "Now, get out of here."

After taking a breath to calm my nerves, I spun around and scanned the poorly lit room for Lucas. I really needed to get better lighting, brighten the place up a bit. He made his way over to me with long, determined strides, completely ignoring the Bitter Hill table. His attention never wavered from me. As he walked across the room, my stomach clenched tight. He had a way of moving through a crowd that announced, without his even trying to, that he owned everyone in it. That he, and he alone, was in control. And everyone who disagreed could go to hell.

"You okay?" he asked, his green eyes skimming over me. The lights in the bar made his hair seem redder, and his arms flexed as he stopped directly in front of me.

Shaking off the warmth coiling through my veins, I rested my hands on the bar and leaned across it. "Yeah, I'm fine, Lucky. But we have company, and they're—"

"I told you not to call me that," he growled.

Then, without a warning, he curled his hand behind my neck and hauled me farther over the bar. Before I could so much as blink, his lips were on mine. He kept the kiss gentle, so it didn't hurt. Despite the fact that he was hot, and I'd been attracted to him since day one, the way he kissed me was so impersonal that it did . . . nothing.

Nothing at all.

His generous lips were hard under mine, and he didn't so much as move his lips softly over mine even once. They were just there, pressed against mine, and then they weren't. He pulled back slightly but didn't let go of me. "I know they're here, watching. That's why I kissed you. They needed to see it before I went over to them."

I blinked. "I don't mean to insult your game or anything, but that wasn't a kiss. I don't know *what* it was, but I definitely wouldn't classify that as a *kiss*."

Instead of looking wounded or injured at my insult to

his moves, he appeared amused. His green eyes danced, and the smirk I'd come to know so well slid into place. "It wasn't supposed to be one. Not really. Run your hand down my back."

He swept his thumb over my jawline, still holding on to me. From a distance, it might look tender and loving, but I knew it for what it really was.

A claiming, intended for those jerks in the corner.

I skimmed my hand down his muscular back. The feeling of his body beneath it affected me much more than that shadow of a kiss had. Not one to follow directions blindly, I slipped my hand down the curve of his ass, cupping it tight. Digging my nails into his jeans, I stared right back at him, not backing down. "How's this? Good enough of a show for you? Why not just write 'Taken' on my forehead for all to see? Or better yet, bend me over the bar and fuck me from behind. Then they'll *really* see I'm yours."

He hissed through his teeth and gripped my chin, holding me still. "Easy, sweetheart. Keep tempting me with that saucy little mouth of yours, and I'll bite. Hard. I don't think you want to go down that road with me just yet."

"Is that a dare?" I smiled at him. "I never *could* back down from a dare, you know."

"Good to know." He leaned close, his lips a breath from mine, and despite myself, my stomach tightened in anticipation. Instinctively, I knew that if he kissed me again, it wouldn't be the mockery of a kiss that he'd given me earlier. "But I told you that I'd make you admit you wanted me before I touched you again, and I meant it. Are you ready to admit you want me now?"

Hell yeah.

"Nope." I laughed and patted his butt condescendingly. "Not in a million years. Hate to break it to you, but you're not really my type, Lucky."

Liar, liar, pants on fire.

He traced an invisible path down my throat and over the top of my shirt. His gaze dipped down to my cleavage, then shot back up as if there was nothing much to see there at all. Man, he was good. Too good. "Yeah, I am. But that's okay. Deny it all you want. We both know the truth."

Scoffing, I shook my head slightly. "You go on and keep thinking whatever gets your rocks off, man. Don't let me sink your battleship."

"Oh, I won't." His grip on me tightened. "Because I'm glad you're not ready for me yet. What would be the fun in winning the fight so quickly? I plan to break you down, slowly and gently, until you finally fall apart in my arms and beg me to fuck you. It'll make the victory all the sweeter, in the end."

Ignoring the surge of lust his words brought out in me, I lifted a shoulder. "Whatever you say."

"Make no mistake. In the end, you'll be naked in my bed." He trailed his hand down the curve of my body, barely touching my breast. But it felt as if he'd stripped my shirt off in front of everyone and had his way with me. My stomach clenched tight, and I pressed my thighs together. It did nothing to ease the empty ache inside me. "And you'll love every second of it, darlin'."

When he dropped his hand on the bar, I released the breath I'd been holding. "Keep chasing that pot of gold at the end of the rainbow, Lucky. You'll have better luck catching *that* than me."

"Who said I wanted to catch you that badly that I'd chase you at all? The way I see it, you're the one who ran into my arms. You're the one who needs me, not the other way around," he said, his cocky brow arched. He gave me a once-over and then lifted a shoulder. "This thing we have between us? For now, it's a necessary transaction and nothing else."

"Is that so?" I slid my hand around the curve of his ass,

over his hip, and brushed against his dick. And what a dick it was, thank you very much. He was hard and huge and unyielding. Much like the man himself. "Doesn't feel like just a transaction to me."

He stepped back, out of my reach. "That, darlin', is called being a man. You cup a guy's ass and talk dirty to him, you're gonna get a reaction. Next time? I'd make sure you're prepared for it, because you can be damn sure it won't end with me walking away empty-handed."

Lucas walked off without another word. Instead of going to the gang members to tell them to leave, he walked by them, nodded once, and sat in the opposite corner of the bar, his back to the wall. When he saw me staring at him, he raised a brow. The small gesture was a hell of a lot more intimidating than the four beefy, hardened gang members tracking me, because unlike with them . . .

I couldn't take my eyes off him.

CHAPTER 7

LUCAS

Damn it all to hell, Heidi was trying to kill me. I'd been sitting there for three hours now, watching her sashay behind her bar. Back and forth, back and forth, all while wearing those tiny-ass shorts of hers. As if that wasn't enough torture, she made it a point to flirt with every single guy who came up to her. Every. Single. One.

I *knew* what game she played, and what she thought she was up to, but even so? It pissed me the hell off. While she might not have admitted it yet, and while I hadn't had her yet, she belonged to me. And I didn't share. Hell, I never kept women around long enough for sharing to be an issue in the first place. But still . . .

I wasn't about to start now.

Some dickhead raised a hand for her attention, and she rested her elbows on the bar and smiled at him, giving him a clear shot of her cleavage. Judging from the way the man shifted on his chair, he took full advantage of that view. If I didn't know any better, I'd swear she didn't even realize she did it. Didn't realize how damn seductive everything she did was, from her laugh, to her walk, to the sexy way her hips swung with every step she took.

But she did.

No one was that sexy without knowing it.

She said something else, laughing and shaking her head. The guy got up and walked to the door, not taking his eyes off her until the last possible moment. The clock on the wall showed me why he'd left. It was closing time. Good.

I'd had enough of this waiting bullshit for one night.

When I glanced back at Heidi, she quickly looked away, as if she hadn't been watching me all along. I involuntarily smiled. Her show of independence was . . . cute. Her attempts at making her disinterest known were even cuter, especially since she thought it would actually work to get me to back off.

Little did she realize, it had the exact opposite effect.

The harder she pushed me away, the more I wanted to pull her closer.

It was in my nature. Who I was, and who I would always be. Tell me I couldn't have something, and damned if I wouldn't stop trying until I proved you wrong with a big *fuck-you* emblazoned in the sky for all to see—after I'd taken the very thing you told me I'd never have. Twice.

Heidi had just made herself even more irresistible.

All last night, I'd sat on the couch, watching both the front door and the bedroom door, where everything I wanted was lying—more than likely *naked*—in my bed. And I'd been a perfect gentleman. Hadn't moved off that couch.

If she hadn't been nearly raped yesterday, I would have taken up the challenge of convincing her to admit her desire for me, before fucking her in every possible position. As it was, it looked as if I'd have plenty of other opportunities. As I'd predicted, those little shits from Bitter Hill were hanging around, just waiting for an opportunity to take her from me.

Waiting to pounce like the dirty vultures they were.

I knew three of the men from past sales, and I recognized the last one from somewhere, too, but I couldn't quite place him. Business with them was a necessary evil. They dealt in drugs, while we did guns, so there was no competition there. Up until now, we'd peacefully worked side by side without issues.

Up until I'd killed some of their guys last night, anyway.

They'd been tailing me all day, and I knew it was only a matter of time until they made their move. What that move would be? I had no clue. But it wouldn't happen in here. Heidi didn't need us breaking up her bar or causing the police to shut her down. If they wanted a fight, they'd get one.

Hell, I'd love to give them one.

Just not *here*.

I lifted my empty glass at Heidi, and she rolled her eyes from across the room. I'd been slowly sipping my whiskey all night, not willing to risk getting shitfaced while we had the enemy in our midst. They weren't here to drink—that much was obvious, since their still-full beers sat on their table untouched—so I couldn't afford to be stupid.

Again.

After Heidi had a low conversation with her bouncer, who had reappeared a few minutes ago, the boy looked over at me, frowned, and went back upstairs. I could just barely make out the steps before a door closed behind him. I had a feeling that his dismissal had more to do with keeping him out of trouble than with the time. Judging by the worried glances she'd been throwing at him ever since he'd come down and seen the Bitter Hill Crew still hanging around, she had a soft spot for the boy.

If that was the case, she shouldn't be so obvious about it.

It was rule number two in this life. Never show your weakness. If you did, it gave them a chance to exploit it . . . and you. A lock clicked as his footsteps climbed higher and higher, and then I heard him walking above us. So did the four men in the opposite corner. Heidi stared at the closed door, let out a sigh, swiped her hands down her shorts, and nodded at me once.

We were the only people left in the bar.

She carried over a glass of whiskey, shooting the men in the corner a narrow-eyed glance as she passed, snapping at them, "It's closing time. Time to go home."

Her steps faltered when one of the pricks lifted his hand, made a gun figure, and pulled the "trigger." It was the guy I couldn't quite place. It took me a second, but then I finally recognized him. It was the one I'd let go—the one with a star tattoo on his neck. I should have popped him. I'd correct that lapse in judgment tonight.

Growling, I lurched to my feet. "Outside. Now."

"Don't." Heidi slid the glass across my table and shook her head, her lips pressed in a tight line. "It's not worth it."

She rested a small hand on my chest. It burned through my shirt, and some foreign emotion swept through me. I shook off the unfamiliar feelings she caused, not even sure what the hell they meant, and filed them away for a day when I was ready to examine my emotions more closely.

Aka, never.

Behind her, the leader, Phil, kicked the one who'd upset Heidi and whispered something to him. The other man lowered his head. I glanced down at her, and she stared back, her blue eyes crystal clear but shadowed. They were still missing that sparkle that had intrigued me initially.

That pissed me off even more than the fucker's actions did.

"The hell it isn't," I snarled. The other four men stood, hands resting on their pieces. Pieces *we'd* sold to them.

Heidi stepped in front of me for the second time that night. "Get out of my way before you get hurt."

Curling her hands in my shirt, she held on tight and didn't budge. *"No."*

"I don't take orders from you, darlin'." I gripped her hands and forcibly removed them from my shirt. "In fact, you're supposed to take them from me."

"I'm not one of your men," she argued, her hands stiff under mine. "So you can take your orders and shove them up your—"

"Heidi." Amusement trickled past my irritation at her resistance, but it wasn't strong enough to win the battle. Didn't she see I was trying to help her? "Get out of my way."

When she didn't move fast enough for my tastes, I picked her up and set her aside. But she didn't let go of me. In fact, she curled both hands in my shirt and shoved me against the wall. If anyone else had done that, they'd be dead on the floor right now.

I stumbled back. "What the f—?"

Throwing her arms around me, she kissed me. Unlike my cold, calculated kiss . . . she was all fucking in. Her mouth moved over mine, and her tongue swept inside my mouth, seeking mine. I kept my eyes cracked open, refusing to let those shits out of my line of sight. They watched us intently, so I cupped her ass and hauled her against me, letting out a groan to make it look realistic.

Oh so slightly, I let my fingers trace the insides of her thighs, barely brushing against the heat of her pussy. Man, I wished we had privacy, so I could actually enjoy this. But we didn't, so I couldn't. She, however, had no qualms about letting her feelings take over, and practically melted in my arms. A moan escaped her, and it distracted me.

Almost dragged me in.

If this had been an actual kiss, one that would end with

her naked beneath me, I'd spin her, press against the wall right now, and my hands would be learning every inch of her body. Every. Delicious. Inch. It wasn't real, though.

And that would have to wait.

If she wanted to sell the story to these guys, I would let her. We were together, and fucking—as far as Bitter Hill knew, anyway. Whatever. But I'd be damned if I lost myself in her, in fiction or real life. I wanted her, yes. But that was it.

No matter how she made me feel, or how much I liked her, it would never become anything else. It couldn't. She'd have to know that before I touched her for real.

Breaking the kiss off, I pushed her behind me. Miraculously, she didn't fight me this time. In fact, she clung to the back of my shirt, shuddering slightly behind me. "Holy shit," she muttered under her breath.

I almost smiled. Almost.

"You need to back off my girl," I said, my voice low and hard. I didn't need to shout to get my point across, and all six of us knew it. "Find somewhere else to drink and cause trouble. I let you off with a warning last night. It won't happen again."

The lieutenant motioned for his boys to stay back, and rounded the table. "You consider last night a *warning*? You killed two of my guys."

"It could have been three, Phil." I shrugged and stared at the man who'd dared to "shoot" my girl. "Still could be. Tonight."

Phil laughed and ruffled his brown hair with his left hand. "We have four guns, and you have one. It's hardly a fair fight."

"You're right." I eyed them and just as quickly dismissed them. Easy. "You should have brought at least two more guys. We all know George and Patrick aren't the best in a fight, and I already bested this idiot last night."

"Fuck you," said idiot snapped.

He came a step closer, and I lifted my shirt a bit, resting my hand on my Sig. It was a violation of my parole to carry, but I didn't give a damn. In my line of work, doing business unarmed was a death sentence. "That's close enough. You want a fight? I'll give you one, gladly. But take it outside my girl's bar."

Phil laughed, and the other three joined in. Admittedly, their laughter sounded a little forced. "You talk a big game, but you let a hot piece of pussy stop you from fighting?"

"Excuse me?" Heidi tensed behind me and let go of my shirt. I knew without looking they'd managed to piss her off. And once she was pissed off, there'd be no shutting her up. In the time I'd frequented her bar, I'd learned that. She came out from behind me, her finger raised as she pointed to them. "You can take your untouched beers, and kiss my a—"

"Enough." I grabbed her and propelled her toward the bar with a gentle shove between her shoulder blades. "Finish closing up. I've got this, darlin'."

She shrugged free of my hold. "The hell you do. I refuse to be shuffled aside like a good little—"

"Heidi." I locked eyes with her, giving her the look that Chris always said could scare the clothes off a nun. *"Go."*

For a second, I thought she wasn't going to listen. Her eyes flashed with anger, and she jabbed a finger at me. "We'll talk about this later." And then she spun on her heel and went behind the bar, slamming things around as she finished closing up.

I sighed. Tonight was going to be a bitch.

Phil laughed again. I'd never wanted to kill someone for laughing as badly as I did right now. "Shit. If I had any doubts about your relationship, they just went away," he said, amusement clear in his tone.

"Oh?" I turned around and raised a brow. "Why's that?"

"Because she yelled at you and you didn't shoot her." He grinned. "Also, the evidence that you're pussy-whipped is there for any fool to see."

The hell I was.

But I wasn't about to argue with this fucker. His misconception worked to my benefit. "You need to clear out and consider this place off-limits. You're lucky I only killed two of your guys this time." I gave a curt nod toward the asshole I let live and had the satisfaction of seeing him pale. "Or would you be okay if I let one of my guys come to your house and rape your girl?"

Phil postured, trying to look intimidating, and his voice could have cut steel. "Is that a threat, Mr. Donahue?"

"Since you have to ask, the answer's obviously a no. If I make a threat, there will be no doubt it's a fucking threat." I smirked at him and leaned against the wall casually, crossing my ankles. "Besides, the Sons get plenty of willing pussy. We don't have to go out and *take* it."

Last night's asshole now turned red in the face and stepped forward.

"Stay right there, Tom," Phil said. The little fucker obeyed instantly. "Speaking of the Sons, does Tate Daniels know that you killed two of my guys last night?"

"I told him, yeah." I shrugged, pretending nonchalance. "He, of course, understood why I did what I did. What's ours stays ours. It's always been that way in Steel Row. Anyone thinks otherwise, they get taught differently. As you learned last night."

It was true. I'd made sure to go see Tate first thing this morning, and I'd briefed him on what had gone down, skipping over the fact that my relationship with Heidi was still more fantasy than reality. For a little while, anyway. And we both knew it. I glanced over at her. She was sitting on a barstool now, arms crossed and clearly still not happy.

She tilted her head at me and shook it, as if she could hear my thoughts.

Maybe she could. I wouldn't put it past her.

"So. Like I said." Returning my attention to the Bitter Hill guys, I stared the lieutenant down. Alpha to alpha. And I didn't back down. "Get out and stay the hell away from my woman and her place. And you can wash that damn tag off her building, too."

After a valiant effort, he reluctantly looked away. I could practically see his tail tucked between his legs. "Shit, whatever. I hear you."

I nodded once. "See yourself out. Now."

"Of course." He walked past me and motioned for his guys to follow him. He kept walking as he talked. "But we're watching you." He stopped at the bar and trailed his fingers over Heidi's arm. She jerked away, nearly falling off the stool, and glowered at him. "And we're watching *her* even closer. I'll allow the kills from last night. Collateral damage in a territory dispute. But if you cross us again? We'll come back in force and . . . take what's yours."

With a lingering look at Heidi that left no doubt as to his meaning, he walked out the door and into the snow. The three assholes with him leered at Heidi, clearly hoping I'd fuck up, before following him outside. Every fiber of my body pulsed with rage and the desire to *kill*. I'd been trained to ignore baiting such as this. Trained to keep my cool in a heated situation, no matter what occurred. But they threatened Heidi, and I was ready to flip my shit.

They were going to die.

Every single one of them.

My mind flashed image after image of what they could do to Heidi. . . . It *did* things to me. It turned me into a murderous beast that needed blood *now*. And I'd damn well get it, too.

I walked after them, pulling my gun out of its holster as I went.

The door shut behind them, and I reached for the knob. Before I could close my palm over it, someone shoved me back. I growled and lifted my gun, pointing it at the object that stopped me from getting what I wanted: to see their blood pooling on the sidewalk because they'd challenged me and endangered what was mine. *"Get out of my way."*

Wide, bright blue eyes and pale porcelain skin stared back at me. She was so damn beautiful. More beautiful than mere words would ever describe. More beautiful than a guy like me deserved, or would ever deserve, in his whole life.

And I was pointing my gun at her head.

CHAPTER 8

HEIDI

~

The second the cold barrel of his gun aimed at the middle of my forehead . . . I froze. I didn't breathe. Didn't dare to so much as blink, in case it sent him over the edge. I didn't think he'd hurt me—not *really*. Not after the way he'd reacted after they'd threatened my safety. But still, having a murderous man hold a gun to your head, with rage blazing in his eyes and anger making those huge biceps of his tremble . . .

Well, you'd have to be a fool *not* to be scared.

And I wasn't a fool.

Hands held out at my sides, I licked my parched lips. "Lucas . . ."

"Fuck." He lowered the gun and stuck it back into the holster before dragging his hand through his hair. If I wasn't mistaken, it trembled ever so slightly. "Don't ever, *ever*, walk in front of me again when I have my gun out. *Ever.*"

I nodded quickly, my hands still held out to my sides. That's something I already knew, obviously. You never messed with a guy when he was intent on murdering someone, especially when that guy was as dangerous as Lucas freaking Donahue. But when he acted all protective and reluctantly heroic, it was hard to remember who he was. And what he did. Stupid, *stupid*, girl.

He cursed under his breath again and reached out for me. Before I could flinch or react in any way, he pulled me into his arms and hugged me, cradling the back of my head tenderly. His hold, while possessive, was somehow comforting, too. "I'm sorry. After last night . . . the last thing you need is another asshole getting in your face."

I closed my eyes, letting myself enjoy the comfort for a second, but then I pushed at his chest and pulled away. He let me. "I'm fine. It's fine. I'm stronger than you think."

"I never doubted that," he said, his tone even. "But still, I'm sorry. I'd never intentionally hurt you. Not like that."

I nodded once, swallowing hard. *Not like that*. What, exactly, was that supposed to mean? I wanted to ask but didn't. "I know."

"Okay. Good." He glanced around at the empty tables and rubbed his jaw, which was definitely harder than usual. "I'll help you lock up, and then we'll go back to my place."

Shaking my head, I crossed the room and grabbed the full beers the gang members had abandoned. "I can do it on my own. You don't have to help."

"Yeah." After straightening a chair, he headed across the room, chugged the last of his whiskey, and let out a long breath. "I do."

When he turned back to me again, that smooth, easy grin of his was back in place once more. I had a feeling he used it as a mask, when he didn't want his feelings to be known. So I was sure he always wore it, because he was a guy, and when did they *ever* show their true feelings? I nodded once. "Okay. Thanks."

He shrugged, as if he didn't give a damn whether I

thanked him or not. I had a feeling it wasn't an act at all. He really didn't give a damn. "Do you need to mop?"

I nodded again. "Yeah."

"I'll do it." He grabbed the beers out of my hands and headed for the bar. "Where do you keep it?"

"Kitchen, in the left corner." I set a chair—the same one he'd straightened—on top of the table before grabbing a second one. "You can set your glass in the sink in the back. I'll have the dishwasher wash it tomorrow. The beers can go in there, too."

He went into the kitchen without speaking, and we finished closing up in companionable silence. Having an extra pair of hands was a pretty big help, so it took me less than half the time it usually did to get the bar shut down and ready for opening. It was Sunday night, so it was the beginning of my "weekend." The bar would reopen on Wednesday.

After I did one more walk-through, making sure I hadn't missed anything, I shut the lights off. Lucas held the door open for me. I walked past him, shoving my hands in my pockets and shivering even before I was outside. It was bitterly cold, and these shorts did absolutely nothing for my legs. Lucas had gone back to my place with me earlier today, so I had clothes at his place. Where I was currently *living*.

Which brought to mind . . .

"How long are we supposed to be, you know, together?" I asked, hunching into myself to ward off the chill.

He shut the door, checked the lock, and turned to me. "Are we already at that point in our fake relationship that we need to talk about our fake future?"

"It's not all that fake when it involves me living in your apartment and us making out in public to prove a point to a bunch of assholes I couldn't care less about." I shivered again, and my teeth chattered. "So, yeah, we're at that point."

"You'll live with me until a sufficient amount of time has passed where we can safely break up, or until I eliminate the threat." He shrugged his brown leather jacket off and draped it over my shoulders, tugging it closed while he looked down at me. "Might be days, might be weeks. No way of knowing."

Eliminate the threat? Aka . . . kill them all. "But—"

"Easy, now. You might hurt my feelings." He gripped the jacket tighter, but his crooked smile contradicted his body language. "Is it so hard to live with me, darlin'?"

He looked so devilishly charming, standing in the moonlight, putting his jacket on me like a gentleman, and looking at me as if I mattered to him. We both knew I didn't. He'd felt sorry for me, he'd saved me, and now he was stuck with me.

I bet he was *thrilled* about that.

"No. Of course not. Your bed is very comfortable." I licked my lips. Images of us together, *naked*, in that bed hit me hard. "You helped me, and it was nice of you. I appreciate it, but—"

He frowned at me, the heat of his body keeping me warm as the chilly wind made itself known. Winter refused to loosen its firm control of the climate, and I was starting to think it never would. "I told you, I'm not fucking 'nice.' Don't call me that. I'm the villain in a fairy tale, not the hero."

The urge to roll my eyes at his self-deprecation was strong, but I managed to contain myself. Barely. "Oh, believe me. I know that. I also know that you helped me, and I don't want to keep taking your bed and complicating your life. Maybe I could still sleep at my place and we could be *together*, but not together. You know?"

He threw his arm over my shoulders and steered me toward his shop. Days-old snow and ice that refused to go away crunched beneath my feet, but I wasn't worried about falling. "No way. First of all, I can't guarantee your safety if you're not with me. Second, it's far too late for that. They've seen you go home with me once, and they would suspect something if it's not a regular thing. My boss was understanding of my little adventure last night, to a point, but he made it very clear that he doesn't want a war. If we give the Bitter Hill guys an opening, and they take it, I can't retaliate. I can't risk pissing Tate, or them, off any more than I already have. If I do, I can kiss my life good-bye—and I don't even wanna think about what they'll do to you."

"But—"

"*No.*"

I would have been tempted to break free of his hold if it wasn't so damn cold out here. Thank God he lived across the street. I'd let him continue being my personal heating pad, but I'd make my feelings clear. "I'm not yours to boss around, Lucky. I've told you, I don't blindly take orders from anyone, not even you."

Something crashed in the alley behind us as he opened the door and pushed me inside gently. "Yeah, you do. In my world, when your man gives you orders, you damn well listen." He raised a hand when I opened my mouth. "And, yes, I know I'm not really your man. And, yes, I know it's old-fashioned and fucked-up. But it is what it is, and it's the life I lead, for better or for worse. If you're going to be my woman, real *or* fake, it's how it's gotta be. End of story."

"The hell it does. I—"

"Enough." He slammed the door shut behind us and boxed me against the wall, leaning down so his face was level with mine. "When we're within these walls, you wanna bitch me out, hit me, whatever, about the rules for out there? Fine. Go for it. But when we're outside of this apartment, and your safety and our lives are at stake? You *will* listen to every damn word I say. There are no other options."

I refused to lower my head or back down. What he said

made sense, but that didn't mean I had to like it. "You're an asshole. We're in private, so I can say it."

"Yeah, you can." His lips twitched ever so slightly. "And I agree. I am an asshole."

"And an idiot."

The twitch stopped. "That I don't agree with, except for in one aspect, but you're entitled to your opinion."

"What's that one aspect?"

"Not telling." He pressed his body—oh my God, that *body*—against mine, grinning down at me. "It's not smart to announce your weaknesses to just anyone."

"I'm not just anyone," I said breathlessly. I could feel *things*, pressed up against my *things*, and it made my stomach clench tight. "I'm your fake girlfriend."

"Exactly my point."

Grinning, he pushed off the wall and walked up the stairs. I followed him because, hey, the view was nice. Lucas Donahue had a hell of an ass. Also, I had nowhere else to go. Lucas swooping in like a modern-day Galahad—and, yes, I know, he was a very bad man, *grrr, argh*—it changed everything. Thanks to Bitter Hill's guys, I was no longer safe out there on my own. So I needed to stay until I was.

And then he'd walk away, and I'd probably never see him again.

Something told me once Lucas Donahue finished with you, he didn't come back to check in and see how you were doing afterward. Once you were done . . .

You were done forever.

He opened his apartment door, motioning me inside. I walked past him, keeping my eyes straight ahead, and flipped the switch on. It looked much the same as it had when we'd left this afternoon, but he'd folded the blanket he'd used last night on top of the couch, and cleaned up the mess I'd made patching him up. My bags still sat by the bedroom door, untouched, next to a black duffel bag of his that had been there last night, too. I stared at them, my heart ridiculously picking up speed when I thought about the next few days I'd be spending here. All day. Alone with him. Turning to face him, I held his jacket closed. It was cozy up here, but I wasn't ready to take it off yet.

It was warm and soft and it smelled like him. Oh God . . .

I was *so* screwed. This wasn't supposed to be happening. I wasn't supposed to want to smell him, for God's sake. Yeah, he was hot. Yeah, he'd kissed me a few times. But neither of those kisses had been real. He showed about as much interest in seeing me naked as he'd show a turnip. Maybe less.

Shrugging his jacket off, I held it out to him. "Here. Thanks."

"Sure thing." He took it from me and flung it over the chair carelessly. His gaze never left my face. "You know, here in Boston, we have this thing called winter. During the winter and most of the spring, it's cold as fuck outside. And it snows. So, generally, in the spring and winter, people wear these things called pants. They're like what you're wearing now, only they go all the way down your legs—like mine do. And while your shorts make you look hot, pants will actually keep you warm."

I placed my hands on my hips and cocked my head, holding back the smile that wanted to escape at his sarcasm. I'd always loved a sharp wit on a man, and, damn, he had one. It wasn't fair. "*Ooooh*. Is *that* what those are for?"

"Indeed," he said dryly. "I suggest you try them."

"I did. The tips were half what I get when I'm wearing shorts." Sitting down on the couch, I crossed my legs and tipped my head back so I could look at him. His gaze was on my legs for a split second before it snapped back to mine. "Men are pigs. They pay more when they can see my legs."

He rounded the couch. "And if they paid more because they saw your ass, would you come to work naked?"

"No. That's a whole different establishment."

Sitting beside me, he trailed his finger up my bare thigh, smiling when goose bumps followed his touch. "Yeah, it is."

"One you've probably frequented."

He shrugged. "For work, sure. But I generally don't spend my free time there. I'd rather get a lap dance for free. And when it's over, I can finish the job right here, on my couch. Or against the wall."

My pulse quickened. If that had been an invitation, my instinctual reply would've been a *hell yes*. A really loud *hell yes*. "Is that a request?"

"Like I told that asshole in the bar, if you have to ask . . ." His green eyes sparkled, and he took his hand off my leg. I missed it instantly. "Want a drink?"

"God yes." I stood up. "I mean . . . I'll get it myself, if you tell me where it is."

"Nah, I'll get it for you for once." He stood, too, and trailed the back of his knuckles over my cheek. I bit down on my tongue. "Wine or whiskey?"

"Wine."

He ran his finger over my lower lip gently. "How's the mouth feeling?"

"It's fine. Barely hurts." My throat felt swollen and aching. It wasn't the only part of me that was aching, thank you very much. I tried to ignore that, though, considering what I was about to say. "Look, if I'm staying here for a while . . . you can't sleep on the couch every night. You should sleep in your bed."

He gave me his back and pulled down a wineglass and a tumbler. "I might not be a white hat, but I refuse to let you sleep on the couch while I take the bed. My ma might have loved me, but she'd rise from her grave to kill me if I did that. No lie."

"You don't have to sleep on the couch." I tucked my

hair behind my ear. "It's a king-size bed, and we're both adults. We could sleep in it together."

He froze, his hand tight on his glass, and backed up a step. Actually backed away from me as if I'd threatened to kill him or something. "You want to sleep in my bed with me?"

The way he said it, half shock, half terror, struck me as odd. "Not like that. I already told you that you weren't my type." I dropped my hand to the counter and tapped my fingers. "But it makes sense, really, for both of us to use it, if we're stuck with each other for a while."

He pulled the whiskey down, poured himself a healthy dose, and finished it all with one swallow. Then he poured himself some more and picked up the wine. He narrowed his eyes and frowned, and I couldn't help but feel as if he was watching me as if I'd suggested he should kick himself in the nuts, rather than suggest a logical solution to our current sleeping arrangements. "I don't think that's a good idea."

"Why not? Do you snore?"

He poured the wine, his face dead serious for once. His skin took on a little bit of a green hue, as if his mere thoughts literally *sickened* him. "No fucking clue."

"Then why—?" I cocked my head to get a better look at his eyes. "Wait. Have you never slept with anyone before?"

He didn't look at me, and, judging from his silence, he didn't intend to answer. Instead, he handed my glass over and picked up his own drink. Then he stared me down. He did that a lot. Spinning the amber liquid in his tumbler into a little whirlpool, he leaned back. "Doesn't a cellmate count?"

I choked on my wine. Once I could breathe again, I gasped in air. "Y-you were in *jail*?"

"Why are you surprised?" he asked dryly, stopping the

whirlpool. "Look at my lifestyle. Of course I was in jail. Just got out, actually. Still want me in your bed?"

For once in my life, I was speechless.

I mean, I knew what he did for a living, and I knew he didn't live on the right side of the law. But still . . . *jail*? I tried to picture him in one of those prison jumpsuits instead of jeans and a blue shirt, and failed. "Like I said, it's just a platonic sharing of the same bed. I promise not to kick you in the middle of the night. Or slit your throat."

His grip tightened ever so slightly on the glass, and he shook his head once. "It's not smart to be around people when you're at your weakest. I don't open myself up to that shit. That's a death wish in my world, sweetheart."

"Yeah, well, not in mine." I rested a hand on his hard biceps. "It'll be fine. I'll keep to my side of the bed, and you can keep to yours. We can even put pillows between us, if you want."

"I don't want anything between us," he said, a hint of a smirk coming into play. "But you're not ready for that yet."

Oh, I would beg to differ. My body was perfectly ready for that. I just wasn't going to give it what it wanted. It would be too risky. Crazy. Insane.

And oh so *stupid*.

"I'm not interested in that at all, and time won't change my mind." I leaned close and trailed my fingers over his jawline, much like he had done to my cheek earlier. His eyes narrowed, and I had the distinct impression that he was like a tiger, ready to pounce at the slightest provocation on my part. "Like I said a million times: Not. My. Type."

He caught my wrist, his grip firm but gentle. "Give me one minute of your time, and I can show you just how not your type I am, sweetheart."

When he said that with his Boston accent, the round sound catching on that *ar* syllable, it made my heart skip a beat or three. I tossed back the rest of my wine before I smiled up at him, batting my lashes. "Oh, honey, you'd need to do a lot more than that to impress a girl like me."

"Oh, *honey*, I highly doubt that. Ask me to do it. Ask me to touch you." He stepped closer, setting down his glass and taking mine out of my hand, too. "You won't regret it."

"Nope." I shivered and pressed my legs together to try to assuage the ache between them. It didn't help. "Not happening."

"Squeezing those hot little thighs together won't help you, sweetheart. Only I can make you feel better. Only I can take that ache away . . . and all you have to do is ask." With his voice lowered, he dropped his head down so his mouth was pressed to my ear. "Ask me, darlin'. I *dare* you."

Damn it, why had I told him I never backed down from a dare? Even now, I wanted to do it. Only because he'd dared me to, of course. Not because I wanted him—oh hell. Who was I kidding? I wanted him to. And that was why this whole thing was so scary. I knew he'd bring me nothing but trouble, and yet I still wanted him with every single breath I took. I pressed a hand to his chest. "I—oh my God."

He nibbled on my ear, his hand dipping between my legs to brush against my core before pulling away teasingly. "No more till you say it, Heidi. Say the word I need to hear. Say *yes*."

It was on the tip of my tongue to say no. To protect what little bit of strength I had to keep him at arm's length. To reject him. But after that half-assed kiss he'd given me in the bar, followed by the kiss he'd just barely tolerated later on, and now that soft caress between my thighs . . .

A part of me wanted to feel what a *real* kiss from him would be like. And I also wanted to know what it would feel like to be wanted by a man like Lucas, even if only for a minute. Even if only on a dare.

He cupped my hip, stepping even closer. "Go on. You know you want to. I'll make it worth your while."

"I don't want you."

"I know," he said, lowering his mouth to my earlobe. He bit down on it, his hand creeping over my butt at the same time. "You said that already . . . repeatedly."

"I don't—" When his fingers brushed my core, I broke off. Everything inside of me tightened and screamed out with need. Need for *him*. "Screw it. You get one minute, and one minute only. After that, we're—" Before I'd even finished my sentence, his mouth was on mine, and words were no longer possible.

CHAPTER 9

LUCAS

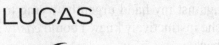

The instant she gave me the green light, I was on her. I wasn't gonna waste a single second of the minute I'd been given to blow her socks off. While I had no intention of fucking her tonight, she needed to stop fooling herself into thinking she didn't want this. Didn't want me.

And after this, she wouldn't be able to.

My tongue swept into her mouth, and she moaned, gripping my shoulders as if she was afraid she might fall. She should have known better. I wouldn't let her hit the floor. She tasted like cotton candy and wine, and it was an intoxicating combination. If I was a different type of man, I could easily become addicted to her taste.

Luckily for both of us, I wasn't.

Backing her against the wall, I let my hands roam over every square inch of her, like I'd wanted to do earlier in her bar when she'd kissed me. It had taken every ounce of my control to keep myself in check that time, and I didn't have any of it left. But this time, I didn't need any of that control. This time . . .

She was *mine*.

Growling low in my throat, I slid my hand over her flat stomach, going lower and lower until I cupped her wet pussy. She moaned into my mouth, the sound desperate, and needy, and hot as hell. Just like her. Her hips rolled against my hand urgently, trying to find the release that she instinctively knew I could *easily* give her, and I pulled back.

She started to turn her head, likely to yell at me for stopping, but when I undid the button of her shorts and slid my hand inside, she stopped.

And she yanked me even closer.

Pulling me closer like that, her nails digging into my shoulders as if she didn't want to let go, it did weird things to me. It was like the feeling you get after coming inside from a long day out in the snow and standing in front of a fireplace. You hold your hands out to the fire, and eventually . . . you thaw out.

Slowly, the pain, numbness, and cold you felt dissipates until you're filled with glowing warmth, spreading to the tips of your fingers. That's how she made me feel.

Whatever the fuck that meant.

Knowing my time was running out, I thrust my hand inside her panties, grunting when I felt her heat. And softness. She was shaved with a small landing strip, and was so wet it killed me that I wasn't going to bury my cock inside her tonight.

But a challenge won easily wasn't much of a challenge at all.

I jammed my leg in between hers and spread her thighs, giving me better access to what I wanted. As soon as she gasped, I thrust my tongue inside her mouth while I inserted a finger inside of her. Her tight walls clamped down on my finger, and when I rubbed my thumb over her swollen clit, curses exploded from her lips.

Breaking the kiss off, I lowered my mouth to the gentle curve of her throat, biting down just enough to hurt so good. "You're so fucking hot, sweetheart. Scream for me. I need to hear you scream . . ."

"Oh my God. *Lucas.*"

After withdrawing my finger, I thrust two fingers inside of her and kissed her again, my lips hard and urgent over hers. Her entire body surged with need and then she cried out into my mouth. I moved my fingers inside her, pressing my thumb even tighter against her. "That's it, sweetheart."

Her nails scraped over my chest, digging in through the thin cotton of the T-shirt I'd thrown on before meeting up with her tonight, and then her muscles seized up. "Oh my God. Oh my God, oh my god, *oh my God.*" Her pussy tightened on my fingers, and then she sagged against the wall, her breaths coming hard and fast.

I dropped my forehead on hers, my own breathing less than steady. I'd started this whole thing to prove a point. And I'd wanted to see what she felt like in my arms, what it was like when she came apart. Turned out? She felt pretty fucking amazing.

I wanted more, but my time was up. I'd asked for a minute, and she'd given it to me. The challenge was over, and I'd won. Forcing myself to let her go, I stepped back, slipping a grin into place. It wouldn't do to let her know that I'd been as affected—if not *more* so—as she had been by that one minute in heaven.

More affected than I wanted to admit. Or ever would.

"Now, *that* was hot, darlin'."

Her cheeks turned bright red. "You . . . how . . . ?"

"You want to know *how*?" I cocked a brow. "Okay, I can walk you through it, if that's what gets you off."

If anything, her cheeks got even redder. It was adorable.

No one should be so adorable with their shorts undone and their lips swollen from my kisses. *"Lucas."*

"Well, first, I kissed you. And then I opened your shorts and thrust my fingers inside of your hot little p—"

Lurching forward, she slammed a hand over my mouth. "Oh my God, stop it."

"What? I was only—" Realizing my words came out more like *Whe? I wav ooooney*, I flicked my tongue over her palm, and she snatched her hand back as if I'd bitten her. I almost had. That had been next on my list. "I was only trying to help. You did ask me how I—"

She swiped her hand across her tee and then glanced down with wide eyes. Frantically, she buttoned up her shorts before glaring at me. "I don't need you to explain my orgasm to me, thank you very much."

I grabbed the whiskey and poured myself a glass. Before I could ask her if she wanted more wine, she took my glass and chugged back its contents. I was impressed. That shit was strong enough to put hair on a man's chest.

"Please. Help yourself," I murmured dryly.

She ran the back of her palm across her mouth and watched me, those bright blue eyes of hers sparkling with desire and irritation and . . . *life*. "Don't mind if I do."

I laughed. "Obviously."

"So, uh." Her gaze dipped down to my cock, and I swear she did more than just look. If I hadn't been watching her so closely, I'd swear she touched me. "What now?"

I poured myself another glass. Judging from the raging erection she'd given me, I'd need it. And more. Maybe a whole bottle. I dumped some more whiskey into her wine-glass and handed it to her. She took it but didn't drink. "What do you mean?"

"You made me . . . you know. *Finish*." She licked her lips, and her gaze dipped down again. I followed her bad example and chugged back my whiskey, my heart pounding in my ears. "What about you?"

"What about me?"

"Don't you need . . . ?" She bit down on her swollen lower lip. It was sexy as hell. Damn her. ". . . to finish, too?"

"Is that an offer?" I asked, turning and facing her completely. I leaned against the counter and gripped the granite edges so tightly it hurt. "Because I only asked for a minute, and that minute is up."

"No." She straightened, her normal self-assurance slipping back into place. I'd thrown her off for a bit, but she was back now. The sparkle had returned to her eyes and it was like the events of the last day had never happened. I liked that about her. She kept her cool under fire and bounced back quickly. "But I can give you a few minutes of privacy if you need to take care of things."

I choked on a moan. When I managed to swallow it down, I chuckled. It came out raspy. "Wow. Thanks."

"Anytime." Her mouth quirked up into a tiny smile. "Speaking of privacy, you won't really have any. I'm off for the next two days. So I'll be here all day, every day. Is that okay?"

No. I needed to distance myself from her. After that short time I'd spent making her cry out in pleasure, I knew one thing. I couldn't let her get inside my head.

"Of course. This is your safe house for now." I swallowed back the remainder of my drink and slid the glass across the counter. "Let me know if you need anything."

Anything at all.

She nodded once. "Okay."

An awkward silence fell, and I knew why. I'd dismissed her, and she didn't know what to make of that. One minute, I'd been all over her, making her come. The next, I was acting as if she was a complete stranger. It's what I did.

And that wasn't about to change.

"Look, I—," she started.

At the same time, I grabbed a shop rag off the counter. "I've got something—"

We both stopped talking.

"Go on," she said, giving me a smile. It looked forced. "You first."

"I was just going to say that I have some work to do downstairs." I rubbed the back of my neck and glanced at the clock. It was after three a.m., and I was exhausted as hell, but I knew I wouldn't be getting any sleep until she was tucked away in my bedroom, safe and sound. "I have a Mustang down there that needs to be finished by nine."

"Oh." She wrapped her arms around herself, her untouched whiskey hanging from her fingers. "I didn't know you actually worked on the cars, considering . . . you know. Your real job."

"I don't have to. I like to. And no one knows I do it." I dropped my arm to my side. It was true; no one else knew. Just one of the guys who worked for me, and he kept his mouth shut. Unlike me. Why had I told her that about myself? She didn't give a damn what I did for a hobby. No one did. "Anyway, go to bed. I'll be down there till it's done."

She watched me, those blue eyes of hers seeing too much. Her blond hair rested in front of her eyes, and she flicked it out of the way with a toss of her head. One strand stuck to her lips, and I almost moved it for her. But I forced myself to stop midreach.

"What about sharing the bed? Will you do that?"

Panic rose, choking off the words I tried to get out. I couldn't open myself up to attack like that. Not even for her. "Not happening," I said, my voice harder than before. She was asking me to let her closer than I'd ever let anyone before. To let my guard down and have her by my side when

I was at my most vulnerable. It wasn't going to happen. I gave her a grin, knowing I was showing just how badly I didn't want to let her in. "Just sleep in my bed and stop worrying about me. I'm fine on the couch. It's a hell of a lot more comfortable than the bunks in lockup."

"But—"

I headed for the door, cutting her off midargument. "Be ready to go out late tomorrow afternoon. We need to sell this relationship."

"What? Where are we going?"

I scanned my brain for date ideas. Damned if I knew of any good spots to hit. I'd been out of the game for longer than I could remember. A couple of years in lockup did that to a man. "Ball game." I winked at her. "Wear something nice for me."

Her cheeks flushed. "I'll show you something nice, but then you can shove it up your—"

"Gotta go. That car isn't gonna fix itself." I headed for the door, whistling as I went. I broke off to add, "I'll lock the door behind me. Don't leave this apartment. Got it?"

She pressed her lips together. "Yes, sir."

"That's more like it," I said, grinning. "Sweet dreams, darlin'."

I closed the door, putting a very real barrier between us. As I walked down the stairs, I kept up my cheery whistling tune. Once I was in my shop, in front of the car that needed a new radiator, I dropped the act. This was the one place I could be myself. The one place I didn't need to pretend for the rest of the world.

Working on cars cleared my head.

Saving Heidi was a nice distraction, but it was a distraction I didn't need right now. I needed to focus on bigger issues. My little brother was trying to kill me, and I needed to decide *exactly* what to do about that. Of course, first I needed to verify Chris's intel. Then, and only then, I needed to create a plan. I no longer had an easy escape. I had cash, sure, but it was enough for only one. Not two.

And I wasn't about to leave Heidi to the mess I'd pulled her into.

Rolling under the Mustang, I sighed. Whether I liked it or not, I had to believe that Chris was right. He'd been right about the promotion part, anyway. When I'd gone to see Tate this morning, he'd hinted at giving me the position Chris had mentioned, and he'd invited me to some big dinner as a guest of honor at the end of the week. That meant I had a week, at most, before Scotty took steps to get me out of the way.

The stakes were higher than ever. I had to stay alive, keep Heidi safe, and attempt to avoid killing my brother, all while conducting business as normal. It had been twenty-four hours since I'd learned of Scotty's plan, and I'd made absolutely no progress on a solution. I didn't want to kill him. I wasn't going to let him kill me. And I couldn't talk sense into him without escalating this to a level I wasn't sure I wanted to visit just yet. Scotty had always had a hell of a temper, just like me. But unlike me, he didn't know how to control it.

If I made him snap, there would be no going back. No stopping him . . .

Or me.

By the time I came back up from underneath the car, my eyes burned with exhaustion. I rolled out and grabbed the rag off the side of the hood, wiping my hands clean. As I lay there, I squinted up at the clock. The numbers mocked me, in their bright red colors. It was well after five, which meant I had four hours until I had to be at the warehouse. We had a big shipment of AK-47s going out, and I was supervising.

Tate had dropped that bomb on me this morning, too, likely some sort of audition.

I pushed myself to my feet and made my way to the door. After one last look over the shop, I shut the lights off. Wearily, I went up the stairs, each step heavier than the last. Once I entered my apartment, I froze. The TV was still on, and I could see the top of Heidi's blond head resting on my pillow.

What the hell was she still doing awake?

I made my way over to her. "Shouldn't you be—?" I broke off, coming to a stop at her side. "Sleeping," I finished on a whisper.

Because she was.

Her hands were folded under her cheek, and her blue eyes were hidden from me in slumber. Her cheeks were rosy, and she had my blanket pulled up over her shoulders.

She looked like an angel come to earth.

Gently, I reached down and swept her hair off her face, smiling when she scrunched her nose in response. I wanted to sit there, staring at her, watching her sleep. But then I realized how creepy that sounded, so instead, I opened my bedroom door. After turning the sheets down, I went back out into the living room and swept her into my arms. She barely weighed more than a box of gun parts, for fuck's sake.

As I carried her into my room, she snuggled up against my chest, murmuring something in her sleep. I carefully laid her down in the center of the bed, arranged her hair behind her, and pulled the blankets into place. For a second, I stood there, staring at her perfect beauty. She was almost ethereal in her innocent sleep . . .

Without that devilish spark in her eyes.

I swept my hand across her soft cheekbone and forced myself to turn away. After I closed the door behind me, I headed into the shower. The hot water washed over me, and I closed my eyes. I pictured Heidi and the way she'd come apart in my arms earlier, and pretended my hand was hers. I slowly pumped my painful erection, picturing her tits and smile. The way she cried out, her mouth parted as she came . . .

It didn't take long for me to come, her name on my lips. I rested a forearm on the tiled wall, my breathing erratic as I came back down. It eased the ache, but it wasn't enough. My hand was a poor substitute for Heidi Greene, and my body knew it. It demanded her touch. Her kiss. *Her*.

I had to be careful, though, with how much I let myself want her. I was a dead man walking, and it was only a matter of time till this earth was rid of me. I would be just another dusty police file, just another forgotten name. No one would remember me.

She wouldn't be any different.

As soon as I was gone, she'd move on. Go back to hustling tips out of weak-willed men in her bar, fighting her way to the top of the food chain. And I had no doubt she would succeed. She was strong, smart, and brave. She wouldn't give in to this world without a fight, and the world didn't stand a chance against her. Hell, neither did I. I might not be willing to let her get too close to me, or to trust her . . .

But damned if I didn't want to.

CHAPTER 10

HEIDI

The next afternoon, we walked down Yawkey Way, toward Gate A at Fenway, hand in hand. Red-and-blue banners with the Red Sox's championship years listed on them lined the buildings, and people drank freely while chanting loudly about the upcoming victory. Every time someone pushed into us, I was concerned they were a threat, but Lucas hadn't listened to me when I'd told him this date thing was a horrible idea. There were men out there looking to kill us, and we were going to a freaking baseball game?

Yeah, that *totally* sounded like an *excellent* idea.

I hated baseball. And crowds. And dates.

Lucas hadn't let go of me yet, and I had a feeling he somehow sensed that I wanted nothing more than to run in the other direction, away from him. Ever since he'd blown my socks off last night, I'd been in a weird place. And by weird place, I meant I hadn't been able to stop thinking about him. And by thinking about him, I meant fantasizing about his lips on mine and his fingers doing magical things to me.

The same fingers that were securely latched onto mine right now.

He sighed, long and drawn out. "What's wrong? You're pouting again."

I glanced at him. He looked handsome as the devil in his dark brown leather jacket, dark blue jeans, and Converse sneakers. He wore a Red Sox hat and a five-o'clock shadow to die for. He looked unassuming and . . . normal.

It was kinda freaking me out.

I glanced down at my own jeans and black puffy coat. It was only mid-April, and it was still unseasonably chilly, so I'd opted for a wool hat instead of a Red Sox one. "Does it matter why?" I muttered.

After all, I'd already made my feelings on this outing quite clear back at his place.

"Heidi," he growled, using that warning tone of his he loved to pull out and throw in my face. "Don't make me—"

"*Fine.* I think this is stupid. Why are we even bothering with the act? No one believes it. Going to watch a bunch of grown men in tight pants playing with their tiny balls isn't going to make anyone feel differently, let alone those guys."

"Because—" His phone rang, and he dug it out without letting go of me. "Shit. Hold on. Yeah?" Silence, and then, "Yeah, we got the air filters squared away by ten thirty this morning. They're all with their buyers now, and we made a better profit than expected."

Air filters? He was obviously speaking in code because there were people surrounding us. A woman shoved her elbow in my back and glared at me, as if I'd done something wrong by being near her in the first place, then pushed her way past the huge dude in front of me. Enough of this touristy crap. I rolled my eyes and tugged Lucas down a back road, next to the Boston Beer Works on the corner of the street.

He followed me, talking about car parts and sales reports, but dug in his heels and frowned when I headed down an alley I knew like the back of my hand. "Hold on, man." Then, to me, "Where the hell are you going?"

"This way." I yanked on his hand again, harder. "It's a shortcut."

He held the phone to his chest. "It's a fucking ambush waiting to happen. No."

He might think he knew the city better than me, but he was dead wrong. This was *my* city, thank you very much. I knew the streets to avoid and the ones that were safe to use. It was the rest of the world that got scared of dark alleys they didn't know. "I used to sleep down there because it was close to the stadium. Vendors give out free food after the games sometimes, so it's a popular spot for the homeless. Even the cops avoid alleys like this, so trust me. It's fine."

His grip tightened on his phone. I could hear a masculine voice calling his name from the other end. "You *slept* down there?"

My cheeks heated. Guess I hadn't told him about that yet. Oops. "Later. Get back to your call," I said, shaking my head. "And follow me."

"Heidi—" The muscle in his jaw ticked. "We'll talk about this later."

No. We wouldn't. "Yeah, sure. Whatever."

He gave me a dark look while lifting the phone to his ear. "Dude, take a fucking Xanax. I told you to hang on a second."

I tuned out the rest of his conversation, tensing as the familiar smell of sausages and onions washed over me. Whenever I came to Fenway, a rush of memories and forgotten emotions always hit me. I'd run away from my foster home when my foster dad had decided that by taking me in, he owned the rights to my body. Rights no thirteen-year-old girl should have to give to a sweating, overweight, balding forty-year-old.

He'd been on the verge of raping me, so I knew I had to get out. One night of inappropriate touching sent me running. The feeling of that man's clammy hands running over my skin still haunted me. He'd touched my thigh—way too high up to be appropriate—and then grunted before whispering, "I'll be at your door tonight. If you tell anyone or don't let me inside, I'll kill you like I did the last one. They never found her body, and they won't find yours, either."

It hadn't taken me more than five minutes to be out that window with all of my meager belongings slung over my back. I never looked back. To this day, I wished I'd castrated him before running. Lucas hung up and side-eyed me. He was obviously thinking about my earlier admission. I hadn't meant to tell him about my past, because it didn't matter. Everyone had a past, and chances were, they were never worth talking about. End of story.

"Don't."

He cocked a brow. "Don't what?"

"Look at me like that."

His bright green eyes locked me down. "How, exactly, am I looking at you, darlin'?"

"Like I'm something to be pitied. You don't like when I look at you like a hero, and I don't like it when you look at me like *that*." I turned away and focused on the spot where I used to sleep, between two big black Dumpsters. "Got me?"

"Got you," he replied, his grip tightening on me.

I couldn't help but feel he meant it in more ways than one.

We fell silent, and I led him toward the end of the alley, my heart picking up speed when I saw a tag on the wall. It didn't match the one on my bar, but it still sent chills down my spine. Lucas followed my line of vision. "It's not Bitter Hill's."

"I know."

"But even so . . . I don't like walking down here." He pulled me closer, scanning the shadows as we walked. A man grunted and rolled over, pulling his newspaper blanket higher. "We should have stuck to the main roads, and once we get out there again? We damn well are."

I peeked over my shoulder. For the first time, I had to admit he was right. Considering the circumstances, we needed to stay out in the open. "It's just the crowds . . . they don't agree with me."

He shrugged. "Well, suck it up, buttercup. We need them right now."

"Yeah, yeah." I rolled my shoulders and forced away the tingling sense of doom making the hair stand up on the back of my neck. "So, air filters, huh?"

He scanned the alley again. "Yeah. What of it?"

"Nothing. I just never thought I'd be dating a car parts salesperson, is all. Ugh, what a dull career to fake-have." I forced a laugh. "Why not be an astronaut? Or a nuclear scientist?"

He chuckled. It came out raspy sounding and way too sexy. "Darlin', that's exactly why we picked it. I'm trying to sound inconspicuous, not intriguing or sexy."

"Well, job done. I don't find you sexy at *all*."

One second I was walking, and the next, I was against the brick wall, the breath whooshing out of my lungs. He trapped my hands between one of his and the rough wall, dipping his face down to mine. "Excuse me?"

"What's wrong?" My heart picked up speed, pounding so fast and hard that it hurt. "Did I hurt your ego?"

The smirk I was all too familiar with crept into place. "The only thing you're hurting, darlin', is your chances of me getting you off again." Lucas slid his thigh between mine, pressing ever so slightly against me. "Tell me. Have you been able to stop thinking about that one minute we shared? I'll be honest. I haven't been able to."

My core ached at the mere mention of the things he'd done to me last night, but I refused to show it. "Sorry about that. For me, it was entirely forgettable."

"Is that so?" he asked, his Boston accent doing odd things to my insides. "So if I tell you how much I want to feel your wet pussy against my fingers again, to make you scream my name, right here?" He slid his hand over my core, cupping me through my jeans. "You wouldn't be interested?"

Yes. God yes.

"Nope, not at all."

He lowered his mouth to mine, not touching but close enough to do so with one small lift onto my toes. "Liar," he breathed. "You want me. You want me so bad that you can't think about anything but having me. One thing you don't realize, darlin', is that I know you. I know all about you."

I shook my head. "You don't know me. You don't know anything about the way my brain works."

"You don't want to like me. You want to push me away and pretend that the desire isn't there, because I'm not a good guy." Lucas brushed his lips against mine. "You don't want to want a guy like me, because what would that say about your character? But you do, anyway. And you're ashamed of that."

He was right about one thing. I did want him, and I didn't want to. The rest, he had wrong. I wasn't *ashamed* of wanting him. I just knew it was a *horrible* idea. I bit down on my lip. "I'm not ashamed of the way you make me feel."

Something akin to shock with a dash of hope crossed his face, but he quickly shut it down. So quickly I wondered if I'd imagined the whole thing. "Bullshit." He pushed off the wall, letting go of me and taking those magical fingers of his with him. He dragged them through his hair and checked out the alley again. "They always are."

"They?" I pressed a hand on my stomach. Butterflies still erupted into flight inside it. "What's that supposed to mean?"

He caught my hand and towed me out into the sunlight, the other hand resting on his gun, each step harsher than the last. It was clear he was agitated, though I wasn't exactly sure why. "Next time, don't drag me down dark alleys when I'm on the phone. That was a bullshit move."

"Sorry. I didn't know you were scared of the dark," I shot back, beyond irritated at him and his attitude. "Next time, I'll bring a flashlight along if it'll help you feel better."

"Quit the bullshit, Heidi. You know why I didn't want to go down that alley, but you pulled some tidbit of information out of your past, threw me off, and I allowed you to—"

I held my hands up. "Hold up. *Allowed me to?* You have no say over what I do, or where I—"

"You're fucking *killing* me." He covered his face. "I'm done. Done fighting you over every damn thing, when all I'm trying to do is keep your pretty little ass alive."

"I can take care of my own ass," I shot back, hands on my hips. "I've been doing it all my life, and I'm not about to stop now. And furthermore, I—"

Growling, he caught me behind my back and hauled me against his chest. I barely had time to register that he'd pulled me into his arms before his lips were on mine, moving over my mouth as if he'd been dying to kiss me for years. And I felt it, too. The need. The want. I curled my hands into his leather jacket, holding him in place.

Because if he stopped kissing me, I might die.

Lucas slanted his mouth over mine, slipping his tongue between my lips until he found what he wanted. The second his tongue touched mine, it was like sparks went off all around us, exploding into fireworks or something equally corny sounding. He let out a tortured-sounding groan and nibbled on my lower lip, and he could have had me, right then and there on Yawkey Way, in front of all the tourists swarming around us.

But then he stopped.

We both drew in a ragged breath, desperate for air. He rested his forehead on mine and pushed my hair off my face with a not-so-steady hand. "Jesus, sweetheart. What the hell are you doing to me?"

"I don't know," I admitted honestly. "But you're doing it to me, too."

He tensed. "I—we—shit." Shaking his head slightly, he pulled back. By the time I could see his face, any hint of vulnerability to me, or *anything*, was gone. He looked as unaffected as ever. "Sorry that I kissed you without warning. I thought I saw a guy from Bitter Hill watching."

I stiffened, knowing a sorry-ass excuse when I heard one. But if he wanted to pretend nothing had happened between us, then fine. He could. And so could I. "Oh yeah?"

"Yeah. False alarm." He let out a breath and ran a hand through his hair. Staring up at the stadium, he hunched his shoulders and shoved his hands into his jeans pockets. "You ready to go in now?"

I swallowed and nodded once. "Yeah."

He offered me his arm, not taking his hands out of his pockets, and stepped closer. "Hold on tight, in case anyone's watching. When we get inside, I'll get us some Sam Adams, franks, and Cracker Jacks."

I groaned. "You're pulling out all the stops, aren't you?"

"Yep."

I slid my hand into the crook of his arm and trudged along beside him. I couldn't shake the sinking suspicion that this game was going to be, hands down, the longest three hours or so of my life. Especially since he'd kissed me again, and then proceeded to go on with his life as if he didn't give a damn about anything . . . especially me.

We walked up to the portly guard in blue. Lucas exchanged a few words with him and handed him a wad of cash to buy our way inside with a pistol. Lucas had refused to go out in public without it, and I didn't blame him. We had no way of knowing when or how they would strike. Going out without protection would be foolish.

The man nodded, stepping back to let us inside without using the wand on Lucas. The security guard and I locked gazes for a split second, and what I saw there left a sour taste in my mouth. He looked . . . *ashamed* of himself and his association with the Sons of Steel Row. Much like Lucas had accused me of, earlier.

Is that what he thought he saw in my eyes when I looked at him? After I kissed him, or admitted I wanted him, like I had the other night? Of course not. He couldn't see it if it didn't exist . . .

Could he?

CHAPTER 11

LUCAS

Heidi leaned back in her chair and adjusted her knit cap, her face impassively placid, but her eyes . . . ah, her eyes told another story. In all the moments leading up to this, Heidi had whined, pouted, and even threatened to castrate me over this date. She'd told me she hated baseball and wouldn't last ten minutes in the "stupid, idiot-packed stadium."

Well, the game was almost over, and she was still alive. Imagine that.

It was the bottom of the ninth, with a tied game, bases loaded, and Ortiz had stepped up to the plate, stretching and swinging his bat in circles. The Phillies' Ken Giles lined himself up, eyeing Ortiz across the expanse of the field. Even from here, I could feel the tension between the two men. "Damn."

Heidi bit down on her lip and leaned forward. "He's good, right?"

"Giles or Ortiz?"

"Ortiz." She waved a hand. "I can *see* Giles is good. I've been watching him off and on all night."

I forced back a grin at her attitude. "Some say so, yeah."

"And you?" She darted a quick glance at me before turning back to the game. "Do you say so?"

"Yeah."

Ortiz swung and missed, making Heidi let out a string of curses. As they lined up for the second pitch, she pressed her lips against the rim of her beer, murmuring something under her breath. I thought I heard the words *please* and *hit it*, but I couldn't be sure.

I chugged back the rest of my draft beer. "You know, for someone who doesn't like baseball, you sure are—"

Ortiz made contact with the ball, and it flew out past the third baseman. The crowd went wild, and Heidi leapt to her feet, completely ignoring me to *whoop* loudly. It was a double, so two men made it home, putting the Red Sox officially in the lead.

She turned to me, a bright smile on her face. "That means we won, right?"

"Yep." I pointed at her beer. "Finish that, and we can head out if you want. I'll put you out of your misery."

She glanced at the pitcher on the field. "But it's not over yet. He's still out there."

"Yeah, but I know you don't like baseball, and I wouldn't want to torture you needlessly," I teased, smirking. "Unless you *want* to stay."

"You know I do," she said, her voice curt. She chugged back the last of her beer and tossed her empty cup at me. "And I'd like a refill, please."

I cocked a brow at her and raised my hand. A guy nodded and turned to get us another beer. "Damn, darlin'. You're gonna drink me under the table tonight."

"That's because you're drinking to blend in but still

staying sober, so you can keep me safe." She tossed a grin at me. "I'm drinking to get light-headed and a little bit stupid, because I've got you to keep me safe. I'm not used to having someone at my back. It's a treat to let loose and forget for a little while."

I gripped the arms of the chair. "Forget what?"

She stilled, then turned to me slowly. She shook her head, and her blond hair blew a little in the breeze. The sunset framed her face, shadowing it slightly, but not so much that I couldn't see the raw honesty in her expression. Or miss out on how pretty the dim lighting of the dusk make her eyes look. "Being alone all the time."

My chest tightened. I knew that feeling all too well. I didn't have many people I trusted to have my back, either. I had Scotty and Chris—but now it looked like I *only* had Chris. And my childhood had been nothing like Heidi's.

While she'd grown up and made something of herself, from having nothing, I'd wasted away all the love and care my mother had raised me with. I'd thrown it in her face and taken what she'd worked so hard to give us—a stable, safe environment—and turned it into something tarnished and ugly.

But that's what I did.

I ruined things.

"You're not alone anymore," I said, locking gazes with her. "You have me."

Her cheeks flushed. "For now."

"Yeah." I shifted in my seat and pulled out some cash and handed it off to the guy who brought her beer without bothering to glance at him. Then I gave her the beer, and she held on to it tightly with both hands. "For now."

She stared out at the field, not glancing my way, and took a big swallow of beer. I couldn't take my eyes off her. She'd been homeless—actually *lived* on the fucking streets—and had come out squeaky and clean in the end. She owned a bar and was seemingly happy.

How? How had she done it?

"You're staring at me." She finally looked at me again, but this time it was with a frown. "Stop it."

I held both hands up. "Well, sorry."

"It's not okay," she snapped.

"I'm not allowed to admire your beauty in the sunset?" I tugged my hat lower. "Sorry, darlin'. I didn't know that was off-limits."

She pressed her lips together. "You're not looking at the sunset or waxing poetic about how pretty my eyes are in the waning light."

Cocking a brow, I drawled, "Actually . . ."

"You're thinking about what I said back there. About me being alone on the streets." She shook her head. "I don't want to talk about it—about why it happened or how. I shouldn't have even told you."

"All right." I rested my left ankle on the opposite knee. "Funny, though. I don't remember asking a question about it."

"You didn't need to. It's written all over your face."

I had to be more careful, then. I didn't make it a habit to let people see my thoughts, and she shouldn't be an exception. Even if it felt like she was. "Sorry, darlin'. I hate to disappoint you, but I wasn't thinking about that. I was thinking about that little moan you made when I kissed you in the alley, and the way you clung to my biceps as I tasted you. And how much I wanted to taste you again."

If possible, her cheeks went even redder than I'd see them go before. "Is that so?"

"That's definitely fucking so," I said, grinning.

She settled back into her seat. Cheering broke out in earnest, and people stood. The game was over. "Well then, sorry for misreading you."

"Maybe you did." I tugged on a piece of her hair. "Maybe you didn't."

Heidi stiffened again. "Which is it?"

"I'll leave you to figure that out on your own." When she started to stand, I placed a hand on her thigh and pressed down. "Sit tight, darlin'. Let the masses clear out first."

She stared down at my hand, her thigh hard underneath my fingers. "Okay."

"How old are you?" I asked. It hadn't occurred to me before, but I didn't even know. I could guess, but that wasn't the same.

"Twenty-four." She side-eyed me. "You?"

"Twenty-seven."

She nodded. "I'd guessed around there."

People pushed out of the stadium, talking loudly and bumping into one another. I didn't like that many men at my back, where I couldn't see them. I'd rather wait. I didn't take my hand off her, even when the first raindrop hit my skin. "Tell me the truth. Have you ever been to a baseball game before, in all your twenty-four years?"

She sipped her beer, watching the emptying field. The crowds. The sky. Anything but me. "It's raining."

"Then we'll get wet," I said dismissively. "I've never run from a little bit of rain on a cool spring day, and I'm not about to start now. Answer the question."

"Lucas—"

"Heidi," I said right the fuck back at her.

She blew out an exasperated breath. "Fine. Whatever. I've only caught bits and pieces on the TV behind the bar. I didn't care for it."

I caught her chin and turned her beautiful face toward mine. I'd never get sick of seeing her small, pert nose, or the gentle curve of her cheekbones. A raindrop landed on one of those cheekbones, and I swept it away with my thumb. "And now?"

"And now." Her tongue darted out to lick a drop off her red lips. It made my cock harden, but even more important, it made something else inside of me grow warm. Something I didn't want to recognize. "I still won't like it at the bar, but it was fun tonight. Here. With you."

That funny warmth she always brought out in my veins spread over my body again. I leaned in, so close I could smell her soft peach scent, and she held her breath. "I liked tonight, too. With you."

Her lids drifted shut.

I didn't need more of an invitation than that.

Closing the distance between us, I pressed my mouth to hers, savoring the moment. She leaned in to me, all softness and sweetness, and I took what she offered.

And for once, I didn't take more.

I traced my tongue over the seam of her lips, gently, and she parted them on a sigh. Permission granted, I slid my tongue in the warm sweetness of her mouth. She melted into me even more, one hand holding on to her beer, the other latched onto my leather jacket. Everything about this moment, this woman, screamed something unique.

Something new.

Something terrifyingly *real*.

Pulling back, I swallowed hard and stared down at her. Her eyes were still shut, and her rosy cheeks were charmingly innocent. Something neither of us was.

Her lashes drifted up, and when she caught me staring, she bit down on her lower lip. "What are you thinking right now?"

That she was utterly, breathtakingly beautiful. "I—*shit*."

The skies chose that moment to open up, pouring buckets of water on us instantly. I cursed under my breath and ripped my jacket off, tossing it over her head like an umbrella. She laughed and set her beer down on the ground, holding my jacket in place. The rain drenched through my shirt in seconds. "I thought you didn't mind a little bit of rain."

I stood and held my hands out to my sides, laughter escaping me because, *fuck*, it was pouring. "Does this look like a 'little bit of a spring rain' to you?"

Still laughing, she stood, too, wobbling on her feet a little. "Sure does."

I shook my head like a dog, splattering her with wet drops. "Then, here, have some more."

"Hey, that's—" I did it again. She squealed and leapt back, knocking over her beer. "Oh, crap."

When she bent to pick it up, I shook my head and grabbed her elbow, straightening her back to her full—but *short*—height. "The rain will wash it away." I held my hand out to her, still grinning like an idiot. "Come on. Follow my lead."

She hesitated, looking at my hand as if I held out a gun or something even more lethal. Then slowly, she lifted her arm and slid her fingers inside mine. There was no denying that this moment felt heavier than it seemed, as if by taking my hand, she said something more.

Something I wasn't sure I fully understood. I latched onto her and didn't let go. Didn't even want to. We made it out of the stadium in silence and were soon on Yawkey Way again. I was so lost in her, in the moment, that I almost missed it.

Almost missed what was staring me right in the face.

Halfway past the huge bay window, I froze. Inside the dingy bar, I saw the one thing I didn't want to see. Blinking the rain away, I stared through the window, heart thudding loud enough to drown out the crowds around us. My stomach hollowed out, then squeezed tight, and for a second I thought I was gonna hurl.

Because sitting in a booth, clear as day, was my brother,

Scotty. And he was with Bitter Hill guys. But if he was in league with the men who'd attacked Heidi, then . . .

No. It couldn't be true.

"Lucas?" Heidi asked from beside me. "Are you okay?"

I could feel her eyes on me, but even so, I didn't look away from Scotty. I couldn't. Why was he here, with *them*? Scotty laughed, and money changed hands. After the Bitter Hill lieutenant tucked the cash into his pocket, he shook hands with Scotty, then tossed back a shot of vodka. Damn it all to hell, Chris was right.

Scotty couldn't be trusted.

When I didn't answer, Heidi stepped closer and peeked inside the bar, too. "What's wrong? Is someone you know in there?"

I stepped in front of her, blocking her view. "No. I'm fine." I rolled my shoulders and turned away, catching her hand again. The last thing I needed was Heidi seeing Scotty and asking questions. We might not be twins, but we were clearly brothers. If Scotty was dangerous, there was no way in hell I'd let him anywhere near Heidi. I looked her dead in the eyes and said, "I thought I saw someone I used to know."

She licked her lips and glanced over her shoulder as I dragged her toward the curb. "Okay . . ."

Lifting my arm, I hailed a cab. One pulled up, and I glanced at the driver to make sure he wasn't a threat. He looked innocent enough. Opening the back door, I motioned Heidi in first. Once I settled in, I told the driver my address.

She shivered and huddled over herself. "God, it's cold out there."

I forced a grin for her benefit, but it was hard. "The cold never really bothered me. It's the heat that usually gets to me. There's no escaping it."

"I love heat. Heat is my best friend."

I dragged a hand through my soaked hair. "Says the girl who wears shorts in winter . . ."

She laughed. It bubbled out of her. "Touché."

Her hair was plastered to her face in wet, snaky tendrils, and her eye makeup ran down her cheeks in black streaks. I'd just found some concrete evidence that suggested my brother couldn't be trusted, and it hurt. But there she was, still hugging my jacket to her head, looking as if she'd walked through a tornado and lived to tell of it. I still hadn't shaken off that moment we'd shared in the stadium, and my heart thudded. Even with all that . . .

I'd never heard, or seen, anything more beautiful than Heidi laughing in my whole life. And I didn't think I ever would, either. I didn't know what to do with that.

So I did, and said, nothing.

Not even when we got home.

CHAPTER 12

HEIDI

The next night, I juggled a baking dish of lasagna in one hand and my phone in the other. It had been ringing for a good ten seconds, and Lucas hadn't answered yet. It was close to five o'clock, and I had no idea what time he'd be home. Ever since our pseudo-date, after which he'd escaped downstairs the second we'd walked inside the building, I felt like we needed something to get through this evening in each other's company.

So, I'd decided to cook dinner for him.

Also, I didn't do idle well. And that was *all* I'd done all day.

Surprisingly enough, I'd found all the ingredients I'd needed to cook the meal from his cabinets and fridge. It made me wonder if he cooked himself. If he did, when had he learned? How? Maybe his mother taught him before she'd died, or maybe he'd learned as a necessity for survival, since he obviously lived alone.

Or did he simply enjoy it?

I had no idea, but I had so many unanswered questions about him that I could fill a novel with them. Questions I'd more than likely never get the answers to. Yesterday, we'd barely spent more than a minute talking after we'd gotten home from the game, but I'd briefly mentioned I liked drinking tea when I was stressed-out. He'd left while I'd been changing into dry clothes and came back with three different boxes for me twenty minutes later. I'd thanked him, and he'd gruffly reminded me that he didn't need any "fucking thanks."

Then he'd gone downstairs to work on cars again.

And that had been that.

The ringing stopped, and the phone on the other end got shuffled before clanging against something hard. Somewhere on the other end of the line, someone cried out and cursed in a Boston accent. And he sounded as if he was in pain.

Lots of it.

"Son of a bitch, shut your mouth, Ian," Lucas growled.

I licked my lips. "Uh, hello?"

"Yeah, I'm here." More shuffling, and the phone got picked up. "Who is this, and why the hell are you calling me?"

"It's me," I said, before mentally face-palming. I hadn't given him my number, so he probably didn't know who I was. I had his only because he'd scribbled it down on a piece of paper before he'd left yesterday morning, along with instructions that if I left the apartment, he'd drag me back by my hair. "Um . . . Heidi."

"Oh." His voice softened slightly. "What's up, darlin'? Is something wrong?"

"No. I just—" Someone cried out in the background again, and I gripped the phone tighter. "What was that? Is everything okay?"

"Everything's fine," he said impatiently. Something clicked

behind him, and the screaming silenced. "Just doing something at work. What do you need?"

"Are you torturing someone?"

"I'm a car parts salesperson." He paused. "Why the hell would I be torturing someone, darlin'?"

I closed my eyes. "Lucas . . ."

"Do you really wanna know?"

I thought about it. "No."

"That's what I thought." He sighed. "Why are you calling?"

I shook off the millions of questions I had. "I wanted to know when you'll be coming home tonight. I cooked dinner, and I didn't want to have it ready too early . . . if you were planning to come home at a reasonable time, that is. And if you wanted to, you know, eat with me."

"Dinner?" he asked, his voice tinged with amusement. "Are you going all domestic on me?"

"Yeah. Maybe." I frowned. "And if I am? What of it?"

He chuckled. "Nothing. Nothing at all. I'll be home around six, so if you'd like to hold dinner for me, I'll be there."

So he wouldn't be avoiding me again. "Okay." I paced across the living room floor. "Also, can you bring home a few things, if I text them to you?"

Sighing, he muttered something under his breath. "This is what being married feels like, isn't it? No sex and all orders."

Oh, we might not have had sex, but we'd had that one incredible moment in the kitchen together the other night, followed by those kisses at the stadium yesterday. The ones that, no matter how hard I tried, I couldn't stop thinking about. "I wouldn't know, seeing as I've never been married."

He laughed. "Well, you had parents at some point, right?"

"No. I mean, I lived in foster homes, and then later on in life . . . on the streets, as I already mentioned yesterday." I bit down on my lower lip, wishing I could take that back. Why had I told him that? He didn't need to know my life history. This wasn't a *real* relationship. *Ugh*.

His voice softened even more. "Heidi . . ."

"Don't." I walked over to my computer and stared down at my shopping list. If he went all pity-boy on me again, I'd put an entire container of salt on his half of dinner. "Will you do it, or would you rather I run out and—?"

"Hell no." *Annnd* there went the softness. Good. I didn't want or need it. It made him way too . . . approachable. "Don't even think about leaving that apartment." A door opened behind him, and I heard a muffled voice. He let out a long breath. "Yeah, I'll be right in." Then, to me, he said, "Send me the list. I'll see what I can do."

"Thanks," I said, staring at the photo on his fridge. It was of a man who had red-tinged brown hair and green eyes who looked like Lucas but definitely wasn't actually him. I'd place him around my age, maybe twenty-five or so. It was the only personal photo he had in his whole apartment. "See you later."

"All right."

He hung up without saying good-bye, which didn't surprise me in the slightest, and I leaned against the counter, still staring at that photo. Was that his brother? The one who had thought Lucas was half fish? It very well might be him, but if so . . . he was very different from Lucas. While Lucas was cautious and guarded, he still had that spark of life inside him that told you exactly how alive he was. But this guy looked cold and dead in the eyes. As if nothing and no one mattered to him at all.

Like all he cared about was himself and what he could get out of life.

I sat down on the couch and pulled up the drink recipes

I wanted to try out later tonight. I always had lots of guys in my bar, but now it was time to try to draw in the ladies. So I had researched a slew of fruity cocktails to test out. After I sent my shopping list to Lucas, I put the lasagna in the oven, dusted off my hands, and smiled. This might not be a real relationship, but tonight felt . . . nice.

I scanned the apartment. I'd cleaned today, too. I was never one to sit around twiddling my thumbs, so this wasn't any exception. Sure, I'd been forbidden from leaving, but I had to do *something* to keep myself occupied. I'd spent the better half of the morning pacing, bored out of my mind. I'd been about five seconds from going into the shop downstairs and begging to do some clerical work, before I'd decided to try my hand at being productive up here. And it had been—

A knock sounded on the door, and I jumped.

I stared at it, not moving. I wasn't supposed to leave, or answer the door, for *any*one. I was under strict orders to avoid contact with the outside world at all costs, unless Lucas was at my side. I found it all to be a bit over-the-top, but I'd decided to honor his wishes. So I wasn't opening that door.

Holding my breath, I didn't dare move.

The person outside knocked again. "Open up, Lucas. I know you're in there. I can smell the garlic from out here, and I'm hungry as hell, so you're gonna share. It's been years since you cooked for me." The doorknob jiggled. "Stop fucking around and let me in. We need to talk. *Now.*"

I tiptoed into the kitchen, grabbed the biggest butcher knife I could find, and backed myself into the corner. I didn't open my mouth or make a noise, because I was hoping whoever was out there would go away. Give up and—

Metal rubbed up against metal, and the distinct sound of a key sliding into place made me stiffen. Shit, he had a *key.* I bolted for Lucas's room at the same time the door opened, hoping to hide before I was sighted, but I was too slow to make it before I was seen. A muffled masculine curse came from somewhere behind me, and I ran faster, but not fast enough. Strong arms closed around me from behind, and I slashed at him with my knife, missing pathetically.

Screw being quiet. It was time to make some noise. "Let *go* of me! *Help me!*"

"Fucking—" He grunted and slapped a hand over my mouth with one hand, while yanking my wrist painfully to the side with the other. The sharp pain almost caused my fingers to let go, but I bit down on the attacker's hand as hard as I could. He jerked away before I could do any real damage, shaking his hand off, then slammed it across my throat, cutting off my supply of oxygen. "Son of a *bitch*."

I gasped in a breath. It was hard, because he was crushing me. "Get off me, or I'll—"

"You'll what?" he growled in my ear, twisting my wrist even more and tightening his arm across my neck. "Who are you, and why are you in Lucas's apartment? Tell me, as quickly as possible, or I'll kill you."

"Go to hell," I gritted out between struggling breaths. It hurt more than I'd like to admit, or ever *would* admit. "As quickly as possible."

"Have it your way, then," he growled, yanking on my wrist even harder.

I lost the battle to hold on to my weapon. The knife hit the floor with a clang, and I followed it. He slammed me into the floor, trapping my hands behind my back and holding on with a death grip. My pulse skyrocketed, and I was sure that this was going to be it. The Bitter Hill gang had come to finish me off.

And this time Lucas wouldn't be able to stop them.

Leaning down, he pressed his elbow into my upper back and said, "I repeat, who are you, and where is Lucas? What have you done to him?"

"N-nothing," I stammered. "Get the hell *off me*."

He yanked on my wrist even more, and I hissed through my teeth. He let up slightly. "Answer me."

I rolled my head to the side so I could look at him out of the corner of my eye. An attractive man with dark brown hair and matching eyes had me pinned to the floor. He had a bit of a five-o'clock shadow going on, and from what I could see of them . . . his muscles were hard and defined under his brown leather jacket.

The same Steel Row jacket that Lucas wore.

Were they friends, then?

Since he had a key, the possibility was likely. But Lucas had told me to trust no one. I shook my head as best as I could with him on top of me, and the floor pressed up against my face. "Who are *you*?"

"Don't worry about who I am," he growled. "Convince me why I shouldn't fucking kill you, right here, right now, for being in my boy's apartment."

"*Fine*. He invited me here," I said, keeping my voice as calm as possible. "I'm living here for a little while. We're—"

"Bullshit," he said, snorting. He tightened his grip on my wrist. "Lucas would never let a girl move in with him. Ever."

I bit down on my tongue to keep the groan of pain from escaping. "He did. I swear it."

"Why would he do that?" he asked, jerking on my wrist a little more.

The pain blinded me, and despite my most valiant efforts, I gasped. "Twist my arm any harder, and you'll break it."

He let up on me a little bit. "Answer. Me."

"I'm his . . . girlfriend."

He laughed. Actually *laughed*. "Sure. And I'm the pope."

"But—" Footsteps on the stairs sounded, and I grinned. "You'll see. He's home, and he doesn't like it when other men threaten me."

It might have been my imagination, but the man straddling me stiffened.

The door flew open, and Lucas came charging in, gun drawn. As soon as he saw me on the ground, with my attacker on top of me, he froze. "Chris. What the *fuck* are you doing?"

The man shot me a look, and for the first time since he'd attacked me, he seemed a little less sure of himself. "I came to talk to you and used the key you gave me. When I came in, I caught her running through your place with a big-ass knife, so . . ." He didn't finish the sentence but shrugged casually.

Lucas rubbed his jaw, staring Chris down with stony silence. "So you tackled her to the floor and straddled her? Get the hell off her, man."

Chris loosened his grip on me. "But who is she, and why is she in your apartment alone? She claimed to be your girlfriend, which we both know can't be true."

"*Shit.*" Lucas kicked the door shut but didn't lower his gun. "Get off her, or I'll kill you. *Now.*"

Chris blinked. "But—"

Lucas crossed the room, his lip curled in anger. Every step he took vibrated with fury and frustration. "I said, *get. The. Fuck. Off her.*"

"All right, man. Easy." Chris got off me instantly, lurching to his feet easily. I rolled over onto my back so I could keep an eye on him, cradling my wrist in my uninjured hand. When he caught sight of me, he froze. "Well, shit. If I'd gotten a real look at her, I wouldn't have questioned why you let her stay with you."

I was about to tell him that that *her* was right here, and he needed to stop talking about me as if I wasn't, but Lucas shoved him backward. His face was red and his movements were jerkier than usual. I'd never seen him look so pissed before. "Don't even think about her like that. She's *mine*. Understood?"

"Dude, I wasn't trying to take her or anything. I was just saying she's—"

"Mine," Lucas repeated, shoving him against the light blue wall. "And if you touch her again, I'll fucking gut you like a fish."

Chris held his hands up, a skeptical look taking over his expression. "Seriously, man?"

"Seriously." He let go of his friend and backed off but gripped the butt of his gun. "Understood, *man*?"

Chris stared back at Lucas for a few seconds, and I held my breath. Finally, Chris let out a breath and nodded. "Okay. I get it. She's yours."

A muscle ticked in Lucas's jaw, and he held his hand down to me. When he glanced at me, I could still see the anger seething in the green depths of his eyes, but they gradually softened to the mist green hue I was so familiar with. "Are you okay, sweetheart?"

"Yeah." I slid my hand into his, shooting Chris a nervous look. Lucas trusted this man—obviously, since he'd turned his back on him—but he'd been holding me to the floor moments ago. I didn't trust him at *all*. Cradling my injured wrist to my chest, I rubbed it absentmindedly. "I'm fine."

"No, you're not." He skimmed his fingers over my wrist, his jaw flexing. "Damn it. It's going to bruise."

Chris cleared his throat. "Uh, sorry about that."

"It's fine," I said. When Lucas merely glowered at Chris, I wiggled my fingers in his. "Hey. I said I'm fine. He was just trying to protect you."

Lucas didn't answer me. Just went on looking pissed as hell. A muscle in his jaw ticked, and I swore I could literally see him plotting Chris's murder.

And it was ugly.

Chris cleared his throat. "Look, man, I'm sorry, okay? I thought she was trespassing—or worse, working for Scotty."

"She's not," Lucas said quickly, dragging his hand through his wavy hair and shooting a quick glance at me. "She's not in the life at all, so shut up."

"Well . . ." Chris tipped his head toward me. "She kinda is now."

That muscle in Lucas's jaw ticked again.

"Who is this Scotty guy, anyway?" I asked, studying them both.

Neither one answered me.

I crossed my arms and tapped my foot. *"Lucas."*

"Heidi," he said back, using the same threatening tone I'd used with him. The smirk I was all too familiar with slipped into place. At least he no longer looked murderous. "He's no one you need to worry about, darlin'."

Chris shifted his weight. "We need to talk." He paused. "Alone."

"Of course." Lucas tipped my face up with his fingers under my chin. His touch was tender. "Hey, dinner smells delicious, but I didn't get those things you asked for, so I'm gonna run down the street and get them with Chris. I'll be home in five minutes."

Chris made a choking sound.

Lucas glowered at him.

"Okay," I finally said.

He let go of me and motioned for Chris to follow him. They walked out the door, and I was left there alone, with my arms wrapped around myself, wondering what the hell was going on, who this Scotty guy was . . .

And why Lucas looked so upset at the mere mention of his name.

CHAPTER 13

LUCAS

I shut the door behind me, stepped outside, and leaned against the brick wall. The freezing night air seeped through my veins almost instantly, and I huffed out a breath. Impact wrenches buzzed behind me, and something clanged on the concrete floor of the shop. Across the way, I could make out the lights of the stadium, and I could smell the stench of the docks if I tried hard enough. Snow fell from the sky again, the kind that fluttered down majestically in big white tufts.

It looked so pure and fresh until it hit the ground . . .

And everything got muddled together in a big fucking mess. Just like life. It all looked good till the shit hit the fan, like it inevitably did.

"Okay, time to talk." Chris shoved his hands into his pockets and sighed. "What the hell are you thinking, man? Bringing a girl like *that* into this world?"

"She's tougher than she looks," I said, still watching

the snow falling from the black sky above. "Don't under-estimate her."

"Oh, I won't," Chris muttered. "But still . . . why?"

"I don't know," I admitted honestly, for once in my fucking life. "I wasn't thinking at all. She needed me, and I came to the rescue like an idiot."

"Wait." Chris scratched his head. "*You* came to the rescue?"

"I know, right?" I shrugged. "But she was about to be raped by some Bitter Hill men. I couldn't just stand there and say nothing. I might be an asshole, but even *I* have to draw the line *some*where."

Chris dropped his hand back to his side. "Damn. You're right, of course, but this new intel makes my news even worse."

I blinked. "How so?"

"Never mind for now." He whistled through his teeth and looked over his shoulder. "What did you do to them?"

"Killed two and sent the other one home with a message."

"You should've killed—"

"Them all." I stared up at the sky. "Yeah, I know that now."

Chris shook his head, his irritation seething off him in waves. "Does Tate know about all of this?"

"Yeah. He was cool with it, but now she's my girlfriend, for all intents and purposes." Lifting a shoulder, I added, "Whether we like it or not."

"You better make sure she doesn't think it's for good." He scratched his chin and glanced up at the window of my living room. The curtains were drawn, so there was nothing to see. "She looks awfully comfortable in your place."

"Believe me—she's as unhappy about this situation as

I am. She's just trying to make the best of a shitty situation, because that's the type of person she is." I started down the sidewalk, and Chris fell into step beside me. "Neither of us wanted this."

That much was true. But if I was being honest with myself, which I wasn't, having her around the apartment didn't exactly make me *un*happy.

"So when you acted as if I'd attacked your most prized possession up there, and you threatened my life if I ever touched her again . . ." He shot me a look out of the corner of his eye. "That was all for show? Does she mean nothing to you at all?"

I didn't answer, and I wasn't going to, because it was none of his damn business.

Yeah, I'd lost my shit up there when I'd found him on top of her. She was supposed to be safe inside those walls. Not threatened and thrown on the floor by someone who was a stranger to her. Seeing Chris on top of Heidi like that . . .

It had messed with me.

At first, I'd been terrified she'd be dead. Chris was the type to shoot first and ask questions later. And once I'd realized she was breathing, the relief had set in, followed quickly by the jealousy. I'd never been jealous before. Over anyone or anything.

And I didn't like starting now, with her.

"Hmm . . . ," Chris said, side-eyeing me.

"Shut the hell up," I growled. "No one asked you. And I seem to remember a time when you were so sure you wanted to marry Suzy Maxwell, like a fucking tool, after you fell for her in a shady-ass strip club. Where she worked. For *ten* years."

He laughed. "Fair enough. But I was eighteen, and she gave one hell of a lap dance."

"Yeah, I know." I grinned and dug my hands deep into my pockets. "We *all* know."

Chris punched my arm. "Fuck you."

"She always liked doing that, too," I teased, laughing when Chris growled. I shrugged. "But, honestly, it always seemed to me that you had a thing for Molly Lachlan. Every time she came outside when I was over your house, you lit up like a Christmas tree."

Chris stiffened. "No, I didn't."

"Yeah, whatever, man."

"I didn't," Chris argued, his whole body stiff. He acted as if I'd witnessed some big, deep secret of his and not some silly little crush he'd had as a child. "I never liked her, and never would. She's a fucking kindergarten teacher."

"Yeah." I snorted. "Maybe you're right. The two of you would be a disaster. Suzy the Stripper's more your speed."

He punched my arm and laughed, but it sounded strained. "You're lucky I swore off her, as well as any and all relationships." He gave me a meaningful look, his forehead wrinkled. "We both did. In this life, marriage just isn't a smart idea."

"Yeah, I know." I lifted a shoulder. "Believe me—we're not getting married. For real, or for show. She's a temporary distraction, and that's all."

He nodded. "Just make sure she's not distracting you too much. Now's not the time to let your guard down."

"Noted," I said dryly. Stopping in front of the store, I opened the door and Chris went in first. After I grabbed a basket, I headed straight for the liquor. "Why did you come by? What's up?"

Chris rubbed the back of his neck. "I saw *him* earlier today. He was at Charlie's, and he was in a small group of guys—about four. One guess who they were."

I tensed but forced a nonchalant shrug, even though I had a feeling I knew exactly who they were. After all, I'd seen it yesterday, too, even though I didn't want to admit it. "I have no idea."

"Bitter Hill."

I froze midreach, dread hitting the bottom of my stomach like a fucking anvil. All the suspicion, all the doubts . . . yeah. They'd just blown up in my face. "Shit."

"Yeah, I know," Chris said, his voice so low I almost didn't hear him. He glanced around the empty store before continuing on. "They were in the corner, whispering and drinking. And I saw money exchanged. Looks like he's been watching you and decided to use the enemy to take care of his own issues. If Bitter Hill takes you out, no one will suspect him. Especially after what you did to them. It's ingenious, really. Don't you think?"

"Son of a bitch," I muttered, grabbing vodka off the shelf.

My phone buzzed, and I pulled it out. It was a text from Heidi. Don't forget the grenadine.

I jotted off a fast reply. I won't. Almost done.

It felt weird typing that to someone who was waiting for me to come home. Weird . . . but not in a bad way. She'd cooked dinner for me. No one had cooked a meal for me since before Ma got sick. After she died, I'd had to take over the duty. Someone had to feed Scotty, because he sure as hell hadn't been about to do it himself. Through trial and error, I'd taught myself. And I'd become pretty damn good at it, too.

But Heidi had cooked for *me*.

I tucked my phone away. When I glanced up, Chris was watching me with a frown. "What?" I snapped, grabbing a bottle of rum, too.

"You just smiled at a text message like a little girl, right after I told you something that should have you breaking shit." He shifted on his feet, something shadowing his eyes. "What the hell is up with you, man?"

Had I smiled? I hadn't even noticed. I yanked down

some Pucker before grabbing another. "I wasn't smiling at the message. I was smiling at the thought of ripping your throat out with my bare hands."

"While drinking an appletini?" Chris rolled his eyes. "Yeah. So threatening, man."

"How do you know this Pucker shit goes into an appletini?"

He lifted a shoulder. "They're good, when you're in the mood for something sweet. I'm not ashamed."

We both laughed.

He sobered first.

"Look, Lucas, it's going down. You should really come up with a plan of defense. Go to Tate and tell—"

I stiffened. "No."

"But—"

"No." I slammed a bottle of grenadine in the basket. "I'm not ratting out my little brother. End of story."

"Even if he kills you?"

"If he kills me, there will be no need to decide anything at all." I grabbed the last bottle I needed before heading for the register. "Problem solved."

Chris made an angry sound I couldn't even begin to describe. "That's not funny."

"I never said it was," I snapped. "But I won't turn on him."

"Fine, then." He held his hands out. "Tell me your plan. Go on. Let me hear it. I'm sure it's brilliant as hell, right?"

I stayed silent, because I didn't *have* one. Not yet.

I'd only *just* accepted that he was actually trying to pop me.

"Yeah. That's what I thought," he said, his tone hard. "You're just going to be the dutiful older brother you've always been, and what? Hold the target on your chest so he can aim properly when he kills you, and praise him on his aim as you fall to the ground?"

"Better that than dying slow. Don't underestimate the importance of a clean shot."

Chris slammed his fist on the counter. *"Luc."*

I knew why he was frustrated. I got it. But if he thought I hadn't been racking my brain nonstop over the past day and a half over what the hell to do about this whole mess, then he didn't know me at all. It had been *all* I'd been thinking about.

But I didn't know what to fucking *do* about it.

"I'll fix it, damn it," I growled.

"There's nothing to fix. You can't cure him from being a jackass."

I smirked. "I dunno. With advancements in modern science, there's gotta be a pill for it by now. Maybe I'll ask around."

"Whatever. Go ahead. Let him kill you. I won't come to your funeral." Chris pushed off the counter and strode toward the door. "Asshole."

After he left, the cashier came up, and I paid for my items. As I walked down the sidewalk, I dialed and lifted my phone to my ear. It rang three times before he answered.

"Hello?" he said.

"Hey, Scotty." I cleared my throat. "It's me, Lucas."

He laughed. It sounded fake as hell. "Yeah, I know. I can read the caller ID. What's up, bro?"

Someone laughed, dishes clanged together, and loud music boomed in the background. He was still at the bar, more than likely. "Just checking in. We haven't chatted much since I've gotten out. How are things going on your end?"

"Good."

That was it. Just a one-word answer. I gripped the phone tighter and stopped in front of the shop. "Where you at?"

"Oh, you know." He took a while to answer. "Just hanging at home with some of my boys from my crew. Shooting the shit."

"Is that so?"

"Yeah." He paused. "That's so."

Gritting my teeth, I closed my eyes. I knew that soft tone of voice Scotty was currently using. It was his lying voice. I'd always teased him about it as a kid. When he lied, his voice rose in pitch just the slightest bit.

I'd first noticed it when he'd eaten my last chocolate bunny from my Easter basket. He'd still had the chocolate on his face, all over his chubby cheeks, and I'd asked him what had happened to it. He'd looked me flat in the eye and said he didn't know—with a hitch to his voice. From that point on, I'd noticed that every time he'd lied to me or Ma, his voice would change. It was doing it now, too.

And it hurt like hell.

I looked down at the snow. It was already gray and filthy. The purity hadn't lasted long. It never did. "You want to meet up for drinks? Shoot the shit? Haven't seen much of you since I got out."

"I can't. Maybe some other time."

I nodded once. "All right, then. Hey, have you seen any of the Bitter Hill guys hanging around our territory? There's been a rumor that they were stirring up trouble earlier, and Tate wanted me to check into it before I went home for the night."

A long pause, and then: "Nah, man. I haven't seen a single one. But I stayed home the past two days with that chick I hooked, so I'm not the most reliable source for that type of intel."

I stiffened and glanced up toward the window again. Another lie. But I didn't need my trick to know it this time. After all, I'd seen him with my own two eyes. As I turned away, something red and black caught my eye. I crept around the side of the building, my heart thudding loudly in my ears, echoing like some sick kind of ticking clock, counting down to D-day.

My shop had been tagged by Bitter Hill.

Son of a bitch. Scotty, the same boy whom I'd told fairy-tale stories to until three a.m. whenever he had nightmares as a kid, had put a price on my head. I glared up at the sky, forcing myself to keep my tone neutral. *Motherfucker.* Out loud I said, "Okay, good. Let me know if you see anything suspicious."

"Sure thing."

Scotty hung up, and I gripped my phone so tightly I'm surprised it didn't crack under the pressure. If I'd had any doubts about his true loyalties . . .

They'd just been torn to shreds.

What the hell had happened when I'd been serving my time? What could have changed my little brother so damn much that he wanted to kill me? Scotty had always been a bit selfish and shortsighted, but fratricide? When had he become someone capable of *that*?

A small—okay, *huge*—part of me blamed myself.

I couldn't help it, since I'd practically raised the little fucker and all. Maybe it was something I'd done or said. Maybe I hadn't been enough of a parent figure to him after Ma died. I'd been all he had after she'd passed. I'd tried my best, but I'd been nothing more than a kid myself.

When I joined the Sons of Steel Row after Ma fell ill, we finally had the money to pay our bills and put food on the table, but she hadn't approved of where the money came from. Had refused the money I'd tried to give her, so instead, I'd bought groceries and paid off her mortgage behind her back . . . whether she'd liked it or not.

I'd done what needed to be done.

But she'd died, and all Scotty had was *me* to look up to.

No wonder he was fucked-up like he was. I wasn't a role model and never would be. I'd joined this life because it had been a challenge, and we'd needed money, so I'd accepted the challenge. I'd worked my ass off to gain their trust, and then

I'd worked even harder. When Scotty had followed in my footsteps and joined, too, I'd welcomed him into the fold with open arms. And look what had come of it. *This*.

I had no clue what to do with him now, but turning him in to Tate wasn't an option. In the end, he might need to die, but he didn't need to be ripped to shreds by the Sons. And I wasn't ready to give up on him yet. There had to be a way for me to redeem him. To show him what he was doing was wrong and guide him down the correct path . . . whatever the hell that was. He was my little brother. I'd practically raised him. I couldn't just give *up* on him.

It couldn't be too late, damn it.

I tore my gaze off the tag that changed everything, made one more quick stop at the hardware store across the street, then opened the downstairs door, climbing the stairs one slow step at a time. Music played, and the welcoming scent of lasagna hit me halfway up. I paused for a second, taking it all in.

Outside, life was hell and dark. But in here . . .

It was like a whole other world. One I *liked*.

She sang along to whatever song was playing, her voice soft, musical, and intoxicating. The way she acted, the way she was, was so different from anyone else I'd ever known, besides my ma. Maybe that's why I'd rescued her from Bitter Hill. She had a freshness to her that drew a dirty soul like me in. She wasn't from the same twisted world that I was from.

Not until I'd pulled her in.

But what else should I have done? Let her get raped, killed, left for the rats and the roaches . . . or worse? Bitter Hill had their hands in human trafficking, too. There was no telling what they would've done with her once they were finished.

There hadn't been any other choice. I'd had to save her.

And now I had to save her from myself, too.

I might not be able to run anymore, but *she* could. I could give her my one-man escape plan and send her on her way. Kiss my chance at starting a new life good-bye.

Scotty had taken that from me.

But Heidi needed to get the hell outta Boston, and I was going to do everything in my power to make that happen before Scotty launched his attack. I couldn't let her get caught in the cross fire.

No matter what I decided, what I did, I couldn't let Scotty hurt Heidi.

I pushed the door open and walked in, forcing a grin to my face as I juggled the door and the bags. "Honey, I'm home."

"Now who's being domestic?"

"Yeah, yeah," I muttered, kicking the door shut behind me. "When in Rome . . ."

Laughing, she motioned me into the kitchen. Her resilience constantly amazed me. Minutes ago, she'd been attacked, and now she was singing, dancing, and cooking as if nothing had ever happened. She was so strong and fierce, and she needed to stay that way. If push came to shove, I'd do what I needed to do to keep her safe, whether she was willing or not.

I'd do what needed to be done, like I always did.

And she'd damn well take my escape plan and run.

"Did you get everything?" she asked, pulling the lasagna out and setting it on the waiting potholders she'd put out on the counter. "I know it was quite the extensive list."

"Yeah. It was practically the whole store," I said, nudging her with my elbow playfully. I loved how the top of her head came up only to the bottom of my shoulders. "Are we having a party I don't know about? Or did our fake relationship drive you to drink already?"

Closing the oven with her hip, she took the mitts off and blew her hair out of her face. She wore a black tank top and a pair of yoga pants. She had little to no makeup on, and her blond hair fell in soft waves over her shoulders. If I wasn't mistaken, she didn't have a bra on underneath her shirt. She looked relaxed and at home. I'd never seen her look more gorgeous.

And I was dying to see if I was right about the no-bra situation.

"Neither option. I want to try to get more women into the bar, so I want to try out a few 'Girls' Night Out' drinks to put on special a few nights a week." With her forearm, she swept the lingering hair out of her face. "I'm going to make them tonight and see which ones are a hit."

"So you'll be shitfaced before nine." I crossed my arms and gave her a once-over. A steaming mug of tea sat on the counter, half-empty already. I'd gone to three different stores before I found some tea that would fit in my Keurig, since she'd mentioned she liked to drink it when stressed. I'd have to dump it all in the garbage when she left, because I hated the shit. "Sounds like an excellent plan."

She rolled her eyes and grabbed her wallet off the counter. "How much do I owe you for the booze and the tea?"

"Nothing."

"Lucas—"

"I said nothing." I pushed off the counter and took two plates out of the cabinet. "I'll be drinking tonight, too, so it's only fair I pay, since you're making them for us."

She blinked at me. "You want to drink cocktails? Call me crazy, but they don't seem like they're your thing. You're more of a whiskey guy."

"Yeah, but you can't have a successful experiment without test subjects." I pointed to my chest. "And I am your *very* willing subject."

She didn't talk for a second, just stared at me, all rosy cheeks and blue eyes. I was two seconds from taking it back. It was a stupid idea and an even stupider sentiment. What the hell had I been think—?

"Thank you," she said softly. Her sapphire eyes glowed with that certain something that told me she was thinking how *nice* I was. "I'd appreciate that."

I frowned. "Stop it. You're doing it again."

"Sorry, sorry," she mumbled. She didn't need to ask what I was yelling at her for anymore. I didn't know if that was a good thing or bad. "Want to punch me in the face to remind me how horrible you truly are?"

I cupped her chin, gently guiding her face toward mine. She joked about it, but it wasn't a joke to me. "I might be an asshole and a killer and a criminal . . . but I'd never, *ever* lay a finger on you. Not in a million years."

She nodded. "Yeah, I know."

"Yeah, but I don't think you really do." I skimmed my fingers over her soft skin. "I'd die before letting anyone hurt you, whether that person's myself or someone else."

She licked her lips, those eyes of hers still glowing that same damn way. But for once, I didn't care. "Lucas . . ." Hesitantly, she lifted up on tiptoe, rested her hands on my shoulders, and pressed her lips to my cheek. I caught her hips in my hands, holding on to her tightly, but I didn't pull her closer. Didn't try to make it into something it wasn't. As she pulled back, she pressed her palm over my heart and smiled up at me. "You might not be a nice guy, or someone I should like, but tough shit. I *do* like you. I like you a lot, and nothing you say or do will change that."

I swallowed hard. My throat felt dry as the Sahara. "You shouldn't."

"Yeah, well. I do."

She kissed me one last time, on the mouth this time. Her lips barely touched mine, in all reality, and the whole thing lasted two seconds, if that. It had been the slightest of touches, barely a kiss at all, and innocent as the fresh-fallen snow I'd been watching earlier. It had been a gesture of gratitude and friendship, and I knew it. But even knowing that . . .

It affected me more than any other kiss I'd ever had before.

And that scared the hell out of me.

CHAPTER 14

HEIDI

A couple of hours later, I mixed the next drink on my list, tapping my foot along to the music I'd started playing after Chris and Lucas had left. Surprisingly, Lucas had kept it on throughout dinner, and even after, while we'd talked. And we'd certainly talked. A lot. Maybe he'd sensed that when I was nervous, I needed a beat to distract me from the shit storm my life usually was. It soothed me and made me less jittery. And after that attack from Chris, I'd needed to soothe my nerves way too freaking badly.

Tea hadn't been enough.

I stole a quick peek at him. He sat at the dining room table, his legs stretched straight under the table, slouched back in his chair. He'd changed into a pair of jeans and a tight T-shirt—blue, of course—and his reddish-brown hair stood on end from him dragging his hands through it all night long. He'd been doing that a lot.

I had a feeling that calmed *his* nerves, much like my tea and music.

All night long, he'd been sipping my cocktails and chatting me up over lasagna, all while acting charming and funny the whole damn time. This would be his third drink. An appletini, this time. He'd been the picture-perfect gentleman—despite the slightly dangerous edge he could never completely hide from the world—for the entire evening. The kind of guy I could never resist. As much as Lucas might not be a "good man" by society's standards, he'd been nothing but kind to me.

If that didn't make him a "good man," I didn't know what did. Maybe it was the buzz talking, or maybe it was the way I couldn't stop thinking about how amazing he'd made me feel for the one minute I'd given him the other night, and during the kiss outside the stadium. Maybe it was something I couldn't even begin to name. All I knew was . . .

He was right. I wanted him.

I wanted him *bad*.

Pouring out the drinks, I glanced at him from under my lashes again. His gun was on his hip. I could just barely make it out under the cover of his shirt. He looked so dangerously handsome sitting there, watching me with those Irish green eyes of his. He stretched, and I couldn't tear my eyes away from those damn biceps of his I'd never been able to stop drooling over. His skin was pale, but to the best of my knowledge, he didn't have any freckles. Unless he had them under his clothes.

I kinda hoped he did. It would be like our little secret when I—

Yeah . . . I needed to stop that line of thinking right there. I wouldn't be undressing him in any way, shape, or form. Ever. It was a bad, bad idea. A dangerous one.

And *stupid*. I wasn't stupid, was I?

As I walked across the room toward him, two drinks in my hands, he lifted a brow and readjusted himself in his seat. My heart fluttered. Those arms of his flexed, and I was drawn to them yet again. They were so strong and sexy. Just like him. "See something you like?"

I scoffed, the noise sounding false to my ears. "Just marveling at the size of your ego."

"Uh-huh." He took the green concoction and sniffed it. His nose wrinkled. "This one smells sweeter than the others."

"It is, I think." I lifted my glass. "Shall we find out?"

He lifted his glass. "Slainte."

I had no idea what that word meant, but it sounded Gaelic. We both tipped our glasses back and sipped. At the same time, we lowered our drinks. I licked my lips. "Mm."

"Yeah, I see what Chris meant." He took another sip. "This is actually pretty good."

I blinked. "*Chris* drinks appletinis? The same guy who tried to kill me for being here?"

"Yeah, sometimes." He stood and tipped his head toward the couch. "Want to get more comfy?"

I tugged at my yoga pants. "I think this is about as comfy as it gets. I look like a bum, while you"—I gestured toward him—"look as devastatingly charming as ever."

He sat on the couch and ran his gaze over me, that all-too-familiar smirk in place. It made me itchy, antsy, and hot. It took all my control not to fan my cheeks. "You look gorgeous to me, darlin'."

Sitting beside him, I tucked my foot under my butt and smiled. "You're sweet."

"The hell I am," he growled.

"Yeah, yeah. I know." I waved a hand dismissively and took a big sip. "Monster, killer, blah, blah, blah."

For a split second, he looked pissed. But then he laughed, and I couldn't stop staring at him. God, he was beautiful when he laughed like that. I know that sounds weird, in connection with a criminal and a man such as Lucas, but it was true. There was something about him that was inexplicably gorgeous. No matter what he said or did.

And I was done denying that, at the very least.

"Blah, blah, blah," he echoed, shaking his head and downing the rest of his drink. He set the empty glass down on the coffee table and licked his lips slowly, as if he relished every last drop. If he was trying to be provocative, he was succeeding. "That was my favorite one."

"Obviously," I drawled. He shot me a look. I quickly stared down at my cup and bit down on my tongue, because this close to him . . . those gorgeous green eyes of his were as dangerous to stare into as the sun. "So, who is Chris? A friend? Relative?"

He remained silent for so long I thought he wasn't going to answer me, which wasn't really a shocker. He wasn't exactly an open book. Or even an unlocked one. He sighed. "Brother, in every sense except blood."

I got over my shock at the revelation of a personal detail, took another sip of my drink, and nodded. Because I totally got that. Marco was more like a relative to me than anyone else had ever been—Frankie, too, when he'd been alive—so I knew the feeling all too well. He was my little brother, no matter what our DNA said. "How long have you known him?"

He leaned his head back on the couch and let out another sigh. He looked relaxed, and for the first time ever . . . it seemed as if he had his guard down. His whole body was chilled, and his eyes were closed slightly. His profile was as perfect as ever, highlighted by the dim lighting he'd turned on before dinner. Rubbing his jaw, he rolled his head toward me. Those eyes of his pinned me in place. It occurred to me they matched the appletini I held. "Ever since I was a kid. From the neighborhood. He's the only person I trust completely," he said, his voice low.

I finished my drink and slid my glass next to his. Turning

more toward him, I tugged my foot into my lap and studied him. His memories shadowed him like a ghost. He no longer looked relaxed. "Why's that?"

"My brother is . . . I don't know who Scotty is anymore." He dropped his hand to his lap. Without really intending to, I followed its descent. His fingers curled into a fist, and I forced my attention upward. "If he knocks on the door, don't grab a knife and confront him. Run."

I swallowed. "Oh."

"I'm not kidding. Run like hell if your paths ever cross, and don't look back."

"Okay, I get it." I reached out and touched his knee, squeezing reassuringly. "What happened between you two?"

"I went to jail." He stared at my hand, and his Adam's apple bobbed. "He changed. And now everything is fucked-up."

"What's he doing?"

"It doesn't matter." He shook his head. "Enough about me."

Not even close. But I drew back, settling deeper into the cushions. "All right. What's in the bag by the door?"

He glanced at it dismissively. "A new lock. Tonight made me remember that too many people have keys to my place."

"Oh." I frowned. "You don't have to do that for me. I mean, I'll only be here for a little while more. Right?"

He grunted. "I'm changing them for me—not you."

"Why do you want to change them?"

He stared back at me, not answering.

It didn't take long to figure out he wouldn't.

"Okay . . . ," I said slowly. "So, you don't want to talk about you. Tell me, then—what *do* you want to talk about?"

"You." He rested his arm across the back of the couch, and his fingertips brushed against my shoulder. "Are you from Boston originally?"

"Not much to tell. I'm a system kid." I fidgeted with the drawstring of my pants. "Born and raised."

"But no parents?"

I shook my head once. "They're dead. Have been since I was a baby."

"So that's why there were foster homes all your life?"

"Yeah." I shifted away from him. "Until I was old enough to run. Then I took my chances on the streets, and did pretty good, too. I was always on the move. Always running from one place to another to avoid any trouble. The only place I ever went back to was that alley I took you down."

He cupped my cheek. "Did you ever have to . . . you know."

The fact that he couldn't ask the question struck me harder than it should have. He didn't need to finish the question for me to know what he asked, though. "No."

He sagged. "Thank fucking God."

"I could've. And probably should have." I lifted a shoulder. "But I didn't want to. I hung on to my pride a little tighter than most and refused to sell my body. Instead . . . I just kept going."

Tapping his fingers on his thigh, he nodded. "And you never stopped running, once you started?"

"I stopped once I met the man who gave me the Patriot. Frankie. He found me sleeping under a ratty blanket behind his bar, woke me up, and told me to 'Get the hell inside where it's warm.'" I smiled at the memory of him. He'd been so openhearted and kind. And he'd always smelled like butterscotch candies. He'd been addicted to the things. He was too good for our neighborhood, but he'd refused to leave his bar behind. "Once he took me in, I finally found a home."

"Where is he now?" He dropped his hand. "Did he move down south to Florida like all the other old people seem to do once they hit eighty?"

"No. He died." I drew up my legs, resting my chin on my knees as I hugged myself. I felt a little cold now. "A little over a year ago."

"Oh." Lucas lowered his chin, the planes of his face softening slightly. "I'm sorry."

I shrugged with a nonchalance I didn't feel. "It's okay. You live. You die. That's life. What about you? Still have parents hanging around somewhere?"

"Nah." He rubbed circles on my back. Slow. Comforting. "I never knew my pa, so he's never been alive, as far as I'm concerned. And like I said the other night, my ma died when I was in my upper teens. So I was in charge of making sure Scotty grew up to be a good man." He paused. "I failed."

"No. That's not on you. People make their own choices, and they don't reflect on anyone else besides themselves."

His hand paused right above my ass. "Yeah, I don't know that I believe that. I think Ma would be pissed at me for letting it get this far. For not keeping him outta trouble."

I hesitated. "Do you miss her?"

"All the time," he answered, his voice cracking and full of honesty. "You?"

Not answering, I nodded once.

I missed Frankie. A lot.

I was alone now. Marco cared, but he wouldn't be in my life much longer. He'd leave Steel Row in a few days and do better things with his life than live in the slums of Boston. He'd leave and never look back. I'd be sad to see him go, but I'd be oh so happy, too. He was doing the one thing I'd never do. Escaping.

This hellhole owned me. I was stuck here, with my bar.

"Ever think about running again?" he asked, his shoulders tense.

Cocking my head, I bit down on my tongue. His thoughts were way too similar to mine for comfort. "Why would I want to run now? I told you, I found a home in the Patriot."

"But what if you could just leave Boston?" He caught my fingers. "What if you had enough money to leave this shit hole and the threat of Bitter Hill behind you? And you just . . . *ran*?"

I shook my head, my heart skipping a beat. "I don't. And I can't. I'm not going to lie; I've dreamt about starting over a few times. But I can't."

I couldn't just abandon the bar. It held the only happy memories I'd ever known.

"Even if you had enough money to start new? To buy a house, and get a job, and live in a quaint little suburb in the safest town you could find? Get a blank passport and the number of a guy who could put your photo on it? Then you could go wherever you wanted."

I let out a short laugh. He was living in dreamland, because I never had, and never *would* have, those things. "Where would that be?"

"I have no fucking clue."

Shaking my head, I shot him a rueful smile. "Yeah, me, either. You know why?"

"No." He shoved a hand through his hair and stood, bringing both the empty glasses into the kitchen. "Why?"

I followed him. "Because you and me weren't meant for perfect lives in the perfect suburbs. We're fighters. Survivors. Not *gardeners*."

"But you could be." He gripped the edge of the counter so tight I could see the whites of his knuckles and the hardening of his muscles. "You could be normal."

I picked up the bottle of vodka. "But not you?"

"Nah. I'll be lucky if I survive the week." His voice tried for casual but didn't pull it off.

"Wait, what?" I set it back down. "What do you mean?"

"*Fuck*. Forget I said that." He opened a drawer and pulled out a fat envelope. He handed it to me, and I took it out of reflex. "Run, sweetheart. Take this and go."

I closed my eyes and bit down hard on my tongue. Something twisted in my chest, and it hurt more than any blow I'd ever gotten. "Tell me you didn't just hand me an envelope full of cash."

He flexed his jaw. "And if I did?"

How many times had I dreamt of this? Of finding a buttload of cash and running? God, I didn't even know. But I didn't want it from him. Not like this. I shoved it back, hitting him square in the chest with a *whack*. "Take it back. I don't want it. And I'm not running away."

He didn't take the money. Instead, he leaned down till we were nose to nose and whispered, "I dare you, Heidi. I dare you to run."

"No." I slammed the envelope on the counter. "I'm not leaving my bar. Why are you asking me to? What's going on?"

He stepped back and covered his face before dragging his hands down and letting out an exasperated sound. "You need to go, okay? Right now. Take the money and get out of here."

Suddenly it made sense. He was trying to get rid of me without feeling guilty. So he threw money at me like I was some hooker from a corner. "Oh. So that's what this is about? You want me gone?"

He nodded once. "Yes. You need to go."

"Okay." I tucked a piece of hair behind my ear, tamping down any feelings of hurt. He'd warned me he was an asshole countless times, but I really hadn't believed all his talk about keeping me safe was just bullshit. Guess I was wrong. "But you don't have to throw money at me to get me to leave. I can take care of myself. Don't worry—I won't even ask for your help lugging my bags back to my apartment."

I walked past him, but he caught my arm. His touch burned my skin, searing some deep part of me that would never recover. "That's not what I meant, damn it. You don't need to go *home*; you need to *leave*."

"Okay, God, I am." I jerked free. "I'm *going*."

"*No.*" He gripped my shoulders and shook me slightly. "You're not *listening* to me."

I pushed his chest, and he stumbled backward. I'd obviously caught him off guard. "No, you're not listening to me. I'm going. Right now. And where I go, and what I do, is none of your business anymore. You saved me, so thank you for that. But now I'll take care of myself, like I always do. I happen to be quite good at it."

"The hell you are." He stepped in my path, towering over me. A muscle ticked in his jaw, and an angry vein pulsated in his neck. "The only way you're walking out that door is if you're leaving Boston."

"I'm not leaving my bar," I gritted out through my teeth. "So screw off, Lucky."

The muscle ticked again. "Then you're not going anywhere."

"Oh. My. God." I threw my hands up, and they trembled with rage and something else I didn't want to name. "What is happening right now? You're making absolutely no sense."

He gripped my arms again, resting his fingers on my back. I felt tiny with his big hands wrapped around me like that. Vulnerable, too. And I didn't like it. "You need to leave town because it's not safe here. You're not safe with *me* anymore."

I tipped my head back and met those blazing eyes of his I loved so much, fighting back the nerves bundling in knots in my stomach. "Why not? What's changed all of a sudden?"

"I thought I could be selfish for a little while longer and keep you around, but it's starting to feel like I'm playing Russian roulette with your life. My brother is trying to kill me, and you could end up as collateral damage in a war that has nothing to do with you," he admitted in a rush, his jaw hard and straight and tough. "So you need to leave town."

I swallowed hard. "Wait. He's trying to *kill* you?"

"Yes." He pointed to the door. "Ready to stop being stubborn and start being sensible?"

"I . . ." And leave him alone, with only one man to watch his back? Hell no. I wasn't about to abandon him in his hour of need, when he'd been there for me in mine. My fight hadn't been his. He could have left me in that alley and done nothing. But he hadn't, and I wouldn't, either. "Scotty?"

He flinched and pressed his lips into a tight line. "Yes. Scotty."

"But . . ." I'd been alone my entire life until Frankie, and it sucked, but it also meant there was no one who could hurt me. I couldn't imagine what Lucas was going through. "But he's your *brother*."

His hand flexed on me. He didn't let go, though. "Yes, I know. I had an emergency escape plan in place, just in case, but then I found out about Scotty, and then I saw—" He cut off. "And then everything changed. So now I want you to take the escape route. Take the money and the passport and run."

"Why don't you come, too?" I asked, holding my breath.

He stepped back. "I can't. There's only one passport."

"So we won't leave the country." It was crazy and stupid, but if he went with me . . . I'd go. If it meant saving him from the impossible choices he was facing, I'd go. "We'll find you that quiet house in the suburbs that we talked about, with the garden and the fence, and never look back."

His gaze darkened. "I can't. There's nowhere in the country that I could hide where they wouldn't find me. It's not that easy for me."

"What makes you think it's any easier for me?"

"Because it is," he snapped. "You don't have any real ties here at all, so nobody will come chasing after you. You don't have a gang at your back, a homicidal brother, or a parole officer hanging over your head. I can't just *leave*, Heidi."

"The hell you can't," I said, jerking free again, his words slicing through me. "You just put one foot in front of the other, and keep on walking till you get to your car. You get in and take the first left. Then you just keep driving."

"So do it." He threw the envelope at me. I refused to catch it, so it hit the floor between my feet. "If it's so fucking easy, then take the first left and don't come back."

"No." I lifted my chin and glared at him. "The only way I'm walking out that door is if you leave Boston with me."

It was a good thing he'd reassured me that violence against women was a line he wouldn't cross, because right now, he looked murderous. "I told you—there's only an escape there for one."

"Then take it," I shot back. "What's stopping you?"

He froze, nostrils flaring, and stared me down. It was then that I realized what was stopping him: *me*. I was the thing that had stopped him from leaving, and I was the reason that he might get killed. And that was unacceptable. "Oh my God."

He ignored me. "Why are you being so bullheaded stubborn? You were already attacked once by complete strangers; you're an even bigger target now that people think you mean something to me."

"Don't be ridiculous. I'm not leaving. There's no reason for me to leave. Chris didn't believe me when I said we had a relationship. I'm sure your brother will just think I'm the flavor of the week, too." I crossed my arms. "You're the one in danger—not me. Me abandoning my life won't do anything, certainly not save you. You need to take the money and go. I'll be fine. Your fight has nothing to do with me."

He stilled. "The hell it doesn't." Lucas kicked the envelope to the side as he took a step closer. "And I didn't ask you to save me."

"You didn't need to ask," I shot back, retreating. I couldn't think clearly when he was within touching distance. "Neither did I."

He flushed. "Scotty bought off Bitter Hill. He'll use them to kill me and then they'll come after you. They *tagged* my building, Heidi. It's not safe here." He stalked toward me, and I forced myself to stand my ground. "They'll finish what they started the other night, and then, if you're lucky, they'll kill you."

My heart raced, but I ignored it. My fight-or-flight instinct might have kicked in with his words, like he hoped, but he underestimated me. I wasn't a flight type of girl anymore—I'd stand my ground. "And if I'm not lucky?"

"They'll keep you. Or sell you." He pressed his mouth into a thin hard line again. "And you'll wish you were dead."

I forced myself to shrug. "On the streets . . . people have tried to cage me before. I'm not scared of them."

"I am," he admitted. He pressed close to me. Gently, he cupped my cheek. His words, though, vibrated with anger and frustration, and so much more. "Not for myself, but for you. I don't want you to get caught in the cross fire. It's not a matter of *if*, it's a matter of *when*, and I could be in a position where I can't protect you anymore. You could get hurt. And that's not acceptable to me. That's why I *need* you to take my escape, Heidi. I *need* you to run."

It was then that I realized the enormity of his actions. It was then, also, that I realized that the fact that he was willing to give me his escape—to selflessly risk his own life for mine, time and time again—didn't just make me grateful or anything like that. His actions, and the way he put me first all the time, made me . . . made me . . .

Love him.

Yeah. I loved him, like the idiot I'd sworn I wasn't.

Despite the fact that I knew he would never feel the same, I *loved* him. Completely, utterly, *loved* him. And he would break my heart in the end if I let him. And, God, I was going to let him.

I was going to give him my heart on a silver platter.

Resting my hands on his chest, I knew that this was one of those moments that defined your existence, a moment where two roads forked out in front of you. One was the path you'd choose, and one held the future unchosen. A lifetime worth of people you'd never meet, events that would never happen, emotions that you'd never feel.

But I was confident in my choice.

Digging my nails into his shirt, I shook my head once. "I'm not leaving you, Lucas. I refuse to run unless I'm running with you. And if you don't want to run with me . . . then we fight. Together."

He let out a strangled sound and rested his forehead on mine, closing his eyes. "Damn it, sweetheart. You have to go."

"I'm. Not. Going." Reaching up, I slid my hand behind his neck. Slowly, he lifted his head and stared down at me, his gaze haunted and glowing with something I couldn't pinpoint. "I'm staying with you. I choose you."

His hands slid down my sides, resting on my waist. He didn't pull me closer, but he didn't push me away, either. The way he looked down at me, all heat and passion, sent a coil of heat ripping through my veins. The tension between us had been tugging at me from the first moment we met, pulling me closer to him. We barely knew each other, but I was done resisting. Done fighting. I'd take Lucas as he was, bloodstains and all. He might not consider himself a "good" man, but I knew better. Now he was *my* man.

And I loved him.

Even though I knew he didn't love me.

"Heidi . . . ," he murmured, his tone laced with want and pure sex.

It was stupid, and I knew I'd probably regret it when this was all said and done, but I wanted to have him. Soon enough, this would all be over. If we managed to survive this mess, I'd be alone in my bar again, and Lucas would go back to doing whatever it was he was doing before I crashed into his life. So this one time . . . for once in my life . . . I knowingly chose to be stupid. I decided to take something I wanted, despite the consequences, and to live in the moment.

No fear. No doubts.

Just *us*.

As if he could feel the pull, too, the little space left between us shrank further as his arms tightened around me. He was so close, I could feel his breath mixing with mine. My heart pounding, I lifted my chin. And I said the words he'd told me I'd say, long ago. Although . . . I guess it hadn't been all that long ago, in reality. It felt like aeons, but it had only been days. "I'm going to say it. Those three little words you love to hear . . ."

He stiffened but didn't move away. "Don't. Once you do, there's no going back. You know it, and so do I. There's still time to—"

Any rational person would tell me it was way too soon for this, but I'd never been one to play it safe. "I don't want to go back."

"Jesus." His gaze fell to my mouth. "Heidi . . ."

Heat curled through my body as I prepared to leap, hoping to God he'd catch me before I fell, and I licked my lips. "You were right."

"Damn you," he growled.

I rose onto my tiptoes, but his mouth was still out of my reach. "I want you, Lucas. I want you so bad."

Before I could blink, his lips were on mine. This time felt different from the others. This time, something snapped inside of him, and he growled low in his throat, and it felt . . . *real*. I stumbled backward, our mouths fused together and our bodies straining against each other. The road I'd chosen was revealed, and I liked what I saw.

My back hit the wall, and his hands were *everywhere*.

CHAPTER 15

LUCAS

Honestly, I never really expected it to happen. I was an ex-con weapons smuggler with a bounty on my head. Heidi should have taken the money and run. There was nearly forty thousand dollars in that envelope lying somewhere on my kitchen floor. But what did the fool woman do instead?

She chose *me*.

If I were a decent man, I wouldn't be kissing her right now. I'd be saying whatever it took to make her leave me behind. I'd briefly considered arranging for Chris to "relocate" her, but I knew Heidi was stubborn enough to turn around and wade right back into this shitfest. With no other options left, I decided to hold on for the ride.

With her soft body pressed against mine in all the right places.

Breaking off the kiss, I took a big breath, my chest heaving. "You're being a damn fool," I rasped, my voice way too raw for my own good. "You should forget all about me. I'm going to get you killed, sweetheart."

She scowled, but she didn't speak. Really, what else was there to say? Instead, she gripped the bottom of her tank top and ripped it over her head. My gaze dipped down low. I'd have to be dead and six feet under *not* to look.

Hell, even then, I'd find a fucking way to see her.

It didn't take long for me to see that I'd been right earlier. She didn't have a bra on. And, holy shit, she was gorgeous, standing there shirtless. Her breasts were large—but I already knew that—and would overfill my hands. Their tips were dusky pink and hard. And they were begging for my touch. As I stared, she pulled her pants down and kicked them off.

All she wore was a skimpy red thong.

And her long blond hair.

I swallowed but almost choked on it because my throat was so damn dry. "Shit, Heidi. You're . . . you're . . . fucking *perfect*."

She gave me a sassy smile. "Yeah. And I'm naked."

"If you do this, you're mine. No more games." I flexed my fingers. "You're actually mine."

She tossed her hair over her shoulder. "Then come get me."

I closed the distance between us. I'd tried to do the right thing, tried being unselfish for once in my motherfucking life, but it didn't stick. She wanted me to take her? I would take her. God only knew what the future held, but I knew one thing.

We would go down together.

When I stopped in front of her, I reached out and gently ran my thumbnail across her bare nipple. She shivered and bit down on her lip. Her rosy cheeks matched the tips of her breasts, and it took every ounce of my control not to not take her hard and fast, because it felt like I'd been starving for her for ages. But she deserved better than a quickie against the wall. She deserved my full attention . . .

And so much more.

"So pretty," I said, my voice almost reverent. But, damn it, she was. I couldn't help but worship her beauty in the face of my own depravity. "So mine."

She curled her hands into tiny balls, and slowly relaxed them until they hung limply at her sides. "Take off your shirt, Lucas."

"Excuse me?" I said, cocking a brow. "Was that an order?"

Tilting her head, she stared me down. "Yeah, it was. Inside these walls, I can say whatever I want—your words, not mine—and I want to see what you look like without a shirt on. So . . . *take off your shirt.*"

I curled my hand around her neck, resting my thumb against her swollen lips. "I'll take it off when I'm damn good and ready to take it off. First . . ." I dropped to my knees and placed a kiss right above the waistband of her lacy red thong. "I need to see if you taste as good as you smell."

A whimper escaped her lips. *"Lucas."*

"Shh. I know, sweetheart. I know."

I flicked my tongue over her clit, tasting her through the skimpy material that separated me from what I wanted most—her. She tasted like nothing I'd ever tasted before, but I wasn't ready to remove it yet. Wasn't ready to give myself what I wanted.

It would be too easy.

She fisted my hair and urged me closer. *"God.* More."

Grinning, I cupped her ass and rolled my tongue in big circles. Teasing her, but not giving her enough friction or pressure to actually do anything for her, because she wasn't getting off that easily. Literally.

"Oh my God," she breathed, dropping her head against the wall. Her breaths came out in spurts, and I pressed my tongue against her one more time before I rose to my feet.

Once she realized I'd stopped, she snapped her head back up and glared at me. "No. Lucas, I—"

I yanked her close by the back of the neck and kissed her, my tongue entwining with hers perfectly. She tasted like herself and appletini—and her scent of peaches permeated my senses. It was a combination I'd never forget.

Not even once she was gone.

A moan escaped her, and she ran her hands down my chest and over my abs, stopping right above my belt. Her hands hovered for a second before she dipped lower, gripping my hard cock. I pressed into her hand, growling low. When she rubbed her palm against me, hard and slow, I backed her against the wall again.

She collapsed against it and grabbed my belt, undoing it with trembling hands. She kept trying to take control from me, and I wasn't about to let her. This was my game to play. I'd been waiting for her to give herself to me, and she had.

Stepping back, I shook my finger at her and grinned. Then I took another step back, because she reached out for me and almost caught me. "Uh-uh. Not yet."

"*Lucas.*" She pressed her palms flat against the wall and bit down on her swollen lower lip. "You said no more games. Stop playing, and *take* me."

"Or . . . ?" I cocked my head. "You'll kick my ass?"

"Maybe."

"Maybe I'd like that." I gripped my shirt and lifted it slightly. Her gaze dipped down immediately, her chest rising and falling rapidly. "Maybe I like it rough."

She licked her lips, and her nostrils flared. "Take it off for me." After darting a glance up at me, she bit down on her lower lip seductively and added, "Please?"

"Since you asked so nicely . . ." I pulled it over my head and tossed it over my shoulder. "Sure thing, darlin'."

When I turned back to her, her eyes were wide. "Holy . . ."

She didn't finish that statement. Instead, she took a step toward me, then two. Slowly, she reached out and traced one of my tattoos. I had them from my shoulders down to below my belt. They all mingled together into one big canvas. She traced the one that had my ma's birthdate on it. "I didn't know you had so many tattoos."

I shrugged. "I have more you can't see."

"Show me." She touched the star tattoo on my opposite shoulder. "I'd love to know what they all mean."

When she touched my skin, her fingers featherlight, I forced a noncommittal laugh and remained completely still. "Some other time?"

"Yeah." She ran her fingers over my nipple piercing. "Some other time."

Shivering from her gentle touch, I pressed her hand more firmly against my skin. "You have ten seconds to be in my bed, naked, and waiting for me."

She blinked at me. "Excuse me?"

"Ten." I cocked a brow, because she hadn't moved yet. "Nine. Eight."

"Seriously?" Her fingers twitched under mine. "You're going to count down for me like I'm a—?"

I stroked my jaw. "Seven. Six."

"Fine, I'm *going*."

"Five. Four—"

Tossing a look over her shoulder, she ran for the bedroom. I watched her go, admiring the view for a split second before continuing on. "Three. Two. One."

I heard her hit the mattress just as I finished counting. "That was way faster at the end. Cheater."

I did my best to hide my amusement at the surly tone in her voice. "I have no idea what you're talking about."

I undid my belt as I walked. As I entered the room, I switched the light on. She'd followed instructions well. She lay in the middle of my bed, completely naked. Her red thong was on the floor, and she rested her weight on her elbows. Her knee was bent and folded over her other leg. Her blond hair fell over her shoulders to the pillows and curled angelically.

It was easily the most seductive pose I'd ever seen, hands down.

"Now who's staring?" she teased.

"What man wouldn't at the sight of you?"

I yanked my belt out and dropped it. Walking over to the nightstand, I opened the drawer and grabbed a condom. After tossing it on the bed, I undid my pants but didn't take them off.

She watched me intently, her gaze never wavering from me as she shifted on the bed, her thighs rubbing against each other. "If you don't hurry up, I'm going to self-combust before you even touch me."

My pants hit the floor. "Don't you dare."

"Oh my . . ." She crawled across the bed, completely naked and sexy as hell. Once she reached the edge, she knelt and ran her fingers over my abs. "I knew you were muscular, but damn, Lucas. This is insane."

I glanced down at her, watching her expression as *she* watched her hand on me. It was intoxicating as hell. Usually she did her best to conceal her expressions, so the fact that she relaxed her guard with me was a gift. I could see what she felt, as she felt it.

That meant more to me than it should have.

She lifted up higher on her knees, glanced up at me through her thick lashes, and flicked her tongue over my nipple ring. I let out a strangled groan and buried my hands in her hair. It felt so good to have her lips on me. I didn't usually let the girl make the first move. I remained in control at all times. It was the only way I knew how to fuck.

But with her . . .

All my rules were flying out the window.

She glanced up at me again. Her sapphire eyes glowed mischievously. "I want to touch you. Taste you. All over."

I nodded once, unable to form words. When she cupped my cock again through my boxers, I stiffened. Everything inside of me tightened, demanding more. Now. But I fought down the urge. That irritating instinct to give her anything she wanted made itself known again, and there was no stopping it. If she wanted to indulge herself with my body, I would man up and give her free rein.

She'd get what she wanted.

When she scraped her teeth over the nipple ring, sucking gently, I let my lids drift shut and shut my mind off. She skimmed her hands down my abs and over my ass as her mouth moved over my piercing. My stomach clenched tightly, and my cock begged to be buried inside her *now*. As if she could read my thoughts, she moaned and slid her hand beneath my boxers, closing her fingers over my hard length. She let go way too quickly, but it was only to lower my last piece of clothing. Once my boxers joined my pants on the floor, she licked her lips and lowered her head.

After dropping a kiss to my hip, she ran her tongue over the tip of my cock. I tugged on her hair slightly. "Heidi, fuck . . . Don't be a cocktease. Do it."

"Since you asked so nicely . . . ," she said.

She closed her mouth over me and sucked gently, and I lost my mind. Groaning, I pressed closer to her, wanting— no, *needing*—her to take more of me inside her hot, wet mouth. And she did. Man, she did. Her tongue moved over me, teasing me, killing me, and yet making me feel better than I'd ever felt before.

And that was saying a hell of a lot.

I didn't know what that meant, but I knew it probably wasn't good. Her nails dug into my bare ass, and she rolled her tongue over me, sucking harder with each torturous stroke she made. I made myself stand still. Made myself give her what she wanted—*me*. But the point came where I needed to move, or I'd come.

And it wasn't time for that yet.

"Enough," I gritted out between my clenched teeth. I pushed her shoulders, and she reluctantly let me go. "On your back, darlin'. Open for me."

She fell to her elbows, her legs spread and her breathing erratic. Her red lips were wet and swollen, and I wanted nothing more than to taste her. So I did. Curling my hand behind her neck, I melded my mouth to hers and kissed her hungrily. It was in that second that I realized I'd never needed anything, anyone, this damn badly before. For the first time in my life . . .

I knew I'd feel it when a woman walked away.

CHAPTER 16

HEIDI

The second he pressed his weight onto me, I knew I was a goner. *His* bare skin, pressed against *my* bare skin, was almost enough to send me over the edge. I'd been waiting for this since the first moment I saw him, no matter how much I'd tried to deny it. What had existed before only in scorching fantasies was now unfolding before me. And he was right. There would be no going back.

Lucky for me, I had no desire to go back. I was just fine where I was.

Part of me knew I was being an idiot. He'd literally handed me a fortune and a new start, and I hadn't taken it. How many times, as a kid, had I dreamt of that very thing? Of saving enough money and taking off, never to be seen in Boston again? So many times I'd lost count. And yet I'd been given the chance to do that very thing, free of charge, and I hadn't taken it.

Adolescent me thought adult me was a freaking fool.

He hauled my leg up, and I wrapped it around his waist,

my insides melting when he pressed his erection up against my core, and all thoughts of condescension against myself faded away. Because adolescent me hadn't known Lucas Donahue. In the past, it had always taken me a while to be ready for that kind of contact, but with Lucas, all it took was a smirk and a sarcastic reply, and I was there. This was a bad idea because there was no happy ending here.

But I was going to do it anyway.

I almost hated myself for it.

His hand closed over my breast, squeezing with the perfect amount of pressure, and I arched my back, trying to get closer to him. His mouth moved over mine, stealing all rational thought, and I ran my hands down his hard back. I'd had no idea he had ink and a piercing, but it was hot. So hot I couldn't even process it.

"No." He caught my wrists in one hand, trapping them above my head. With his other hand, he cupped my core, his palm pressed against my clitoris. "My turn."

My heart skipped a beat. "Yes," I breathed. "God yes."

He kissed a path down my neck, over my shoulder, and scraped his teeth over my nipple. I cried out and strained against his hold, longing to pull him closer, but he didn't budge. Not even an inch. He sucked harder, making everything inside of me strain for more. By the time he released me, I was a mess of need and frustration.

"So delicious," he breathed, his tone almost full of wonder. "I could spend all night teasing you. Taunting you. Tasting you."

Unacceptable. Especially when I knew for a fact he could get me off in under sixty seconds. "God, Lucas, I'm going to kick your—"

He nipped the skin right above my hip. "Uh-uh. No talking back."

"But—"

He nibbled on my hip again, and I drew in a breath through my clenched teeth. "No buts, darlin'."

"Lucas."

"Good girls get rewarded." He kissed the spot directly above my hip where he'd bitten, and massaged my butt. "Don't you want to get rewarded, darlin'?"

I did. I *really* did. So I kept my mouth shut and nodded.

When I remained silent, he grinned. "That's what I thought."

He kissed my thigh before he moved in a little bit more. I held my breath, every inch of me begging for him to do it. To run his tongue over me again, like he'd done earlier. Instead, he lifted himself up and grabbed the condom. I watched him roll it on his long shaft, his hands moving over himself seductively. His eyes were slitted and were focused on me. I bit my tongue to keep the curses from flowing out. "P-please," I whispered. "I need you, Lucas."

His jaw flexed, and he kissed me gently. "Sh." He skimmed a hand up my thigh and traced my slit. For a second, he teased my entrance, but he pulled back before giving me what I needed from him. He was trying to *kill* me. "I'm here, darlin'."

He kissed me again, and his hand came back between my legs, stroking me gently. I strained against him, wrapping my arms around his neck. My time exploring Lucas's body had barely taken the edge off my appetite, and now he was killing me with those barely there caresses. His tongue circled around mine before he pulled back, ending the kiss. When he pulled back, he cupped my cheeks and gave me a small smile.

He kissed the tip of my nose, and my whole body warmed. That, right there?

It was why I'd fallen in love with him. He was this hardened, jaded soul, but with me . . . well, he wasn't. And it was only with me, so that meant something. He made me feel as if I was the only person on the earth that mattered to him. The only one he showed this soft, sweet, lovable side to. It made what we had, however temporary it might be, all the more special.

"This is a mistake, but, sweetheart, I'll make sure that I'm the best mistake you've ever made," he said, twisting his lips into a small smile. "That I can promise you."

Before I could form a reply, he kissed me one more time and lowered his body over mine, dropping kisses as he went. By the time he reached where I ached for him most, I was *desperate*. I'd have given anything to have his mouth on me. Agreed to anything. Sold my soul to the devil himself. Lucas didn't tease me this time. Didn't get close before backing off. No, this time he closed his mouth over me right away, and oh my God—

I curled my hands in his hair and moved my hips, closing the rest of the world out and letting myself slip away. When he'd touched me in the kitchen and made me come in seconds with nothing more than a few flicks of his wrist, I'd thought that was heaven. Boy, I had been wrong. His *mouth* on me was heaven. The tension in me coiled tighter, and I moved my hips faster. And when he hardened his strokes against me, his tongue driving me to edges that I'd never known existed, I screamed out, *"Lucas."*

He gripped my hip with one hand and thrust a finger inside me at the same time as his tongue lashed out. I gripped his hair even tighter, yanking on it unintentionally, and he growled. I lifted my hips once, twice, and then . . .

Everything exploded, and I felt as if I flew away.

Before I could crash back down to earth, he lifted my hips. He rubbed his erection against my already sensitive clit, and I stiffened in disbelief. Stars burst in front of my vision and I came again, even harder than before. *"Oh my God."*

"So fucking hot," he growled, his jaw hard and his body even harder. His mouth slammed down on mine and he thrust inside me with one sure stroke. I closed my legs around him, holding on for dear life, because he'd swept me away on a tide of pleasure, and I was scared I'd never be able to catch my breath again. And I didn't want to.

He didn't give me time to adjust to him inside me, and I was glad for it. It had been a long time and he was big, but I was too far gone to care about any discomfort he'd caused. He needed to move, take me, and claim me as *his*. I needed to feel him, needed to see him come as explosively as he'd made me come. His tongue swept into my mouth as his hips moved in a fast, steady rhythm, and I tasted myself on him. When he moved faster, I clung to him, climbing higher and higher all over again. He broke the kiss off and bit down on my shoulder, hard enough to nearly break me from my haze of pleasure.

But it only made it stronger.

Gasping for air, I buried my face in his neck and did the same to him, biting down to keep the cries from escaping my lips, tasting the saltiness of his skin. "Lucas . . . I . . . I need . . ."

"I know what you need, darlin'." He lifted my hips higher and slammed inside of me, hitting a spot that I'd only read about in romance books. "You need *me*."

I choked on a sob and punched his shoulder. "M-more. Harder."

For once, he didn't argue. He just gave me what I needed. Almost more than I could handle. My whole body tingled and went numb, and I dug my nails into his back, dragging them down till I cupped his ass. And I pulled him even closer, because no matter how close we were, I couldn't *get close enough*. My heart pounded, and another sob escaped my lips. He reached between us, his fingers brushing against my clit, and he thrust inside of me completely. Then finally, thank God, all the pressure that had been building up inside of me popped. I'd never felt so incredibly free before.

He groaned and thrust inside of me once, twice, and a third time. His whole body tensed, and he threw his head back, his muscles straining, as he came inside me. The look of complete rapture on his face was strangely moving, and I moaned.

His muscular arms—the ones I'd admired from the start—flexed, and he lowered his body onto mine, cradling me to him tenderly. "Jesus, Heidi. I . . . *shit*."

I nodded, my lips pressed to the side of his neck. "I know. Me, too."

We both fell silent, and I was glad. I was afraid that if I talked right now, I'd turn into a babbling mess and say something really stupid. Something like how that had been the most amazing night of my life, or how he'd made me feel things I'd never felt before. Or how he made me feel special, even though I knew I meant nothing to him at all. How I loved him, and it was okay that I knew he would never love me back. Or even worse, how I wished we could freeze time in this moment.

Stay like this, naked and joined, forever.

But thoughts of reality kept intruding. His own brother was plotting Lucas's execution. Living on the streets had made me tough, but my experience with Bitter Hill proved I was out of my depth in Lucas's world. Quite frankly, his world scared me.

And I didn't want him to die.

Lucas kissed my temple and pulled back. When his gaze latched onto mine, I forced a smile. He didn't need to know I was worried, or that I wished I could save him from the choice he was facing. Because I knew how his world worked.

If his brother didn't kill him . . .

He'd have to kill his brother. And no one should have to do that.

"Regrets already?" he asked, his voice low.

"No, not at all." I brushed his hair off his forehead, damp from sweat. "What's there to regret? Mind-blowing orgasms?"

He laughed. "Well, when you put it that way . . ." Pulling out of me, he pushed off the bed and crossed the room naked. "I can't argue."

I watched him go, because I couldn't *not* watch. My willpower wasn't that strong. He removed the condom and chucked it in the trash. When he turned to me, his arm folded behind his neck as he scratched his back, the dancing laughter was gone from his eyes. I stiffened. "Don't start again. I'm not leaving."

"The sex didn't change anything," he said, looking way too serious for what we'd just done together. "It just paused the argument."

I rolled to my feet and glared at him, his nudity no longer a distraction. "Like hell it was only paused. Nothing you say or do will change my mind."

"We're going around in circles." He stalked over to me, each step angrier than the last. "I'm trying to save your ass, while you seem determined to constantly put it in danger. What is it going to take to make you see reason?"

I crossed my arms. "Since it's *my* ass, I get to decide what happens to it. Not *you*."

"When you gave yourself to me, it became my ass, too." That muscle I was becoming all too familiar with in his jaw ticked again. "You became mine the second you said the words I told you not to say."

I lifted my chin and snorted. "The hell I did. I go where I want, when I want, and you don't own my ass—or *any* part of me. Got it, Lucky?"

He gripped my chin, his touch firm yet somehow gentle. "That's how this is gonna be? That's your final stance?"

"Yes." I pulled free from his grip. He let me. "What are you going to do about Scotty?"

His brows slammed down. "You don't need to know anything about that."

"I think it's a reasonable question. I might not be a part of Steel Row, but I know how it works. I know you have to act fast, and I know it'll be ugly, no matter what you choose." I bit down on my cheek, trying to select my words carefully. "And I also know that both of our lives count on what you decide to do."

"They don't have to." He gripped my shoulders. "You could leave, right now, and start over. You have nothing tying you here. No family. No kids. No lovers."

I ignored the small jab of pain his words caused me. Guess that answered the question of how Lucas categorized our relationship: a mutually satisfying lay and nothing more. Not that it was a huge surprise. Yes, I'd admitted to myself that I loved him, but I hadn't slept with him because I hoped he might love me, too. No, I'd slept with him because I'd wanted to. Nothing more, nothing less.

But still, I felt vulnerably naked.

I crossed my arms in front of my bare chest. "I might not have a man tying me down, but that doesn't mean I have *nothing*. I have my bar, the legacy Frankie left me, the only home I've ever really known. And I have employees who count on me to show up for work."

He ground his teeth together so hard that I heard them scraping against each other. *"Enough."*

Without another word, his mouth met mine, and he kissed me until I was breathless and clinging. By the time the kiss ended, I'd nearly forgotten what we'd been arguing about in the first place. He lifted me in his arms, laid me down in the bed, and tucked me in. "Sleep. We'll talk more in the morning."

"Yes, sir," I mumbled. His high-handed command made me want to go another round, but truth be told, I was done, too. It was like arguing with a wall. It wouldn't get me anywhere. "Are you going to turn in, too?"

"Yeah." He stepped into a pair of gray sweats and walked to the door. When he got there, he stared at me, his hair mussed and his chest marred with scratches. Scratches I'd put there. "Sleep tight."

I yawned and burrowed under the blankets. But then I realized I was tucked in and he was leaving. "Wait. Where are you going?"

"Heidi . . ." Resting a hand on the switch, he gave me an exasperated look. He took a step toward me but then stopped, flexing his jaw. "You know where I'm going."

"To work on cars?"

He shook his head once. "No. I'm going to go change the lock, and then I'm gonna crash."

"Oh." I threw the covers back. "I can help you, and then we can go to bed together. I'd like to—"

He crossed the room and pushed the covers over my legs again. "No."

"But—" I blinked at him. "Why?"

"Because I'm not coming back in here, Heidi. My opinion on sleeping next to another person hasn't changed."

"Seriously?" I lifted up on an elbow. "You *still* won't sleep with me, after all that? What do you think I'm going to do to you?"

He didn't answer. Instead, he shut off the light and walked out, closing the door gently behind him. I stared at it, wondering what the hell he had against sharing a bed. And why I wanted so badly for him to come back . . .

Even though he pissed me off more than any other man ever had before.

CHAPTER 17

LUCAS

I woke up slowly to the sound of bacon frying, and the accompanying delicious aroma teased my senses into full awareness. For a second, I couldn't figure out who the hell would be cooking me breakfast on a Wednesday morning. Then everything came rushing back, and I jerked straight up. The couch had been even more uncomfortable last night than it had been before, and I'd slept horribly. I'd been two seconds from crawling into bed with Heidi.

Then I'd remembered I didn't *spoon* with women, and I'd stayed the fuck on the couch. Rolling my shoulders, I winced and glanced into the kitchen. Heidi tapped her foot as she cooked, her earbuds in, and she sang along silently to music only she could hear.

In the short time I'd known Heidi, I'd learned that she couldn't just be. Silence and Heidi didn't get along, which was funny considering how much silence and I *did* get along.

Lurching to my feet, I stretched, groaning and yawning at the same time. Heidi kept cooking, in her own little world, oblivious to the fact that I was up. Or she didn't give a damn. Either way, she didn't see me slip inside my bedroom with my phone.

Before I'd passed out last night, I kept going over the situation with Scotty, and I'd decided to confront the issue head-on. I was going to arrange a face-to-face with Scotty and let him know his secrets were out. He was getting one chance to get his shit together, or I'd do what needed to be done.

No matter how much I didn't want to.

I sat down on the edge of the bed and sent the text before I changed my mind. Hey, can we meet up for lunch at Charlie's? I wanted to talk to you about a few things.

Chris would tell me I was being a fool, opening myself up for an attack like this. But Scotty wasn't just an enemy—he was my blood, my little brother. I remembered holding his hand when I walked him to school, making a lopsided birthday cake when he turned ten, his grin when I gave him that game system as a Christmas present. I'd saved up all year for that. And now I needed to get through to him, one way or another.

My phone buzzed with Scotty's response. Sure. What time?

I glanced at the clock. It was shortly after nine thirty. I'd slept in. Eleven. Come alone.

He didn't reply, affirmatively or negatively. Shaking my head, I texted Brian, Tate's right-hand man. Meeting up with Scotty in Charlie's at eleven. Need anything while I'm there?

Charlie's was another front for money laundering, and we kept a large quantity of our cash in the safe. This was a dangerous play. There was a slight chance—okay, it was fifty-fifty—that I wouldn't make it out alive. If I didn't, someone needed to know where I'd been, and whom I'd been with.

Nah, but stop by after. Tate wants to talk to you.

I stood and rubbed my jaw, staring at myself in the

mirror. My restless night hadn't done me any favors, and a hint of desperation darkened my expression. I couldn't help it. I was facing impossible choices.

The door opened, and Heidi poked her head in.

She didn't meet my eyes, and her cheeks were flushed. She looked nervous. Why the hell was she nervous? Maybe it had something to do with last night. She'd said she didn't have any regrets, but she could've lied. "You're up?"

"You think?" I asked dryly.

She waved a hand dismissively. Her blond hair was damp, and she smelled like peaches even from this distance. "Whatever. I'm making breakfast, and it'll be ready in ten minutes."

I scratched my stomach, liking the way her gaze dropped to the brief flash of my abs. "Okay. I'll be out in a few."

She didn't reply, and closed the door again. I made quick work of brushing my teeth and showering before walking into the living room and making my way to the kitchen barefoot. Heidi had her earbuds in again, so she didn't hear me come up behind her. She swung her hips, tossing her head back and forth as she danced to whatever the hell it was she listened to.

The whole thing felt so domesticated and so . . . *normal.*

Heidi looked like she belonged in my kitchen. It made me think that she was wrong. That maybe we'd make badass gardeners. My tulips could win the top prize at our fictional town's gardening show. It was entirely possible that we'd kick ass at being normal.

But, really, what were the odds that two fucked-up people like us could pull that off? I'd never been good at following the rules. I closed my arms around her, sliding my hand up her shirt to rest on her rib cage, right below her breasts. Burying my face in her neck, I inhaled her scent deeply. "Mm. Smells delicious, darlin'."

"Thanks." Heidi skated out of my arms, shooting me a

nervous glance as she popped her earbuds out. Okay, then. She didn't want to be touched. Message received loud and clear. "The secret is butter. It makes the eggs richer."

I hadn't been talking about the food, but I didn't point that out. She was throwing up major *back the hell off* vibes. I tried again, lowering my voice, "Can't wait to taste them."

She picked up the plates. "Well, lucky for you, you don't have to. It's ready."

"Thanks." I grabbed the plates out of her hands and carried them out to the table. She followed me with two mugs of steaming coffee. "You do know that you don't have to cook for me, right? I don't expect anything because you're living with me. I'm not that guy."

"I know. But it keeps me busy." She set the mugs down and lifted a shoulder. "Uh . . . the cooking, I mean. I don't sit idly well. I need to do things, or my mind wanders. And when my mind wanders, I get even antsier than before. Like this morning. So, I cooked."

I got that. I was the same way, but with the cars downstairs. I set my fork down, studying her closely for any hint of the reason she was acting so odd. The only thing I could figure it would be was regret. "I have to work today. Want me to get you anything while I'm out? Books? Movies? More booze?"

"I have to work tonight, too." She fidgeted. "So, no, I'll be fine. I won't be here much longer, I'm sure."

I made a mental note to be back before she went to the bar. I wanted to be there, guarding her. If I'd had it my way, she wouldn't leave my place at all.

"What makes you say that?" I asked, half hoping she'd changed her mind and was going to take the cash and go, and half hoping she hadn't. *Selfish bastard*. "Where you going?"

"Nowhere at the moment. But this thing with your brother can't go on for much longer." She picked up her spoon, set it down, and picked it back up again. "So once you handle the situation, I'll be free to go home, and you can go back to . . . doing what you do."

In other words, she couldn't wait to get out of here. What-the-fuck-ever. If she wanted to hit the road the second the coast was clear, I wouldn't stop her. I could go back to enjoying my silent apartment, and my silent life, without any complications. And if I felt a cavity in the bottom of my stomach at the idea of going back to normal . . .

I'd ignore it.

I was good at ignoring shit I didn't want to deal with.

"Working on cars, selling illegal guns, and killing ass-holes," I said, watching her the whole time. She didn't even flinch. "In between being devastatingly charming in bars, that is. Can't forget that part of my life."

She set her spoon down again without touching her food. Her lips didn't even twitch at my attempt at humor to lighten the situation. "Yeah. We can't forget that."

I didn't know what to do with this version of Heidi. I wanted to make her feel better, but honestly I didn't know how. If she was upset she'd fucked me last night, there was nothing I could do to fix that. I couldn't go back in time and *un*fuck her, even if I wanted to. Which I didn't. "I'll be out all day, so you'll have the place to yourself. Got some business to take care of."

She pushed the eggs around on her plate. "Okay."

We fell silent, and I ate quickly. By the time I was done, she'd nibbled on a piece of bacon and had barely eaten a bite of eggs. At some point, she'd given up attempting to look as if she'd actually eaten anything, and instead leaned back in her chair, holding her mug of coffee. Her gaze was on the bedroom door.

"You okay?" I asked.

"Huh?" Heidi's attention flew back to me. "Yeah, of course."

"All right . . ." I stood and grabbed my keys, shrugged into my leather jacket, stepped into my boots, and slipped my phone into my pocket. My gun, like usual, was already in its holster. "Come here."

She stood up and walked over, her blue eyes shadowed. "Yeah?"

"What's wrong, sweetheart?"

She shook her head. "Nothing's wrong. I'm fine."

I snorted. "Darlin', if there's one thing I know how to do, it's spot a liar. Fess up. Tell me what's on your mind."

"No." Heidi averted her face. "It's nothing. Really."

"You're regretting last night, aren't you?"

"What? No." She shook her head. "There's nothing to regret. It was sex. Nothing more."

So she kept saying. Maybe she thought she didn't regret it, but she didn't usually fuck killers like me. If Heidi had no regrets, she wouldn't be acting as if I had the plague right now. "If you say so."

She pressed her lips into a tight line. She did that when she was irritated with me, which was almost all the time. I tried to tamp down my own irritation. "I do. I'm just . . . I'm scared."

Ah. I hadn't expected that. But she hadn't shown much fear up until now, so I guess it was only a matter of time till it hit her. I ran my knuckles over her cheekbone. "You're safe as long as you're here, or with me."

"I'm not worried about my safety." She pursed her lips. "I'm worried about *yours.*"

I blinked. People didn't worry about *me.* "What? Why?"

"Because your brother is trying to *kill* you. I know you're the badass criminal with no regard for human life, but it's your brother. I don't think you'd be able to kill him like it's no big deal." She locked gazes with me. "And that scares me, because from what I've heard . . . your brother *is* that type of guy."

Heidi didn't think I could kill him? She was wrong. Dead wrong. It wasn't the first time she'd made assumptions about me, and it probably wouldn't be the last. "I'm that type of guy, too. When it comes to dying or living, I'll choose life every time."

"I didn't say that you wouldn't do what *had* to be done." She lifted her chin defiantly. "I just meant you're going to do everything in your power to avoid it, and that might be your downfall . . . because he won't."

Jesus Christ. I'd killed men before, and I didn't lose any sleep over most of them. But Chris and Heidi seemed to think that my reluctance to gun down my little brother was a character flaw. I didn't want to kill my brother. Why was that a *bad* thing?

What the hell did they want from me?

I let go of her and stepped back, anger pumping through my veins. "If you want me to be the type of man who can kill family without exploring other options first, well, then it's good that last night was just sex."

"No." She paled. "*No*, that's not what I meant."

I rested my hand on my gun. "If Scotty doesn't leave me any choice, I'll do what I have to. But, no, I don't particularly want to put a bullet in the brain of the kid I used to tuck in at night. I don't want to walk away from a broken body that used to be a boy who was captain of his little league team, and just chalk him up as another enemy eliminated. I don't want to believe that my baby brother hates me enough to plan my execution. But, what, you think I should just write him off now? Is that what I should do?"

She shook her head. "N-no, of course not. I'd never *want* you to kill *anyone*. That's the problem. I don't *want* you to kill him. I can't . . . you can't . . ."

And just like that, I understood what this was about. She knew how this would likely end—even if I wasn't ready to accept it yet—and she was terrified of the fact that she'd fucked a man who would kill his own brother to survive. She was *ashamed*.

Of me. Of *us*.

I'd had my share of women like her in my life, the ones who liked to take a walk on the wild side and blame me for it afterward. They'd sit there and wonder how I'd made them forget their principles and how I'd convinced them to forget that I was a monster.

But I hadn't thought *she* was one of them.

I'd given her plenty of chances to walk away, but she'd agreed to stay last night. She'd told me she wanted me. Last night, during her passionate response, as the chemistry bubbled between us, it felt like I'd finally found the place I belonged.

What an idiot.

I laughed, loud and hard, and tossed my keys on the table. "Yeah, of course not. Because that would make me a murderer. And good girls like you aren't supposed to fuck murderers, are they?"

Her cheeks went red. "What? Last night has nothing to do with this!"

I laughed again, anger at this whole situation making me bitter. Heidi wasn't doing anything to me that hadn't been done to me thousands of times before. The fault was mine for allowing myself to believe she was different. "Yeah. Sure it's not, darlin'. Keep telling yourself that, if that's what it takes to make you feel better."

Fisting her hands, she took a step toward me, her nostrils flared. "Stop being such a jackass."

"Newsflash, darlin'," I drawled. "I *am* a jackass. Always have been."

She shook her head. "Not to me, you're not."

"Yeah, you're right. I was trying to be nice to you, and

look what that got me. With you on the verge of tears just because you fucked me last night." I held my hands out to my sides. "We all know that it's all fine and dandy to have a guy like me protecting you, but when it comes to the reality of what I do, you can't handle it. And now you wish you'd never let me touch you. Admit it."

She shoved my shoulders. "Don't put words in my mouth. You have no idea what I'm thinking, or how I feel about you."

"Ah, but I do. You're just like the rest of them." I caught her wrists and hauled her against my chest. She squirmed but didn't break free. "You fool yourself into thinking that I'm this guy who is soft, caring, and horribly misunderstood. It's why you let me fuck you. You saw the 'good' in me when it was convenient for you to do so. Now, in the light of day, it's a lot harder to see, isn't it?"

Heidi shook her head. I waited for her to tell me I was right. To tell me she regretted letting me have her last night. But instead, she tried to knock me right off my feet with her softly spoken "No. It's not. I still see it."

And, damn her, I was a breath away from believing her. I *wanted* to.

But I refused to let her in. I'd done so once, and it had given me a glimpse of what it would feel like if I did it again, and she later stabbed me in the back.

It had reminded me why I shouldn't let anyone close. *Anyone.* "Whatever you say, sweetheart." I smirked down at her, letting my defenses slip back into place. The ones I never should have let fall in the first place. "Guess you couldn't resist the chance to get your rocks off, even if it was with a scumbag like me, right?"

She yanked free and stumbled back, her face bright red. Her bright blue eyes spit fire at me, and I swore I felt each lick of flames piercing my skin. "Fuck off, *Lucky.*"

I gritted my teeth at the annoying nickname. "Gladly."

I threw the door open. "Oh, by the way, I'm off to meet my brother. You better hope I don't have to gun him down, or you'll have slept with the king of the sinners. I'll send you a text to let you know whether you need to shower a second time or not, to wash off my filthy touch."

"Argh." She made a frustrated sound. "God, you're so . . . so . . . *annoying.*"

She threw a pillow at me. A fucking *pillow*. I caught it easily. "That's what I should bring to the meeting. A pillow. It would solve everything. Maybe he just needs a good, long nap. He always used to get cranky as a kid when he missed one."

She stalked across the room toward me with murder in her eyes, but I closed the door before she could reach me. Dropping the pillow on the stairs, I took them two at a time, needing to get away from her. She'd struck a nerve, and I didn't know how to handle it just yet.

As I opened the door and stepped outside, I took a deep breath, welcoming the icy air in my lungs. It felt good. Much better than the weird sensation slicing through my chest. A weaker man might call it pain.

But I didn't feel pain anymore.

I'd stopped years ago, after Ma died.

I dragged a hand down my face and scanned the sidewalk. I almost walked away, but the glint of sun reflecting off metal caught my attention at the last second. It came from the second-story window of the Laundromat next to Heidi's bar. And I knew what that reflection meant all too well.

The door opened behind me.

I realized, with a sinking horror, that Heidi had followed me outside. Damn her. *"Son of a bitch."*

She came stumbling out, something in her hand, still looking as gloriously angry as before. "You—*oof.*"

Without hesitation, I threw myself at her, shielding her

from what I knew was coming. The second my body covered hers, a shot rang out, and I had no idea if I'd moved quickly enough or if she'd been hit. Either, way, those fuckers would pay. Whether she'd been hit or not . . .

I'd kill everyone who had a hand in this.

Twice.

CHAPTER 18

HEIDI

I hit the wall with a thud, and the sharp edges of the brick ripped through my thin shirt, scraping my skin. Lucas literally threw his body over mine, and I had no idea why he was tossing me around like some maniac. I'd just been trying to give him his—

A loud gunshot rang through the formerly silent street, and I cried out. Lucas cradled me in his arms, curling his body around me protectively. The bullet zinged off something near our heads, the brick, maybe, and I braced for impact. Nothing hit. Lucas spun, pulling out his gun as he did, and took three rapid shots. I cried out again, slamming my hands over my ears. They went silent before ringing painfully from the *bang*. Before the last gunshot dissipated, Lucas was shoving me inside and slamming the door shut behind us. He ran his hands over me frantically, his breathing harsh, and panic written all over his face.

He said something, but I couldn't hear him. I couldn't hear *anything*.

I shook my head, like I could shake away the blockage. "What?" My voice sounded distant, as if I stood at the opposite end of a long tunnel and shouted down it. All I could hear was a faint buzzing sound. "I can't hear you."

He cupped my face and enunciated perfectly. "Are. You. Hit?"

"N-no." I glanced over him. "Are you?"

His hands slipped away from me. "No. Go up and lock the door."

I blinked, because I was trying to read his lips and it wasn't easy. "What?"

He pushed me gently. "Up. Lock. Door."

I ran up the stairs, making it up in record time. When I opened the apartment door, I turned around, waiting for him to rush through it. But he was *gone*. Bolting back down the stairs, I tried to open the door, but something held it shut. And it wasn't budging. Had he . . . had he locked me in? "Oh, hell no."

Throwing my shoulder into it, I shoved all my weight against it, and it didn't shift even a fraction of an inch. Another gunshot cracked through the air, followed by two more in rapid succession. I collapsed against the door, my breathing heavy and tears blurring my vision. He was out there, getting shot at, and he had no one to help him. Because he'd *locked* me in. If he died . . .

I forced myself to stop that thought in its tracks.

Okay, sure, I was unarmed, and even if I'd had a gun, I wasn't that great a shot, but he shouldn't have locked me in here. I knew calling the cops would be an awful idea, because Lucas would go back to jail for violating his parole. I wondered if he might be safer locked up and then immediately dismissed the idea. I knew better. An organization like Steel Row or Bitter Hill had a long reach, even behind bars.

He wouldn't be any safer in jail than he was out there.

Sirens started wailing, and I cursed. Had someone *actually* called the cops, or was it a coincidence? Running back up the stairs, I shut the door behind me silently and locked it, following Lucas's original instructions. Backing away slowly, I forced myself to breathe. Lucas was smart. He'd find a way to get out of there before the cops started poking around. And there was no reason for them to look for me. I'd been outside for only, like, two seconds.

Footsteps sounded on the stairs, and a key slipped into the doorknob. I grabbed a knife from the carving block—just in case—and stared at the door as it opened. When I saw Lucas walk in, I let out a sigh of relief and started talking before he took another step. "Are you okay? Did the cops see you? Are they coming up here? What should we do? What should *I* do? I don't—"

"The Boys didn't see me. I was already policing my brass before they were a block away." Lucas lifted a hand to his head and rubbed his wrist over his temple. He looked exhausted. And pale. And . . . and . . . "They're not coming up here. Relax."

"You're bloody. Are you bleeding?" I took a step toward him, paused, and took another uneven step. Blood soaked through his left sleeve, and his hand hung limply at his side. "Lucas . . . *why are you bleeding*?"

"Huh?" He glanced down at his arm, his brow furrowed. "Oh. Look at that. I got shot."

"Look at—" I closed my eyes and counted to three. He said that in the same fashion that a normal person would say "I went to the movies" or "I have a cold" or something inane like that. As if it didn't even hurt. "We have to get you to a hospital."

"Hell no."

I stomped my foot. "Yes. You're *shot*, Lucas. Freaking *shot*."

"Yeah. I know." He leaned against the door and slid his

gun into its holster. "And if I go to a hospital, they'll have to report it."

"But—*damn it*." He was right. Gunshot wounds always involved cops. "What do we do? Do you know someone? Is there someone on the payroll that can fix you up?"

"Yeah, but I can't go in. I can't trust him anymore. Scotty could've gotten to him."

I pressed my fingertips to my mouth before saying, "Sit down. You look pale." I led him to the couch, and for once, he didn't argue. "God, what do we do now?"

Once sitting, he pulled his phone out. He glanced up at me. "Are you good with a needle?"

"Oh my—" I pressed a hand to my stomach. "No. No way. I'd puke all over you."

He winced. "That wouldn't really help me at all."

"Yeah. I know." A small laugh escaped me, despite the stress of the moment. "But I can't help it. It's true. The idea of pushing a needle through your flesh—" I covered my mouth and swallowed back the bile trying to escape my stomach.

He blinked at me. "Okay, okay. Stop thinking about it, sweetheart."

I nodded frantically, because if I didn't, I'd hurl.

Lifting the phone with his good arm, he waited. After a few seconds, he spoke. "I need you to sew me up. Some Bitter Hill guys got me in the arm." He glanced down at the rapidly growing stain. "Yeah, it's nothing bad. Just a flesh wound, but it's on my arm, so I can't do it myself." He chuckled. Actually chuckled. "No. She's apparently not on board with needles and flesh." Another pause. "Thanks— I'll leave the door unlocked. Be careful. The Boys might actually be doing their jobs and investigating the shots. I heard the sirens."

He hung up and tossed his phone aside. When he looked

up at me, he looked as calm as ever, and that famous smirk of his was firmly in place. "Chris is coming."

I nodded. "Let me help you get your shirt off."

He glanced down. "Damn it. This was my favorite dress shirt."

"You can get another shirt," I snapped, unable to believe how extraordinarily calm he was being about this. "You can't get another arm."

"No shit, Sherlock," he drawled.

I walked up to him and undid the first button. My attention fell to his shirt, and the red blood spread way too fast for comfort. "Did you find them? Did they come out onto the street?"

He flexed his jaw. "I got two, but the sniper got away."

I undid another button. "Oh."

"Yeah. I wish I'd gotten them all, damn it." He shifted his weight and winced. "I'll get them eventually, though. No one takes a shot at you and lives to tell."

"I don't think they were shooting at me," I said, my voice cracking.

"Yeah, well, I don't give a shit." He gripped the arm of the couch. "They still coulda hurt you."

My heart twisted. He'd been shot at and almost killed, and all he cared about was that I was almost collateral damage. What even *was* that? "We need to stop the bleeding."

"Hence the needle," he said dryly. "Chris will be here soon. I'll be fine. It's a through-and-through, and it only skimmed my arm, really. A couple of stitches and I'll be back on my feet. Probably could do without, but I don't want to risk infection."

I choked back the bile rising in my throat and continued unbuttoning his shirt. It was taking longer than it should have, as my hands wouldn't stop shaking. "How do you know all this?"

"Because this isn't the first time I've been shot, darlin'." He dropped his head back on the couch and closed his eyes. "And it won't be the last."

"That's just—" *Lovely.* I bit my tongue and undid the last button. "Sit up. Let's get this off you."

He sat up. I slowly lowered his shirt off his good arm and carefully peeled it back over his injured one. He hissed through his teeth when it stuck to his skin. "Son of a fucking bitch."

"Sorry, sorry, sorry," I murmured, finally getting it off him. There wasn't a whole lot of new blood, because it had clotted up a bit. "Did you get hit when you threw me against the wall?"

"No. I think it was after." He glanced at me, his gaze shadowed. "When I found them."

I rolled the shirt up in a ball. "And you think Scotty sent these guys after you?"

"Yep, no doubt." He smirked. "So much for that lunch date with him, I guess. Good thing I filled up on eggs."

"Lucas."

"What?" he asked, blinking. "I just complimented your cooking."

I threw the shirt aside. Anger pumped through my veins, but it wasn't alone. It mingled with fear. *So much fear.* Knowing I'd almost lost him . . . Yeah, that scared me more than anything else could have. He could have died, and he was cracking jokes and acting as if it didn't matter at all. It did.

He mattered, damn it.

"Stop acting like you're not upset by this by making jokes. Your brother just tried to have you killed." I knelt next to him on the couch and cupped his face, swallowing back the furious words trying to escape. He didn't look at me. "I *know* that has to hurt. I *know* you're upset. And that's okay."

He growled under his breath. "And what will being *upset* accomplish? How will *that* keep us alive?"

"It won't." I climbed onto his lap, straddling him. He didn't move, but the jaw in his muscle flexed. "And that's okay, too."

He let out a harsh laugh. "Everything is okay, according to you."

"That's because it is." I ran my thumb over his lower lip. "That's because it can be."

He finally looked at me, and what I saw in his eyes . . . I would never forget it. Not in a million years. The cold, hard reality of what had happened, and what he would soon have to do, was all there for me to see. "Heidi."

"Shh. I know."

Leaning in, I pressed my lips to his, keeping the kiss gentle. It wasn't meant to initiate sex. It was an act of comfort—the only act I knew that would show him without words that I *cared*. He needed to know that I didn't regret last night, or us, at all. I didn't know why he'd jumped to that conclusion earlier, but he had. And it had *obviously* upset him.

If he ever doubted anything, it shouldn't be my feelings for him. I loved him, and nothing he did or said would change that. I loved how selflessly he took care of those he considered under his protection. I loved the undying hope he had that his brother was a good man, even though I feared it might get him killed. I didn't love him despite his flaws—I loved him *with* them. Who he was. Who I was. We just worked.

And he needed to know that much, at least.

Pulling back, I framed his face with my hands again and smiled down at him even though it hurt to smile at him when he looked so lost. "It's okay. It's going to be okay."

"No. It's not." Something inside of him seemed to break. I saw it. *Felt* it. "It's really fucking not."

But it could be. I was starting to come around to his line of thinking. Except he'd wanted me to run, to be safe. I wanted *him* to run. To stick to the original plan. I wouldn't go with him, because there was only one passport, and he needed to get the heck out of this country. If he stopped worrying about me, he could run. He could *live*. "I want you to—"

The door opened. "Okay, where's the—?" Chris paused midstep, a brow raised. He took in our positions, me on top of Lucas, holding his face, and didn't look too happy. "Am I interrupting something?"

"No," Lucas said, the emotion I'd seen earlier gone in an instant. "Heidi here was just being a doll and taking care of me."

"I see that," Chris said dryly. "Don't expect me to straddle you like that. You're not my type."

"The hell I'm not," Lucas said, smirking.

I rolled my eyes and climbed off him. "I'll get you some whiskey."

"Thanks, *doll*," Chris said.

"It's not for you," I snapped. "It's for him."

He held a hand to his chest. "Ouch. That almost hurt."

"And don't call me *doll*."

"I'm winning you over," Chris said, grinning. "I can feel it."

I ignored him.

Lucas laughed. "Shit, man. She doesn't like you."

"She'll come around," Chris answered distractedly. His gaze was on Lucas's arm instead. "This is barely a bullet wound at all. You called me over here for this shit?"

"I'm high maintenance like that," Lucas said, grinning.

"No shit," Chris said, walking past him and into the bathroom.

I came out of the kitchen, a full tumbler in my hand. "Drink this."

"You don't have to tell me twice." Lucas lifted it to his lips and downed it all. I cringed because he had the cheap stuff that tasted awful. Prison food must have destroyed his palate. When the glass was empty, he handed it back to me. "You might want to leave the room."

Shaking my head, I dumped the glass onto the coffee table, sitting beside him to hold his hand. "I'm staying right here."

"Heidi, you nearly puked just thinking about the stitches. Now you're gonna watch? I don't think so, sweetheart." He locked stares with me. "Go into the bedroom and listen to your music or something. The stuff you were dancing to earlier."

Taylor Swift. I couldn't rock out to that when he was getting stitches and bleeding all over the couch. I just *couldn't*. "But—"

"Look at it." He turned to me fully, and I forced my eyes on it. Just seeing the blood and flesh torn apart—oh my God. "Yeah. That's what I thought. You look seconds from puking, and that won't help Chris focus on the stitches. Go in my room."

He was right. Swallowing back the bile, I nodded once. "If that's what you want."

"It is." He rested his head against the couch. "Go."

Standing, I dropped a kiss on his forehead. It was coated in a thin sheen of sweat. "Okay."

His good hand gently cupped the back of my head before letting me go, his fingers trailing through my hair, and he nodded once. "Thanks. And, darlin'?"

I stopped halfway to the bedroom. "Yeah?"

"Turn it up really loud, and dance for me. I like it when you dance."

I wouldn't be able to dance to music right now if someone held a gun to my head and told me my very life depended on it. "Yeah. That's not going to happen."

As I walked to the bedroom, I stopped at the bathroom doorway. I peeked back at Lucas, but he didn't appear to be watching me. Chris straightened, a bunch of medical supplies in his hands. When he saw me standing in the doorway, watching him, he froze. "You hiding in the bedroom?"

"We agreed that it might be best."

"I heard." Chris studied me, his dark brown eyes seeing way too much. Despite my knee-jerk dislike of him, he really *was* very handsome, if you liked brown hair and brown eyes. Turned out, I preferred reddish brown hair and moss green eyes. "I'll let you know when it's over."

Running my gaze over the supplies, I noticed something was missing. "You'll give him something for the pain, right?"

Chris shifted his weight, focusing on something past me. Lucas, more than likely. "Haven't before, but maybe the third time's the charm."

Lucas had been shot twice before? Somehow in my examination of his body last night, I'd missed the scars. It was something to put on my to-do list. Chris began to move, like he was going to try to squeeze past me, and I took a step to block his way. I glanced at Lucas again. He'd lifted his head and was watching me.

Turning back to Chris, I took a deep breath, Lucas's stare burning into my back. "Look, I'm not good with the blood-and-gore type of stuff, but if something happens . . . if you need an extra set of hands, yell for me. I'll deal."

To be honest, I half expected Chris to laugh in my face. You'd think a street rat like me could handle a little blood, but *nooo*. Yet, instead, he eyed me with respect and nodded. "Fair enough. I'll take good care of him, though. I swear it."

I swallowed past the lump in my throat. I didn't cry, and

I wasn't about to start now. "Good. Now go fix him up for me."

Chris brushed past me, his gaze never leaving mine until he was out of the bathroom. I watched him cross the room, set down the medical supplies, and lean down at Lucas's side. Instead of going into the bedroom, I backed into the bathroom and closed the door most of the way, leaving a small crack for me to see through.

They spoke quietly between themselves, and I strained to hear the words. I couldn't make out a single one. After Chris finished threading the needle and setting up the supplies, he started wiping the wound with a cotton ball doused in alcohol. Completely unfazed by the blood that was soaking the cotton, Chris said something that made Lucas laugh. At the sight of the crimson-tinged cotton, my stomach roiled.

I pressed a hand to my mouth. "Oh my God," I whispered.

"Heidi? Close the damn door," Lucas growled.

Jumping, I slammed the door shut out of reflex. As soon as it closed, I heard a few words, and Lucas laughed again. Clearly, I was the only one thrown by the fact that Chris was doing emergency surgery in the living room. I retreated until I hit the toilet. Dropping the lid, I sat, interlocking my fingers tightly. There was a "Fuck, man, that hurts. Didn't your Girl Scout troop leader teach you any gentler sewing techniques?" from Lucas, and I could taste bile. Three times he'd been shot. I thought I knew what kind of life he led, but as I listened to the boys compete for the filthiest curse, I realized I had no idea.

Things got quiet again, but I refused to go peek. With my luck, Lucas would be passed out from the pain and I wouldn't be able to stay away. Instead, I got up and opened the small window. It was freezing outside, but the cold air was a refreshing wake-up call. Maybe I didn't know all the details of Lucas's life, maybe we'd only scratched the surface of our personal lives, but the fact remained that this was a man I wanted to be with, even if it was only for a short period of time. He was the man I loved.

Gunshots and all.

CHAPTER 19

LUCAS

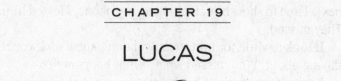

An hour or so later, I was all stitched up and Chris was ready to leave. I sat down on my bed, rubbed my forehead, and let out a long sigh. Heidi walked Chris to the door, talking to him quietly as she went. After he'd patched me up, he'd questioned me on what my next move would be. Would I tell Tate? Go after those Bitter Hill guys unauthorized? What was I going to do about Scotty? And I didn't know.

Truth was, I had no idea what to do.

That pissed me the hell off, too.

I tucked the spare gun Chris had given me under my pillow. The mag wasn't fully loaded, but it would do in a pinch. One gun in the house wasn't enough anymore. Not when Scotty seemed bound and determined to put me six feet under.

Slumping down against the pillows, I ran through everything I knew again. We had a big company dinner Friday night, and I was supposed to be there. According to Chris, it was also the night I'd find out about my promotion.

Scotty would probably be there, too.

Unless he decided to avoid it, because of me.

By now, he had to know that his assassination attempt had failed. He had to know that I wasn't dead. And that meant he'd be biding his time, waiting to see what I'd do next. Time to show him. Picking up my phone, I texted him. They missed.

It took a while for him to reply. I don't know what you're talking about. Who missed what? What happened?

I gritted my teeth. If he thought he could play innocent after that, then he was more of a fool than I'd ever given him credit for. Don't fuck with me, kid.

This time, he replied right away. I'm not. What happened?

You know what happened. My finger hovered over the send button before deleting the message. If he wanted to pretend that I didn't know, then maybe it would be to my advantage to let him think I was still clueless. I thought you heard by now. Bitter Hill attacked me outside my place. You know anything about it?

A few moments, then: No. Why would I? What are you going to do about it?

You'll see. Friday night.

He didn't answer, so I called to let Tate know I wouldn't be able to stop by today. He was pissed until I explained the cops were nosing around the neighborhood after my little shootout and he agreed I should lie low. I promised to be there for the party, so he was good when we hung up. I didn't mention what had prompted the fight in the first place.

Scotty was mine to take care of, no one else's.

I made quick work of my pants and boxers before sliding beneath the sheet. Heidi wasn't the only one who liked to sleep naked, and right now, I needed my bed.

Not my couch.

The bedroom door opened, and Heidi came in. Her pale

cheeks had a bit more color, but there were still shadows in those blue eyes of hers. "Hey."

"Hey." I forced a smile and patted the spot next to me on the bed. I'd had more than a few drinks during and after the stitch-up, so I might have been sliding down the slope to smashed. Hypothetically. "Come here, darlin'."

She bit down on her lip as she crossed the room. Crawling onto the bed from the opposite side, she settled in next to my hip. "Does it hurt a lot?"

Fuck, yeah. "Nope."

"Good." She touched the white gauze Chris had wrapped around it. "Do you have any of the good stuff to numb the pain?"

I chuckled. "I sell guns, not drugs."

"Shit."

"It's fine. I'm fine." It was true. I didn't need any damn pills dulling my brain. Between the fact that I'd been shot in my dominant arm and had already had plenty of booze, I didn't need anything else messing me up. Chris was watching my perimeter and would give me a heads-up if it looked like a threat was approaching. Or he'd just handle it himself. I'd told him to do whatever the fuck he wanted, so long as he stayed away from Scotty.

I focused back on the woman in front of me. "You're pretty, you know."

She'd been staring at my arm with a green tinge to her skin, but my words jerked her attention north. Yeah, my arm had just been shot, but I wouldn't want to be anyplace else right now. "Uh, thanks?"

"No, like, seriously. You're really pretty. Like an angel come to earth." Reaching out, I tugged on a piece of her light blond hair. It was as silky soft as always. "My own personal angel, trying to bring me to the good side . . ."

She blinked. "I'm no angel, I assure you."

"I don't agree." I yanked her down till she sprawled

across my chest. She landed with an *oof*, taking care to avoid my bad arm. "Not at all, darlin'. Just look at you."

Her brow furrowed. "Oh my God, are you *drunk*?"

"No," I whispered back, as dramatically as her. "Certainly not."

But I ruined it by laughing.

Instead of looking annoyed, her lips twitched, and she laughed, too. "You're way too cute when you're drunk."

I ran my thumb over her mouth, watching as it swiped over that full lower lip of hers that had driven me insane countless times. Her breathing quickened. Despite the way she'd been acting earlier, during our fight, she wanted me now. That much was clearly evident. "Cute enough to get away with this?"

Before she could reject me, I closed my mouth over hers, kissing her. Her lips parted on a sigh, and I took full advantage of that opening. My tongue swept inside her mouth, seeking and finding hers instantly. She tasted as good as I remembered.

Hell, probably even better.

And she still smelled like peaches.

I'd expected her to tense. To pull away and tell me to keep my hands to myself. She should have. So when she moaned and climbed on top of me, I reveled in it.

But the stupid, noble part of me wouldn't shut up. Breaking off the kiss, I groaned and gripped her thigh, digging my fingers into the soft flesh. "You don't have to do this. I know I'm not your type. Don't feel you have to take pity on the wounded drunk."

What was it about this girl that made me want to be something I wasn't? Shit, I'd had more moments of regret over the last three days than I'd had in the last fifteen years combined. I was turning into such a pussy.

"About that?" She played with a piece of my hair. "I don't know what the hell's been running through your brain all day, but if you've thought about last night half as much as I have, it would've proved to you that you're totally my type."

Gritting my teeth, I arched my hips up into her. Her heat pressed against me, and it took all my control not to roll her underneath me and take her, hard and fast, right now. The only thing that stopped me was the fact that the excruciating pain I was sure to feel would kill my hard-on.

The reminder about my injury, and how I'd gotten it, made me make one last-ditch effort to get Heidi to see reason. "I'm no good for you, sweetheart. You deserve Prince Charming, not the villain. Whoever the fuck the villain was in that stupid story."

"You're not a villain. Not to me." She rested a hand over my heart. "You're a Prince Charming who's suffered in defense of his kingdom. You did what needed to be done, no matter how dark it might have gotten. And you won. That doesn't make you a villain. It makes you a survivor. It makes you *you*."

Her open acceptance filled the cracks in my soul. I'd needed to hear that. My arm gripped her tighter and she gave me a watery smile. Shaking my head, I swallowed back the words I'd never let myself say. I was drunk, and now was not the time to spill my guts. Yeah, I had some regrets right now, and that was a new feeling. Fucking up Scotty was one of them. But there was one thing I wouldn't regret. Not in a million years. And that was *her*. "I want to take you again. I want to make you mine."

She nodded. "Yes. I am yours, Lucas. All yours."

"God help us both."

I tugged her down and kissed her again, closing my eyes and letting go of all the reasons I shouldn't be touching her. Claiming her. I was in an impossible situation with no way out. We were doomed. Hopeless. *Screwed*. Even so, I couldn't have stopped if someone held a gun to my head.

She was worth dying for.

Skimming my hand down her leg, I slipped my fingers up the inside of her thigh, creeping closer to what I wanted. But she had too many clothes on, and I didn't have enough hands available to take them off properly. "Take your clothes off for me, sweetheart."

"Yes, sir," she teased, straightening and tugging her shirt over her head inch by tantalizing inch. "Are you naked under that sheet?"

I smirked. "Take one guess."

"Good." Tossing her shirt on the floor, she reached behind her back and undid her bra. After shooting me a naughty grin, she let it slide off her arms and hit me in the face. "That's the way I like you. Naked and helpless in my bed."

My bed. That's what she'd said. The fact that she considered my bed to be hers, with everything that had happened between us over the last four days, filled me with that unfamiliar warmth all over again. And it felt good. I dragged her bra off my face and tossed it over the edge of the bed, smiling way too big considering all she'd done was call *my* bed *hers.* "Tease."

"You know it." Shimmying off me, she stood and pulled her pants down. Every inch of skin she bared stoked the fire in my blood higher and higher. "You love it."

The second her pants hit the floor, I yanked her onto my lap with my good hand. Our lips fused and our tongues entwined, and everything felt right. Being in her arms felt like coming home. A home I hadn't had in a long damn time. Growling low in my throat, I deepened the kiss.

Her nails dragged down my chest, circled around my piercing, and then slid under the sheet. When she closed her soft, warm hand over my cock, I knew I needed her. *Now.* I didn't usually rush through sex. The act was a display of discipline and skill. It wasn't a time to get lost in the moment and forget yourself. But with Heidi, I wanted to.

I wanted to lose myself so fucking bad.

Tugging the sheet down, I hauled her onto me so she straddled my hips. Breaking off the kiss, I demanded, "Condom. Now."

For once, she didn't argue with me. She just reached out, opened the drawer I'd used last night, and took one out. Ripping it open, she scooted down my legs and slid it on, licking her lips as she did so. She was killing me. After she rolled the condom on, I buried my hand in her hair, fisted it, and slowly pulled her down.

She followed my guidance until her lips were an inch from mine. Breathing heavily, she straddled me and locked her stare with mine. When she positioned my cock at the entry of her pussy, I tsked. "Not yet, darlin'."

Freezing, she bit down on her lower lip. This close up, I could see the darker specks of blue hidden near her pupils. I'd never noticed them before, but now I knew I'd always see them. She licked her lips, her tongue brushing against my mouth because we were that close together. "Lucas . . ."

"I know, darlin'. I know."

Yanking her closer, I kissed her, and at the same moment, I lifted my hips and thrust inside her. She whimpered into my mouth, her whole body tightening around mine, and tugged on my nipple ring. For once, I didn't hold myself back. My attention wasn't split between the woman beneath me and the environment around me.

I just let my instincts guide me, and I let Heidi take me away.

She rode me, hard and fast, and our lips never parted. Her hands framed my face, and she moaned, long and deep. I knew I was close to the edge. So close that all it would take was another one of those moans from her, and I'd be a goner. So I reached between our bodies and pressed my thumb against her clit, repositioning myself beneath her so her body rubbed against mine as she fucked me.

Her thrusts became more frantic and needy, and each one made her walls close on me even more. Each restless cry, and held breath, made my body tighten even more. Breaking off the kiss, I growled and buried my face in her shoulder, lifting my hips off the bed and thrusting into her even deeper. "Come for me, sweetheart."

"Oh my God, *Lucas*." She clung to my shoulder for dear life. *"Again."*

I lifted my hips again, still pressing my thumb against her. She threw her head back, and that hair I was obsessed with trailed down her back to my thighs. Her big, perky tits bounced, and she stared down at me with sparkling blue eyes that made my heart speed up for no reason at all. I knew, again, that this woman was special. That I'd never find another woman who made me feel this way.

Not like her.

Her mouth fell open, and she came, her pussy clamping down on my cock. I was already primed and ready to explode, so all it took was one more thrust into her wet heat, and I joined her in heaven. Because if ever a heaven existed? This was it.

Knowing she was still soaring high, I pressed my thumb against her clit again, moving it in tiny, gentle circles. She tensed and started riding me again. It was the most exquisite torture I'd ever inflicted upon myself, but I'd be damned if I'd let her leave my bed with only one orgasm. Even if it killed me . . . which it just might.

Biting down on her lip, she let out a shattered breath and rolled her hips in a figure eight, her cheeks flushed red and her entire body a tempting portrait I never wanted to stop admiring. And probably never would, years after she walked away from me. Her muscles tightened, and letting out a groan, she came again.

Grinning, I slowly stopped massaging her, letting her come down slowly. She fell on top of my chest, her breathing hard. After a while, she lifted her face and stared down at me. Her cheeks were still flushed, and her lips were soft and swollen from my kisses. "Holy *shit*. That was . . . wow."

She started to climb off me, but I wrapped my good arm around her, hauling her even closer. Her bare skin on mine felt amazing. I didn't want to read too much into it, or have her think this meant something more than it could, but I definitely didn't want to let go of her, either. So I didn't. The room spun, and I closed my eyes. The damn ceiling fan wouldn't stop moving even though I was pretty sure I hadn't turned it on.

She tried to roll away again, so I held her even tighter. "Where do you think you're going?"

"Nowhere." She rested a hand on my heart. Or, better yet, where my heart would be if I still had one. I wasn't so certain I did, most of the time. "Nowhere at all."

Yawning, I nodded. "Damn right, you aren't."

Exhaustion tried to claim me, but I fought it. In a minute, I'd get up and go lie down on the couch. In a minute, I'd separate myself from the woman who had already claimed too much of me for comfort. In a minute . . .

CHAPTER 20

HEIDI

Three hours later, I sat on the couch, accounting ledger in my lap and my hair pulled back in a loose ponytail. I'd called out of work for the next two nights and asked my manager to cover my shift. I hadn't wanted to leave Lucas alone. Earlier, Lucas had fallen asleep, and I hadn't wanted to spoil the moment by slipping out of his arms and waking him. I'd lain there, enjoying the feel of his arms around me as his breathing evened . . . and I'd accidentally drifted off as well. When I'd woken up in his arms, I'd been torn between wanting to smile and giving in to sheer panic.

If he knew that he'd slept beside me, he'd push me away even more than he already had. Something about that intimacy scared the crap out of him, and I had to respect that. I might have stupidly fallen in love with him, despite his telling me not to, but that love didn't make me stupid. He'd made it very clear that he didn't want to sleep with me, just like he'd made it perfectly clear that he would never care about me.

So I'd climbed out of bed, gotten dressed, and decided to act as if it had never happened. To him, it probably hadn't, since he'd been out cold.

It was my dirty little secret.

Footsteps sounded outside the door, followed by four knocks in a row. "Hello? Heidi? It's me, Chris. Let me in. Lucas didn't give me a new key yet."

I set the ledgers aside, smoothed my shirt over my stomach, and made my way to the door. When I got there, I cracked it open and peeked through, making sure he was alone. He was. "Hey. What's up?"

"I got you guys pizza." He held the white box higher. "Pepperoni, Lucas's favorite. I figured he needed it after today."

I opened the door and crossed my arms in front of me. It felt weird letting him in, even though he was clearly an ally. I hadn't forgotten how we'd met. "Thanks."

"I got beer, too." He walked past me, leaving the faint scent of Old Spice aftershave in his wake. After setting the pizza and a six-pack of Sam Adams on the table, he turned to me. Something of my feelings must have shown on my face, because he rubbed his jaw and said, "You don't like me much, do you?"

I lifted a shoulder and leaned on the closed door, hand on the knob. "Does it really matter if I do or don't?"

He walked over to me, stopping a few feet short. Close enough for eye contact, but not close enough to make me feel the urge to defend myself . . . again. This time, if he made a move, I'd be ready. And he'd get a knee to the nuts. "Look, I'm sorry I tackled you to the floor."

I choked on a laugh. "Uh, thanks?"

"I'm serious." He shoved a hand through his brown hair and stared at me. This close, I saw he had little flecks of dark green in his eyes. I'd never seen anything like it. "I know I came across like a dick, but I was just looking out for my buddy. He doesn't have a lot of people in his corner, but he has me. He's always had me and always will."

Sagging against the door, I bit down on my tongue. What he said, and how he said it, struck home with me. I didn't really know what that felt like. Lucas was lucky to have someone who cared about him that much. "I know why you did what you did. It's fine."

He rested a hand on my shoulder. "Are you sure, doll?"

"Yes, of course."

The door opened and Lucas came out, yawning. He had on a loose pair of gray sweats and no shirt. "Heidi? Where are—?" He saw me and Chris standing together. "Oh. There you are."

"Hey." Chris dropped his hand instantly. "You're up."

"Yeah." Lucas fisted his hands and locked those bright green eyes on me. "Everything okay out here, darlin'?"

"Y-yes, of course." I smiled. "Why wouldn't it be?"

"He had his hand on you," Lucas pointed out. "For starters."

Chris sighed. "Don't go getting jealous, now. I wasn't doing anything like that. We were just—"

"I know." Lucas frowned at both of us. "I didn't think she was. I just wanted to make sure you weren't about to tackle her to the floor again."

We all fell silent.

Chris cleared his throat. "I brought up beer and pizza, so you have good timing. Sorry if my knock woke you up, but I don't have a key anymore."

"Thanks, man." Lucas walked to the window and peeked out, his shoulders hard and straight. "Your key is by the door."

Chris walked over and grabbed the gold key, holding it up and nodding once. "Got it."

Lucas still didn't turn around. "Everything quiet out there?"

"So far."

"Good. Thanks for keeping watch while I slept the whiskey off."

Chris nodded once. "Anytime, man. You know that."

"I do." He turned back to us. "Thanks, again, for coming."

I recognized a dismissal when I saw one.

So, apparently, did Chris.

He headed for the door, zipping his brown leather jacket up. "Hey, by the way, Tate wants you to supervise the drop at the docks tomorrow at eleven, and then you need to be at the meeting afterward. It wasn't a request. He said be there."

I frowned. "He can't. He's still recovering."

"He doesn't have a choice," Chris said.

"I can talk for myself," Lucas interjected, his voice rock hard. "I'll be there."

I gritted my teeth, watching the men say their good-byes. As soon as the door shut behind Chris and we were alone, I let loose on him. "You were literally *just* shot, and you're going to go back out there? Are you insane? What if they attack you again? You're weak. You can't fight back."

"The hell I can't. Besides, I don't have a choice," he said, locking the door. "I already canceled on Tate once. To do it twice wouldn't be wise."

I crossed my arms again, watching him as he slowly turned back to me. I could see he was in pain by the thin sheen of sweat coating his skin. He'd never admit it, but he was. The fight in me receded, and worry took over again. I almost preferred the fight. "Why anyone would want to work with a guy like him is beyond me."

His jaw ticked. His impassive façade had slipped away, and he grimaced as he walked past me. "Because we needed something, and he was willing to give it to us. That's why."

I followed him. "What did you need?"

"Money to pay my mom's medical bills. And to pay our

rent." He grabbed a beer and popped it open. "And to put food in my little brother's mouth. Listening to him cry every night because his belly hurt got really old really fast."

I . . . I had nothing to say to that. I'd been expecting some snarky, smart-ass reply about how it was none of my damn business. Not *that*. "Oh."

He took a swig of his beer. "Yeah."

Not knowing what to say to that kind of honesty, I made myself busy serving pizza. He settled into the couch, grunting once as he adjusted himself, and crossed an ankle over his knee. I handed him pizza on a paper plate. "Here."

"Thanks." He set his beer down and took it. "You're eating, too."

It wasn't a question. I answered anyway. "Yep."

Once I'd gotten myself a slice and a beer, I settled in beside him. We ate in companionable silence, my mind on his earlier statement about joining the gang because he'd needed cash for his mother. I'd assumed he'd always been in that life, because that's how gangs like the Sons of Steel Row worked. Blood.

But with him, that wasn't the case. No, he'd joined to freaking *feed his family*. It only made me love him more, when I already loved him too much.

Especially considering he didn't love me back.

"Typical," I muttered under my breath.

He blinked at me. "What's typical?"

"Uh . . ." I glanced at the pizza. "They didn't use enough seasoning."

"Tastes fine to me," he said, clearly not buying my half-assed excuse, and finished his first slice. "I have oregano in the kitchen if you want it."

"I'm fine."

He cocked a brow. "The one phrase in the English language that never means what it should."

I shrugged but didn't answer. "Did you have a nice nap?"

"Yeah. I was out." He scratched his head. "What did you do while I slept?"

Slept with you, then crawled away like it never happened. "Not much." I motioned to the ledgers on the table, my cheeks hot. "Marco brought these up for me so I could stay home with you tonight. He's covering the bar for me. I don't want you to be alone in case . . . you know. You start bleeding again or something."

His brow furrowed. "Oh, right. You were supposed to work tonight."

"Yeah. I called off tomorrow, too."

He let out a breath and stared out the window again, from the couch. "Probably a good idea. I don't want you out there yet. I want to make sure I can protect you, and my arm still hurts like a bitch."

"But you can go do your job, which is inherently more dangerous than mine." I rolled my eyes. "That makes total sense."

"Heidi . . ."

"Yeah. I know. You don't have a choice." I eyed the bandage wrapped around his arm. His skin was pale and looked a little clammy, but I kept my hands firmly in my lap. My pizza sat mostly untouched. "You scared me today."

"I know." He didn't pretend to misunderstand, but took a sip of beer. His Adam's apple bobbed, and his hard biceps flexed as he lowered the bottle. "This is my life, darlin'. Why do you think I'm single all the time? No one wants to put up with this life. No one I'd want to be with, anyway."

"And here I thought it was because you didn't want to be tied down," I said quickly, not liking the idea of him being shot all the time. It might be reality, but it didn't have to be mine. "That you were too much of a devastatingly handsome rogue to settle down with one woman."

His lips quirked, and he turned to me, scooting a little closer. His thigh touched mine. "That, too, of course."

"What if you met the right woman? One you liked, who liked you, and didn't mind the life you led?" I asked, my breathing picking up speed. "Would that change your stance?"

He hesitated, his gaze skittering from mine. He swallowed another gulp of beer. "No. It's my life, but it's not going to be anyone else's. I refuse to do that to someone."

Sadness hit me, but I wasn't sure why. It wasn't as if I thought *I* could be that woman. I wasn't. He didn't want me to be. Heck, I wasn't even sure if *I* wanted me to be. Sure, I loved him, but could I handle the reality of him being shot at for the rest of our lives? Probably not. But it didn't matter, because I would never get the chance. "Gotcha."

"What about you?" He stretched his good arm over the back of the couch, resting it over me. His cold beer pressed against my shirt. "Why haven't you settled down and made a few little Heidis?"

"Yeah." I snorted. "Not gonna happen."

He stilled. "Why not?"

"Gee, I wonder why not? Maybe because I grew up on the streets, for starters."

He cocked his head. "Yeah? And?"

"And I'd make a horrible mother."

"Because you lived on the streets," he said dryly, the disapproval practically dripping from his words. *"Riiiight."*

"I'm serious. I know nothing about parenting at all. I didn't even *have* a parent."

"Doesn't mean you'd be bad at it." He shook his head. "Can I ask you something you might not want me to ask?"

I stiffened. "What?"

"Why didn't you stay in foster homes?" He shrugged. "You had to have had a few, right? You were probably a cute kid. Someone had to have wanted you."

Years-old unshed tears stung my eyes, not because of his question, but because of how ironically wrong his words were. And he didn't even know it. "Oh, they wanted me all right. Particularly my last foster father. He really wanted me."

"Then why—?" He cut himself off, obviously reading the undertone to my words. Rage, like I'd never seen before, slipped into place. "Tell me his name. Tell me it right fucking now."

I shook my head. "No. I don't even remember anymore." That wasn't true. I'd never forget his name. But I didn't need to be the reason for more blood on Lucas's hands. "He's probably dead by now." He wasn't. "Or in another state." Nope. Still lived on Chestnut Street. "Who knows?" Me.

"I'll find him myself, then. Don't think I won't. If I make it outta this alive . . ." He squeezed my thigh, totally blind to the fact that he'd just stabbed a knife through my chest with those words. "Any man who takes advantage like that—he—how old were you?"

Usually I didn't want to talk about this, like, *ever*. But with Lucas . . . it didn't feel so bad. "Thirteen."

He let out another string of curses that lasted at least another ten seconds. Once he settled down, he threaded his hand in my hair and stared into my eyes. I couldn't look away. "I'm sorry, Heidi. So fucking sorry."

I swallowed hard, the closeness of the moment hitting me hard in the chest. I wasn't sure what to do with that. "It is what it is," I whispered, latching onto his wrist. "I got away before he got me, though. He made the mistake of warning me ahead of time."

"You were handed a life full of shit as a kid," he said, his voice wrapping around me and not letting go. God, I loved his Boston accent. It got a little more pronounced in quiet moments like this, and it made my insides weak. "You took all those bad things and made them something good. You're an incredible, strong, brave woman, Heidi Greene. Don't you ever doubt that, or your ability to be caring at the same time."

I blinked rapidly, refusing to let tears come out. I mean, I hadn't even cried when it had happened. Why start now? But his words, they meant something to me. "Be that as it may . . . I still wouldn't be a good mother."

"I disagree," he said. He readjusted himself, setting his beer down on the table and then resting a hand on mine. "I think you'd make an excellent mother."

I tried not to believe him, or care that he thought that, or get pulled under his spell, because in the end . . . it didn't matter if he thought I'd make a good mom. He'd be gone from my life, and I'd be gone from his. "Oh yeah? What makes you so sure?"

"You remind me of my ma," he said softly, his voice cracking ever so slightly. So slightly I might have imagined it, but I knew I hadn't. "And she was the best mother I know, or will ever know."

My heart twisted into a tight, tiny ball. There went my plan to remain unaffected. He'd smashed it all with a few soft-spoken words, as usual. Stealing my heart without my permission, time and time again. And the worst part was, he didn't even know it. And never would. "Lucas . . ."

"Shh, sweetheart. Just . . ." He cupped my cheek and leaned close, resting his forehead on mine. "Just . . . *shh*."

And then he kissed me.

He slowly leaned back on the couch, and I climbed into his lap, never breaking the kiss off. We made love slowly, tenderly. There was something extremely different about this time, and I had a feeling he felt it, too. Every healing touch, every soothing brush of his fingertips, brought us closer. Closer to what?

I had no idea. But I had an idea I'd find out soon . . .

One way or the other.

CHAPTER 21

LUCAS

The next afternoon, I stood behind the men loading the guns into the truck, my eyes on the horizon. I couldn't shake the feeling that Scotty was watching. Waiting. Plotting.

And sooner or later, he would take another shot.

The only thing in question was how I'd react to it. I flexed my sore arm, hiding a wince as I did so. Heidi was right. I was weak, and if someone came at me right now, I might not be able to fight them off. "This is bullshit."

"What is?" Chris asked. He stood beside me, arms crossed, frowning as the men loaded the second-to-last box onto the truck. "Easy, guys. Those are fragile parts."

I'd been talking about my brother wanting me dead, but I didn't feel like delving into that. "The fact that I'm out here, in the open, vulnerable, and I've only got one working arm. If someone attacks me, or Heidi . . ." I growled, pissed off at the world. Pissed off at everyone in it, too. Everyone except *her*. "This couldn't have come at a worse time."

Chris shot me an incredulous look. "Dude, your arm

isn't hurt because of some work injury or something. Your arm is hurt because someone wants you dead and is determined to accomplish their goal. That 'someone' is your—"

"Yeah." I tugged on my collar. "I know, asshole."

"Coulda fooled me," Chris muttered, walking closer to the truck and leaving me alone. I watched his back, making sure no one from the other gang—the ones buying the guns—made any sudden moves. "Let's go. Move your asses. We have a meeting to go to. It's your dicks on the line if we're late."

I followed him, frowning when I saw one of the guys from our crew standing to the side, watching me intently. He fingered the gun at his hip, his dark shades blocking his eyes from my view, but I didn't doubt my initial assessment. For some reason, he was focused on me. I frowned at the man. "Hey. You. Get to work."

He ignored me. Just stood there.

Not one to back down from a threat, I walked over to him, resting my hand on my own piece. "Is there a problem?"

The man rocked back on his heels. "No, sir, there's no problem here. I was just watching your back. Tate's orders."

Watching it . . . or watching *me*? Either way, I didn't like it. I didn't know this man, and I definitely didn't want him at my six. "Fuck off. I watch my own back."

"But—"

I grabbed the man's shirt and hauled him close, face-to-face. "I said, back the fuck off. *Now.*"

The man held his arms up, swallowing hard. "All right, sir. All right."

I let go of him, and he backed off, letting out an aggravated sound. After one last dirty look, he stormed off. I walked over to the leader of the other gang, who'd been watching us way too intently, and held out my hand. "We all good, Gonzales?"

Gonzales eyed me. This was the moment where, if anything was gonna go bad, it would. Cops. Guns. Fights. This was when it all happened. When money exchanged hands. My pulse skyrocketed, and I scanned the perimeter. So did Gonzales.

After what felt like a fucking year, he reached into his pocket. I tensed, watching for any signs of something hard and gun shaped. Instead, he pulled out a crisp, white envelope, much like the one I had in my home. "We're all good."

He gave me the envelope, and I immediately tucked it into my jacket pocket. No sirens blared. No gunshots boomed. The deal was complete. I inclined my head toward the other lieutenant. "Have a good one, man."

The man walked away without another word.

Chris immediately came over. "What was that about, earlier, with MacKenzie?"

Was that his name? Shit if I knew. "Tate had him watching me."

"Shit," Chris muttered. "I don't know if that's a good thing or a bad thing."

"Me neither, but there's only one way to find out." The trucks pulled away, and the crew piled into cars. I tipped my head toward Chris's Porsche, since we'd ridden together. "Let's go to the meeting."

We rode the short distance to the office in silence. My mind was on Tate and whether he was looking to get rid of me, and Chris seemed just as lost in thought as I was.

The second we walked through the doors of the office, Brian approached us.

Chris nodded. "Hey. How's it going?"

"Good. Arms up," Brian, Tate's right-hand man, said to me.

Gritting my teeth, I did as ordered. "If you wanted to feel me up, you could've at least bought me a drink first."

"There's one in there waiting for you." He patted me

down, checking for wires or any weapons I'd failed to leave outside the meeting room with my phone. After a few moments, he nodded once. "Go on in."

I gave him a cocky grin. "Thanks."

He moved on to Chris, who stood behind me, and I went in. I'd never been in this particular room before, since I wasn't up high enough on the food chain to warrant an invitation. I wasn't sure why I'd gotten one now, either, unless I was about to get that promotion that Chris had warned me about. Either that . . .

Or they knew about Scotty.

My pulse sped up, and I sank into one of the chairs that had a whiskey sitting in front of it. I could only assume it wasn't taken, since everyone else had a glass in their hands except me and Chris. I stared down at the drink but didn't touch it. Instead, I scanned the room. Polished wooden circular table. Five matching chairs. A few generic paintings of flowers and landscapes. Everything looked boringly white-collar.

But I knew better than to believe it was.

"All right," Tate said, settling into his chair. He wore a dark blue suit and a light blue dress shirt and looked every inch the professional businessman he pretended to be. "Let's get this meeting started. First, let's welcome our visitor today, Lucas Donahue."

Everyone sat, murmuring quiet welcomes in their designer suits and ties.

Chris just raised a brow at me.

I stared back at him.

The men took turns speaking and solving problems. One by one, they discussed territories and deaths and errors. It was a management meeting, and I had nothing to add, because I didn't manage a damn thing besides Heidi, and I even sucked at that.

Leaning back in the wood chair, I watched my companions through my lowered lashes. Tate sat kind of separated from the rest of us, and Brian was to his left. Chris sat on the right, and I was next to him. Across from me was Tommy, and he watched me with skepticism, as if he couldn't figure out why the hell I was sitting at this table in the first place.

Hell, neither could I.

But I'd been summoned, and so here I was.

"The crew in Center City is having a hard time locking down sales. They keep getting busted and think we need to move away from the high school," Tate said, rubbing his forehead. "So we need to come up with a better place to deliver."

Chris smirked at me. I stiffened, knowing this wasn't gonna go anywhere good. "You got any thoughts on this, Luc?"

"Uh . . . yeah." I sat up straighter and tapped the fingers of my good hand on the table. "Center City is heavily policed. We need to move away from it."

Brian nodded. "That's what we just said. So what do you suggest?"

"Yeah." Chris leaned back and crossed his arms. "Whatcha got, Luc?"

I shrugged, not liking the way my blood brother put me on the spot like that. This was obviously some sort of test, and the stubborn asshole part of me didn't want to fail it. An earlier conversation with Heidi came to mind, and I sat up straighter. "I don't know. Maybe . . . maybe we throw the badge for a loop and move closer to Steel Row High rather than farther from it. There's an alley near it, right?"

Tate leaned forward, his lips parted. "Yeah. It's got a few. And there's a deserted Laundromat, too, only a block out."

"So what if we use those alleys to our advantage?"

Brian shook his head. "Too dangerous. We'd be vulnerable to an ambush."

"Agreed," Tommy said quickly.

"But the police usually avoid the alleys if the homeless are in them. They don't waste their time with them, since all they want is a place to sleep." I leaned on the table and locked gazes with Tate. "A few wads of cash and a couple prepaid phones here and there, and we can not only have that alley empty and waiting for us, but we'll have people who can warn us if the Boys are coming."

Brian shook his head. "I don't know. Too many risks."

"It could work, though," Tommy said, eyeing me with new respect. He rubbed his jaw and slapped his hand on the table. "It could actually fucking work. He's right. The Boys avoid the usual homeless haunts."

Tate cracked a smile. "All right. Then I say we should case the place, see how it looks. Take a few days to make sure we're right, and then we make the move, if all the pieces line up the way I like."

Chris nodded once. "Seconded."

"Third," Brian said.

Tommy nodded. "Fourth."

They all stared at me. I shifted in my seat. "I came up with the idea, so obviously . . . fifth . . . or whatever the hell I'm supposed to say."

Tate laughed, his blue eyes shining like sapphires. The guy could be a ruthless killer, but there was no denying his charismatic charm. It was a dangerous combination, if you were on his shit list. "You'll get the hang of it. Don't worry."

"The hang of what, exactly?" I tugged on my collar and picked up my whiskey, which had been previously untouched. "Why am I here?"

"That's a conversation we're going to have alone." Tate nodded at the other men. "If you'll excuse us, gentlemen?"

The other three men grabbed their drinks and left without another word. As Chris passed, he winked at me. I flipped him off under the table. He laughed. As soon as the door shut, I set my glass down. "Is there something I can do for you, sir?"

Tate shoved a hand through his red hair. "You've been loyal to us for over thirteen years now. A member since before you were old enough to grow hair on your chest."

I laughed. "With all due respect, you're only two years older than me."

"Yeah." Tate smiled slightly. "But I was born into this life. You weren't. You chose it, embraced it, lived it."

I stared down at my glass. "Really? Most of the time, it feels like it chose me."

"Which is the sign I needed to know I made the right choice." Tate leaned back and steepled his fingers, watching me over them like a hawk about to pounce on its prey. "You did your time, and when you came out, you integrated back into our life without a hitch. Some might even say you've shone like a fucking lightbulb."

"Call me Rudolph, if you must," I said, smirking.

"Call yourself whatever the hell you want, but I call it ambition. Street smarts. Success." He stood and went to the window, pulling the blinds apart to look outside. It was a sunny day in Steel Row, and the light reflected off the tip of the cathedral. There were birds singing out the window, telling of the coming spring, but I wasn't holding my breath. Mother Nature was a major bitch this year, and there was still snow on the ground. "I'd be a fool not to reward that."

I also stood, smoothing my button-up shirt over my abs. "What are you saying, sir?"

"You know, I haven't been on a date with a normal girl in ten years." Tate dropped his hold on the blinds and turned to me. He ran his hand over the buttons of his suit jacket. "I feel like I've been in this life too long sometimes, you know. Like it's changed me, but not for the better. Do you ever get that feeling? Like normal life is something beyond your reach?"

I swallowed. "Yeah. I know the feeling very well."

"But you have Heidi now." He cocked his head. "She's normal."

I nodded once. "Indeed."

"And you make it work."

Tugging on my collar again, I shrugged. I didn't like him focusing on her. The less the gang knew about her, the better. Then once we were over, she could break free of it all, once and for all. "So far, sure. But I'm a guy, so I'm sure I'll fuck it up at some point."

Tate laughed. "Sure. We all do. But they usually forgive us."

I shifted uncomfortably. "No offense, but did you really bring me in here to chat about the status of my relationship?"

Tate quit laughing. "No, of course not. Sorry."

"Don't mention it . . . sir."

"I called you here because"—he came up to me and placed a hand on my shoulder—"I'd like you to take over the exporting and importing sector of Steel Row. Be my head lieutenant."

I'd known it was coming, thanks to Chris's intel, but it still sent a hollow ping through my chest, because it reminded me yet again that Scotty wanted me dead over a position. I said the only thing I could say if I wanted to walk out of there alive. "I'm honored."

Tate clapped me on the back. "I'll take that as a yes?"

Not like I had a choice, really. If I turned it down, I might as well sign my own death warrant. Anyone who turned down advancement in this gang was suspect. "Yes, of course. Thank you."

"Excellent." He sat back down and pulled out his Mac-Book Air, opening it and staring down at the screen with a furrowed brow. "We'll announce it at the party, then."

I bowed. "See you then, sir."

"Oh, and bring Heidi." He glanced up at me again, his expression leaving no room for argument. "I want to meet this paragon of a woman who can handle this lifestyle of ours, without even knowing what the hell she was getting herself into."

"Oh, she knew." I headed for the door, my body tense. "But I don't think she can come. She owns a bar, and she has to work."

Tate leveled a frown at me. "I want to meet her."

"Again." I shrugged. "I'm sorry, but she's busy, sir."

"Another time, then."

I left without answering, shutting the door behind me with a soft *click*. A bunch of guys sat at the bar, drinking and shooting the shit, but I walked out without so much as a wave in their direction. After I got behind the wheel of my Mustang, which we'd dropped off earlier so Chris and I could carpool to the docks, I gripped the shifter and snarled, "Son of a fucking whoreson cocksucker."

He wanted me to bring Heidi into the mix and introduce her to a roomful of people she had no business knowing? And even worse, Scotty would be there. If I brought Heidi, it would take Scotty all of five seconds to put two and two together.

And she'd be vulnerable to attack.

I had to find a way to get her to leave me. To push her away, once and for all, before my life dragged her down. If I was a dick, she wouldn't like me anymore. And if she didn't like me anymore, maybe she wouldn't feel guilty about taking my cash. And if she took my cash, she'd run. She'd be *safe*.

I slammed the car into reverse, making it back to my apartment in record time. As I climbed the stairs, I heard Heidi talking animatedly. I stiffened, stopping outside the door to listen. "No, of course not. You have to go." There was no reply, and then Heidi said, "I know, I'll miss you, too. But you'll be fine, Marco, I promise. I'll come in tonight and work. Yeah, at four." She jumped as I walked in, then waved at me. Turning her back, she nodded. "Of course. We'll talk soon, okay?" After she hung up, she spun back to me, her phone pressed against her chest. "Hey, how did your job and meeting go?"

"Fine." I tossed my keys on the table and rotated my sore arm. "Everything okay with Marco?"

"Yeah, he's just finished packing and is heading out for dinner with a few friends. He wanted me to come with him, but I declined." She nibbled on her lower lip. "He doesn't need me around him right now, considering . . . you know." Considering I'd turned her into a walking target, she meant. "Plus, I have work to do at the bar, since you're feeling better."

I crossed the room and opened the cabinet to the left of the sink. It had my gun-cleaning supplies, and after firing it yesterday, I needed them. Especially since she was determined to go to work tonight. "Yeah. I know."

Heidi came closer, her thumb pressed against her lip. "Whatcha doing?"

"Cleaning my gun, in case I need to kill more assholes to keep you alive," I said, keeping my tone caustic and surly.

She blinked, clearly taken aback at my behavior. "Okay, then. Someone woke up on the wrong side of the couch this morning."

Pushing past her, I sat at the table and rolled the white cloth across it, lining up my supplies and ignoring her. She watched with wide eyes as I took my gun apart with practiced ease. When I set it all down and pulled out the barrel brush, she still hadn't moved. I frowned. "Don't you have something better to do than stare at me?"

She stiffened. "Yeah. Sure. Whatever."

With that, she walked past me, into my bedroom, and

slammed the door in my face. I sat there, staring down at my gun, and felt . . . shame. Over the past thirteen years, I'd killed, stolen, bribed, and fought my way to the top. And for what? Power? Money? Notoriety? What the hell good would any of that be when I was six feet under, or anchored to the bottom of the Atlantic? Yes, I'd been trying to push her away to save her, and yes, I had noble intentions for once in my life. But even so, I'd been a dick.

And for the first time in my life, that didn't sit well.

CHAPTER 22

HEIDI

Later that night, I stood behind my bar, watching the door nervously. It was the first time I'd left the apartment since Lucas had been shot, and I couldn't shake the feeling that something terrible was going to happen. None of the Bitter Hill guys were here yet, but nothing was stopping them from coming in. Lucas was here, brooding in the corner seat at the bar, but a group of guys could still barge in here and do some serious damage before Lucas could take them down.

If he could take them down.

He had some mobility in his arm again, but it certainly wasn't a hundred percent. How could it be? A little over thirty-six hours ago, he'd been *shot*. I had no idea if it was still painful, but I could only assume it was. He'd been throwing off majorly cold vibes, so I hadn't asked. I knew better than to poke a man who didn't want to talk, so I'd given him some space all day long.

He glanced at his phone and muttered a string of curses under his breath.

"That was a mouthful," I said dryly, leaning on the bar. "What's wrong?"

"Nothing," he muttered. He shot a look at Chris, who sat in the back corner watching the door, and hunched over the bar. "Just thinking out loud."

"About . . . ?"

"Shit you don't need to know about." He rubbed his jaw. "Shit you don't want to know about."

Cleaning the bar with a rag, even though it was spotless already, I kept my voice purposely calm. "Where did you go earlier today?"

He tensed. "Out."

"Wow, that was so informative," I snapped. This attitude of his . . . I'd had enough. He needed to explain himself, and do it now, or he'd answer to me. "Thanks."

Something inside him eased a bit. I had no idea what, but it did. His muscles relaxed, and he sighed. "I was searching for Scotty, if you need to know. To stop this shit before it gets out of hand. I went to his place, but he was gone."

My heart seized as if someone had grabbed it and squeezed as hard as they could. "You can't just go *looking* for him. What if he killed you? What if—?"

"I don't give a damn." He locked his gaze on mine, and for a split second, I saw all the emotion he was so good at hiding from the world in those green depths. But he turned away, and it was gone. "He's my brother, Heidi. My *brother.*"

I pressed my lips together. "But—"

"There are no buts to this situation. And you have no idea what this feels like, because you don't have any family to stab you in the back like this." As soon as the words were out of his mouth, he stiffened. "I mean . . . shit. Heidi—"

Okay, that hurt. I didn't need his reminder that I was alone in this world, thank you very much. I knew it all too well. But I refused to show him he'd hurt me, so I scowled. "Stop. Don't you dare apologize to me."

He ran his hands down his face. "Fine."

"And you're right. I don't know anything about this life you lead. This whole kill-or-be-killed thing."

He dropped his hands to his lap. "That's everyone's life, darlin'. Most people are just too blind or naïve to see it."

"People like me?"

He shrugged. "Your words, not mine."

"Why don't you tell Tate about this? He's the boss, right?" I leaned in close. "He could, y'know, *handle* the situation, and then you won't have to. Common sense says—"

"No." He reared back, his nostrils flared. "I will never turn him in. *Never.*"

"But . . ." I knew it was harsh, but if it came down to Scotty or Lucas, I'd always champion Lucas. I didn't even know his little brother. And anyone who could plot to kill his own blood deserved what he got, really. But that didn't mean Lucas had to be the one to pull the trigger. "So, what, you'd rather Scotty die by your hand? How is that better?"

"I'd rather he hadn't started this goddamn mess in the first place." He pushed back off the bar. Resting his palms on the bar, he leaned in and stopped when we were just nose to nose. God, he loved getting all up in my personal space during an argument. It was equal parts intimidating, annoying, and *hot*. "But he did, so I'll take care of it. Not Chris. Not Tate. Not you. *Me.*"

Shaking my head, I forced myself to remain calm. "I don't understand your reasoning. I'm trying, but I don't."

If looks could kill, I'd be dead. "If Tate kills him . . . I know what happens to rats and traitors. Being my brother won't save him from a slow, torturous death, and after he's finally dead, his body will just disappear. But he should be with my ma. When she passed, I bought another plot, figured I could use it for a dead drop, so we have the room. He should be with Ma."

The heartbreak was clear in his voice and I fought back tears. "Maybe you could ask Tate to jump him out and exile him? On the account he's your brother?"

"He's a traitor. If you turn on one of us, you turn on all of us. And you die." He lifted a shoulder. "That's the way it is."

"That's why you want to do it yourself," I said, finally understanding. "You want to give him a merciful death. Fast and quick."

He gritted his teeth. "He's my *brother*."

"And if he kills you first?"

He didn't meet my eyes. "Chris will make the arrangements. All you'll have to do is get out of Dodge before Bitter Hill comes sniffing around again."

I crossed my arms, moving away from him. He acted as if his death would mean nothing. Like the only reason I cared whether he lived or died was because I didn't want to be without protection. As if I'd just shrug and move on as if he'd never existed. I didn't know whether to be pissed, insulted, or sad. "Wow. Just . . . wow."

He stared at me, looking cold and aloof. "I need some peace and quiet."

And then he walked away.

I watched him, anger burning red-hot through my veins, but didn't follow him. If I did, I'd hit him. And if I hit him, I'd kiss him. And I didn't want to kiss him right now.

I wanted to *hate* him. Too bad I loved him instead.

Chris came over, his beer empty, and set it down on the bar. "Trouble in paradise already?"

"As if you'd expected anything else?" I asked, my tone as neutrally passive as I could manage. "Want another?"

"Yeah." He sat down and looked at Lucas—who glared back at him. "You need to back off him. He's not your knight in shining armor."

I poured his beer, trying to ignore the stinging behind my eyes. God, I hadn't cried in years. *Years*. And now here

I was, worrying about a man who didn't give two shits about me, seconds from tears for the millionth time in a short handful of days, and I couldn't stop. Lucas was trying to break me. "I never said he was."

"You don't need to say it. I can see it." Chris tossed cash on the bar. "But you can save him, for once, if you're willing."

I slid his beer toward him and stole a look at Lucas. He watched, those green eyes of his burning into me, as I took the cash off the bar. "Oh? How so?"

Chris leaned closer. "There's a party tomorrow night. Tate asked for you to come, but Lucas told him you had to work. Word is, Tate's pissed."

"I do have to work, but I could get out of it, if I need to." I curled my hand into a fist, crinkling the crisp five-dollar bill. "But why would your boss want me there?"

"He wants proof that you're real and that this isn't just a ruse. Lucas caused a shit-ton of trouble when he swooped in and rode away with you on a white horse." He tapped my hand. "Tate wants to know it was worth it. He wants to see the two of you, hand in hand, madly in love with one another. And if he doesn't . . ."

"Lucas gets in trouble." I swallowed hard, my chest aching. "Why didn't he tell me?"

"He's still protecting you. Like always." Chris shrugged. "Even if it gets him killed, which it might, he'll refuse to bring you along."

No. *No.* I couldn't let that happen. "But—"

"Now that you got your beer, can you go back to the corner to watch the door?" Lucas sat down directly next to Chris, anger seething from him. "I need to talk to Heidi. Alone."

Chris grinned. "Sure, man."

As he walked away, Lucas turned back to me. "What was he saying to you?"

"Nothing." I cleaned the spot on the bar I'd cleaned ten times already, not meeting his eyes. I couldn't right now, because he would see the truth in my eyes. "What's his story, anyway? He an orphan like you?"

"Nah, his pa's in the gang, and he followed in his footsteps. I did, too." He tapped his fingers on his untouched glass of scotch. "Well, I followed Chris. Not my pa."

"So no one from your family was ever in it?"

"No. We needed the money, Ma was already sick, though we didn't know it yet, and she couldn't work as many shifts at the restaurant. I knew from hanging out with Chris that you could make a decent living as a Son, but I also knew that you had to be a legacy to get in. Tate's way of weeding out rats and undercover cops." He shifted in his seat but kept talking. "So I found a way to meet with Tate and convinced him to let me in the Sons of Steel Row. Trial basis at first, petty-ass shit, but soon enough I was climbing up the ladder, faster than any other new recruit."

Shaking my head, I finally turned to him. He watched me intently, those green eyes of his locked onto me without fail. "What about him?" I glanced at Chris again. He watched us way too closely. "How did he feel about you finagling your way in?"

"He didn't give a damn." The smirk faded away. "Why are you asking so many questions about Chris?"

"Curiosity."

His jaw flexed. "You lookin' to move on from me already, darlin'?"

"Because I need another man like you bossing me around, thinking he owns me?" I asked, snorting. "Thanks, but no thanks. I was just curious. That's all."

"He's not—" His phone buzzed, and he glanced down at it. His brows lowered, and he pushed off the stool, grabbing his glass. "Speaking of Chris, I gotta go talk to him."

He walked away without giving me another glance, his attention fixed on his phone.

I knew, then, in that moment, that he would do the same thing when this was all said and done. That he'd walk away from me . . .

And never look back.

CHAPTER 23

LUCAS

A few hours later, the bar was empty, minus me, Chris, and Heidi. She kept eyeing me up like she was planning on hauling me outside before ensuring I met a gruesome end. I'd annoyed her earlier, apparently.

Not a huge shocker.

I never had been good at understanding women, which was why I generally avoided them unless we were naked and not speaking at all. But there was no avoiding Heidi. I'd tried. It was like trying not to breathe or blink. If she was near me, it was inevitable I'd seek her out.

But I'd been trying my damn best not to.

I'd even tried to be a dick to her for a few hours, but the thing was—it wasn't *working*. And I didn't really want it to. I liked her. I didn't want to be a dick. For some reason, it mattered to me that she liked me, too, and that only made me even more of a selfish prick than I already was. I should be pushing her away so she'd run.

Instead, I was too busy making sure she liked me.

Asshole.

Besides, I must have misjudged Heidi when I'd decided she'd run if I was a dick. She wouldn't.

Chris came over to me. "I'm going to head out. You two good to make it across the street alive?"

"I think I can manage," I said dryly. "Thanks for doing me a solid, man. I appreciate it."

"Yeah, I know. I rock." He clapped me on the back harder than necessary. "I'll see you tomorrow night for the ride to Tate's."

I glanced at the kitchen door. Heidi hadn't come back out yet. "I didn't tell Heidi about the party, or Tate's request that she come, so don't bring it up in front of her. If she knows he wants her there, she'll insist on coming, and I don't want her within ten miles of that house—or Scotty."

"Uh . . . about that . . ." Chris rocked back on his heels. "I might have already mentioned the dinner. And that Tate wanted her to come. I told her I'd see her tomorrow night because I was planning on riding with both of you."

"You've got to be kidding me." I rubbed my temples and leaned against the wall. "I'm gonna punch you so hard in the nuts that you won't be able to fuck for a week." I growled and tightened my hands into fists.

Chris held his hands up and stepped back. "Okay, okay. Sorry. But how was I supposed to know you didn't want her to come?"

"Why the hell would I *want* Heidi to come with me to Tate's?"

Chris glanced over my shoulder, cleared his throat, and tugged on his collar. I knew without looking that Heidi stood behind me and had heard my last sentence. "Uh . . . and that's my cue to leave. Nice seeing you again, Heidi."

"Shit," I muttered under my breath. Looking over my shoulder, I said, "Hey, darlin'," with a fake-ass grin on my

face. "Have I mentioned how pretty you look tonight in those shorts?"

She didn't answer me. Instead she walked Chris to the door. "Thanks for coming."

I couldn't hear Chris's reply, but he glanced at me one more time before leaving. I didn't move. Just watched Heidi as she locked the door behind him. We were alone. She leaned her hands on the door and took a deep breath. By the time she turned around, I knew I was in for a fight. The look in her eyes only confirmed it.

"What's happening tomorrow night at Tate's?" she asked softly. "And why don't you want me there?"

"Nothing. And because it's nothing you would want to go to." I rubbed the back of my neck and tried my best to look innocent of any possible wrongdoing. I had a strong poker face with everyone else, but with Heidi, I wasn't any good at it. If she even suspected that her being there would help my case with Tate, it would be impossible to get her to stay home. "It's just a stupid work party."

She nodded as if she wasn't pissed off at all. "And by work party, you mean . . . what? Champagne and lobster? Caviar and mousse? Only the best gourmet treats for the crème de la crème of Boston's criminal elite?"

It sounded ridiculous when she said it like that, and that was probably the point, but Heidi didn't know Tate considered himself something of a foodie. The mousse would probably be salmon. "Tate uses these parties to network and build alliances. Half the invitees are probably on some agency's most-wanted list. You have to practically provide a DNA sample to get past the security, but once you're inside the house, anything goes." I cocked a brow. "Everything illicit that you could possibly conjure up. It'll be there."

Her cheeks flushed. "Drugs? Murder? Prostitution?"

"Drugs? Sure. Murder? Hopefully not. Girls? Yeah,

there'll be some." I shrugged. "But not for us. Tate doesn't mind if we party a little, but bottom line, it's a business event. The women are for the clients."

"Oh my God." She crossed her arms. "Seriously?"

"Don't worry—I'm not interested in them, or anyone else." I skimmed my knuckles over her soft cheek. "I only want you."

She licked her lips and stared up at me, her wide blue eyes locked on me. She looked so soft. So hesitant. As if unsure of her welcome, and that made me feel like even more of a dick, because I'd made her doubt herself by being a prick for a few hours. "Oh . . ."

"I'm sorry, sweetheart."

She blinked at me, clearly thrown off. "For?"

"Being an asshole." I pulled her into my arms. "I thought . . . actually, it doesn't matter why I did it. It was a stupid idea, and you deserve better."

"I thought you were just in a bad mood." She softened and rested her hands on my shoulders. "Tell me the truth. Why did you do it?"

"I wanted to scare you away. Send you running with my cash with a few callous remarks." I rested my forehead on hers, gripping her hips, and breathed in her scent. "It didn't work, though. It's so fucking easy for me to be an ass to everyone. Everyone but you."

A smile lit up her face. "Even if you managed to be the biggest jerk in the world, it wouldn't have changed a thing. I told you I'm not going anywhere, and I meant it." She skimmed her fingers over my jaw. I could barely feel her touch, but it soothed the beast inside me. "I'm not leaving till this thing is over."

What she meant by *this thing*, I didn't know. But I wasn't about to ask. It wouldn't be fair of me. Not when I was standing at the entrance of the Valley of Death. And something inside of me, deep, deep down, below all the anger and knowledge, believed her. That scared the shit out of me.

Not trusting myself to speak, I let go of her, walked to the door, unlocked it, and motioned her through it. She wore short denim shorts, a tight sweater, and a pair of knee-high boots, so like usual, she shivered as soon as she stepped outside, even though it was slightly warmer tonight.

Shrugging my jacket off, I tossed it over her shoulders without speaking.

We walked home in silence, and after I checked that the apartment was clear, I walked right back out. I wasn't going to push her away by being a dick anymore, but that didn't mean we'd live happily ever after. Not with my life. She didn't bother to ask me where I was going, either because she already knew, or because she just didn't give a damn. Either way, it didn't matter.

Switching the light on, I walked into the garage and eyed the cars waiting to be repaired. Rotating my aching shoulders and wincing at the pain in my arm, I walked over to the Camaro in the corner and read the file. All it needed was a routine oil change. Perfect. That's about all I could handle with one lame arm.

Rolling my sleeves up, I tried to force everything that was upsetting me to the back of my mind. That's why I did this. Working with my hands made my mind clear, and it soothed me. Like Heidi with her music—

Damn it, could I spend one fucking moment *without* thinking about her and her damn smile and bright blue eyes and fresh, clean peach scent? Part of me—a very, *very* small part that I'd deny till I was blue in the face if anyone ever asked me about it—wished I'd taken Heidi up on her offer the other night.

I *almost* wished we could run away together.

Take the money, find the quaintest, smallest town in

America, and start over. One with a zero point nine-nine percent crime ratio. She could open another bar, and I could open up a legit mechanic shop. Live life on the right side of the tracks for once, and see how it felt. With her by my side . . .

I had a feeling it would feel really nice.

Sweat rolled down, stinging my eyes, and I cranked the torque too hard. Straightening, I swiped my forearm across my forehead and let out a low curse. The image of Heidi's blue eyes flashed in front of me, and I tossed the rag aside. Working on cars wasn't quieting my mind tonight. I couldn't stop thinking about *her*.

I was still avoiding thinking about Scotty and his attempts to kill me, but Heidi hadn't left my mind yet. I didn't know what to do about that, damn it. Or what it meant. Shaking my head, I sat on the hood of the Benz behind me with a groan. I could still hear little Scotty's laugh as I chased him around Ma's house.

He'd always worn that damn Batman cape, and I'd always been delegated to don Robin's tights. I'd hated Robin. But I'd worn them for him anyway.

And now he wanted to *kill* me.

Life was too short to mess with this shit, but it was also too short to ignore the one thing that was staring me in the face: Heidi was upstairs, waiting for me, and I was downstairs pretending I didn't need to go up there because I didn't *want* to want her.

Admitting I did made me weak. It's what I'd been told my whole life. What I'd told myself. But now, with Heidi in my life, I found myself questioning those values.

Questioning everything.

Tossing the torque wrench aside, I walked away from an unfinished car for the first time ever. Someone else could fix it tomorrow, and that someone wouldn't be me.

Shutting the lights off, I headed up the stairs and tossed

the apartment door open, scanning the room for any signs of life. The living room was dark, and so was the kitchen, but the bedroom light was still on.

I could see it shining underneath the crack of the door.

Without breaking stride, I threw open the door. She lay in the bed, a book in her hand, and jumped when I came barging in. "Lucas? What the—?"

"I want you." I took her book out of her hands and set it down, being careful not to lose her page. Then I threw the covers back and crawled on top of her, right where I belonged. All she had on was a baggy shirt and a pair of satin underwear, and she managed to make that sexy as hell. She immediately closed her legs around my waist. "But even more than that? I need you, sweetheart. I fucking *need* you."

She didn't hesitate. Didn't shy away. Instead, she cradled my face and smiled up at me. "So take me. I'm all yours."

Groaning, I melded my mouth to hers, taking what she offered me so freely. The second our lips met, it was as if everything else faded away. The worry. The pain. The betrayal. My whole life—it just went away until all I felt and knew was Heidi.

She *was* my life, in that moment.

And nothing had ever felt more right.

Her tongue slipped over mine, and she let out one of those sexy-ass moans I loved so much. And it felt like home. I'd found a home. It wasn't a building or a town or even a room. It was *her*. And I didn't want to leave it.

Rolling my hips against hers, I slipped my hands under her loose shirt and cupped her breasts, running my thumbs over her hard nipples. I could feel her wet heat pushing against my cock, demanding more without words. She writhed beneath me, making small noises, and dragged her hands down my back until she cupped my ass. Everything inside me answered to her cries and her movements.

Everything.

Breaking off the kiss, I buried my face in her neck, letting her peach scent wash over me, and tenderly kissed the spot where her pulse beat, fast and strong. At the same time, I thrust my hips against hers, cursing the clothes we hadn't yet removed. I hadn't lied or exaggerated. I needed her. But even as I did, I knew it wasn't right, me needing her like this. It wasn't fair. "I'm sorry, darlin'. So fucking sorry."

"I know." She locked her ankles behind my back, holding me still. "But I need you, too, Lucas. I need you so bad. I . . . I care about you, Lucas. A lot."

Instead of the surge of satisfaction I'd expected to feel, it felt like she'd shot me and I was bleeding out. She cared about me. Actually cared. What the hell was I doing, making her care whether I lived or died? She didn't deserve this.

She didn't deserve *any* of this.

And I'd remembered that way too fucking late.

"Don't," I said, my voice hard and yet still somehow broken. I gripped her hips. "Don't care."

"Too late." She gave me a sad smile. "But don't worry. I know how this ends. It ends with you leaving, one way or another, and me staying in my bar, doing my thing. This thing we have, it's not for the long haul, and we both know it. We're not going to live happily ever after, and that's just how it's going to be."

Everything she said was right. We wouldn't ride off into the sunset in my car, holding hands and smiling at our bright, sunshiny future. More than likely, this would end with me dead and her crying while identifying me at the morgue . . .

This, right here, was everything I should have never let happen.

Just a few days ago on the Freedom Trail, I'd sworn to myself that I'd never fool myself into thinking that I could have a "normal" life. That I wouldn't corrupt someone into caring about my dark, blackened soul—and just as important, that I'd never care back.

I was beyond hope in this world. *She* wasn't. This was getting too real. Too fast. She didn't need this shit in her life. Didn't need me.

"Shit, darlin'," I managed to say through my suddenly, oddly tight throat. "I'm not gonna be a dick, or try to scare you away, but this thing we have between us? It's gonna hurt in the end. We both know it."

Something flashed in her eyes. Pain? Maybe something deeper. Harder. Darker. Whatever it was, it made me want to cling to something that wasn't meant for me.

My very own happy ending.

She nodded once, her gaze never wavering from mine. And no matter how hard I tried, I couldn't look away. "So what are you saying? That it should end now?" she asked.

"Yeah. It should."

She swallowed hard. "What if I don't want it to?"

"I don't want to hurt you, sweetheart." I kissed her shoulder, my lips lingering. "I don't want to make you cry."

"Then don't." She buried her hands in my hair and tugged till she had me where she wanted me—nose to nose. "Kiss me instead."

Shaking my head, I tried to resist, but it was futile. With a groan, I did it. I kissed her again. And this time, I didn't stop. Heart thumping hard, I yanked her panties off, tossing them over my shoulder, and slid down till my head was between her legs. The second my tongue touched her, she fell apart in my arms. Her thighs trembled, then clamped down on either side of my head as she let out a long guttural moan.

She rocked her hips against my mouth desperately. "*Lucas*. God, harder. More. *Yes*."

Moaning, I dug my fingers into her soft ass cheeks and deepened the intimate kiss, tasting her impending orgasm before it even hit her. Her whole body tensed, she lifted her hips, and she cried out unintelligible words.

She managed to make that hot as hell, too.

As soon as she crested, I dropped her to the mattress, let my pants hit the floor, took care of protection, and thrust into her before she even had time to come back down. She screamed and dug her heels into my lower back, thrashing beneath me, her hot pussy clamping down on me until I was sure I'd died and gone to heaven. And if I had, I never wanted to go back.

The harder I thrust my hips, the more she cried out beneath me, chasing the pleasure I could give her. My own orgasm crept up my balls and into my aching cock, and something unfamiliar, warm and strong, rolled through me, starting somewhere in my chest until it all centered and became something I recognized more . . .

The carnal needs of the flesh.

But even after that familiar need took over, there was still that warm, sinking feeling that after I finished making love to her I'd never be the same again.

And strangely enough?

I was okay with that.

CHAPTER 24

HEIDI

Friday night, I stood outside a huge brick mansion, wearing the fanciest dress I owned, clutching a purse that was so tiny, it was ridiculous to even bother carrying it. I knew that this was a big mistake. A colossal, life-ending, game-changing type of mistake . . . and yet I was going to go ahead and do it anyway.

It was time for *me* to protect *him*.

Tate wanted to see me, so he would. Then I wouldn't have to worry about Lucas being attacked from three corners instead of just two.

Wringing the absurdly small purse in my hands, I walked up to the front door. I could hear what sounded like a small orchestra playing Mozart. Freaking *Mozart*. It sounded as if the party was a hell of a lot like I'd guessed last night, but I'd been joking. I hadn't really expected ball gowns and caviar, despite Lucas's alluding to a high-class affair when we'd talked about it last night.

After taking a calming breath that did nothing at all for

my nerves, I knocked. The door swung open immediately, and two large men in designer suits stood there.

They looked me up and down, the appreciation in their eyes all too clear.

The one on the left raised his brows. "Are you one of Suzy's girls? I haven't seen you around here before."

"N-no." So. The prostitutes were already here. *Lovely.* I forced a smile and stopped strangling my poor purse to death. "I'm with Lucas. Lucas Donahue. I'm his—"

"Girlfriend." Chris came up behind the two men, looking hotter than ever in his suit. His brown hair was gelled and styled to perfection, and I swore he had the whole five-o'clock shadow thing down to a science. "And he wouldn't appreciate your insinuation."

The man on the left flushed and stepped back. "Of course. I apologize."

"Come in, miss." The one on the right scowled at the other man. "Ignore Frank here. He's always been an idiot who doesn't know how to treat a lady."

Chris stepped forward, his whole body tense and ready to pounce. "Maybe he needs to be reminded to think before he fucking speaks."

"It's fine, really." I glanced at Chris, then at the pale man to my left. "It was obviously just an honest misunderstanding."

Chris walked up to me and placed a hand on my lower back. "Make sure it doesn't happen again. Take her coat and go back to your posts."

The man who wasn't Frank helped me slip off my wrap, and they both gave Chris respectful nods before walking away. I returned to strangling my purse. "You didn't have to do that."

"Yeah, I did." He looked at me out of the corner of his eye. "I thought you weren't coming. Does Lucas know?"

I shook my head. "Nope. As a matter of fact, he made it very clear I wasn't welcome."

"Damn, girl." He whistled through his teeth. "You've got balls."

"Not the last time I checked," I said dryly.

He snorted and gave me a gentle shove toward the room where the majority of the crowd was gathered. "Come on. I'll escort you inside and keep you safe when he starts breathing fire."

My heart thumped loudly in my ears, and I let him guide me to the room's entryway. As soon as I caught sight of it all, I froze. Stunning jewelry adorned the most beautiful of women, all clad in evening gowns of the latest fashions. All around me in the marble-floored room, men conversed in small groups, most of them with a woman or two on their arms. It all looked so very civil. If I didn't know any better, I'd think this was a party for the Boston Brahmins.

There was even a cop there. A freaking *cop*. I recognized him from evening news reports, and he'd recently won an award for cleaning up the streets of Steel Row. I felt like I'd fallen straight down the rabbit hole and landed in Wonderland. Eyes wide, I stared at everyone. I knew all the men were armed with at least one weapon beneath those Gucci suits, and all of them could likely kill a person without batting an eye. Including Lucas. Speaking of which . . .

It didn't take me long to find him.

He stood in the corner, facing slightly away from us. A gorgeous woman in a silky red dress ran her hand over his arm, but he shrugged her off, ignoring her completely. As he chatted to her escort, he glanced over at Chris, a cocky grin on his face. At least until he saw *me*.

Then he looked ready to kill. Or breathe fire, like Chris had said earlier. I sucked in a deep breath and stepped back, my heart speeding so fast it hurt. "Oh God."

Chris chuckled. "Too late to back down now. Tate saw you, too, and is coming this way. If you leave, it'll look bad, and all of this will be for nothing. Lift that chin, doll. It's time for a show."

Forcing my attention off the furious man stalking my way, I scanned the room for signs of this "Tate." A young, *way* too hot man walked toward me. But that couldn't be Tate . . . could it? I'd thought he'd be, you know, *older.* "That's not him, is it?"

"Hm?" Chris glanced over at the guy I couldn't stop staring at. Not because I was attracted to him or anything, but because he was the opposite of what I'd expected him to be. "Yeah. That's him. Why?"

I swallowed hard. The incredibly attractive man walking toward me oozed danger. Even more so than Lucas . . . which was saying a lot. He had red hair and blue eyes and was clean-shaven. He looked as if he was more comfortable at a charity gala than in a gunfight, but I didn't let that fool me into thinking he wasn't a dangerous man. "I thought he'd be older. I mean, he's in charge, right?"

"Yeah. His father died recently, and he took over."

I glanced toward the real threat. Lucas. He was almost at my side, and even from across the room, I could feel his stare, as he did his best to glare holes through my black dress. I stepped closer to Chris. I didn't think I'd ever see the day where I thought *he'd* be the safer option, considering how we'd met, but tonight he was. "Oh God."

"You already said that," Chris muttered. "Smile, doll. He's a foot away."

I plastered a smile on.

Chris stepped forward. "Tate, meet Heidi Greene, the now-famous woman that Lucas risked his life to save," Chris said, his voice practically booming over the crowded room. "You can see why, I'm sure."

"Indeed." Tate held his hand out. "It's a pleasure to meet

you, Ms. Greene. I've heard so much about you. Lucas had said you couldn't make it tonight, so I'm pleased to see he was mistaken. If he was trying to keep you away, I can't say I blame him. If you were mine, I'd hide you away, too. And I know exactly where I'd keep you."

My cheeks heated. I threw a fast glance Lucas's way before sliding my hand into Tate's. If anything, Lucas looked even more pissed at the contact. "I was busy, but I cleared my schedule for Lucas . . . and you, of course."

"Excellent." He gave me a once-over, his eyes lit up with male appreciation. The significance of that wasn't lost on me. Another man slipped up to us and whispered something in Tate's ear. Tate turned aside for an inaudible conversation. After a moment, he nodded. "If you'll excuse me for a second?"

"Of course," I said in a rush.

Tate walked away, and I let out a quiet, relieved sigh. One down, one to go. As he walked away, he motioned for Lucas to follow him. Lucas shot me a scowl, promising me that my future would include severe punishment, I was sure, but obediently followed Tate out of the room. I'd been granted a reprieve. A small one, but still.

It was better than nothing.

"Shit," Chris muttered, stepping closer. His gaze was locked on something right behind Tate's head, and he looked like he'd swallowed a box full of screws. "Shit, fuck, *shit*."

"What?" I rose onto my tiptoes. "What's wrong? And where's Lucas going?"

"Come on," Chris said, his voice low. Spinning on his heel, he led me across the room. "I need to hide you until—"

We made it only two steps before a voice stopped us.

"Not so fast, Chris," an unfamiliar, and yet somehow eerily familiar, voice said from behind us. "I didn't even get to say hello to the lady on your arm."

Chris's arm went stiff under my hand. "Didn't you? We were just—"

"I know who she is." The man walked in front of us and stopped. The second he did, I knew who he was. Even if I hadn't seen his picture on Lucas's fridge, I would have known. The eyes were the same, and so was the hair. They even had the same facial structure, the same cocky grin. But that was where the similarities ended. Where Lucas's eyes were warm whenever he looked at me, Scotty's were cold as ice. "Ms. Greene, right?"

I wanted to do something violent. Hit him. Shoot him. Something. *Anything.* He deserved it for trying to kill his brother . . . and me. But instead, I gave him a bright smile and pretended I had no clue who he was. "Yes. And you are . . . ?"

"Scott. Scott Donahue." He cocked his head and caught my hand, raising it to his lips. When he kissed my knuckles, I had to fight the urge to wipe my hand off on my dress. "I'm sure my brother mentioned me once or twice."

"Oooh . . . right." I blinked. "Yes, yes. Of course. I've heard *so* much about you . . . and how much you love your big brother."

The smile faltered a little bit, but not enough. "Right."

"Well, now you've met her." Chris cleared his throat. "We should go find Lucas. He'll be waiting for us."

"What's the rush?" Scotty asked, still holding on to my hand. I fought the urge to yank it back, because if I did, he'd think he intimidated me. He didn't. "He's with Tate, and I want to get to know Ms. Greene here a little bit better. She *is* dating my brother, after all."

Chris's grip on my waist tightened. "You know her well enough, I think."

I nodded. "It was nice meeting you, though."

"Not so fast." Scotty stepped closer and smiled at me.

Chris cursed under his breath. "Tell me more about how you and my brother met."

Chris stepped closer to me, reaching for his gun. "You need to back the—"

"I heard he saved your life, risking his own in the process," Scotty said, watching me closely. He rubbed his jaw, rotating his shoulders and letting out a small laugh. "Which doesn't sound like my brother at all, if you ask me."

I lifted my chin. "Guess you don't know him as well as you think, then, because it sounds like him to me."

"It makes me wonder just how much you mean to him." He tilted his head back, focusing all his unwavering attention on me. I didn't like how his single look almost made my legs quiver. "And letting such a vital piece of information get out to the general public? He knows better."

Even though his words sent a shiver down my spine, I refused to show it. Refused to let him get to me. "I don't know what you mean."

"I mean that you're obviously important to him," Scotty said, scanning his gaze over the crowd. "It was clear from the second he saved you, completely disregarding the ramifications of his actions. In doing so, he revealed his biggest, and perhaps *only*, weakness. You."

"He was doing the right thing," I said quickly, forcing a laugh. "That's it."

Scotty flexed his jaw. "If you say so, sweetie."

Rage, hot and red, flashed in front of my eyes. The fact that he could stand here, idly chatting with me while he plotted to kill the man we spoke of, chilled me to the bone. "Don't call me sweetie. I'm not your sweetie."

Chris chuckled. "Like I said. Balls, doll. Balls."

"Scotty," Lucas said. I'd sensed him before I heard him. He walked up behind me, and the tension rolled off him in waves. *Tidal waves.* "Is there a problem here?"

"Nah." Scotty dropped his hand and ducked his head. "No problems here. We were just chatting."

I dug my nails into my palm. It was either that or scratch Scotty's face off. "It was lovely meeting you, Scotty."

"Yeah." Scotty flushed at the nickname. "Likewise."

When Scotty didn't walk away, Lucas tipped his head. "Was there something else you needed, brother?"

He stared at Lucas, long and hard, and then stepped closer, lowering his voice. I barely heard him, so I knew Chris didn't, though it looked as if he strained to do so. "You shouldn't be so obvious about your feelings, you know. You taught me better. You never know who might be watching."

Lucas slung an arm over my shoulders. He looked relaxed and totally unshakeable. As if nothing affected him, least of all Scotty. But I could feel the tension in his biceps. He was far from unmoved. "I have no idea what you're talking about."

Tate walked out, a glass of champagne in his hand. Lifting it high, he came over to Lucas's side. The cop set his drink down and left the room, as if he knew what was coming and wanted plausible deniability. "Everyone, I'd like to raise a glass to celebrate. As with all loyal members of this organization, Lucas has done his time, kept his mouth shut, and now he will be rewarded. You're looking at the new head of imports and exports."

A few low murmurs spread over the room. Lucas's hand stroked my bare shoulder as if he didn't have a care in the world, but I knew better. That muscle in his jaw was ticking away like a clock. Scotty watched Lucas, but he had a hard glint in his eyes. It legit sent a cold fist of fear squeezing over my heart. Fear for Lucas. Something was *very* wrong with Scotty, and he was fixated on Lucas.

He smiled and held his hand out, but the smile didn't reach his eyes. "Congrats, brother."

"Thanks." Lucas smiled back at him and shook his

hand. "Just goes to show what a little hard work and time can do."

"Is that what you're calling it?" Scotty asked.

Tate watched the two of them, his brow furrowed. "Is there a problem here?"

"Nope," Lucas said.

"Absolutely not," Scotty said. "I was just leaving, actually."

He walked away, his strides long and unhurried. He looked as if he had all the time in the world to kill his brother . . . and didn't mind the delay in the slightest.

It was *terrifying*.

"Ignore him," Lucas said to Tate, still not speaking to me even though his grip was unyielding. "He's been anxious for his shot at the big leagues."

Tate nodded. "He might be a little upset, but you earned it. He'll accept that and move on." He paused and gripped my shoulder. "You okay, Ms. Greene? You look a little pale."

I bit my tongue. I wanted to tell Tate so badly that Scotty was trying to kill Lucas. Yet if I did that, I'd be betraying Lucas, and there would be no coming back from that. "Y-yes, of course. I'm just so happy for Lucas."

"Me, too," Tate said, smoothing his suit jacket. "Now that the announcement's out, time to get down to business. If you'll excuse me?"

"Mind if I cut out early?" Lucas asked. He smirked and ran his hand down my bare arm. "We've got some celebrating to do, if you know what I mean."

Tate laughed. "Of course. But I'll expect you at the office first thing in the morning. We have lots to go over."

"Of course," Lucas murmured.

"It was lovely meeting you, Mr. Daniels," I said quickly, extending my hand. "Thank you for your hospitality."

He kissed it. "Anytime, my dear."

The second he walked away, Lucas dropped his hold on

me like I was a hot potato. And his casual *nothing bothers me* act. "What did he say to you?"

"Nothing," I answered quickly, crossing my arms in front of me. "It was nothing."

He looked at me for a moment, studying my features carefully before his eyes turned to stone. He must have seen the lurking fear in my face.

"You shouldn't have come here," he growled, dragging his hand through his hair. When he focused on me, I took a step backward before I caught myself. He no longer looked at me with warmth or anything even akin to it. No, he looked . . . he looked like Scotty. Cold. Calculated. *Pissed*. "You should *not* have fucking come here."

CHAPTER 25

LUCAS

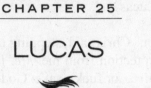

It took all my control not to lose my shit, right here, in front of everyone. To not grab her by the elbow and drag her out of the room like she was an errant child. She'd behaved like one when she'd decided to come here, after I'd expressly forbidden her from doing so. If she hadn't come here, she never would have met Scotty. And if she'd never met Scotty, she'd be in significantly less danger.

Heidi didn't even realize it, but by coming here tonight . . .

She'd signed her own fucking death warrant.

I took a deep breath, clenching and unclenching my fists on the count of five. When it came to her, I wasn't good at acting the way I was supposed to act. I'd saved her when I should have minded my own business. I'd let her creep by the years and years of defenses I'd built around myself, and now I cared about whether she lived or died.

And to repay me, she'd come here tonight and basically thrown her life away.

I was going to kill her myself, and save Scotty the trouble. Growling, I yanked on my bow tie—which was doing its best to strangle me—and jerked my head toward the exit. "We're going home. Now. Get your coat."

Her gaze flitted to the door, then back to me, and she swallowed. "Lucas . . ."

"Now."

"Look, man," Chris said, stepping in front of her, as if she needed protection from me. *Me.* I was the only one keeping her alive, for fuck's sake. God himself knew *she* wasn't. "She didn't mean any harm. She was just trying to help—"

"Help? This was, in no way, shape, or form a help to me. And if you know what's good for you, you'll back the hell off." I stepped up in his personal space, using all of my extra height on him. "This is none of your goddamn business."

Chris flushed. "I'm not your employee, dickhead, and neither is she. You can't boss us around like—"

Us? Since when were the two of them a *team*? Jealousy, as uncomfortable as it was unfamiliar to me, hit me in the gut. Hard.

"The hell I can't," I growled, needing to get my rage out somehow. I needed an escape, and this was it. Chris, my best friend, my *real* brother, was my outlet for this inner hell I was stuck in. "Watch me."

I started to swing, completely prepared to beat the shit out of him in the middle of the crowded room, when Heidi threw herself in front of him. "Lucas, no. Not here. Too many people are watching."

I lowered my arm, but I didn't uncurl my fist. Breathing heavily, I ignored all the angry words trying to escape. Now was not the time, or place, to unleash them. I glanced around the room. Way too much attention.

I was doing it again. Showing weakness.

And there was nothing I could do to stop it. It was like an unstoppable tornado inside me, wrecking years and years of self-control.

Chris gently moved Heidi out of the way, and she let him. "I'm not the enemy here, and you know it. Neither is she."

I slowly uncurled my fist, my blood pumping through my veins at breakneck speed. My knuckles practically ached with the need to crush bone, but I ignored the primal urge. "Get. Your. Coat."

"Okay." Heidi lifted her chin high. She looked infinitely calm, when I was anything but. "Okay. Come on."

I'd told her not to come. She shouldn't have come. She shouldn't have—

She held her hand out, those soft blue eyes of hers calling to me in ways that no one else ever had. "Come on. Let's go home."

Home. Such a simple word.

Without speaking, I reached for her hand and led her toward the coat area. Several people watched us go, their intent gazes making me itchy, but I didn't look back. No more looking back. It was too late for that. It was too late to keep her hidden and safe from the life I led. And it was definitely too late to make sure she ran for it and stayed alive. Too late to keep her safe from me. It was time to look forward now.

Time to plan.

After I'd helped her into her coat, we walked out into the dark night, and she kept shooting me glances out of the corner of her eye. I ignored them. I wasn't ready to talk about it yet, so I wouldn't. "How did you get here? Is your car here?"

"No. I took a cab." She tugged her jacket closed. "I don't have a car."

I ground my teeth together as I gave the valet my ticket. "You came here alone?"

"Yes."

Yeah. I wasn't gonna touch that one. Not yet, anyway. The fact that she'd ventured out alone, when she knew Bitter Hill was looking for any chance to get to her, was enough to make me want to go all Hulk Smash in my rage. Scanning the shadows for any threat as the valet pulled up, I opened the passenger door and stared her down. Clearly a smart kid, the valet didn't wait for a tip and made himself invisible.

She didn't shy away or avoid my stare. Just slid into the car, her body stiff. After I seated myself behind the wheel and put the car into gear, she buckled her seat belt. We pulled out onto the road in silence, and I'd never been more grateful for the lack of conversation. Checking the rearview for a tail, I stole a quick glance at her. She gripped her purse tightly and stared straight ahead. She looked upset.

Good. She should be upset.

As if she sensed my eyes on her, she broke the silence. "I'm sorry you're angry, but I heard that Tate wanted me to come, to prove that what we had was real, or you'd be held accountable." She gripped her purse tight. "And I didn't want you to be in even *more* trouble over me. God knows I've made enough problems for you."

My lip curled up, and I gripped the wheel so hard my hand hurt. "So you just had to play the part of a hero, huh? You just couldn't resist trying to save me."

She gasped. "I wasn't—"

"Enough." Rage pumped through my veins—hot and fast. I was seconds from exploding, and I didn't want to. Not all over her, damn it. "Just . . . *enough*."

Luckily, she took the hint and got quiet.

I tried to ease my grip on the wheel and failed. How

could I relax when I *knew* that Scotty was going to go after her now with a vengeance? All because she'd had to be a hero and show up at the party. That's what being a hero got you. A target on your back.

Well, screw that.

I wasn't a hero, and I never would be.

"Why are you so angry with me?" she asked. She'd finally stopped staring out the windshield, and focused on me instead. "Is it because I came to the party even though you didn't want me there, or is it because I didn't blindly listen to your orders?"

Gripping the wheel tightly, I silently counted my breaths. *In, one. Out, two. In, three. Out, four.* I would not snap, and I would not lose control. Not with her.

"You can't keep trying to protect me, no matter the cost to yourself, like this," she said. "I refuse to let you do it anymore."

I counted to ten this time, breathing heavily. It didn't help.

"Now you're going to ignore me? Really?" She tossed her purse aside. "How old are we, five?"

When I still didn't answer, she gave up and stared out the window.

By the time we pulled up to my shop, the tension in the air was thicker than oil. I shut the engine off and checked the parking lot for any signs of movement. There was nothing. "We are going directly inside. No talking, just walking."

She glanced over at me, her eyes wide as if she was shocked I'd actually spoken. "Oh, so we're speaking to each other again?"

"This isn't a fucking game," I snapped. "Shut. Up. Get. Inside."

She rolled her eyes and threw her door open, hopping

out in one smooth motion. Gun in hand, I followed her, watching for any threats. We made it inside without attack, but I didn't let my guard down. After locking the door, I went to the window and glanced out. I'd keep watch all night long. It wasn't as if I had any other options now. The bedroom door closed behind me, and I rested my forehead on the cold glass. Thank God she'd decided silence was the better option.

It really fucking was.

What the hell was I supposed to do with her now? How was I supposed to keep her safe, when Scotty knew for a fact now that she was my weakness? Straight ahead, I could see the top of St. Stephen's. It was partially ensconced in fog. Where was "God" now? Where was he when my brother decided he'd be better off without me in his life? And where was he when Heidi had been attacked and I'd had no choice but to save her—and in doing so, gotten her wrapped up in this life?

I looked away from the tower, which would give me no answers and no absolution. The clouds obscured any signs of stars I'd have seen, and I had a feeling we were in for a storm. I hadn't had time to watch the weather in between dodging bullets and keeping Heidi alive, but I could read the skies well enough.

As if on cue, flakes of snow fell from the clouds above.

The bedroom door opened behind me, and I tensed. "Go back to bed."

"I'm not going to bed." She headed across the living room, but I didn't turn around and look. I didn't trust myself to look at her right now. "I'm going to work."

It took me a minute to process the fact that, once again, she was trying to *kill me*. Technically, she was trying to kill herself, but if she died, I'd . . .

It was one and the same.

"You're not going anywhere."

She threw her hands up. "Why not?"

I set my gun down on the table by the door and leaned against it, blocking her only exit. "You just had to go and show your pretty little face at that damn party."

"I told you. They needed to see me." She lifted her chin defiantly, looking as foolishly brave as ever. "*Tate* needed to see me."

Everything I'd been holding back, everything I'd been trying to keep at bay, came slamming out of the dam. There was no stopping it. I slammed my palm against the door. "I don't give a flying fuck what he needed. *I* wanted to keep you safe, and out of this life. And you ruined it."

"By going to one single party," she drawled. "Yeah. Sure. I totally won't be able to resist the lifestyle now. I'll be at every party you ever go to, being a regular social butterfly. Ruining everything with my presence."

I walked into the kitchen and grabbed the whiskey with a shaking hand. Rage filled me more with every single word she said. She was now the prime target for Scotty. It was only a matter of time till he struck.

And he'd strike hard.

"You won't be alive to do that." I flipped the cap off and brought the bottle straight to my lips. After I finished, I slammed the bottle on the counter with so much force that it was a miracle it didn't shatter into a million pieces. "You don't get it. You really don't get it, and that pisses me off more than you could ever know."

She came up behind me and snatched up the bottle. She did the same as me, raising it to her lips and setting it down on the counter. "Dammit, Lucas. I was already in the cross-hairs, thanks to Bitter Hill. How could me going to some stupid party make it any worse?"

"You went to a party where my brother, who is dead set on killing me, was scheduled to attend." I leaned on the counter, scowling at the wall. "You walked up to him, introduced yourself, and let him see who you were."

"Yeah . . ." She blinked. "And?"

"This all started because I wanted to keep you safe," I muttered, shaking my head and laughing. It sounded slightly maniacal. "And you are constantly ruining it. You're trying to get yourself killed, I swear. That's the only possible explanation."

She made a frustrated sound. "You're not making any sense. What does the party have to do with any of—?"

"When I rescued you, I had nothing to gain from it. All my life, I've existed by only doing things that helped me get what I wanted. I was tired of being poor, so I joined up with the Sons of Steel Row. I let Scotty join because it was the easiest way to keep an eye on him. Hell, I went to jail rather than work with the cops because I wanted to stay alive. Everything I've done, I've made the smart decision, the safest decision." I dragged my hands down my face. "And then for the first time, I did something where the cons greatly outweighed the benefits."

She bit down on her tongue or cheek. I couldn't tell which, but I knew she had a habit of doing it when she was thinking really hard about something. "Me."

"Yeah. You." Holding my hands out to my sides, I laughed again. "And if you'd been just a casual fuck, no way I'd let you meet Tate. Scotty knows that. But you didn't. So, darlin', what better way to get me to show up like a lamb to a slaughter than to have you show up to that party? Scotty's gonna know that you're the best way to get to me, since now he thinks you're the most important person to me on this planet."

And he might be right, but I still refused to admit it. Out loud, at least.

It wouldn't do us any good.

"But that's . . . I'm not . . . I'm not your weakness. You've been trying to get me gone since day one." She licked her lips and shook her head. "What you did in that alley, it was just temporary insanity on your part."

I opened my mouth to tell her how wrong she was. To tell her I'd been drawn to her from the first moment I'd seen her. Why else had I gone back to her bar, time and time again? I could drink at home easily enough. I'd gone to see *her*. To be near *her*. It was on the tip of my tongue, all the words I'd been keeping locked inside.

But what good would it do for me to say them?

I shook my head. "It doesn't matter what I really did, or why. It matters how it looks to him. What he believes."

She turned away and took a deep breath. Right before she twisted away, I saw a glimpse of something shadowing her stare, but I couldn't get a close enough look to know what. "That's why you didn't want me to go to the party. Because you knew what Scotty would think."

"Yes," I managed to say.

"Why didn't you tell me that?" She faced me again, her cheeks flushed and her whole body held taut. "Why didn't you just open up and treat me like a partner instead of forbidding me to go like I was a child?"

"Because I didn't want you getting hurt, damn it. I didn't want you showing up and drawing attention to yourself." I looked her up and down, curling my upper lip. "But you did it anyway. You interfered and killed us both."

"You're forgetting one small detail," she snapped.

I raised a brow. I knew she hated it when I did that. "Oh? And what would that be, darlin'?"

"You didn't save me because you cared about me, or because you loved me."

I crossed my arms and leaned against the wall, doing my best to act as if I wasn't seething inside. "And?"

"And . . ." She walked right up to me and tipped her head back, staring up at me without a sign of any emotion whatsoever. "Since there's no love lost between us, if they take me . . . who cares? I can't be used against you if you don't come after me."

"So, after already going to the trouble of rescuing your ass, I'm just supposed to . . . what?" I smirked. "Write you off as a loss? Not give a shit if you're gone and he has you? Pretend I don't know how Bitter Hill treats women, what they could be doing to you? I should just not give a damn? Is that what you're saying?"

She pressed her lips together, not backing down. Usually her tenaciousness made me want her even more, but not this time. This time was different. "I think it's up to you how you feel. Not him. And not me. If you don't care, you don't care."

"Is that what you think of me?" I asked quietly, my chest tightening with each word. This was the closest I'd ever come to admitting I had feelings for her, and it scared the shit out of me. "Do you honestly think I would—*could*—abandon you if you were in trouble?"

She stared at me, not speaking. I stared right the fuck back at her, letting her see me. Really see me. It was about damn time, too. Slowly, she shook her head. "No."

"You're my weakness," I said, dragging my hands down my face. "And now he knows it. He fucking *knows it*, Heidi. You handed yourself over to him on a silver platter. And me, too."

She backed up, shaking her head. "No. I'm not . . . you don't . . ."

"Yes." I locked eyes with her, my chest rising and falling faster than it did after I ran five miles. My heart beat a rapid staccato in my head, drowning out the voices telling me to shut the hell up before I said something I'd regret. "I do."

She covered her mouth. "Lucas . . ."

I stepped closer to her. "Run."

"Run with me." She took a shaky breath. "If you run with me . . . I'll go."

Another step. "No."

"Then *no*."

I grabbed her by the waist and hauled her against me. "Damn you, Heidi. *Damn you*."

And then I kissed her.

CHAPTER 26

HEIDI

Lucas spent all this time warning me off, like I couldn't see what kind of man he was. All the examples of his "self-ishness" were bullshit. He joined the gang to provide a better life for his family. He let Scotty jump in because he thought it would keep his little brother safe. He didn't cut a deal and took the jail time because his loyalty was bone-deep. And now he was hinting that he felt something for me . . . something real . . .

But I didn't believe him.

He was only saying these things—feeling these things—because he'd *saved* me. And now, as a result, he wanted to keep me alive. He was invested in my survival. That was all. My foolish heart might have wanted to attach a deeper meaning to his actions, to believe him when he looked at me as if I *mattered*, but I knew better. He didn't love me. Or want to spend the rest of his life with me.

He'd just done the right thing because despite every-thing, he was a good man.

Just because he kissed me like he couldn't live without me didn't mean he actually couldn't. Just because I wanted more, against all reason and logic, didn't mean *he* did. He spun me so my back pressed against the wall, and growled deep in his throat. His hands roamed all over my body, touching everywhere. Leaving trails of fire in their wake. His tongue danced with mine, and I lost myself in him. As usual.

But in the back of my mind, even as he made me cry out in pleasure, was the pain that, this thing we had going between us? Yeah, it was dead.

It had been since the moment I'd called him Lucky in my bar.

Tears stung the backs of my lids. After what I'd seen at that party, there was no doubt in my mind that this whole Mexican standoff he and his brother had been stuck in was about to end. And it would end in a haze of bullets and blood. Maybe our blood. I could only hope it ended with Lucas still standing, because if it didn't . . .

I didn't know how I'd go on.

In the short time we'd been together, he'd woven himself into my life, into my heart. He'd made me realize that when it came to certain aspects of my life, I was still a dreamer. Last night, I'd dreamt about him and me. And we'd been happy. *So* happy. I'd dreamt about us making dinner in a normal kitchen, in a normal house, and we'd been leading a normal life. He'd come up behind me and kissed my neck, wrapping his arms around me and hugging me close, as if he never wanted to let me go. Despite the fact that I knew it was a dream and it would never be anything more, I couldn't shake the feeling that . . .

We could have been *happy*. In a different life, we really could have been.

He gripped my pants and yanked them down to my ankles, his hand immediately dipping between my legs to cup me. The second he closed his fingers over me, I moaned. The things he did to me . . . they were crazy. And addicting. And oh so dangerous.

Just like him.

He let go of me and undid his trousers, letting his pants hit the floor, too. Breaking the kiss off, he dropped to his knees in front of me. Gripping my hips, he stared at me. He'd never looked more vulnerable than he did now, kneeling at my feet. "I'm sorry I yelled, sweetheart. I'm sorry I got you in this mess, too."

I'd never get sick of the way he said *sweetheart*. He could tell me the world was ending, but as long as he added on that *sweetheart*, his voice jagged on that second syllable, I wouldn't even care. And that was the God's honest truth, right there. "I know. It's okay."

"No, it's not." He pulled my panties down. "But I know how to make it better."

He closed his mouth on me, not wasting a second before blowing my mind. He cupped my butt from behind with his big hands, holding me where he wanted me. I collapsed against the wall and let out a long, strangled moan, burying my hands in his thick hair. Lifting my leg, I rested it over his shoulder and rolled my hips in a figure-eight pattern, needing him to send me to heaven for a few minutes. Needing him to make me forget everything that had happened, and everything that would still happen.

I needed to forget it all, just for a second.

He scraped his teeth against my already sensitive clit, his tongue rolling around me in wide, sweeping circles. My breathing came faster, and I fisted my hands in his hair, pushing him even closer to me. It still wasn't close enough, and it never would be. "Lucas, *oh my God*."

He deepened his strokes, thrusting a finger inside me at the same time. Stars burst in front of me, and I came explosively against his mouth. Growling, he spun me so my ass was in the air and gripped my hips from behind me. After a few moments, he pressed his erection against me, right where his lips had been earlier, and I came again, even harder than before. Grunting, he gripped my hair and pulled my head back tenderly.

His mouth pressed to my ear, and he nibbled on it. "I love fucking you with my mouth, darlin'. Love the way you taste when you come, and those breathy little cries you make. I love—" He cut off, his grip tightening in my hair. "I could live the rest of my life with my head between those creamy thighs of yours and die a happy man, but right now? I need to fuck you."

I nodded. "Yes. God yes."

He plunged inside of me with one long, hard hit. My nails scraped over the countertop, searching for purchase, but I came up empty. He gripped my hips and moved inside of me, each stroke harder than the last. I arched my back and pushed against him, straining to get even closer to him.

"Heidi." His hips moved faster, and he moaned. "You're gonna kill me."

I cried out, the pressure building inside me until it boiled over. And the second it did, he was there with me, his body tensing as he came, too. Breathing heavily, he collapsed against me, but he didn't crush me between him and the counter. "Lucas . . ."

"I know." He kissed the top of my head. "Believe me. I know."

We stayed like that for a short time, him holding me close, till he swept me up without a word and carried me into the bedroom. His pants were stuck on one ankle, so it was almost comical. Almost. Instead, it felt bittersweet. Gently, he laid me on the left side of the bed and pulled the covers over me.

Yanking his shirt over his head, he threw it on the floor. He stood there, gloriously naked, and I couldn't stop staring at him. I would never get sick of looking at him. Admiring those tattoos, and muscles, and—

Oh my God, were those *freckles* on his shoulder?

"What?" He glanced down at his shoulder. "What's wrong?"

"Are those"—I got up on my knees and crawled over to him. He watched me, his chest rising and falling as I got closer—"freckles?"

He covered his shoulder immediately, his cheeks slightly flushed. "Yeah. Why?"

"I want to see them." I tugged his hand down, and he let me. Reaching out, I traced the pattern of his freckles. They were in the shape of . . . of . . . "Is that a star?"

His cheeks turned even redder. "Yeah. Ma always said it was a sign I was destined to be a star. She was obviously wrong."

I drew the star on his shoulder. I hadn't known the significance before, but he had a matching star tattoo on his other shoulder, right above his piercing. A memorial to his mother. The love I had for him, pure and strong, punched me in the chest. It choked me, catching in my throat, but I swallowed it down. "Your mother was a very wise person."

"No. She was wrong. I'm not a star; I'm a criminal." His Adam's apple bobbed. "She's dead, and Scotty wants me dead, and if I'm not careful, you'll be dead, too."

My heart twisted. "Lucas—"

"Don't." He ruffled his hair and let out a long sigh. "Just don't."

I wanted to argue, to beg him not to shut me out again, but what was the point? As real as all this might feel to me, it wasn't real to him. He didn't want to open up to me, and any connection I felt was one-sided. He reminded me of the fact that this was temporary enough times to get *that* point across. "Are you going to run off to work on cars again?"

He lifted a shoulder. "I should. I think best when I'm alone, when my hands are busy and no one talks to me."

"Is that why you only work on them in the middle of the night, when no one else is there?"

"No. I only work on them in the middle of the night when no one else is there because I'm not actually a mechanic." He stepped out of his boxers and stretched. Every lean muscle of his taunted me. "But if I was, I'd still want to work alone. I do everything best when I'm alone." He shot me a smirk. "Well, minus one thing, anyway."

I rolled my eyes and snorted. "Wow. Smooth." I faced the wall and curled up on my side. I didn't want to watch him leave me again, even though I'd never expect anything else from him. "Have fun with your cars."

He sighed. "Good night, sweetheart."

"Night," I murmured.

Closing my eyes, I waited for him to walk away. To do what he did best, to retreat behind a wall of loneliness and ice. So when he cursed, and the bed dipped under his weight . . . I almost missed it. He lay down beside me, pulling the blanket over himself, too. He rubbed his cheek against mine. "You can relax, sweetheart. I don't bite . . . hard."

I held my breath, sure if I breathed, he'd remember I was here and leave. But he didn't. He pulled me into his arms and curled his body around mine. I still didn't move. Instead, I lay there, blinking at the wall. I'd never been so shocked to have someone touch me before. I forced my muscles to chill the hell out. ". . . What are you doing?"

"Um." He chuckled, the sound innately sexy as hell. "Last I checked, but don't quote me on this, it's called 'spooning.' I believe it's what people do when they sleep together. I've never done it before, but I figured I'd give it a go." He rolled his hips against my ass, his erection brushing against me insistently. "Turns out, it feels good."

I laughed, too. "Well, yeah. But why are you doing it with *me*?"

"Because we fucked, and now I'm tired, and this is my bed, too." He nipped at my shoulder. "Though this position isn't exactly conducive to sleep, is it?"

A moan escaped me. "Not when you're doing that."

His hand slid down the curve of my hip and slid inside my thighs. "Damn. You feel good, darlin'."

"Lucas . . . ," I whispered, my voice breathy.

"Don't make this into something huge." His hand stopped its descent. "I'm just sick of sleeping on the couch."

Glancing over my shoulder, I tried to read his expression, but it was too dark. "I can sleep out there, if you want."

"I don't want that." His arms flexed around me, holding me even closer. "You know why I'm here tonight," he said gruffly. "I'm not gonna fucking say it."

But, God, I wanted him to. I wanted to know if what he was saying was what I wanted him to say—or if this was just one moment of bliss before we parted. Because my gut told me it was the latter, as much as I might hope it was the former. Despite the doubts plaguing me and the questions running in circles in my mind, I snuggled in closer, hiding my smile in my pillow, and went to sleep.

CHAPTER 27

LUCAS

Warm, naked skin was pressed against me, and an arm was thrown over my chest. If I wasn't mistaken, a leg was over mine, too, and it felt like I'd died and gone to heaven. The Saturday-morning sun shone through the curtains, warming my bare shoulders, and the slight hint of a peachy scent teased my senses.

Smiling, I kept my eyes closed, enjoying this once-in-a-lifetime experience for what it was. It was the only slice of normalcy I'd ever get.

While it had been a mistake to spend the night with her, I didn't give a damn. I didn't have much longer with her in my arms, so I'd decided to live life for once, instead of just surviving it. I'd decided to see what all the fuss was about and slept with a woman curled up in my arms. Turned out, sleeping with a woman was . . . nice.

Better than nice.

But it was daytime now, and it was time to find my brother and end this, one way or the other. And to do that, I had to make sure Heidi stayed out of my way and out of danger. I skimmed my fingers over her bare arm, and she made a soft sound in her sleep, burrowing closer to me. My smile widened.

I couldn't help it.

She felt *good*.

Run with me. If you run with me . . . I'll go. My heart picked up speed as her words replayed in my head for the millionth time. Ever since she'd spoken them, those blue eyes of hers shining at me with so much emotion it had choked me, I hadn't been able to get them outta my head. Hell, I'd even dreamt about them. *Run with me. If you run with me . . . I'll go.*

It was the one solution I'd refused to accept.

The one solution I'd ignored, because I didn't fucking run.

It wasn't me. But with her . . . could I do it? Take one of life's ultimate challenges and turn a guy like me into a law-abiding citizen. Start a mechanic shop and try life on the legal side of the tracks. But could I really *be* that guy? Could I—

The downstairs door to my apartment opened slowly.

I stiffened, every nerve in my body awakening at the sound of the creaking hinge, keeping my eyes shut in case someone was watching me already. Sliding my hand under my pillow, I felt around for my pistol . . .

And then remembered I'd set it down by the door while fighting with Heidi last night. I still had the one Chris had given me, but that meant I'd left a weapon out there. A weapon that could be used *against* me, instead of *for* me. "Shit," I muttered.

"Hm?" Heidi asked, stirring beside me. "What's—?"

I slammed my hand down on her mouth, and she came to with flailing arms. One managed to clock me on the side of the head before she finally focused on me. The second she did, I held a finger to my mouth in a *shh* gesture and cocked my head toward the door, hoping she'd get the message. She looked terrified, but she nodded.

I lowered my hand and whispered, "Get under the bed. *Now.*"

She didn't argue with me. Within a second of my command, she threw the covers off and crawled under my bed, wearing nothing but a shirt she must've pulled on during the night. I wore nothing at all . . . and we were under attack.

I never should have let my guard down.

Making sure to move silently, I rushed to my nightstand and pulled out the loaded Glock I kept hidden there. My pulse raced, and adrenaline pumped through my veins. Looked like I didn't have to find Scotty after all. He'd found me.

"Whatever you see or hear, don't come out." I stepped into a pair of sweats. The last thing I needed was my cock hanging out as I fought for our lives. I glanced down at the floor. There was no sign of her, but I knew she was under the bed. "Not even if they kill me in front of you. Got it?"

She peeked her head out, locking eyes with me. I saw so much in hers that it made me even more determined to get the hell out of here alive . . . no matter the costs. I saw my fucking future. My life. My past. It was all there, staring back at me. For the first time in my life, I truly, fully, completely regretted something.

I regretted not running with her when I had the chance.

"Lucas . . . ," she whispered.

"Don't. Come. Out." I tipped my head. "Now, get back under."

She nodded and slid back under the bed as far as she could go. "Be careful."

I tightened my grip on my gun, sent a quick prayer upstairs in case that God everyone always talked about actually gave a damn, and crept to the door. Heart racing, I plastered myself against the wall next to it, gun held at the ready.

The second they opened it . . . I'd be on them.

With any luck, I'd have the element of surprise since they'd expect me to be asleep in bed. Footsteps crept up to the door, and hushed whispers came through the door. The knob jiggled, and then the door flew open. A man came bolting through it, gun raised, so without hesitation, I pulled the trigger. Blood sprayed all over my face and splattered all over the wall behind the first bastard trying to kill me today.

I didn't have time to check and see if I knew him, because there were more.

Before I could get off another shot, a fist connected with my temple. My vision blurred, and I cursed under my breath. I stumbled back and lifted my arm again. Too late.

At least two hundred pounds of pure muscle launched itself at me, and I hit the floor hard. My head knocked into my dresser as I went down, stinging like a bitch, but I didn't have time to cry over shit like this. I had to *fight*. Lifting my gun, I managed to get a shot off, but the man on top of me lunged to the side at the last second. My vision was even more blurred from the hits I'd taken, but I didn't let that slow me down.

I couldn't.

A fist hit my stomach, and I fought the nausea trying to take over me. I struggled to get a lock on the man attacking me, but my damn vision wouldn't cooperate. At the last second, I saw black metal pointed at me, and kicked at it with a curse. My bare foot connected with bone and metal, and it skittered across the floor to the foot of the bed.

Toward Heidi.

From my position on the floor, I had a second to meet her stare directly, but that was all I had. She was still hidden, covering her mouth to stifle any sound she might make, and still safe. Lifting my gun, I fired off another shot. This time, I didn't miss. The fucker hit the floor, convulsing and choking on his own blood.

I rolled to my feet, gasping in a deep breath and pressing a hand to my stomach. Jesus Christ, this had to be hell on earth. Fighting not only for my own life, but for the life of the woman I loved. How could I—? Wait, *what*?

Maybe that fall had affected more than my vision.

My ears rang from the gunshots, and I blinked rapidly in an attempt to clear my vision and my brain. I was nearly certain I had a concussion, and the dizziness was as unwelcome as it was dangerous. As were my inner thoughts, so I shut them the fuck down. But still, all I could hear was the thumping of my racing heart, echoing in my head. A quick glance confirmed what I already knew.

Neither of these men was my brother.

But I recognized them . . . even though my bullets had blown their heads apart. They were two of the Bitter Hill guys from Heidi's bar the other night, George and Patrick. Where George and Patrick went, Phil went, too. There was at *least* one more guy out there, waiting to pounce. I'd have to pounce first.

It was the only way we'd get out of here alive.

I lifted my gun and crept toward the door. I didn't hear anything from the living room, but the pounding of my heart told me I wasn't safe yet. I'd always trusted my instincts when it came to shit like this, and I wasn't about to stop doing so now, when they had never failed me before. Ignoring Heidi in case anyone was watching, I tiptoed through the door and peeked out into the living room.

No sign of anyone, but I knew he was there. The second I stepped through the door, someone pressed the business end of a gun to the back of my head. The asshat had been hidden against the wall, just like I'd been. And I'd fallen for it.

"Freeze, fucker," he commanded, his tone as mocking as mine would have been, had the roles been reversed.

I did. He was behind me, holding a gun to my head, so for now, he had the advantage. I wouldn't let that last for long, though. The stakes were too high. I had to win, or die trying. And if I died . . . Heidi died. That wasn't acceptable.

"Don't even blink. Gun up."

"Phil. How nice of you to come play," I said slowly, holding my hands out but not relinquishing my gun. "I was wondering when I'd get to reunite you with your buddies."

"Face the window."

I turned toward the window. "You want to let me watch the bright blue sky as you shoot me?" I sighed. "Wow. I hadn't taken you for a sentimental guy. Maybe I'll be nice when I kill you, too." I paused, as if thinking about it. "Then again, I never was any good at being nice."

"You're gonna kill me?" Phil asked, laughing.

I nodded once. "Yep."

"I'm not the one with a gun to my head," Phil said, sounding out of breath already, when he hadn't even done a damn thing yet. He pressed the barrel into the back of my head even harder, twisting it, managing to find the spot I'd slammed into the dresser. It hurt like a bitch, but I clenched my jaw to keep any telltale signs of weakness from showing. "And you're already bleeding."

"What? That?" I chuckled. "That's just a scratch. You want to see blood, look at your buddies. They're ruining my hardwood floors with all that brain matter."

Phil growled. "Shut the fuck up."

"I'll tell you what. How about I give you one chance to run for it. I'll count to three, and once I finish, if you're still here, I'll blow your brains out and ruin my floors out here, too." I grinned. "Don't worry about it. I know a guy who can get the stains out."

The gun shoved in the back of my head wavered. "Go to hell."

"Gladly. One."

"Stop it," Phil warned, the gun wavering even more. "Stop counting."

"Two." I tensed, ready to whirl and hoped to hell that Phil wasn't quick enough to fight me off. It was all I had going for me. "Th—"

"Three," Chris said, his voice loud in the silence of the room.

"Chris." Relief hit me, hard and fast, and my knees threatened to give out on me. After all this tension and fear, my blood brother had swooped in to save the day. I wasn't fighting alone. "Thank God. Kill this little shit."

Chris laughed. "Yeah . . . I can't exactly do that. I kind of hired him."

"What do you . . . ?" I curled my hand that wasn't holding the gun into a fist, unable to believe what I was hearing. "You hired him."

It wasn't a question. Not really.

"I did." Chris laughed again, walking closer. His steps were slow. Unhurried. *Steady.* "Oh, right. Surprise. Your brother isn't trying to kill you. I am."

My stomach rolled into a tight ball. A bird flew by the window, singing a cheerful song, and I wanted to fucking shoot it. Because the one man I'd trusted was going to be the one man who brought me down. He knew all my secrets. Knew saving Heidi hadn't been an act of kindness. He *knew.*

And if he'd found Heidi . . . *Please, no.*

But he couldn't see my fear. Couldn't see me panic. I uncurled my fist, one finger at a time, and forced myself to relax. "So all that shit about Scotty?" I asked, keeping my voice neutral. "You made it up?"

"Yeah." He leaned against the wall, crossing his ankles and looking as if he didn't have a care in the world—even though he'd just blown mine to pieces. "Scotty has no idea what's going on, and it'll stay that way."

I swallowed hard, my stomach still threatening to eject its contents, and tried to figure out the big picture. If Chris had been plotting to kill me along—and he clearly *had*—then why were we standing here, shooting the shit? Why wasn't I lying on the floor with a bullet in my brain? "Why?"

"The original plan was to convince you to kill your brother. I would, of course, be there with you. The second you pulled the trigger, I'd pull mine. I'd go back to Tate, tell him you were working with the police and killed your own brother in cold blood before I could stop it. I'd be the hero. And you'd be dead, like you should have been long ago."

"Wow." I swallowed hard. "That's pretty fucking cold, man."

Chris lifted a shoulder. "It never should've been you."

"What shouldn't have been me?" I slowly rotated a little to the left. "The—?"

"Don't even think about moving another inch," he snapped. "I know all your tricks, brother."

"Brother." I snorted, rage finally taking over the shock that had punched me in the throat. "Fuck you. You're not my brother."

"Ouch. That almost hurts." Chris stared down at Heidi's purse, a smirk taking over his face. My other gun sat on the table behind him. "You shouldn't have gotten promoted, or even gotten in the gang. If I'd known then that you'd swoop in and take my position from me, I'd have shot you as a kid."

I forced myself to smirk. "As if you could. You never could beat me."

Chris's face flushed, and he stepped closer, anger and jealousy coming off him in thick, tangible waves. It made me wonder how I'd missed it before—the jealousy. "Funny, because I'm winning now. When my original plan didn't work quickly enough, I had to come up with a new one. I couldn't risk you talking it out with Scotty and realizing it was me who wanted you dead."

I refused to ask him what his new plan was. I wouldn't give him the satisfaction. "I fail to see how that means you're winning."

"That's because you didn't even see the fourth guy come in."

Fourth guy? Shit. I clenched my jaw, knowing the answer to my question but playing along anyway. "Where is he?"

"He was retrieving something for me while Phil distracted you with the pretty view of Boston you've got there." Chris cocked his head. "Bring her out, Tom."

I stiffened, knowing what I was going to see and hating it. Hating that it had come to this. The second I'd found out it was Chris, not Scotty, who wanted me dead, I'd known how this would end. He knew too much.

I should have run with her last night. Should have run, to keep her safe.

I'd do anything to keep her safe, damn it.

And Chris knew it.

The man I'd let live the other night came out of the bedroom, one arm clenched around Heidi's throat way too tightly, and the other holding a gun to her head. She had both hands wrapped around the man's forearms, and stumbled forward as he nudged her with his knee. He laughed and pressed his lips to her forehead. "Easy. Wouldn't want you to get hurt . . . yet. Not before we finish what we started the other night."

"My, my." Chris grinned and dusted his hands off. I knew that grin all too well. It was the one he'd always worn right before he did something that would get him, and *me*, in trouble. "Welcome to the party, doll. Good of you to join us.

Please contain yourself, and save the begging for your lives for later."

She glanced at me, then back at Chris. Her lip was swollen, and blood trickled out of the corner of her mouth. They'd *hit* her. "Go to hell," she snarled. "I don't beg."

"Let go of her right now," I said, my tone deceptively quiet. Rage hit me hard, slamming into my chest and stealing my breath away. "And I'll let you—oh, who the hell am I kidding? I'll still fucking kill you."

I swung my gun toward the man holding Heidi, but Chris sprang into action. I pointed my gun at him immediately, ready to find out who the hell could shoot the fastest, but he didn't threaten *me*. No, he pointed his gun at *her*. "Easy. If you shoot me now, I'll still fire as I go down. And so will Tom. And let's not forget the gun held to your head by dear old Phil . . ."

I blinked. Blood ran into my eyes, stinging, blurring my vision even more. "I don't give a damn. It'll be worth it."

"You might not give a damn about yourself." Chris stepped closer to Heidi. "But you care about her. You care about her so much that you'd die to keep her safe, and we both know it."

I didn't look at her. I couldn't afford to. "You're wrong. She's nothing to me."

"Oh?" He tsked. "Tom. Go ahead and taste the goods, since he doesn't give a shit."

"Gladly." He lowered his hand and cupped Heidi's breast, squeezing cruelly. "I've been waiting a long damn—"

Heidi squirmed, struggling to get free. Her hair fell in front of her face, obscuring her. "Get your hands *off* me."

The nausea hit me even harder. And the rage . . . oh fuck, the rage. I tried to keep my cool, but it was impossible with that little shit threatening my woman. I stepped forward, but the man behind me clocked me on the head. "Don't move again," he warned, "or I'll shoot you in the leg."

I'd forgotten all about that little shit. I'd been too busy watching Tom asking to be killed. Slowly. "Touch her again, and I'll cut your hands off."

Tom grinned and squeezed her breast again. "It'll be worth it. These are some fine tits. I'll—"

That was it. He was *dead*.

"Enough, Tom." Chris flexed his jaw, looking uncomfortable for the first time since he'd announced his betrayal, and headed across the room. "That's no way to treat a lady."

Heidi lifted her chin, those blue eyes of hers blazing with so much strength and courage that I wanted to cross the room and kiss her . . . before hiding her. "As if you know how to treat one?"

"Oh, but I do." Chris caressed her chin, and Heidi flinched away. His back was to me, which was a bold move on his part. Cocky, too. Like always. "It should have been me who saved you that night. God knows he doesn't know what to do with a woman like you. If he did, you wouldn't be here right now."

"Go to hell," she snapped, spitting in his face.

Chris laughed and swiped his forearm across his cheek. "I gotta say, I love that feisty spirit of yours. It would be so much fun to break it . . ."

I swallowed back the curses trying to escape. "Touch her, and I'll kill you so slowly you'll be crying for your ma like you did that time you fell out of the tree."

Chris snorted. "As if you could." Then, to Heidi, "Easy, doll. I'm not gonna hurt you. Just your lover . . . as long as he's a good boy and does what I say."

She glanced at me. She looked terrified now.

Because they'd threatened *me*?

No one was watching me besides the man behind me, so I took a calculated risk. They hadn't killed me yet, so Chris obviously had some elaborate plan B. Something that would make it look as if he had nothing to do with this mess. And Heidi was part of it . . .

Just like I was.

Slowly, I turned my gun and aimed. The man behind me didn't even notice. I took a deep breath and steadied my hand. I couldn't be even a fraction of an inch off, or Heidi would die. Inhale. Exhale. *Boom*. I squeezed the trigger, and Tom stood there for a second, not moving, before the gaping hole in his head spurted blood.

Heidi screamed and covered her ears, and Tom collapsed back into my bedroom. For a second, time held still. No one moved. Not even Chris. "Heidi! *Run!*"

Then everything exploded, because Heidi ran for the door. Chris chased her, and I whirled to fight the man behind me, who still stared at his dead friend stupidly. Lifting my gun, I squeezed the trigger—and nothing happened. *"Shit."*

The click of the empty gun firing jerked the fucker out of his trance, and he snapped to attention. I tossed the useless gun aside, cursing Chris for giving me a gun without a full mag and myself for not taking the time to reload. Phil clocked me in the temple with his gun . . .

And the world blackened.

When I came to again, blinking against the pain wrecking my head, Phil held a gun to Heidi's head and Chris stood over me, arms crossed. Heidi held herself stiffly, her gaze locked on me intently, as if she was terrified I might not wake up at all. It probably would have been better if I hadn't.

Whatever these guys had planned for us . . . it wouldn't be good.

When Chris saw me come to, he straightened and smiled. "Ah . . . Sleeping Beauty awakens."

Heidi sagged against Phil, her pale face gaining a little bit more color. But not enough. I rose onto my elbows, taking in the scene. The three dead bodies hadn't been moved, but there was a chair sitting next to me. And my gun was still on the table by the door. It was almost in reach, too. "You don't have to do this, Chris."

"Ah, but I do." He smiled a chilling smile. "If you want something, you have to take it. You can't wait for someone to give it to you. It's the only way to get what you want out of this miserable life. You taught me that."

"Bullshit," I snapped. "You want something, you need to *earn* it."

"Nah. It's more fun to take it." Chris pointed his gun at Heidi. She glared back at him. "And now, I'm gonna take it from you. And you're gonna give it to me."

I sat up and pressed a hand to my throbbing head. Chris frowned, watching me for any signs of a threat. He kept his gun pointed at Heidi, and so did Phil. "What's the plan here? How are you hoping to pull this off?"

"The job should've been mine, Lucas. I was here, putting in the time, *earning* it. But then you waltz back in, after years away, and steal my promotion. So you need to die. With you gone, I'll finally get the position I should have gotten all along."

I laughed and ran my tongue over my split, dry lips. All I could taste was blood, but I didn't give a damn. "The hell you will. Scotty will, dumbass. He's my brother, and I'm not gonna shoot him like you'd hoped."

A crazy light lit his brown eyes. "You don't need to anymore." Chris walked around Heidi and Phil, looking completely evil. He didn't even look like the boy I'd grown up with anymore. I didn't know this man. Not anymore. "You're going to walk over to that table, real slow, and sign this will that I so kindly typed up and had the notary stamp. It says that you're leaving everything to me—your blood brother—including your position. Heidi will witness the transaction, sign it, and then . . . well, you know what comes next. You fought off Bitter Hill as long as you could, but in the end . . . you failed. With your endorsement from beyond the grave, Tate will have to give me the job."

I looked at the chair he'd set up. Sure enough, there was a pen and a piece of paper, too. "Not gonna happen. I'm not signing anything."

"Yeah, you will." He stopped next to Heidi. "You'll do it, or I'll kill her, right here. Right now. In front of you. And you know I will, too. But if you do it . . . she lives."

"Let her go first. She can sign it and leave," I said quickly. "Then I'll do it."

"Yeah . . . not a chance." Chris snorted. "I'm not an idiot. You just want her gone so you can kill us both without risking her life."

"You're wrong." I struggled to my feet. Chris watched me closely but didn't tell me to stay on the floor. "I don't want to kill you at all. Why do you think you're still alive?"

He laughed. "Because I'm the one with all the guns."

"Keep telling yourself that," I said, forcing a smirk even though it hurt like hell. "I don't want to kill you. I didn't even want the job. As a matter of fact, you can have it. No killing necessary. Just let us go, and you'll never hear from us again. We'll leave Boston. You'll live the life you think you want so badly."

"I'm not the one whose life is in danger." Chris straightened. His confident smile wavered. "It's over. I've won."

"Am I dead?"

Chris's jaw tightened. "No."

"Then it's not fucking over." I held my hands up and took another step. I was one step closer to my gun now. One step closer to getting Heidi and me out of this mess alive. "But it doesn't have to end that way. Just let us go. Let us run."

"What? You'd give it all up, all that *power*, to be normal? Scrambling around, trying to make ends meet, poor and powerless and alone? Go back to the way you grew up?" He gestured toward Heidi with his gun. "Live a normal, *boring* life?"

I curled my hands into balls. Heidi watched me closely, one eye swollen shut, and blood still trickling from the cut by her mouth. Tears ran down her face, and she'd never looked more terrified than she did now. Because of me. I had to fix this.

And for the first time, I knew without a doubt what my answer would be.

"Yes. I would run away from here forever, so long as I was with her, and we'd never look back." I locked eyes with Heidi. "I'd live any kind of life to be with this woman, and be the luckiest bastard alive, poor or not, if she'd have me."

CHAPTER 28

HEIDI

I swallowed past the aching lump in my throat. He'd said those words so passionately, so realistically, that for a second . . . I believed him. But I was so conflicted. I'd asked him to leave with me numerous times, and each time he'd rejected the idea. It had to be a ploy, to throw Chris off-balance, to give Lucas an opportunity to attack.

Chris laughed. "Damn. Most guys come out of lockup mean sons of bitches. But not you. Look at you, a pussy-whipped little bitch."

Lucas cracked his knuckles, his face flushing with anger. The muscle in his jaw ticked, his telltale sign of being pissed off. For once, it wasn't directed at me. "Call it what you want. All that matters is that neither of us has to do something we'll regret."

"Nah." Chris shook his head. "I'm not buying it."

Just like I didn't buy that if Lucas signed the papers, and I witnessed them, I'd walk out of here without another scratch. We were both dead, unless Lucas did the killing first. But even after all this, and after seeing the lengths Chris had gone to . . . Lucas hadn't shot him. I was sure he could've. But he hadn't.

He was looking for a way to end this that didn't involve Chris never seeing the light of day again. When he'd been on the floor earlier, lying motionless and pale, I'd gone through an emotional roller coaster of grief and fear. And when I'd thought he might be dead . . . I'd died.

The pain and fear had crept into my heart, grabbed hold, and hadn't let go.

Which was exactly why his words hurt so much.

I *wanted* them to be true. I *wanted* him to want me. Need me. Love me. But I just couldn't believe him. Even last night, when he'd pulled me into his arms in bed, he'd warned me not to read into it too much. I'd listened. I wouldn't stop now.

"It's the truth. Right, Heidi?" He held my stare before slowly looking to the left. I believed he was telling me to dodge left when he made his move . . . and hoped to hell that I was right. We couldn't afford any miscalculations right now. "Weren't we just talking about how we wanted to get out of here, make the first left we found, and keep driving?"

While I didn't think his plan could possibly work, it wouldn't stop me from trying to help him in any way possible. Licking my sore, raw lips, I nodded. "Yeah. It's true. We were talking about it last night. We were gonna run for it this morning. Start over."

Phil's arm tightened on my throat. "Bullshit. It's a trick. He's going to kill us, just like he killed them. Who'd walk away from this? The Sons own this town and now Lucas is up there at the top."

"Shut up," Chris growled. "I didn't ask for your opinion, nor will I *ever* ask for your opinion."

"No." Phil shook his head, swinging the gun from my

temple to Lucas. "*No*. If you won't kill him, I will. I won't let him get away with—"

No, no, no, no.

I kicked backward, knowing Phil was distracted, and that it was now or never. When he grunted and loosened his grip, I threw myself to the left, like Lucas had wanted. Gunshots boomed over me, and I had no idea who shot whom, or who missed whom, or if Lucas was still alive. I rolled to my knees, my ears ringing, and lifted my head in time to see Phil lunge for me. I cried out and scrambled to my feet. The second I steadied myself and turned around, another gunshot boomed. Phil froze, arm extended toward me. I stumbled back, sure he was going to grab me.

But he made a gurgling sound, spat out blood, and hit the floor. I covered my mouth, watching as his eyes glazed over and all signs of life left him. I couldn't look away. I had no idea if Lucas was dead or alive, or if Chris was about to kill us both, but I *couldn't look away*. No way. I'd just watched a man's soul leave his body.

How had my life come to *this*?

Shaking my head, I stumbled back more, until I hit the wall. Finally, I snapped out of it and scanned the room. "L-Lucas? *Lucas!*"

"Here," he said from the left. "Are you hit?"

I turned my head and found him. He had blood running down his face and it looked as if he'd ripped the stitches open in his arm, but otherwise . . .

He looked uninjured.

Besides the fact that Chris had a gun aimed at him and he was defenseless. And we were both about to die. Yeah, besides that, he looked *great*.

"No." I forced myself to breathe. I'd forgotten how. "You?"

"I'm fine." He looked at me and smiled. Actually smiled,

as if we weren't seconds from being as dead as the guy at my feet. My heart twisted so hard I was sure I would fall over dead, or that I'd been shot in the chest. But I wasn't bleeding out. I was just dying because I knew how this ended. "Four down. One to go."

Chris clamped a hand over his shoulder, which gushed blood. "I'm not going down. You might have shot me, but I'll be walking away from this alive. Sign the fucking will."

They stared each other down, neither one moving. I didn't know what was happening here, but I could feel the energy charging through the room. After what felt like months of silence, Lucas spoke. "You let her walk out of here after she signs it, and then I'll sign. But not till she's clear of here. After that, you can try to kill me. If you succeed, you'll be set. That's the only way you get what you want."

I blinked at him. "*No*. You can't—"

"Yeah. I can," he snapped. "Well? What's it gonna be, Chris?"

Chris didn't answer at first. He stared at Lucas, opening and closing his fist, gun pointed at the man I loved, but otherwise remained motionless. "You seem to think you have some sort of bargaining chip over me. That you're the one with the upper hand. You're not. And I'll prove it."

Aiming at Lucas's shoulder, Chris squeezed the trigger. In what seemed like slow motion, I screamed and threw myself in front of him at the same time as the boom of the shot exploded in the silent room. I didn't think. Didn't hesitate. Didn't even breathe.

I just *moved*.

As I flew toward him, I saw Lucas's face—the shock clearly written across it as I did my best to save his life. As if he couldn't believe I'd do so.

I hit the ground hard, slamming my right shoulder into

the table by the door as I slid. The whole time, I didn't take my eyes off Lucas. I watched him, making sure he didn't fall to the floor with lifeless eyes. He just stood there, mouth wide, and then fell to his knees at my side. "Jesus fucking Christ, Heidi. What the hell are you doing?"

His hands roamed over me, taking in every inch of me, and I finally breathed in. The oxygen filled my lungs, burning, but it didn't matter. He was *alive*.

"Are you hit?" His hands trembled as they ran over me. He didn't come back with bloody hands, and I didn't feel pain, so I was pretty sure the answer was no. "Jesus, Heidi. You can't . . . *Christ*." He hugged me close, his arms strong and steady.

"I'm fine. I'm not hurt." I finally managed to find my voice, gripping his shoulders tight. Then I whispered, "But you need to finish this."

Lucas lunged for his gun, but he was too slow. Chris cocked his gun and aimed right at my head, freezing Lucas midreach. "Do it, and she dies. Right here. Right now. I won't miss this time. And her blood will be on your hands."

Lucas held his hands up, swallowing so hard I saw his Adam's apple bob. He didn't take his eyes off Chris. "I'll sign the fucking papers, okay? Don't hurt her." Lucas picked up the paper and pen. "Sign it, darlin'."

Blinking back tears, I did as I was told, knowing it would be the last thing I ever did. My hand shook so hard that it was barely legible, but I did it. "Lucas . . ."

"I know, sweetheart." He took the pen out of my shaking hands. "I know. And I'm sorry. I'm so fucking sorry." He signed the paper, but his hand didn't waver. After he finished, he set it on the table and pushed me behind him, blocking me with his own body. "You got what you wanted. Let her go. She has nothing to do with this."

Chris smiled. "Told you I'd win. That's what happens

when you care about someone else—you lose. You knew that already, though, didn't you?"

I swallowed hard. "Go to hell."

Chris smiled even wider. "Gladly. But you'll go there first." He pointed the gun at Lucas's head. "Any last words, brother?"

"Fuck you," Lucas snarled. "Those are my last words."

And then he lunged for Chris. The men fell to the floor in a tangle of legs and arms. They moved so fast, both fighting for their lives, that I couldn't tell who was who. A gunshot boomed, and they both froze, neither one moving.

I struggled to my feet, wheezing for air because *I couldn't breathe*. "Lucas! Oh my God, *Lucas!*"

"No one move," a familiar voice said from the doorway. I hadn't even heard him arrive, but apparently he was the one who'd shot the gun. He held it aimed at the pair of men, his grip steady and his eyes locked on them. "Get up. Hands in the air."

Lucas rolled to his feet, hands up. He had another bruise forming on his left eye, and it had swollen shut already. Blood covered his face, and he looked as if he struggled to breathe, but I didn't see any bullet holes in him. "Scotty?"

Chris struggled to stand, looking a lot worse for the wear than Lucas.

He didn't say anything.

"What's going on here?" Scotty asked, aiming for Chris. Well, at least we had someone on our side, and not the other way around. "Give me one good reason not to shoot you in the head, right now."

Chris laughed. It sounded maniacal. "Go ahead. See if I care."

"Why are you here?" Lucas asked. "How did you know . . . ?"

"I didn't." Scotty's finger flexed on the trigger. "I had no idea any of this shit was happening. I was just in the neighborhood and heard the shots."

Lucas stared at Scotty, knowledge in his eyes. Knowledge of what? I wasn't sure. But it looked as if he watched Scotty with . . . with . . . *pride*. And a little bit of fear, too. Lucas wiped away the blood that rolled down across his mouth. "Don't shoot him. He's gonna walk out of here, and so are we. Everyone's walking away alive."

I pressed a hand to my chest, my heart thudding loudly. *"Lucas."*

"I know, sweetheart." He spared me a quick glance, running his gaze over me before turning back to Chris. Picking up the paper, he handed it off. "You're still gonna have to actually fight for this, even with a note, but my position is now yours. I'm dead. Now, get the fuck out of here before I change my mind."

Chris clutched the paper to his chest.

Scotty watched them both, eyes narrowed.

"He'll never play along," Chris said, tipping his head to Scotty. "What's to stop him from telling everyone what he saw here?"

"Nothing," Scotty answered. "You remember that, little fuck—"

"He won't tell anyone," Lucas said quickly, his gaze darting back and forth between his brother and Chris. "Right, Scotty?"

"Damn it, Lucas." Scotty frowned but said, "Fine. Whatever. I'll keep my mouth shut."

Chris shifted on his feet. "But—"

"He said he wouldn't tell anyone," Lucas growled.

Scotty hesitated but nodded. "As long as you stay away from Lucas . . . and Heidi . . . yeah. I'll keep my mouth shut."

"I don't understand," Chris said slowly. "Why are you giving up everything when you could kill me instead?"

"I'm not giving up everything," Lucas said, watching me with warm green eyes. "I'm keeping the thing that matters most, and I don't want more blood on my hands."

My heart wrenched. I didn't know what to say to that, and I wasn't about to question him in front of the other men, so I said nothing.

Chris rolled his eyes. "You can't be serious."

"I've never been more serious in my life," Lucas said, still watching me as if he waited for . . . I don't know. A sign from me? "We'll be gone within the hour. Now, get the fuck out."

Chris nodded and walked to the door. There was a tense moment when Scotty didn't back out of the way, not letting Chris pass, but then he stepped aside, gun still trained on Chris. "One wrong move, and you're dead. You remember that."

Chris nodded, took one final look at Lucas, and then left. The door closed below us. I collapsed against the wall, my heart thudding in my ears faster than a racehorse. "Oh my God. You did it. We're alive."

"Yeah." Lucas set the pen down and turned to me. He pulled me into his arms, those strong muscles I was so familiar with closing around me and hugging me tight, but it didn't stop the trembling. "*We* did it. Together. Thank you, Scotty."

Scotty closed the door and walked to the window, watching. "I didn't do anything. But you guys need to get out of here. He could come back with more guys."

Lucas let go of me. It took all my strength not to cling to him.

"How long?" Lucas asked.

Scotty stiffened. "How long for what?"

"How long have you been a cop?"

"Wait. What?" I asked, mouth open. "Scotty's not . . ." Oh, crap. He totally was. The guilty look on his face said as much. "Oh. Wow."

Scotty dropped his head back on the glass. "How did you figure it out?"

"The way you spoke. The way you held yourself. And the way you lied when I asked how you knew what was going on here." Lucas shrugged. "I put two and two together. Am I wrong?"

"No." Scotty shook his head slowly. "You're not wrong."

Lucas's chest puffed out with pride, but that fear was still there. "If they find out . . ."

"I'm a dead man. I know." Scotty dragged his hand through his hair. "You think I don't know? I don't care. I have to make this town clean again. For Ma."

Lucas staggered back a step but caught himself. "I know."

"Why didn't you rat me out?" Scotty asked. "You could've. Still could."

"I'm not going to do that to you."

I watched them, unable to take my eyes off the two of them.

Scotty dragged his hands down his face. "Thank you."

"I gave Chris the paper so you could keep your cover. If you arrested him, your cover would be blown. You'd be done. And if we killed him, you'd have to answer for two deaths. At least this way, it looks like Bitter Hill attacked, and I lost. Bitter Hill took me, abducted me, and killed me off. Never returned the body. You both saw it happen but couldn't save us. Easy to explain, clear-cut. No one will suspect a thing. You can keep an eye on Chris, and he'll steer clear of you out of fear for what you'll say, or you can kill him off later. But whatever you decide, you better watch your back."

"Thank you," Scotty said, his voice low. His green eyes, which had once chilled me to the bone, looked fraught with emotion now. "I know you thought that I wanted you dead . . . it killed me to let you think that. All I've ever done is try to keep you safe."

Lucas nodded. "I know. Were you really trying to get me in jail again?"

"Yeah. I put you there the first time, too." Scotty scratched his head and shuffled his feet. "But only because I wanted you to be safe. To stay out of trouble. I could keep an eye on you there. Not because I hated you."

The men stared at each other.

When Lucas said nothing, Scotty cleared his throat. "You need to pack. Get to it. I'll keep watch outside."

And with that, he walked out.

We were alone.

Lucas stared at the closed door, not moving. I wrapped my arms around myself, swallowing hard. "It wasn't . . . Scotty didn't . . . We *lived*."

My words seemed to snap him out of his trance. "We lived." He came up to me and cupped my cheek. His touch was so tender, but just seconds ago, he'd been killing men in front of me. He was splattered with blood and God only knew what else, and so was I. "But it's time to get moving, or we won't be alive for long."

I shook my head. "This still doesn't make sense to me."

"I can't live that life anymore. I don't want it. Not now that I . . ." He pressed his lips together, seeming to struggle with words. "We don't have time to talk about this. It's time to pack."

I collapsed into a chair. "Right. Pack."

He was leaving. I'd never see him again. I'd known it would happen, and I'd known it would hurt when he did leave. But I hadn't expected it to hurt *this* much. The threat was over. The Bitter Hill guys who'd been after me were dead, Scotty was actually a cop—which I still hadn't wrapped my head around—and Chris had gotten what he wanted.

Lucas had given everything up to save me.

Everything.

Lucas dug out the envelope full of money from a kitchen drawer and shoved it into a bag, before walking into the bedroom. As he passed me, he frowned. "Move your pretty little ass, darlin'. As soon as Chris gives that will to Tate, there will be people coming here to look for my body, needing to confirm my death. We're done here."

Blinking, I stood up. It hadn't even occurred to me to, you know, leave. He was done with me, and I was sitting here like an idiot, watching him pack up and walk out of my life. As if I'd expected a tender good-bye. A kiss or a hug, or *something*. But no. I got a "Move your pretty little ass, darlin'." Maybe it was stupid, but I really expected something more, after all we'd been through. "O-oh. Right. I'll . . . yeah. I'll get going."

"Good. Don't forget—" When I walked past him and headed for the door, he broke off, blinking. "Wait—where the hell are you going? Just because Scotty's out there doesn't mean it's safe out there. We can hit the bar and your apartment next."

"I know," I said quickly. "You have to go, and I get that. I don't want to slow you down. I need to—wait, the bar and my apartment?"

"You . . ." His grip tightened on me. Something haunted him, something dark and raw and real, but he turned away before I could figure out what. "You want me to go alone?"

"I thought you *wanted* to go alone." I pulled free. "Why would I go with you now? It's over."

"I thought . . ." He cleared his throat and rubbed the back of his neck. "I thought you would come with me. I said those things to Chris and Scotty, and you didn't . . . you agreed."

"Yeah, but you didn't *mean* any of that, right?" I laughed, expecting him to join in and say something cocky like usual. He didn't. "Lucas?"

"I—I don't know how to do this. How to say the shit I

want to say to you, Heidi. I . . ." He dropped his hands to his sides, fisted them, and closed the distance between us. "Fuck it. I'm going all in."

The confusion inside me only increased. "What—?"

He cupped my face in his hands and kissed me.

CHAPTER 29

LUCAS

The second her lips touched mine, I put every single fucking feeling that crashed through me into that kiss. The feelings I didn't understand yet, the feelings that frankly scared the shit outta me, and even the belief that we could be happy together. It was all there for her, laid out as simply as possible, in the form of a kiss.

I knew I needed to say the words, too, but this was a start.

Earlier, in front of two other men, I'd put my heart on the table and let her know just how badly I wanted to be with her. I'd said I wasn't losing because I got her. But now it seemed like I didn't have her, because she hadn't even believed me, and I had to fix that. When she'd said she was going to run with me, she'd made me the happiest man on this planet. I'd thought she actually wanted to be with me. But she hadn't really meant it.

She hadn't even *believed* me.

Heidi moaned into my mouth, her hands clutching at

my shoulders as she twirled her tongue around mine. Breaking off the kiss, I rested my forehead on hers, breathing heavily. Her breaths matched mine. "I know I'm not a good person," I said. "Not even close."

She blinked up at me and pulled back. "Yes. You are."

"No. I'm not." I shook my head. "But you make me better. You make me want to be good. I know I'll fuck it up, and I know next to nothing about life outside of"—I gestured to the dead bodies on the floor—"well, this hellhole. But I also know what it feels like to be with you. And it feels good, sweetheart. You can't stay here, with them. You have to come with me. I *need you* to come with me."

Biting down on her lip, she stepped out of my arms. They'd never felt so damn empty before. "I like being with you, too—"

"Let me finish. I know it's asking a lot, but I want . . ." I gestured between her and me impatiently. "I want this. With you. I want to spend the rest of my life protecting you. Taking care of you."

"Is that what this is?" She blinked rapidly, but she looked less than convinced. If anything, she looked even more skeptical. "Is this just you finding yet another way to keep me safe?"

"You'll never be safer than when you are with me," I argued.

"The thing is, you already gave up everything for me. Walked away from everything you know. Everything you wanted." She gestured at the apartment. "You don't have to spend the rest of your life keeping me safe because you think it's the right thing to do. You did enough for me."

"No." I shook my head. She didn't get it. "Please, darlin'."

She gripped the top of my couch, keeping it as a barrier between us. "Please, what?"

"I'm not asking you to run away with me because I want

to save you, like a hero. I already told you, I'm not one. And I never will be."

"Lucas . . ."

"I'm asking you to run away with me because I *want* that life. And I want it with you. I want it so fucking bad. Run with me, sweetheart. Live a normal life, in the safest town in America, as far away from here as possible. Live in a normal house, with a fence. Plant an ugly garden with me." I stalked across the living room. "I know you can do better than me. I know you deserve better, too. And I know you love that shitty little bar across the street, but you know what? I . . . I . . ."

She let go of the couch, her mouth parted. "You what?"

I swallowed the acrid taste of acid rising in my throat. Was I actually going to do this? Say this sappy shit? Yeah. I was. And I wouldn't regret a single word. "I love you, damn it. So that's why I dare you to run away with me. That's right. I fucking dare you to run."

She gasped. "Wh-what?"

I'd wanted to vomit before I'd said those words, but once they came out . . . damned if it didn't feel amazing. I walked around the back of the couch and yanked her into my arms. She sagged into me, barely breathing. "I love you, okay? You made me realize I wasn't as dead to the world as I thought, and I want to embrace it instead of killing it. I want to live in that little house with you, probably killing lots of flowers, and spend the rest of my life loving you. Making you smile. Making you as happy as you've made me, if that's even possible."

Tears streamed down her cheeks, and she smiled up at me. How the hell did women do that—manage to look both brokenhearted and ecstatic all at one time? "Say it again. I want to hear it one more time."

I cocked a brow. If she was asking me to say it again,

that had to mean one thing. I'd gotten my *yes*. "I love you, Heidi."

She let out a sob and threw her arms around my neck. "I love you, too."

For a second, my arms hung limply at my sides. Not because I didn't want to hug her, but because I was so stunned that she could possibly love me back. She was . . . she was *her*, and I was *me*, but she loved me *anyway*? "You love me?"

She nodded, her face buried in my neck. "I do. I didn't want to admit it for the longest time, but I knew I loved you that night we first made love. You kept telling me not to want you, or fall for you, but it was inevitable. I fell, and I fell hard."

I finally closed my arms around her, hugging her close to my chest. She clung to me, and I stood there for a second, just taking it all in. She'd said she loved me. Really loved me. *Me.* "Yeah, well, you fucking tripped me."

She laughed, pulling back and smiling up at me with shining blue eyes. "We're really going to do this? Run away together and be *normal*?"

She said that as if it was this horrible, dreadful thing, so I couldn't help but laugh.

And I couldn't believe it, either.

"Hell yeah, we are. So hurry up and pack before Steel Row gets here . . . or even worse? The Boys—not counting Scotty, of course." I kissed her forehead. "Even though this is the shittiest section of Steel Row, someone might have called it in."

She nodded and let go of me, but her eyes held on to that sparkle. "Okay, let's do this."

We scrambled around the apartment, packing clothes and computers but tossing the phones in the trash—all while stepping over dead bodies and pools of congealing blood. At one point, she stopped and frowned down at them. "Won't they wonder why your body isn't here, with theirs?"

"Nah. Scotty will take care of it and Chris will play along. He won't have a choice."

"Oh. Right." She smiled at me. "He's a cop."

For the first time since the crazy revelation, I let that sink in. My brother wasn't a bad man at all—he was a *good* one. One with morals and a soul. I'd raised him right. I'd never been so proud of something I'd done before, and I'd never been so proud of him. It scared the shit outta me, knowing he was undercover among a bunch of ruthless killers who skinned cops alive, but still . . .

I was so proud of him.

Ma would've been, too.

"I know." A smile broke out on my face, too. "I didn't fuck him up."

She came over to me, rose on tiptoe, and kissed me. It took all of my control not to hug her close, but we had to get moving. So I didn't. "That's because you're a good man, Lucas Donahue."

For the first time . . . I almost believed her.

The door opened, and I turned to it, gun held at the ready.

Fully reloaded, this time.

"Don't shoot," a voice I recognized all too well called out. "It's me. Scotty. Are you guys ready yet?"

"Yeah." I slipped my bag onto my shoulder, my gun into the holster, and held my hand out for Heidi's. She slid her small, soft hand inside mine and hugged my arm close to her side. We were bloody, bruised, and dirty—but we were *free*. "We're ready."

Scotty looked at our joined hands and the bags on our shoulders. "Not so fake anymore, huh?"

"I don't think it ever really was fake," I admitted. "We're

running, and we're never coming back. I'm . . . I'm gonna miss you."

"I know." Scotty shoved his hands in his pockets. "I'm going to miss you, too. There's one problem, though."

I stiffened. "Yeah?"

"They'll want a body, and so will the cops. You know it. No one leaves this life unless it's by the gun, and they'll want proof." He took his hands out of his pockets. "You have to be dead, and everyone needs to know it. It's the only way you'll be free."

Heidi peeked at me, her cheeks pink. "But how do we do that?"

"There are a bunch of dead bodies in here. Who's to say one of them isn't Lucas's?" Scotty asked.

She snorted. "DNA. That's who. You of all people should know that."

"That's why we have to torch the place and remove any evidence that one of these bodies isn't mine," I said, understanding where he was going.

"Exactly. But even more than that, we need there to be two more bodies."

Heidi blinked. "Us?"

"Yeah. I got in contact with one of my buddies at the morgue, and we're getting two cadavers sent in—a male and a female—so it looks even more real. We'll falsify the dental records so you can escape without anyone questioning anything." Scotty crossed his arms. "You will be, for all intents and purposes, dead. No cops will come looking for you, and neither will Steel Row. CSI will confirm it's you, and you'll be free."

There was that word again. *Free.* "They would do that for you?"

"I got people." Scotty nodded. "So, yeah. They would."

Heidi trembled. "And then we just drive away."

"Yep." Scotty stared at Heidi. "I'll tell Steel Row I saw

you go down in a blaze of gunfire and smoke, which the evidence will corroborate, and hung around to make sure it was you. Chris will back me up because he doesn't have a choice." Scotty lifted a shoulder. "Not if he truly wants the crown."

"I'm proud of you, brother," I said. And I meant every word. "I'll never forget what you're doing for me now. I'll never . . ."

Scotty didn't say anything, but he dipped his chin in acknowledgment.

Emotion swelled within me, but I swallowed it back. He knew I loved him. And now I knew he loved me, too. But I had so many questions. "Why were you meeting with Bitter Hill the other day? I saw you."

"I have a guy in there. He was keeping me informed of Chris's plan. It was all a setup." We walked down the stairs, and he asked, "Where will you two go?"

"I don't know yet." I squeezed Heidi's hand. This whole thing felt like a dream. The best fucking dream ever, and I never wanted to wake up. "We'll hit the road, turn left . . . and just keep going."

"And just keep going," she echoed, smiling.

"Jesus, you two . . ." Scotty made a frustrated sound. "Okay, off you go. I'll take care of this. Go, before someone sees you."

I opened the door of my Mustang for Heidi, and she slid inside. She gripped the handle and looked up at Scotty. "My bar . . . and Marco . . ."

"I've been watching you, so I'll take care of them both."

She nibbled on her lower lip. "He's on his way to Boston College."

"I'll make sure he gets, and stays, there." He rolled back on his heels, and the wind blew his brown hair. "Don't worry about life here. I'll take care of it all."

She sagged against the seat. "Thank you . . . for everything."

"Don't mention it."

"I'll be right in." I closed the door and turned to Scotty. "Make sure there's nothing left."

He nodded. "You know it, man. You're sure this is what you want? That you're willing to walk away from everything you built and fought for, for a woman?"

I glanced through the window. She watched us, her cheeks flushed with excitement as she nibbled on her lower lip. "I've never been more sure of anything in my life."

"Then go." He patted me on the back in that man-hug we all did. "Go be happy. You deserve it. I'll make sure Chris straightens his shit out . . . or I'll have to finish what you didn't."

Not willing to let him leave with a lame-ass hug, I pulled him into my arms and kissed his temple. "I . . . I love you, brother."

He hugged me back, his arms stronger than I remembered them being. "I love you, too. Take this start and make a real life. One Ma would be proud of—because she would be so fucking proud of you right now."

I swallowed past my aching throat. "I hope you're right."

"Oh, I am." He let go of me. "Now, go."

"Okay." I walked around the trunk of the car and tossed our bags in. As I shut it, I nodded at Scotty once, memorizing his face one last time. "You do what you gotta do, man. Just stay alive."

He saluted me. "Always."

"If you ever need me . . . well, find me. I'll be there."

Without answering, he headed back into my apartment. As I settled into the driver's seat, I gripped the wheel tight. Last time we'd been in this car, I'd been so sure we wouldn't walk away from this shit hole alive, let alone together and in love. I kicked the engine into gear. We backed out of the parking spot and drove down the road.

We passed the Laundromat next to her bar and slowed in front of the Patriot. She ducked her head and stared up at it, resting a hand against the cold window, her shoulders hunched. "Good-bye, little bar."

I rested a hand on her thigh and squeezed. "You sure?"

"Yeah." She laid a hand over mine. "I'm sure. Where to?"

"How's Georgia sound to you?"

"Georgia?" She turned to me, her plump pink lips wet and looking way too damn kissable. "Why Georgia?"

"If they see through the whole death thing, no one would ever think to look for two city rats in the country." I smiled. "Plus, you smell and taste like peaches, so it seems fitting."

She choked on a laugh. "I do?"

"Yeah." I slid my hand up her thigh. "Everywhere."

Her cheeks pinked. *"Lucas."*

"Yeah, darlin'?"

"Make a left, and keep driving . . . till we hit Georgia."

"Okay, but first . . ." I curled my hand around the back of her neck and dragged her close. Our lips met, and we smiled as the kiss ended. "Any regrets? It's not too late to go back."

"Keep driving, Lucky." She let out a little laugh. "You're stuck with me, whether you like it or not."

Closing my eyes, I hugged her close and breathed in her scent like air. A scent that I'd never have to stop breathing in. "Oh, I like it. I like it a lot."

We settled back into our seats, and I pulled up to the stoplight. When it switched to green, we smiled at each other, the joy in the car overwhelmingly sunshiny bright. If it had been anyone else, I'd have gagged and told them to go get a fucking room—or better yet, shoot themselves in the head or something equally harsh.

But it was *us*. So I turned left, and just kept driving. Out of Steel Row, out of the city limits, and out of Massachusetts, too. Somewhere around the mountains inside Pennsylvania, I finally let myself believe that this was actually happening.

For the first time in my life . . .

I believed in happy endings, even for a villain like me.

EPILOGUE

LUCAS

One year later
Georgia

I lifted the shovel and slammed it into the rocky soil. The salty sweat rolling down my forehead stung my eyes like a bitch, but I didn't let it slow me down. The sun was shining down on me, and it felt as if it tried to bake me alive, but I didn't give a damn. I had only a few more minutes to get this shit right, and I didn't want to fuck it up.

If Heidi came home too early and caught me, my whole plan would be ruined. I couldn't risk her finding out my secret before I was ready to confess it all to her.

Swiping my forearm across my forehead, I eyed the bagged item I was supposed to bury. This wasn't my usual job, but I was determined to do it anyway. To prove myself, somehow. Bending down, I hauled the item into the hole and spent the next few minutes covering it up with dirt. I stood back, surveying my handiwork. Brown branches extended from the freshly tossed dirt, green leaves bloomed from the stems.

Peach tree . . . *planted*.

Take that, garden.

Striding over to the picnic table we'd built together, I picked up my bottle of water and chugged it back, not leaving so much as a drop behind. The hot sun was trying to kill me, and it was only spring. I knew from experience that it would only get worse.

And we both loved every second of it.

We'd spent the last year trying our best at being "normal," and it turned out . . . we were both a hell of a lot better at it than we thought we would be. I owned a mechanic shop that did a lot of business—though mostly because I was the only mechanic shop in town—and Heidi owned a bar right next door to my shop.

Just like old times, only a hell of a lot better.

She'd called her bar "the Dare."

Once, we'd gotten a card from Scotty. He hadn't written his name, or ours, and he'd mailed it from a different state, but I'd recognized his writing. It had contained a lot of money—from the bar, more than likely—and that was it. Despite the fact that we'd ditched my car just over the Massachusetts border and changed our last names, he'd figured out our location.

How? I had no fucking clue.

But he had, and if anyone was gonna know our location . . . well, I was glad it was him. I trusted him, and so did Heidi. And that was good enough for me.

I'd never been happier.

"Lucas?" Heidi called out from inside the house.

I set my water down. "Out here."

The back door opened and Heidi came out into our fenced-in yard. "Hey, I got home a little early. I thought it would be fun to head out to the movies and—" When she saw the rosebushes—all ten of them—and the peach tree I'd planted, she stopped in her tracks, her jaw dropping. "Oh my God. You planted a garden."

"We kept saying we would have that normal garden in our normal house in our normal town." I gestured to the house. "And we got all of that other stuff, but we never planted our garden . . . until now."

She walked over to the tree I'd planted and touched its leaves. "What kind of tree is this?"

Smirking, I walked up directly behind her. "Guess."

"I don't—" She turned around and gasped.

I stood directly behind her, holding a peach in my hand. Lying on top of the peach was something shiny and bright. I grinned. "It's a peach tree, of course."

"Of—" She covered her mouth with a shaking hand. *"Lucas."*

"I thought of a million fucking ways to do this, you know. In a fancy restaurant, or on one of those ridiculous kiss-me cams at a baseball game, or in bed while naked. I thought of a million ways, and none of them felt right." I dropped to one knee in front of her, peach in hand . . . and my heart, too. "And then it came to me. None of it felt right because that wasn't how it was supposed to go down. A piece of the puzzle was missing."

She laughed and shook her head. "The garden."

"The garden." I offered her the peach. She took it with trembling hands, her gaze locked on the ring on top of it. "I love you, darlin'."

Reaching up, I grabbed her hand in between mine to steady it. Mine weren't trembling, because I wasn't nervous or uncertain. I knew what I was doing, and I was one hundred percent ready. "This is the second smartest thing I've ever done in my life. The first was daring you to run away with me."

She nodded frantically. "Yes."

"And I—" I frowned. Wait. "You can't answer me before I ask you, darlin'."

"You don't need to ask me. And you know that." She fell to her knees in front of me, set the peach down between us, and framed my face, smiling brightly up at me. "But if it makes you feel better, go ahead and—"

"It does," I muttered. "I want to do this the traditional way, damn it."

Her lips twitched. "Go for it, by all means."

"Thank you." I took a breath. "Heidi Greene *Buchanan*, light of my life, love of my heart . . ."

She laughed. "Laying it on a little thick, huh?"

"Darlin'," I teased, kissing her briefly, "you're ruining my proposal."

She mimed the act of zipping her lips.

"I know you deserve better than me, and that I'm not a good man. I'm definitely not a good enough man for you." She opened her mouth to argue, and I pressed a finger to her lips. "Sh. My speech. I get to say what I want, and you're not allowed to argue." I paused, waiting to make sure she'd let me talk. She stayed silent. "But since I know you deserve better, that's why I'm the best man for you. I'll constantly be trying to do better, to be better, because you deserve the best in everything."

"And I have it," she whispered. "I have you. I know you think you're not good, but to me . . . that's all you've ever been. You've always been good to me, for me, and I love you with all my heart. And I love our normal life, and I love this garden."

I grinned so wide my face should have cracked. "Well, then, in that case . . . Heidi Greene Buchanan, will you do me the honor of becoming Heidi Donahue Fischer?"

"Yes. Most definitely yes," she said, kissing me again.

Ending the kiss before I forgot about the ring and left it out here to rot, I picked it up from on top of the peach.

"This was my mother's ring. She asked me to keep it for when I decided to get married. I never thought I'd use it . . . but then again, I'd never thought I'd meet someone like you, either."

She held her hand out. It still trembled. "It's beautiful. Perfect. I love you," she said in a rush. "I love you so much."

Laughing, I slid it onto her finger and helped her to her feet. "I fucking love you, too," I growled in her ear, backing her into the house. "And I'm gonna show you how much."

She clung to me, and our lips melded together perfectly, just like they always had. I'd known, after that first real kiss in my kitchen, that this thing we had going between us was forever. I hadn't recognized the warm feelings she gave me for what they were, but deep down . . . I'd known. And it was why I'd refused to let her go.

Kicking the door shut behind us, I lifted her onto the counter in the kitchen, stepping between her thighs and deepening the kiss even more. She undid my shirt, and within seconds it was on the floor. A minute later, the rest of our clothes were there, too.

I broke off the kiss and stared into her blue eyes, unable to believe that this was my life now. I'd lucked out, won the jackpot in life. Not too long ago, I'd been so sure I'd never be free. That I'd never have the same freedom that everyone else in America had. But . . . I'd been wrong. I'd found that freedom. Heidi was it. And I was hers. I'd never forget that or take it for granted. "I love you, darlin'."

"I love you, too."

She kissed me again, her hands skimming over my chest. When she moved lower, closing them over my cock, I hissed through my teeth and rocked into her hand. She let out that husky laugh of hers that was sexy as hell, her fingers moving over the tip of my cock. "You like that, Lucky?"

"I'm feeling pretty fucking lucky right now, so, yeah,"

I said kissing a path down her body. Her neck. Her collar-
bone. Her breast. When I reached the hard pink tip, I took
it into my mouth, sucking hard and scraping my teeth across
it exactly like she liked it. Letting it go with a pop, I smirked
up at her and knelt so I was head level with her hot, wet
pussy. "How about you? Feeling *lucky*, darlin'?"

Spreading her legs for me, she arched her back and
buried her hands in my hair. "Yes. God yes."

Chuckling lightly, I closed my mouth over her clit, rolling
my tongue over her in wide, light circles. By the time I
reached the third circle, she was panting and clawing at my
shoulders, begging for me to hurry up and *just take her.*

So I moved even slower, of course.

Her hips rocked against my mouth, and I could taste the
sweetness of her orgasm coming, so close it was making
her legs quake on either side of my head. I increased the
pressure just enough to send her flying over the edge, and
thrust two fingers inside of her at the same time. Her walls
clamped down on me, and she stiffened, her mouth forming
that perfect O that never failed to drive me insane.

Growling, I stood and drove inside of her in one smooth
motion. The second I was fully inside of her, she came
again, her screams filling the kitchen and echoing off the
tile floors. I thrust inside of her, again and fucking again,
harder each time. Her nails scraped over my back and my
balls pulled up tight to my body. Everything screamed for
me to finish—to come, too—but I held back.

I wanted more from her.

Tossing her head back, she screamed out in frustration,
closing her legs around my hips and digging her nails into
my shoulders so hard it stung. "God, Lucas. *Please*."

Biting down on her neck, I lifted her slightly and plunged
inside of her, hitting the spot that was guaranteed to make
her come at least three times. She screamed, choked on a sob,

and came, tightening all around my aching cock. Growling, I caught her mouth with mine and kept moving inside of her, hitting the same spot over and over again.

By the time she came down from her second orgasm, I was fucking lost. I needed to reach completion inside of her more than I needed air, or water, or life.

If I didn't have her . . .

I'd be nothing.

I moved my hips faster, grunting as the orgasm took over my entire body, mind and soul. And she joined me, soaring through the clouds one last time before drifting back down to my arms. Burying my face in her neck, I struggled to catch my breath.

It was useless. Around her, I'd always be breathless.

And I wouldn't have it any other way.

She rested her head on my shoulder, sighing and tapping her fingers on my heart. I watched her, the diamond ring glistening in the sunlight that streamed through the windows. She still smelled like peaches. Sucking in a deep breath, I let her sweet scent wrap around me, hugging me close, and that all-too-familiar warmth spread through my veins all over again. Only now I knew what it was called.

It was *love*.

ACKNOWLEDGMENTS

First and foremost, I would like to thank my husband, Greg, for always being there for me. You never doubted that I could get what I wanted, or succeed in this writers' world, and your undying faith in me means everything.

And my kids—Kaitlyn, Hunter, Gabriel, and Ameline— once you're old enough to read these (if you *ever* read these), know that every book I wrote and every word I slaved over, I did it so I could be the best mom I could be. I hope I succeeded in that!

To the rest of my family—Mom, Dad, Tina, Cynthia, MeeMaw, PeePaw, Carole, Greg, Danny, Riley, Connor, Erick, and Ashley—you're all awesome! Thanks for always asking about my career, and what I was working on.

To my friends—Liz, Jay, Cora, Jen, Chelsea, Tiffany, Megan, and so many more of you that it would take twenty pages just to write all your names . . . but you know who you are—thanks for always being there with me at conferences and in real life, to laugh, talk, and hug.

To my agent, Louise, you've never given up on the fact that you would get me exactly where I wanted to be. You told me you would do it, and you did. I'm here, and I couldn't be any more grateful for everything you do for me on a daily basis.

And, Kristin, thank you for being such an awesome editor and sounding board. Without your tireless devotion to my books, I wouldn't have gotten where I am, either. You're always there when we need you, and that's, like, a superhuman power.

And to my editor here at New American Library/Signet Eclipse, Laura Fazio, thank you so much for your love for this book and my writing! It's been such a pleasure to work with you, and I look forward to many more books with you! Ever since we met at RT, I knew it would be a match made in heaven. Thank you for thinking the same!

To everyone at Penguin who has worked or will work on this book, thank you for being such a great company to work with. You all rock!

Lastly, to anyone reading this: *Thank you*. I wouldn't be here without you. I'll see you next time.

Read on for a sneak peek at the next
heart-pounding novel
in *New York Times* bestselling author
Jen McLaughlin's
Sons of Steel Row series. . .

DARE TO STAY

Coming soon from Headline Eternal.

CHAPTER 1

CHRIS

Sometimes you had to take a look at your life—a good, hard, brutally honest look—and admit that somewhere along the way, you fucked up *big-time*. Just as important, sometimes you had to accept that the reason you were in an alley, bleeding and dying behind a busted-up Laundro-mat, was because . . . those choices you made? The screwups, the wrong turns, all the things you wish you could take back?

Yeah. Those were the reasons why you deserved this.

To die alone as violently as you lived.

I turned my head to spit out blood, painting it across the dirty concrete wall next to me, and laughed at the almost smiley face it made, because why the hell not? But my laugh made my aching ribs hurt more than before, so it ended on a groan. Clutching my ribs, I gingerly rolled over and glowered up at the sky. The uneven cement under my back dug into my already aching spine. The docks were nearby, the smell of week-old garbage and rotting rat corpses surrounded me.

The moon was absent tonight, and there wasn't a cloud to be seen in the sky. The stars shone down on me—never changing, always steady—mocking me with their bright futures. While I probably wouldn't last the night.

Because I tried to kill my best friend . . .

And he let me live.

Lucas Donahue should've killed me, instead of just shooting me and cracking my ribs in self-defense. He was the closest thing I had to a brother and I'd engineered a bloody coup that had nearly cost him everything. He should have shot me down in cold blood, should have put me down like the rabid dog I was. I deserved it. But instead, he showed me mercy. He let me walk away.

What the hell was I supposed to do with *that*?

The moment he'd let me walk out of his apartment with a crumpled-up, bloody note in my hand giving me everything I wanted, I knew I made a huge mistake. I should never have attacked my blood brother to get ahead in a gang that—more likely than not—would end up killing me anyway. I'd stupidly wanted to prove to Pops that I could be the man he wanted me to be.

Cold. Ruthless. A killer.

I *was* all those things, but not to Lucas.

Betraying Lucas was the single biggest regret in my life. Normally, I didn't wallow in the what-ifs or the shoulda-beens. I didn't waste my damn time with what I could have done, or what I could have been. But if I could go back in time and undo all the shit I'd done to Lucas . . .

Man, I would turn that damn clock back so quickly, it'd snap in half.

The bloodstained note in my pocket burned against my thigh. It named me Lucas's successor, just like I'd wanted. And just like I'd wanted, Lucas was out of the picture, out of the gang. When his younger brother, Scotty, showed up, gun in hand, at his place, I knew that no matter the outcome, I wouldn't win.

But truth be told, even before that, I'd known I'd made a mistake.

Lucas had looked at me with hope, thinking I'd come to help him, and a part of me died back in that apartment with the rest of the men who dared to attack Lucas. When he had realized *I* was the mastermind all along . . .

There'd been no coming back from that.

It had been too late.

Too late to say, *"You know what, man? Never mind. We're cool."* The second Lucas had found out I was trying to kill him to move up the ranks—I'd known I was a dead man, whether he pulled the trigger on his gun or not. Angry at what I had become, I'd lashed out at Lucas. Tried to get him to pop me to put me out of my misery. But he hadn't. He'd done the honorable thing and let me live. He hadn't wanted to kill me, even after all the shit I'd done to him. He'd told Scotty to let me walk away . . . and I had.

Now, with Scotty's help, Lucas was gone.

Dead. Only he wasn't. By now, he was probably miles outside Boston and away from this slum we called Steel Row—while I would die in the worst section of Southie, knowing I put power above brotherhood.

I should have lived the life that Lucas led. He was the type of guy who put friends first. Family first. The type of guy who saved a guy's neck, even if that guy had just tried to kill him, because he'd made a promise he'd be blood brothers with him when they were kids.

And here I was, a fucking fool.

Any minute now, my phone would ring with the news of Lucas's "death," and I would be expected to be shocked. Raging. Grief-stricken. And the thing was, even though I knew he was alive and well . . . I *was* all those things.

Because I'd become a monster.

I laughed again. "Rest in peace, Lucas Donahue."

As if on cue, my phone buzzed in my pocket. Wincing, I dug my sore fingers into my pocket and pulled out my iPhone. Squinting at the screen, I sighed. It was Tate, the head of the Sons of Steel Row, my gang. Time to put on a good act. "Hello?"

"Where are you?" Tate asked, his voice hard.

I struggled to sit up, resting my back against the concrete wall, right next to my bloody smiley face. "I ran into some Bitter Hill guys, and they did a number on me. I'm just trying to recover a bit before I head back in. Why? What's wrong, sir?"

"We just got bad news . . . about Lucas."

I rubbed my forehead. It hurt like a bitch. I didn't know what Scotty had or hadn't told him yet, so I didn't want to say too much. "Where is he?"

"I'm sorry, but he's gone." Tate made a growling noise. "Fucking Bitter Hill took him and his girl out. They burnt the place down, leaving nothing but bones and ash, but the dental records match. Lucas is dead."

I blinked. How the hell had they managed to pull off a damn dental records match—and so quickly? I'd hung around after the attack to make sure Lucas and Heidi had actually kept their word and left. They had. Scotty had waved them away with a smile. They weren't dead, and yet . . . *Oh, shit.*

Son of a fucking bitch.

It all made sense now.

Scotty had seemed so sure that Lucas and Heidi could get away, just as he agreed to keep my secret. And when he'd come barging into Lucas's apartment, the way he'd held the gun had been telling. It had screamed his true identity, clear as day. And the way he'd stood, straight and at attention with a firm grip on his pistol—like they teach at the academy. Scotty was a fucking cop.

In the eyes of Steel Row, that was worse than what I'd done. It was worse than a betrayal. Beyond a death sentence, it was a *mutilation* sentence.

If I told Tate about this, Scotty would be dead within the hour, and no one would ever find all the pieces that would put him back together. My position in the gang would be more secure than ever before, if I helped take him down. I would successfully take over Lucas's position, and Pops would finally be proud of me.

It was the perfect way to secure my future.

But it was Scotty Donahue, Lucas's little brother . . .

The brother of the man I'd wronged.

"Chris?" Tate said, his voice raised. "Are you there?"

I must've been silent too long. But my shock over Scotty's occupation would double as my grief over Lucas's demise. I cleared my throat. "Y-yeah. I just . . . I can't . . . I'm gonna fucking kill them all. Every last one. Right now."

"No." Something slammed down on wood. More than likely on Tate's walnut desk. He loved opulence as much as I loved women. "We need to be smart about this. We've got enough cop focus on us right now, and we don't need more by bringing a gang war down on Steel Row. All that'll do is land our asses behind bars. I think we've all done enough time."

There it was. The opening to mention my suspicions about Scotty's side job as an undercover. It would be so easy to do. A hell of a lot easier than shooting Lucas had been. "Then what am I supposed to do? They killed my best friend. I—I . . . *Shit*. I can't let that go."

"You have to, until we have a foolproof plan. Until then . . ." Tate slammed something else down, and I heard someone speak in a low voice. "Okay, yeah. Your pops called in from the airport. He suggested you take some time to yourself, and I agree. Lie low. Heal. Drink. Fuck it out of your system. Whatever works for you."

I gritted my teeth. Of course my pops immediately assumed that I was weak and would need time to heal. And worse than that, if he knew I had tried—and *failed*—to kill Lucas, and that his death was a ruse, he wouldn't be so quick to protect me. And I would get one of his legendary beatings that would make a gunshot to the shoulder and a few cracked ribs look like a walk in the park. "Are you sure? Don't you need me there? I mean . . . Christ. *Lucas.*"

"I know." Tate sighed. "You do you. We've got this. We'll make plans, and when we have anything concrete—"

"I'll be the first to pull the trigger."

"I promise," Tate agreed.

"Thank you, sir," I said, glancing down at my blood-soaked T-shirt and brown leather jacket. If I didn't sew up that bullet hole soon, I would go from dying to dead. "I appreciate it."

"Sure thing."

The line went dead, and I dropped my hand to my thigh. Holding up the phone took too much effort. Hurt too much. But it was nothing compared to the guilt trying to choke the life out of me. Banging my head on the wall hard enough to see stars all over again, I said, "Son of a bitch, Scotty."

Didn't he know how much danger he was in by doing this? By pretending to be in the gang while reporting back to the boys? If Tate found out about Scotty . . .

Gritting my teeth, I struggled to my feet, wavering.

I'd lost a lot of blood, and unless I truly wanted to die in this alley, I needed to get moving. There was a closed pharmacy in the swanky part of town, outside of Steel Row, which Southies generally avoided. But this one was in the Sons' employ, thanks to Pops and his fondness for gambling. If I could get in through the back door, I could grab supplies and pain meds, stitch myself up, and then . . .

Then *what*?

Fuck if I knew.

Trust that Scotty, the *cop*, didn't turn me into Tate? Trust that he wouldn't tell the man of my deceit and betrayal? If he told them, they would kill me, no matter what Pops said. I would be a dead man.

Even worse, what if Scotty used the other side of his advantage—and turned me into the boys? Told them all the shit I'd done and locked me away behind bars?

Maybe I *should* tell Tate about Scotty's dirty little secret first and be responsible for yet another "disappearance" in the Donahue family.

Or . . . I could just hide out.

Wait and see how all this blew over.

Nothing good ever came from rash decisions, and after the death of four Bitter Hill guys, there was more than likely going to be some reaction. And that backlash would circle around to me. I'd sworn Phil and his men to secrecy when I hired them to take Lucas out, but that didn't mean they hadn't blabbed to someone.

Men like them always did.

I stumbled down the alley, each step hurting more than the last. Lucas had kicked my ass within an inch of my life, and he should have killed me. I should be *dead*. Maybe I should just lie down and wait to bleed out. It was a fairly peaceful way to go for a guy like me. I could just let my blackened blood spread across the grimy cement until nothing remained of me but a dried-up shell.

But that damn survival instinct in me refused.

I fucked up big-time by betraying my best friend—that much was true. But to just give up and let the devil drag me to hell? I couldn't do it. And Scotty, fool that he was, had a lot riding on this whole affair, too. If he wanted to remain undercover, he would need me to back his story up. Vouch for him.

If he told them I was there, too, I needed to agree.

It was the only way to keep Scotty whole.

I had to play my part. Tate and the rest of the guys at Steel Row would expect me to be vengeful, bitter, and upset. I could do that. It might be too late to make it up to Lucas, to let him know how sorry I was for what I did, but I could save Scotty.

Because I owed it to Lucas.

It was a small thing to do, really. Not even close to big enough to make up for all I did, or the lies I told in my quest for power and Pop's approval.

But it was *something*.

And it had to be enough.

Rounding the corner, I clutched my bleeding shoulder and rested against the wall, breathing heavily. The world spun in front of me, and I rested against the rough brick. I needed a few seconds to gather some strength.

To make sure I didn't pass out—

"Well, well, what do we have here?" a man said from the darkness. I recognized that voice, damn it. Reggie, a lieutenant in Bitter Hill, was the only other man who knew about my plot to kill Lucas. Therefore, he was the only man who knew why Bitter Hill guys had died, and *how*. He probably hadn't shared that information, because working with Steel Row would get him and Phil killed, too. "Chris O'Brien, bleeding and alone."

Forcing my eyes open, I smirked. "Reggie, great to see you, man."

"Where are *my* men, O'Brien?"

"Yeah, about that . . . ." I shrugged, ignoring the pain blazing through my shoulder from the small gesture. "Turns out, Lucas isn't as easy to take down as I thought. It got ugly, and there were losses, but he's dead."

Reggie rubbed his jaw and walked closer, his black hair as black as his eyes. He'd been walking behind me, and I stiffened. I didn't like anyone at my back. Especially not guys like him—guys like *me*. "Let me guess. Steel Row thinks we're to blame while you're free and clear."

"Shit if I know. Haven't heard word yet. I'm kinda recovering from the op, in case you can't tell." I straightened and pushed off the wall. "But as soon as I hear who they're looking to pop, I'll let you know."

Reggie chuckled. "Yeah. Sure you will. You must think I'm a fucking fool."

Well, actually . . . "Nah, man."

"Why should I believe you?"

I shrugged, even though it hurt. "Why not? You lost some men, but you took down Lucas Donahue. I call that a win."

"Know what I'd call a *win*?" He flicked a finger, and two guys came out from the darkness. "Kill him, and make it painful."

He walked away, not bothering to turn around to see if his men followed orders. I reached for my gun—till I remembered that Lucas had taken it from me. *"Shit."*

Reggie's guys grinned, and one pulled out a Glock. "Any last words?"

I'm sorry, Lucas. "Yeah." I inched closer and forced a grin. The man's hold on his weapon trembled, and I knew I could take him. A man who hesitated was a man easily overtaken. "Never fuck with someone who's got nothing to lose."

I threw myself at him, and we hit the ground with a bang—literally. The gun went off, and the bullet miraculously hit the man who leapt forward to help his buddy. He hit the ground, convulsing and choking on blood. The guy under me cursed and let loose a mean right hook that solidly connected with my nose. I rolled to the side, blinking away the impending blackness, but I knew I would be too late.

I really was going to die in this alley . . .

And I deserved it.